tillie walden

are you listening?

First Second
New York

:01
First Second

Published by First Second
First Second is an imprint of Roaring Brook Press,
a division of Holtzbrinck Publishing Holdings Limited Partnership
120 Broadway, New York, NY 10271

Don't miss your next favorite book from First Second!
For the latest updates go to firstsecondnewsletter.com and sign up for our enewsletter.

Library of Congress Control Number: 2018953552

Paperback ISBN: 978-1-250-20756-2
Hardcover ISBN: 978-1-62672-773-1

Our books may be purchased in bulk for promotional, educational, or business use.
Please contact your local bookseller or the Macmillan Corporate and Premium Sales Department
at (800) 221-7945 ext. 5442 or by email at MacmillanSpecialMarkets@macmillan.com.

FIRST EDITION

First edition, 2019

Edited by Connie Hsu
Book design by Molly Johanson
Printed in China

Paperback: 10 9 8 7 6 5 4
Hardcover: 10 9 8 7 6 5 4 3 2

BY ART WE LIVE

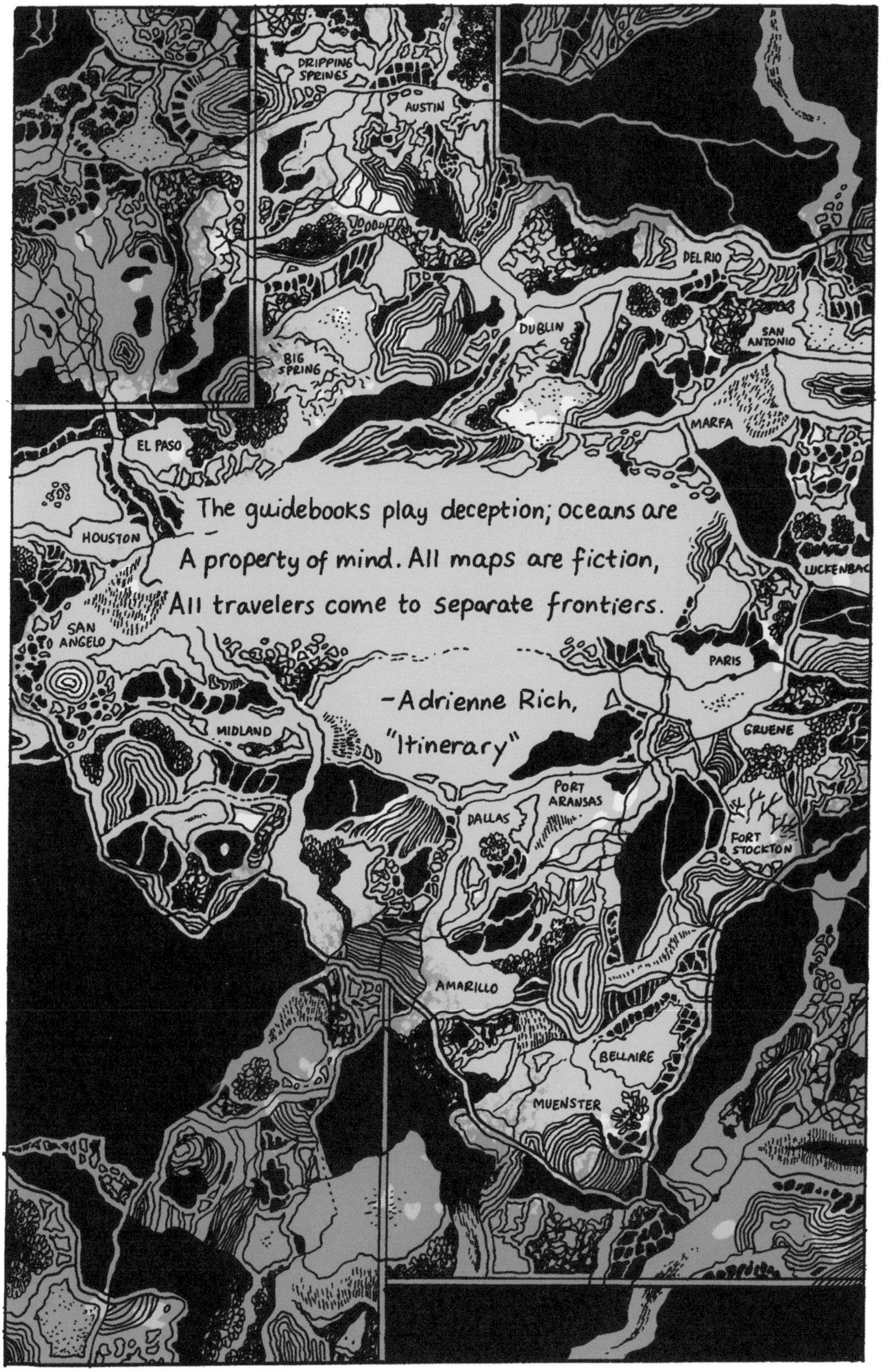

The guidebooks play deception; oceans are
A property of mind. All maps are fiction,
All travelers come to separate frontiers.
—Adrienne Rich,
"Itinerary"
DRIPPING SPRINGS
AUSTIN
DEL RIO
DUBLIN
SAN ANTONIO
BIG SPRING
MARFA
EL PASO
HOUSTON
LUCKENBAC
SAN ANGELO
PARIS
MIDLAND
GRUENE
PORT ARANSAS
DALLAS
FORT STOCKTON
AMARILLO
BELLAIRE
MUENSTER

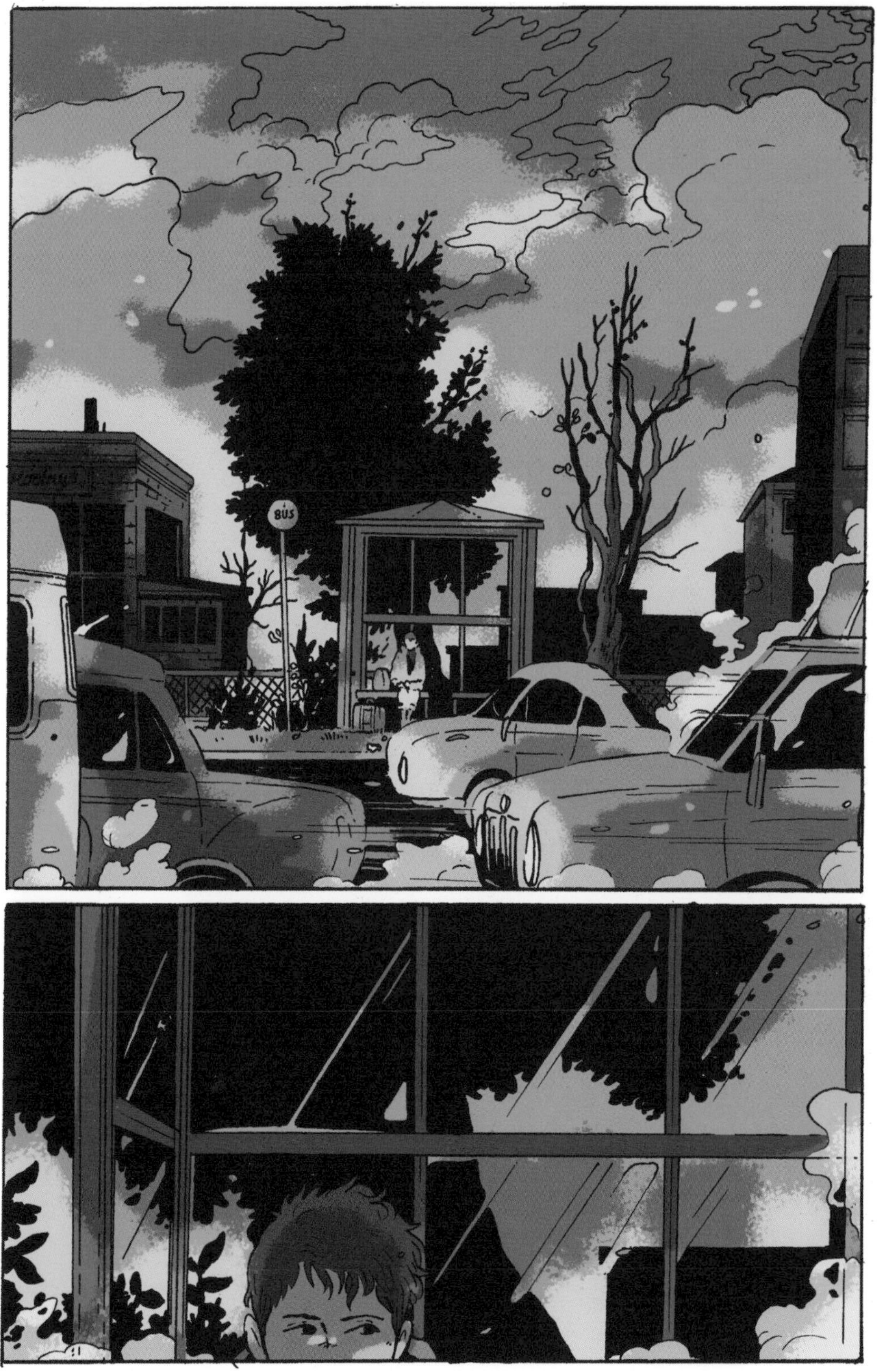
BUS

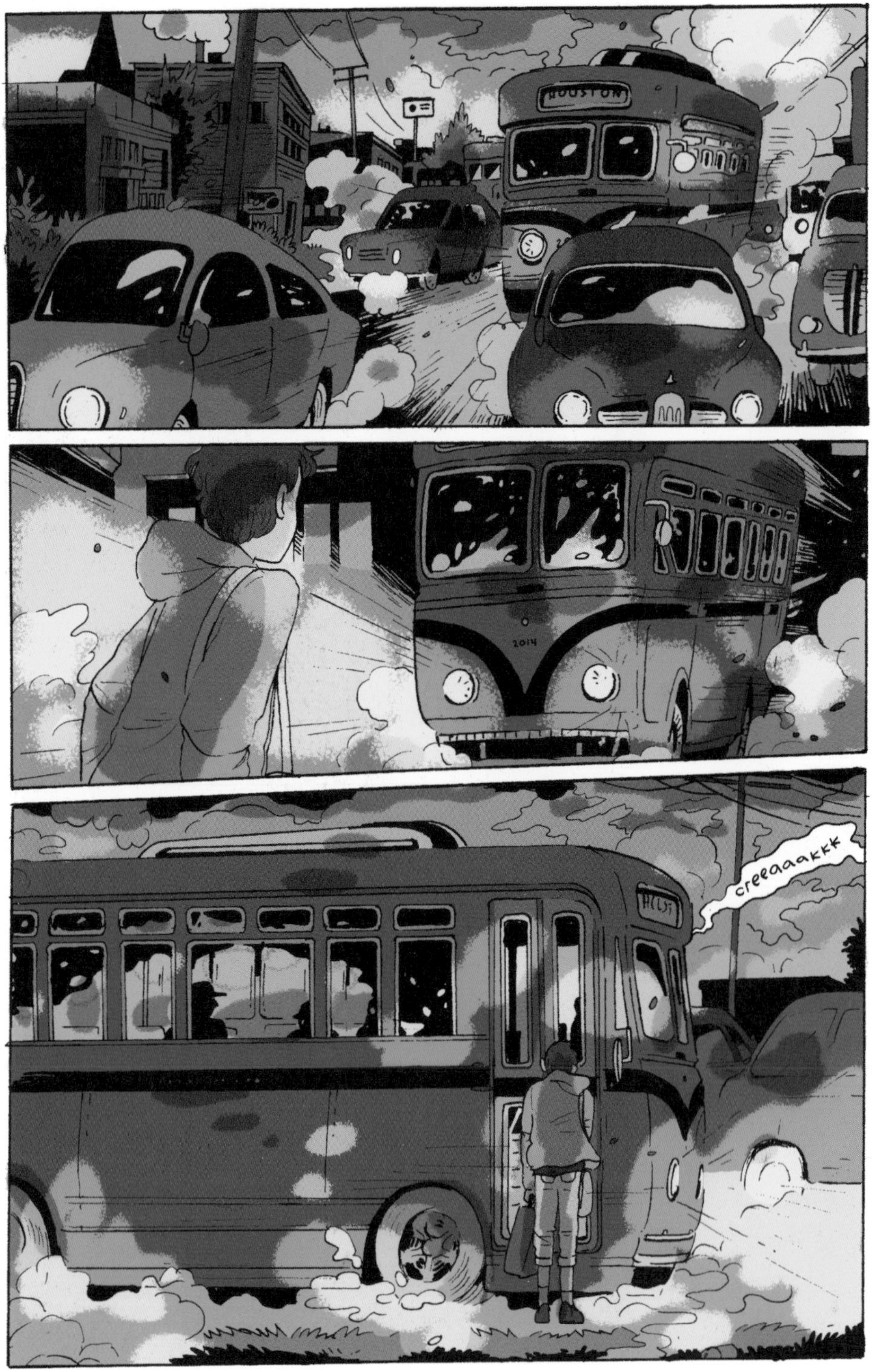
HOUSTON
2014
creeaaakkk

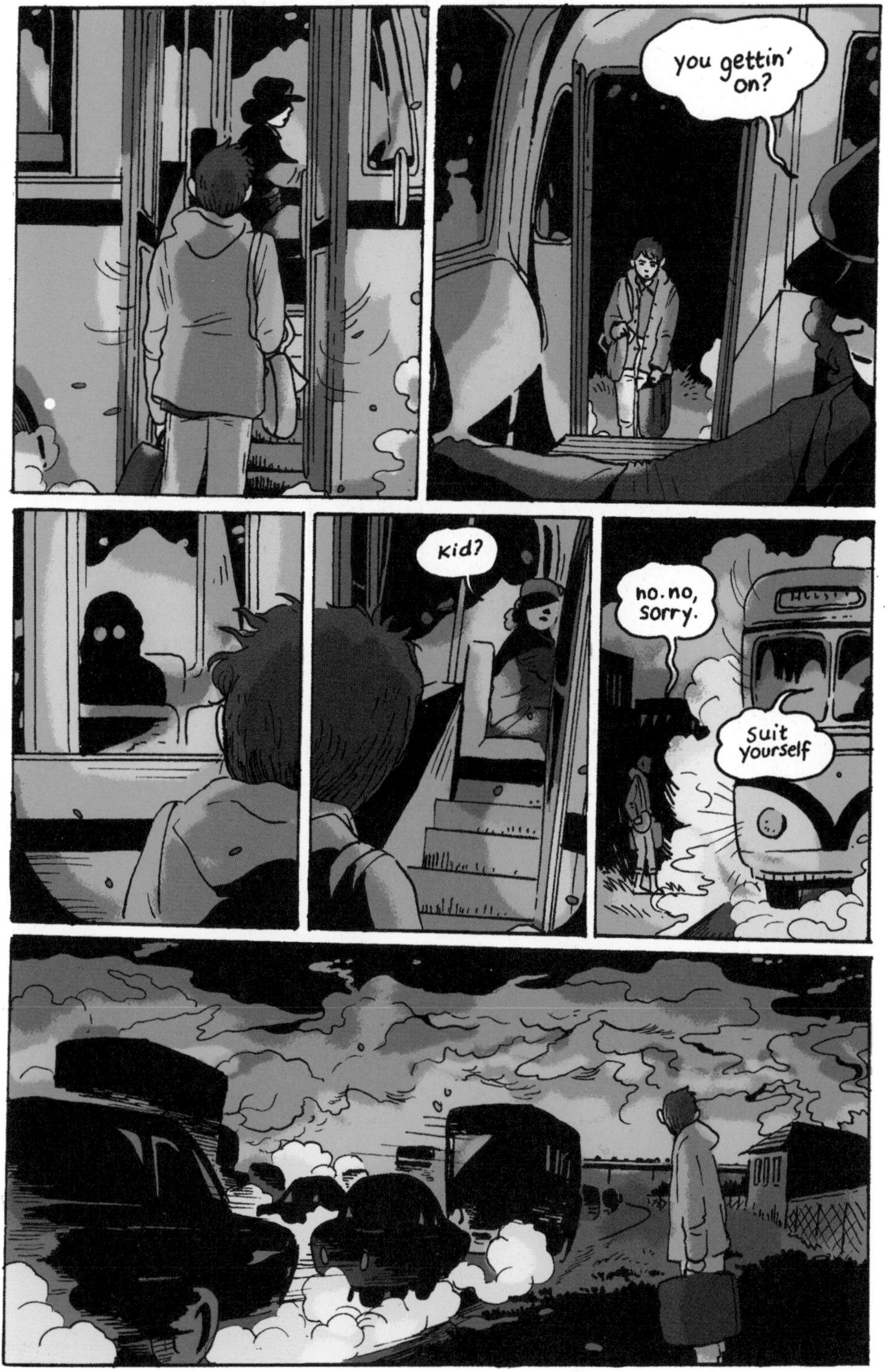
you gettin' on?
Kid?
no. no, sorry.
Suit yourself

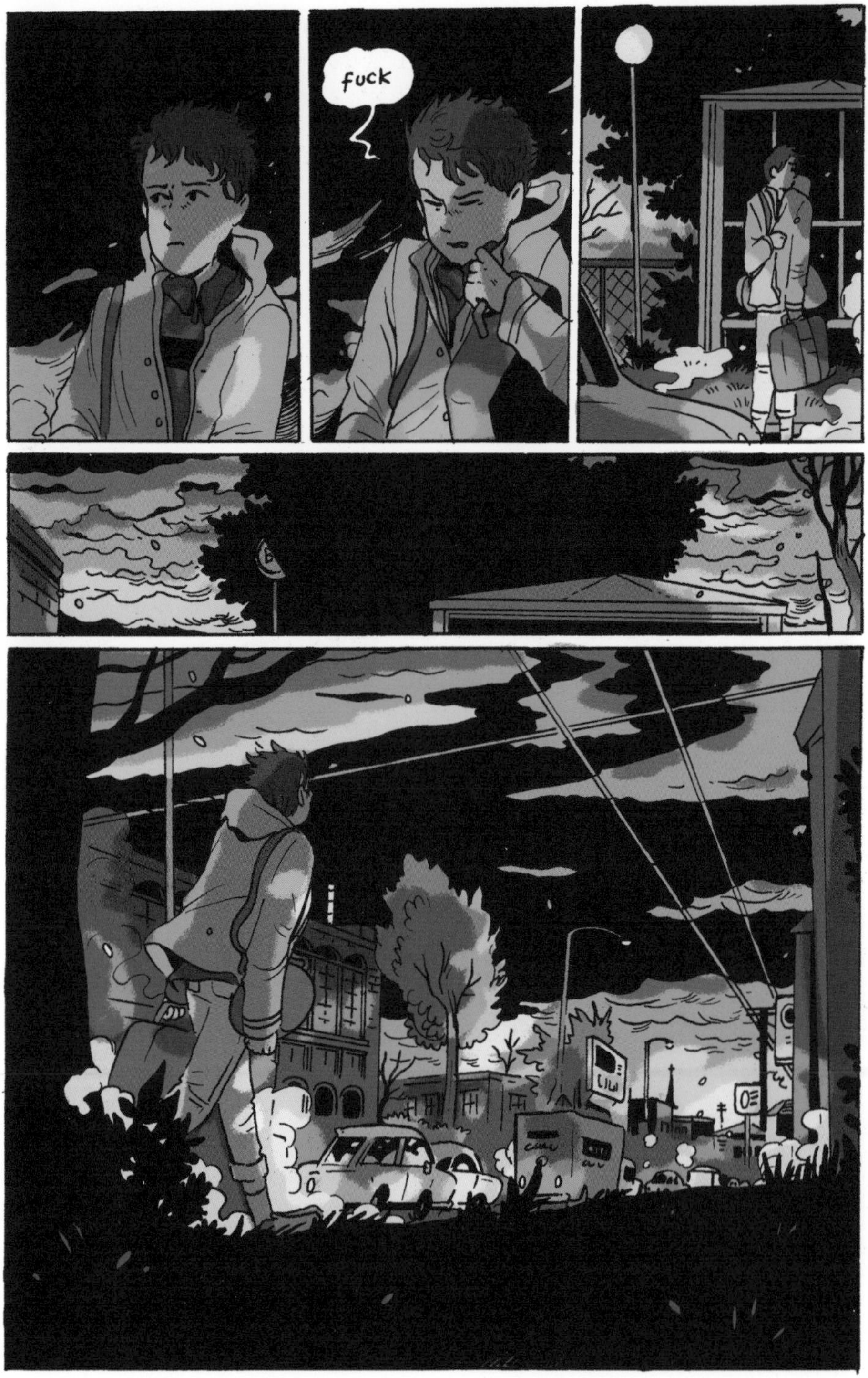
fuck

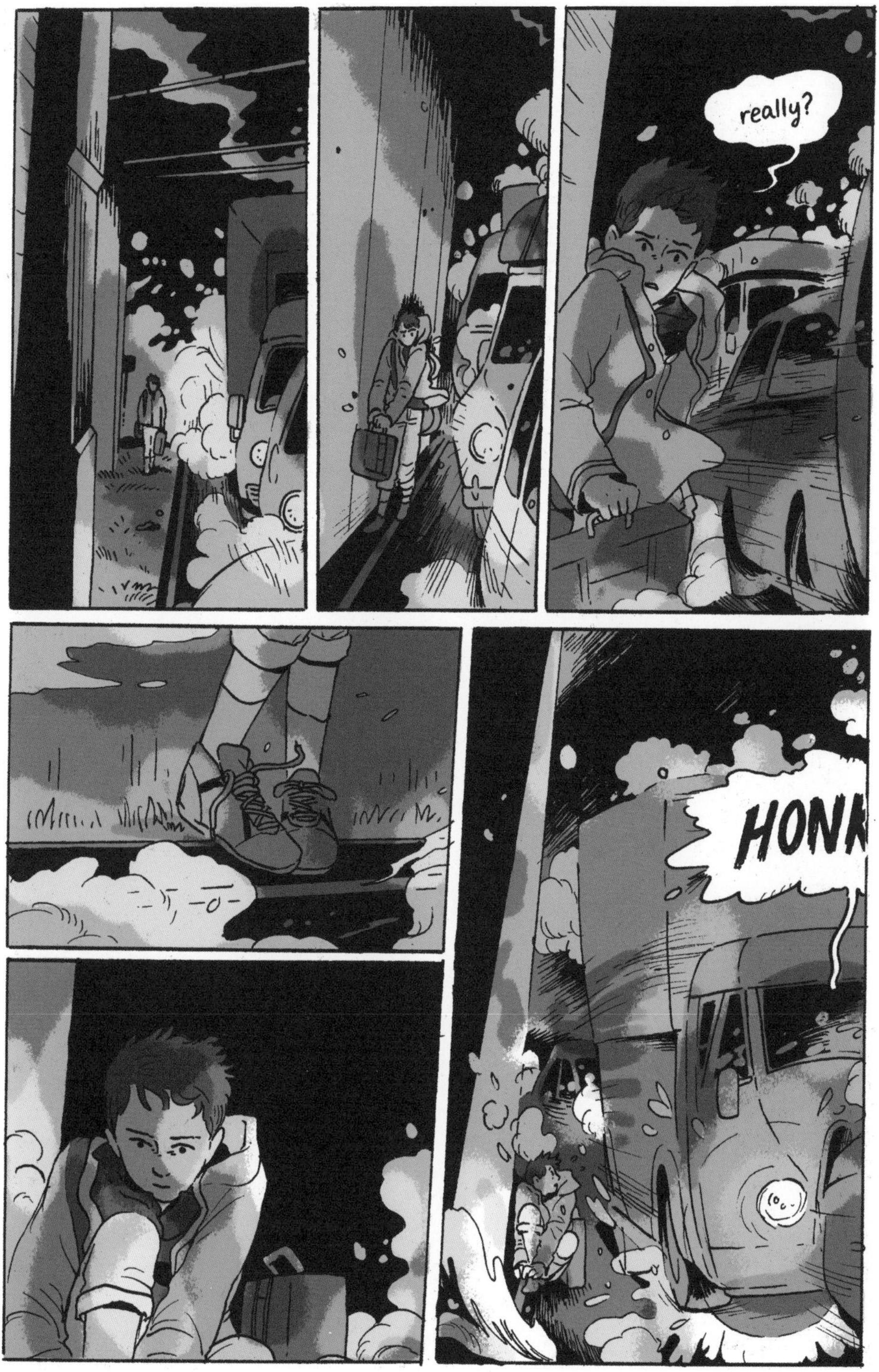
really?
HONK

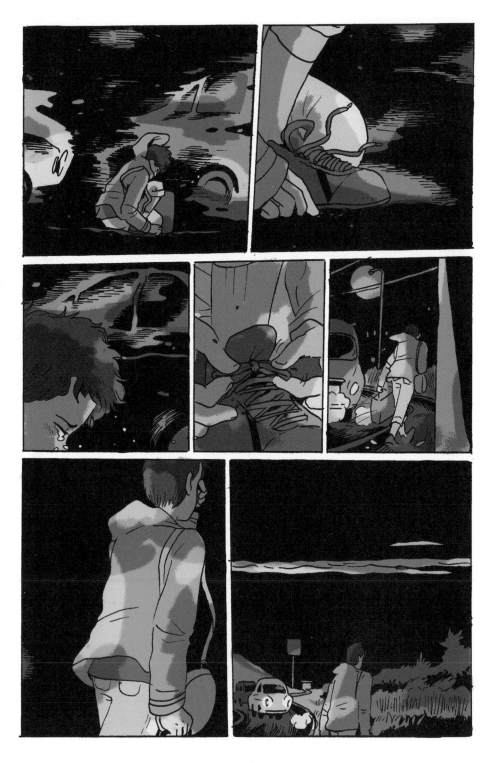

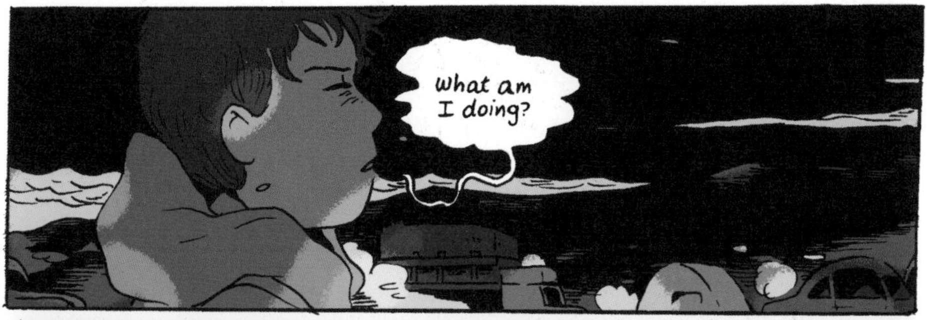
What am I doing?

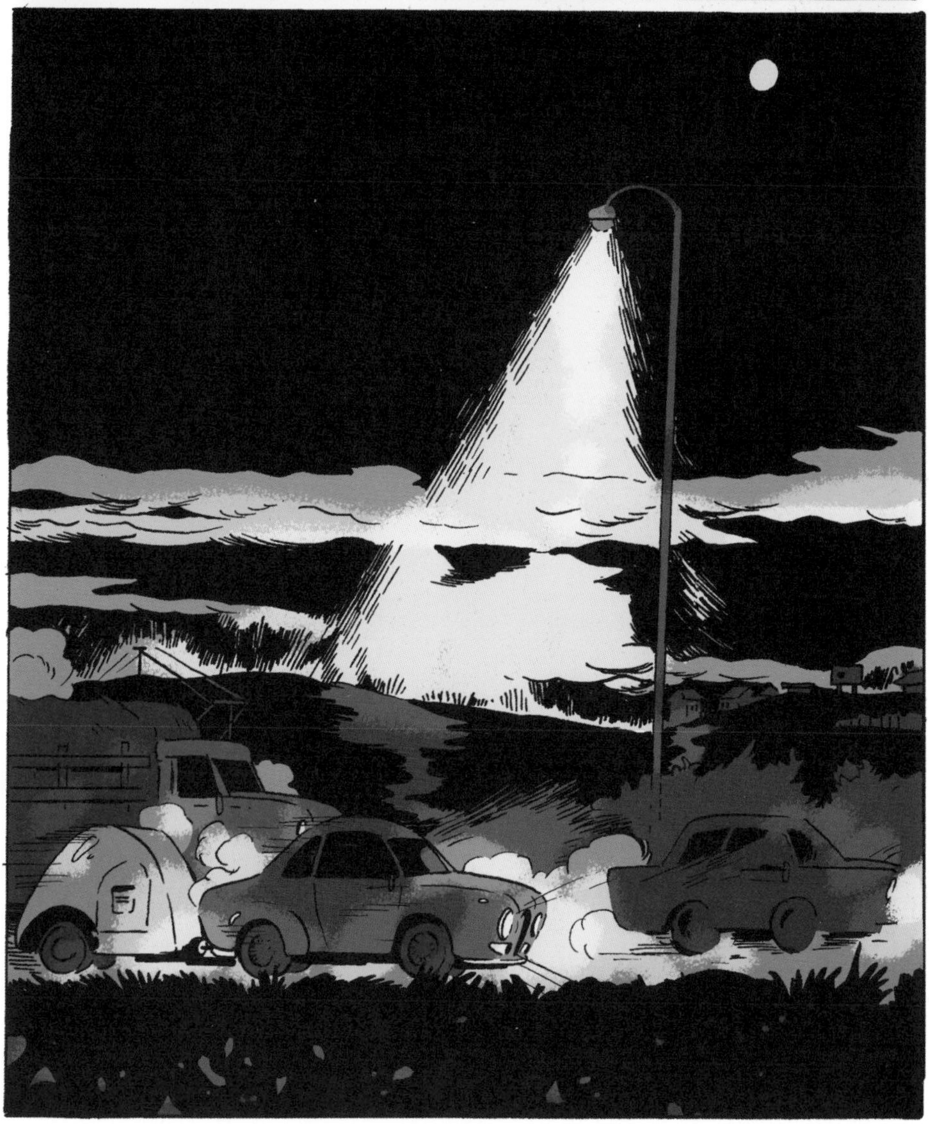

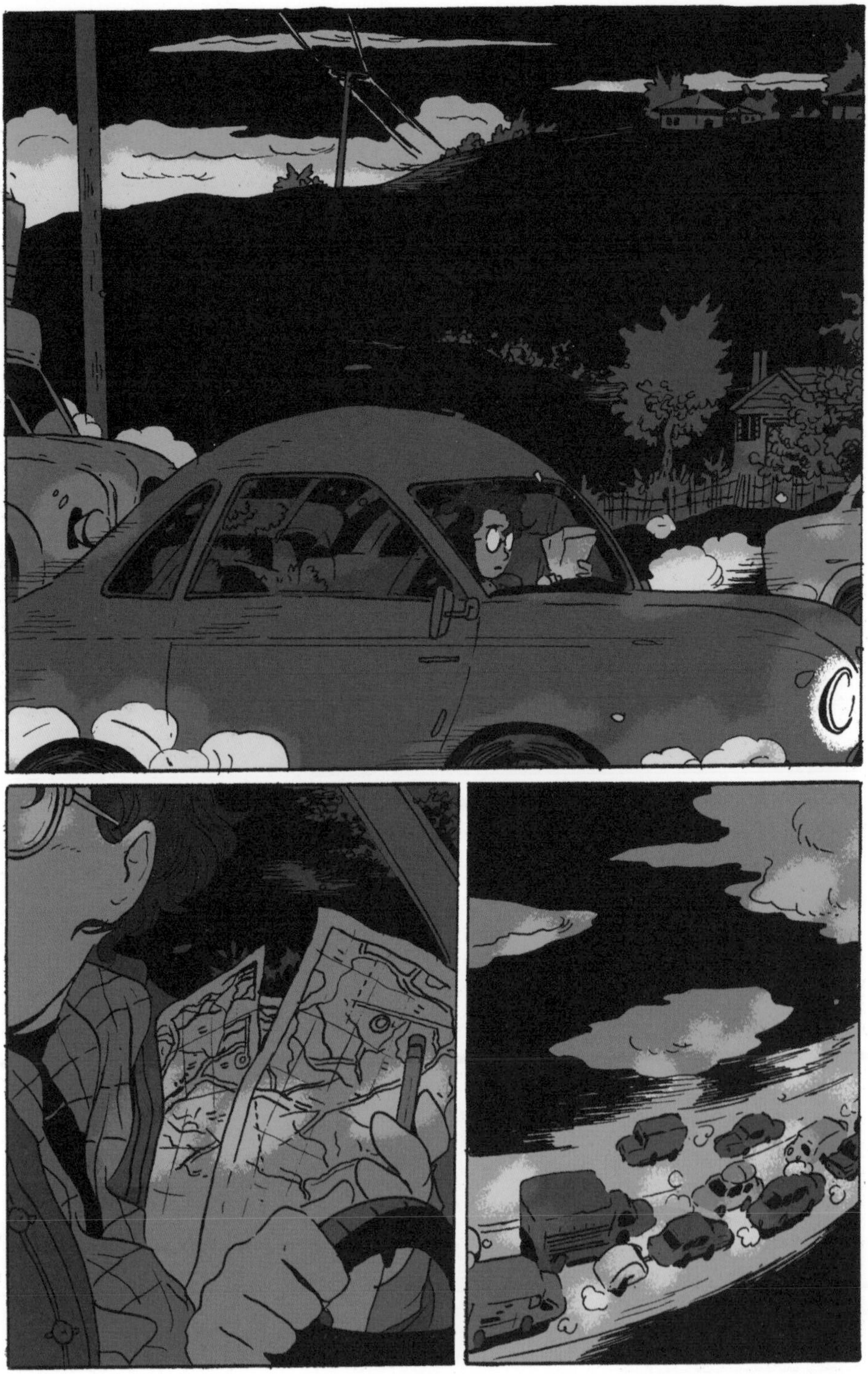

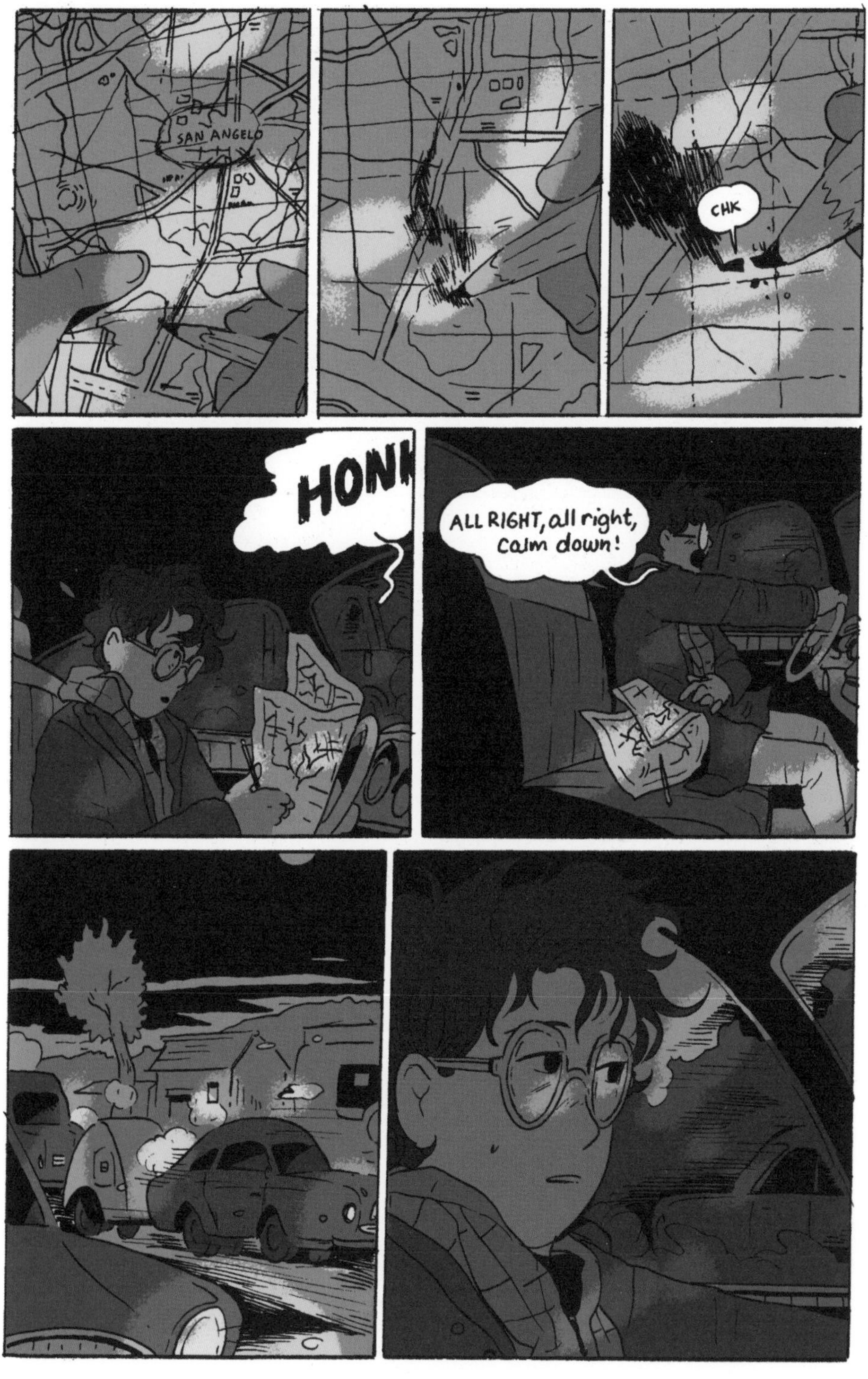
SAN ANGELO
CHK
HONK
ALL RIGHT, all right, calm down!

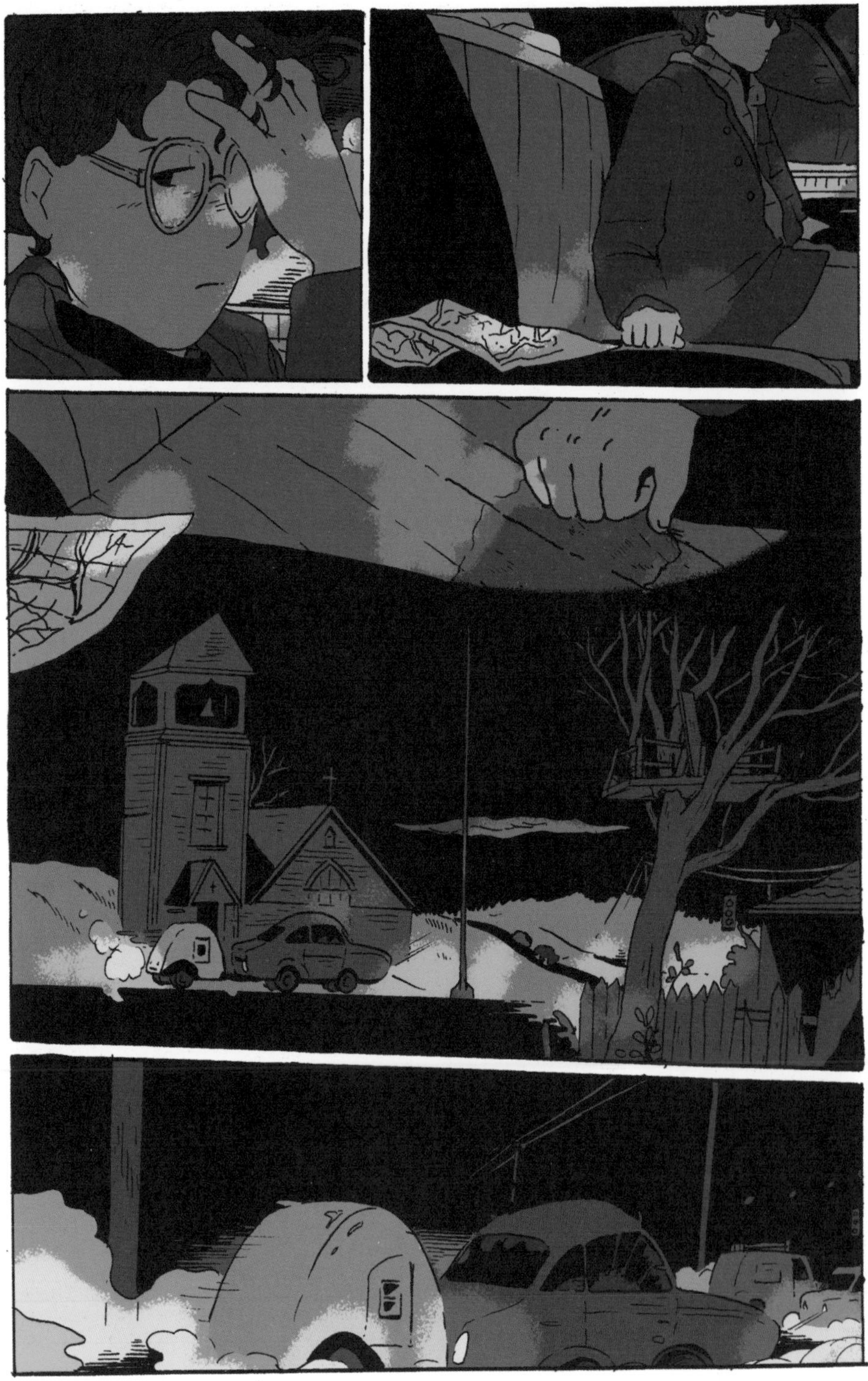

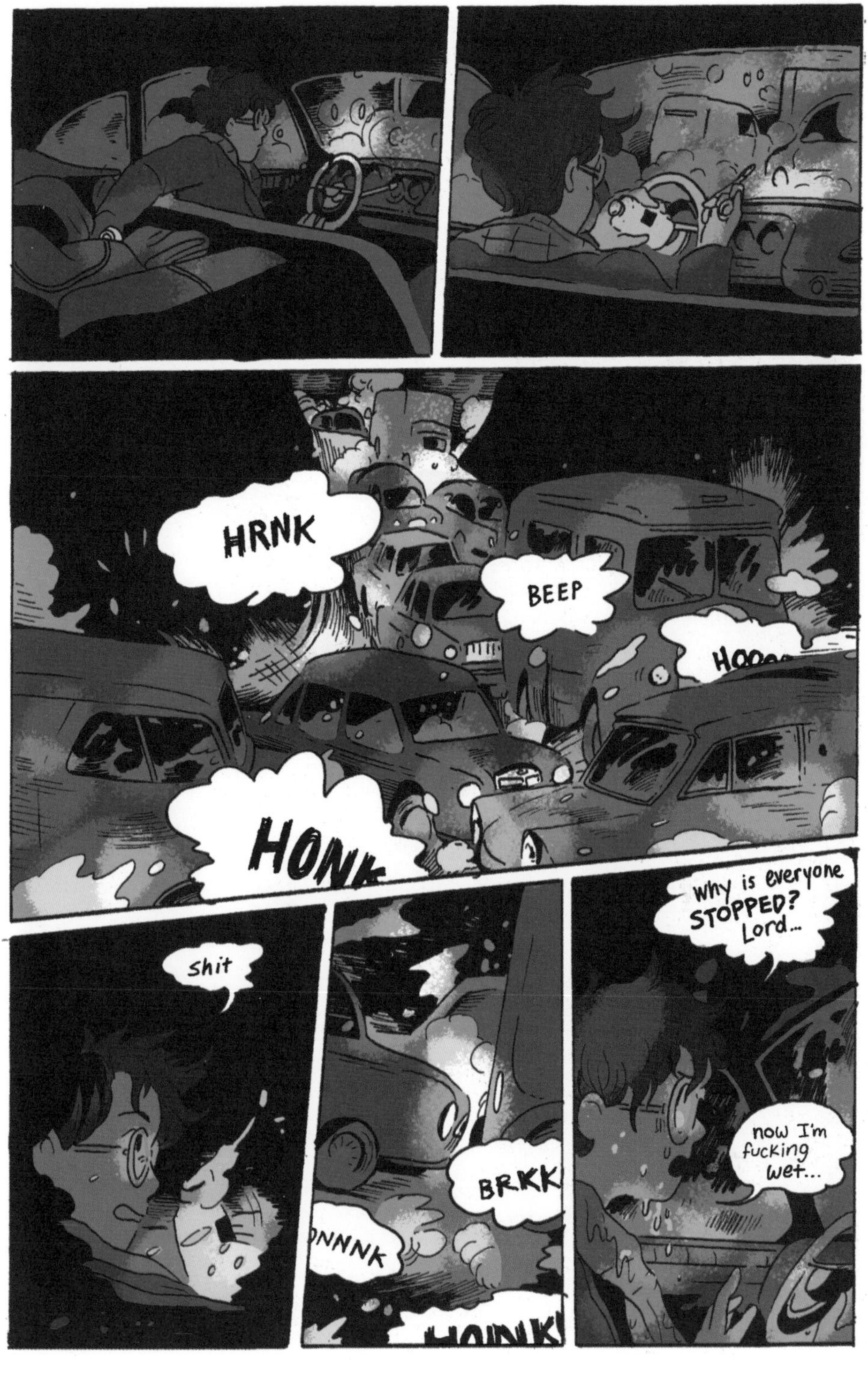
HRNK
BEEP
HOOO
HONK
shit
BRKK
NNNK
HONK
why is everyone STOPPED? Lord...
now I'm fucking wet...

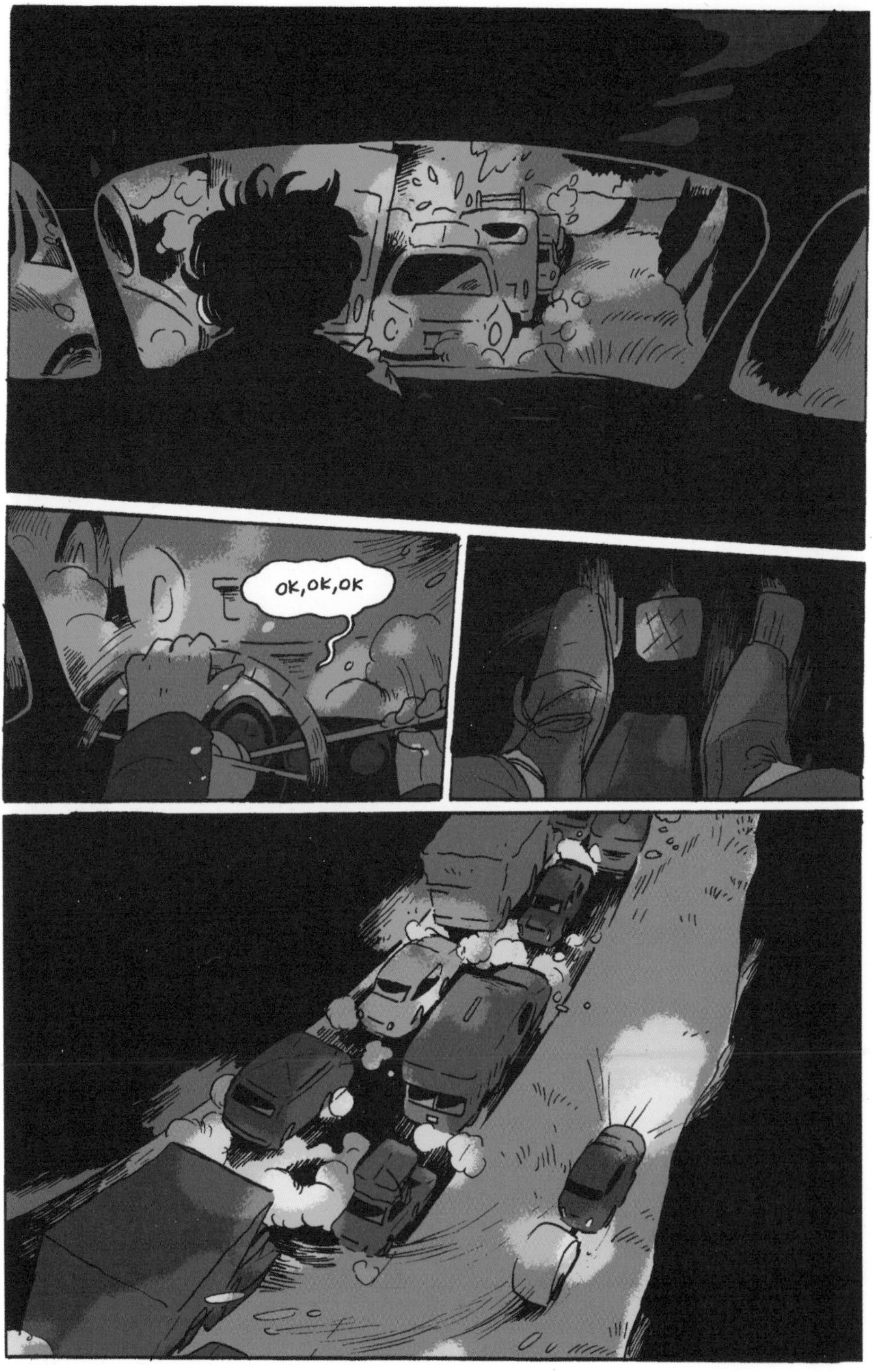
OK,OK,OK

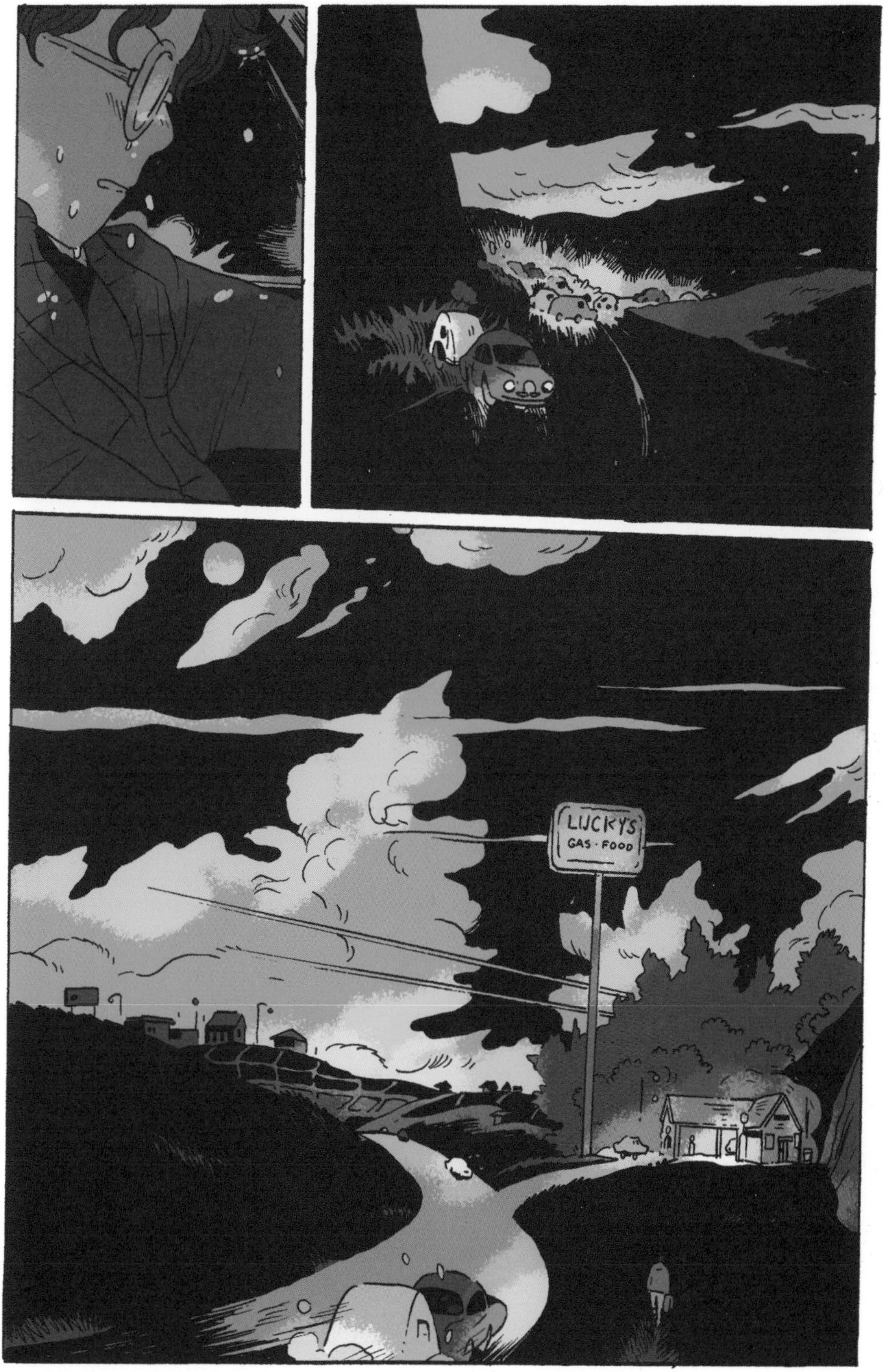
LUCKY'S
GAS · FOOD

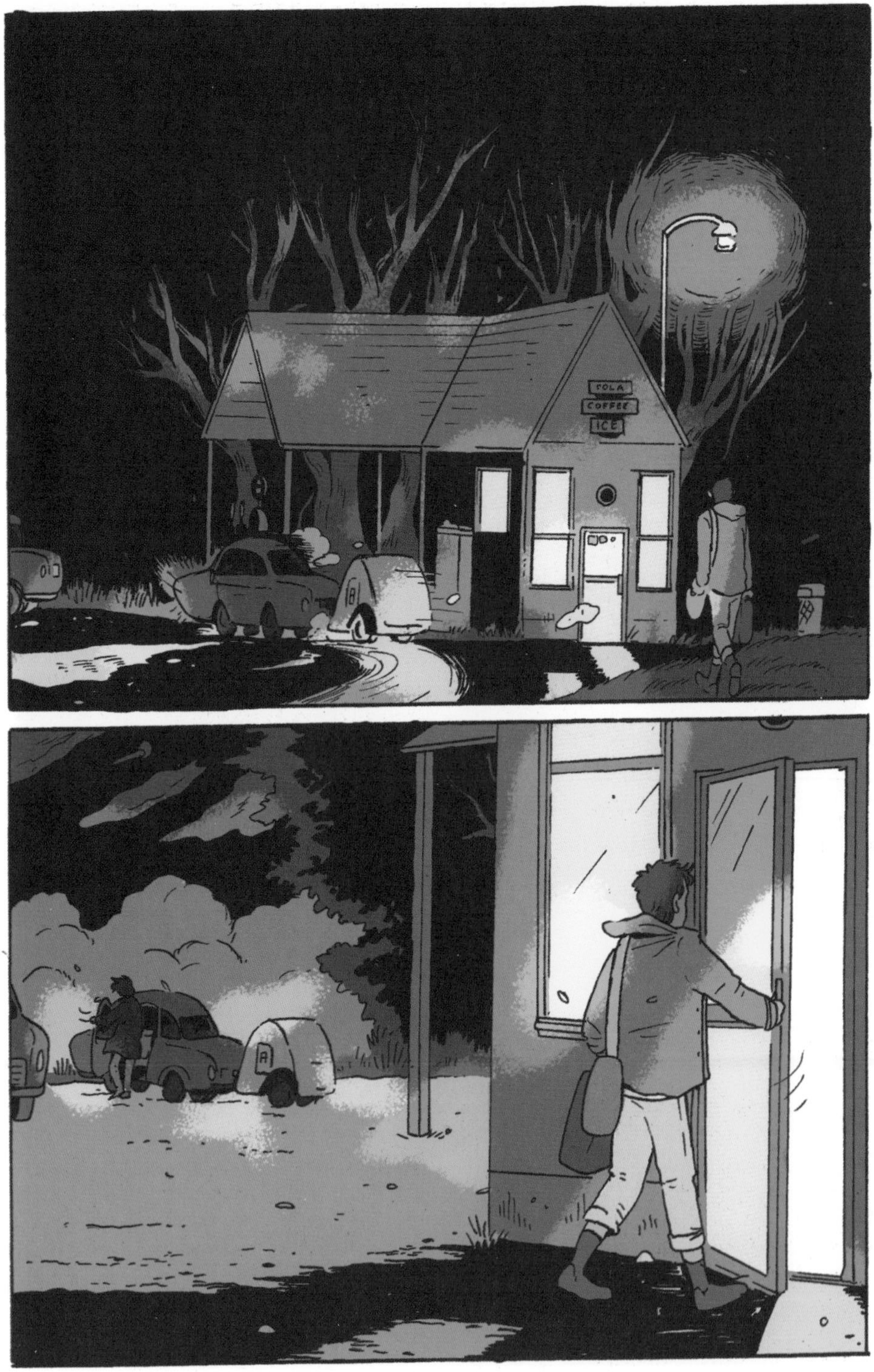
COLA
COFFEE
ICE

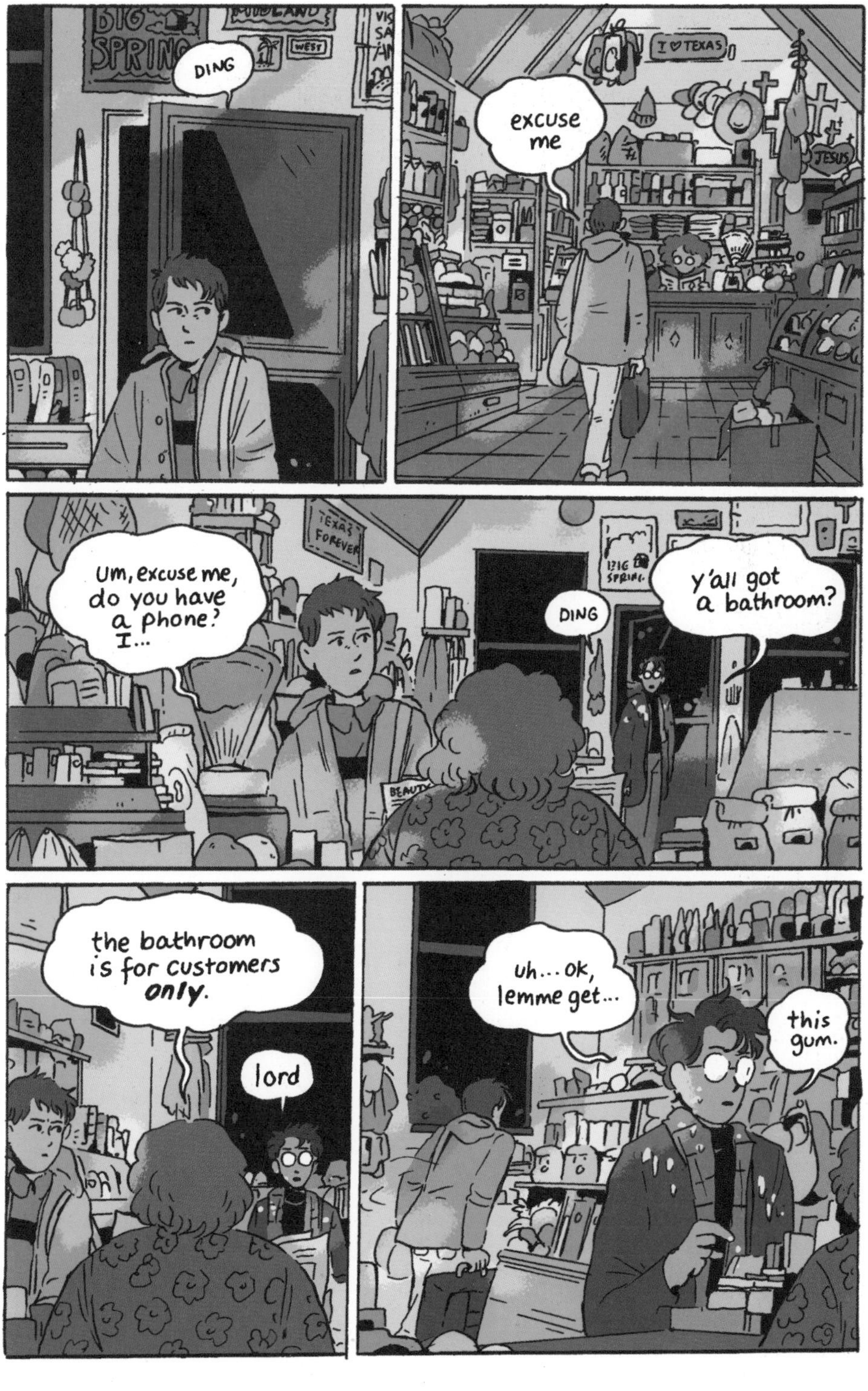
BIG SPRING
MIDLAND
WEST
DING
I ♡ TEXAS
excuse me
JESUS
TEXAS FOREVER
BIG SPRING
Um, excuse me, do you have a phone? I...
DING
y'all got a bathroom?
BEAUTY
the bathroom is for customers *only*.
lord
uh... ok, lemme get...
this gum.

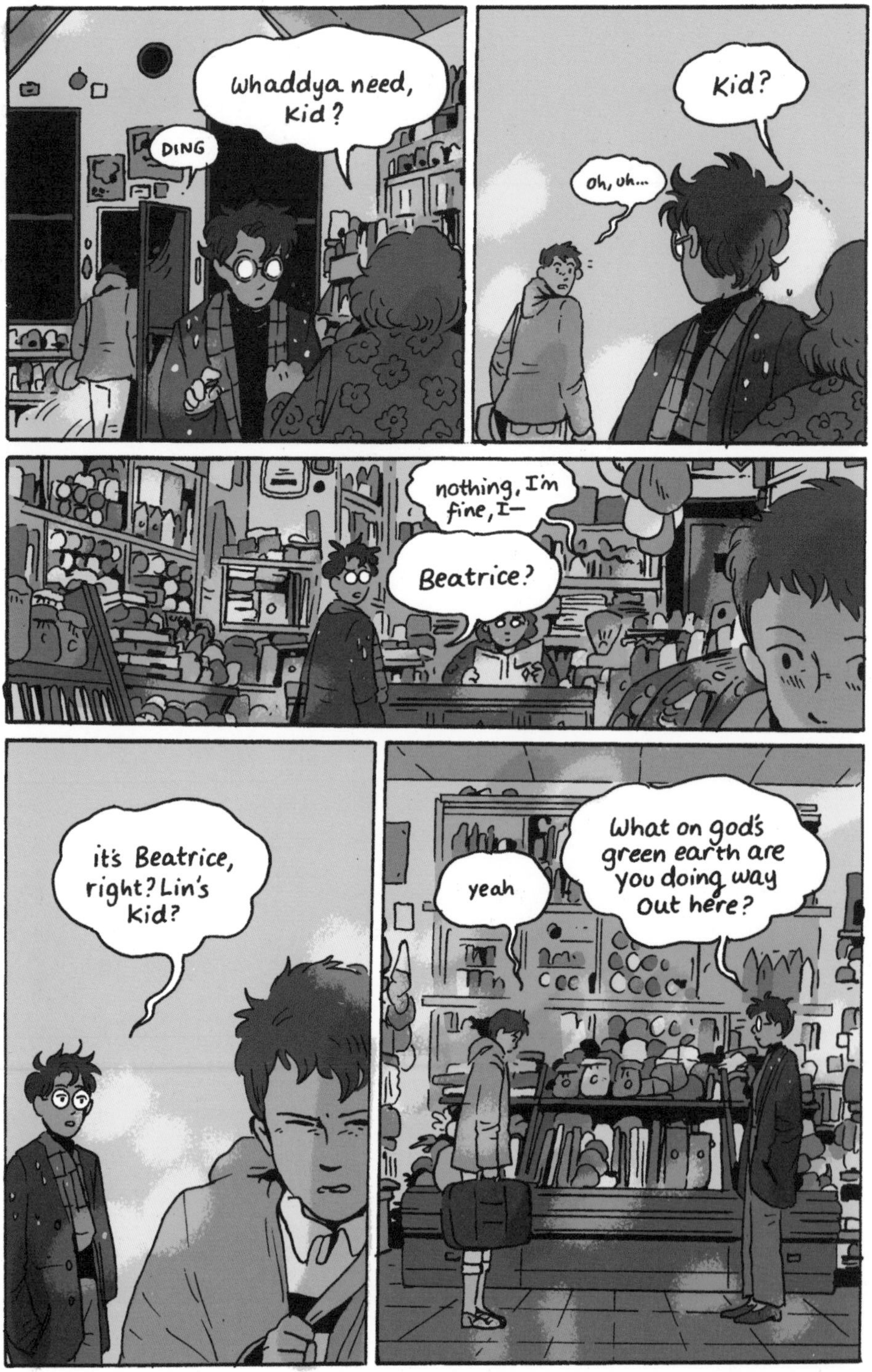
DING
Whaddya need, Kid?
Kid?
Oh, uh...
nothing, I'm fine, I—
Beatrice?
it's Beatrice, right? Lin's kid?
yeah
What on god's green earth are you doing way out here?

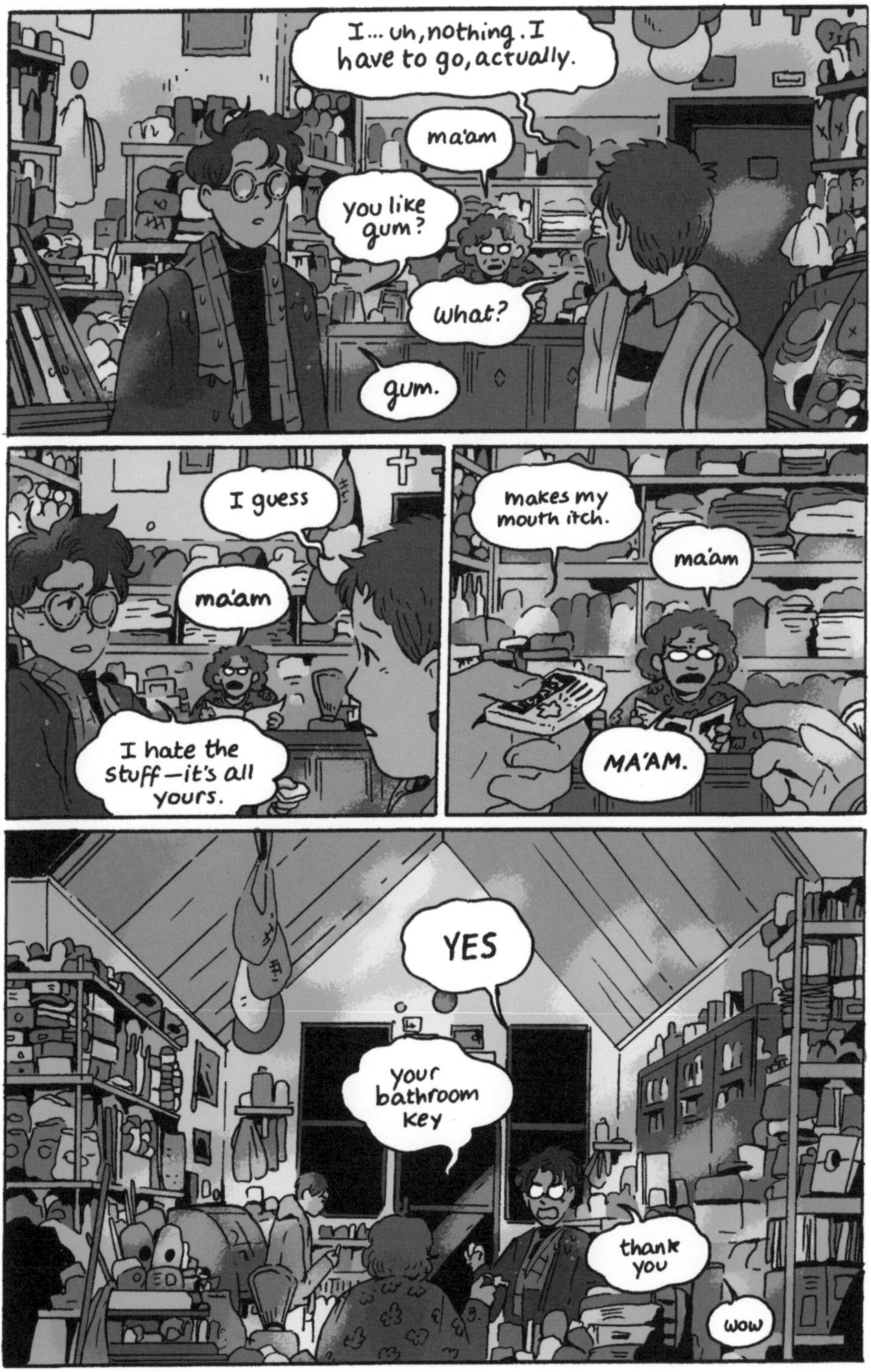
I... uh, nothing. I have to go, actually.
ma'am
you like gum?
what?
gum.
I guess
ma'am
I hate the stuff—it's all yours.
makes my mouth itch.
ma'am
MA'AM.
YES
your bathroom key
thank you
wow

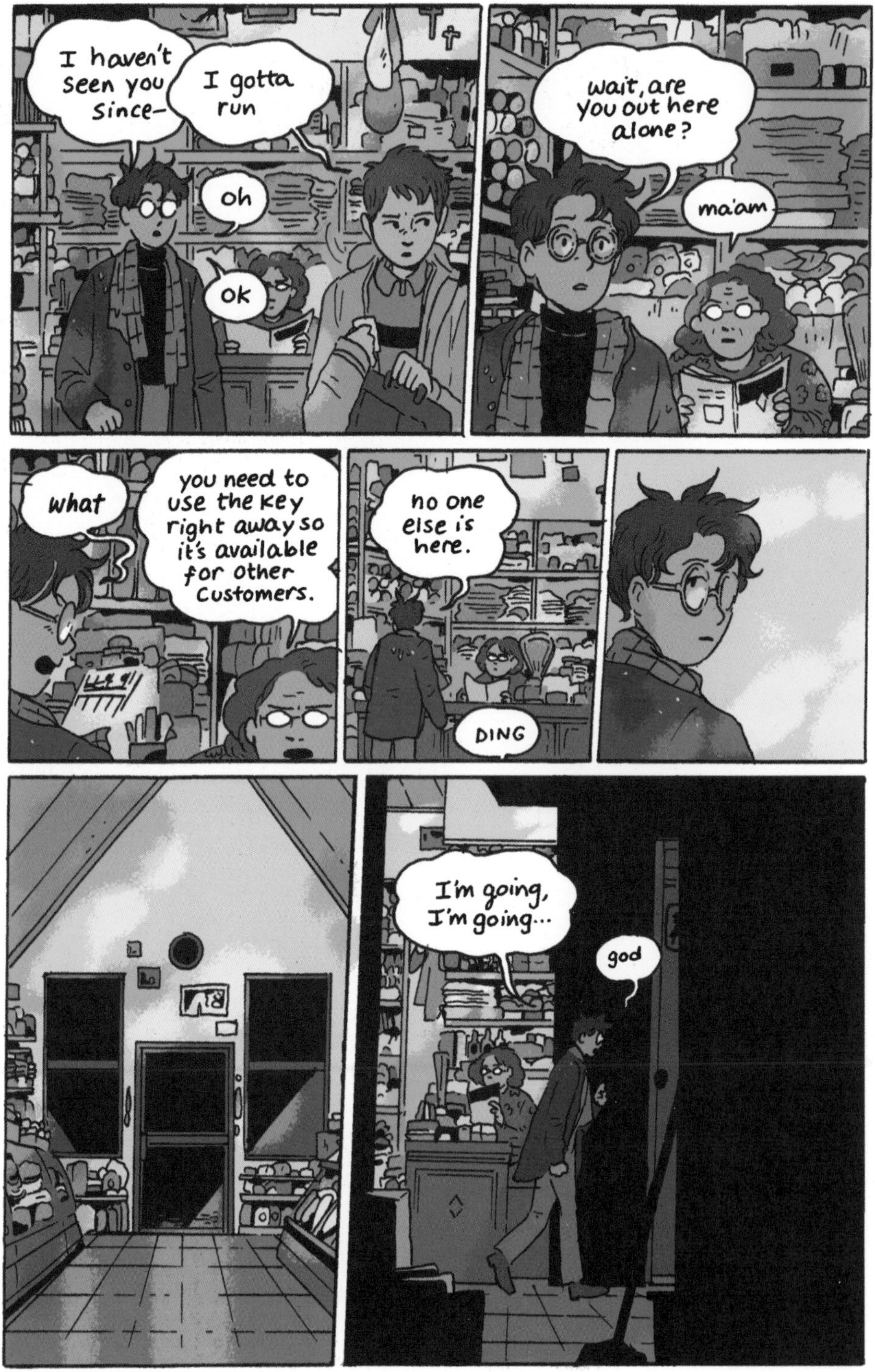
I haven't seen you since-
I gotta run
oh
ok
wait, are you out here alone?
ma'am
what
you need to use the key right away so it's available for other customers.
no one else is here.
DING
I'm going, I'm going...
god

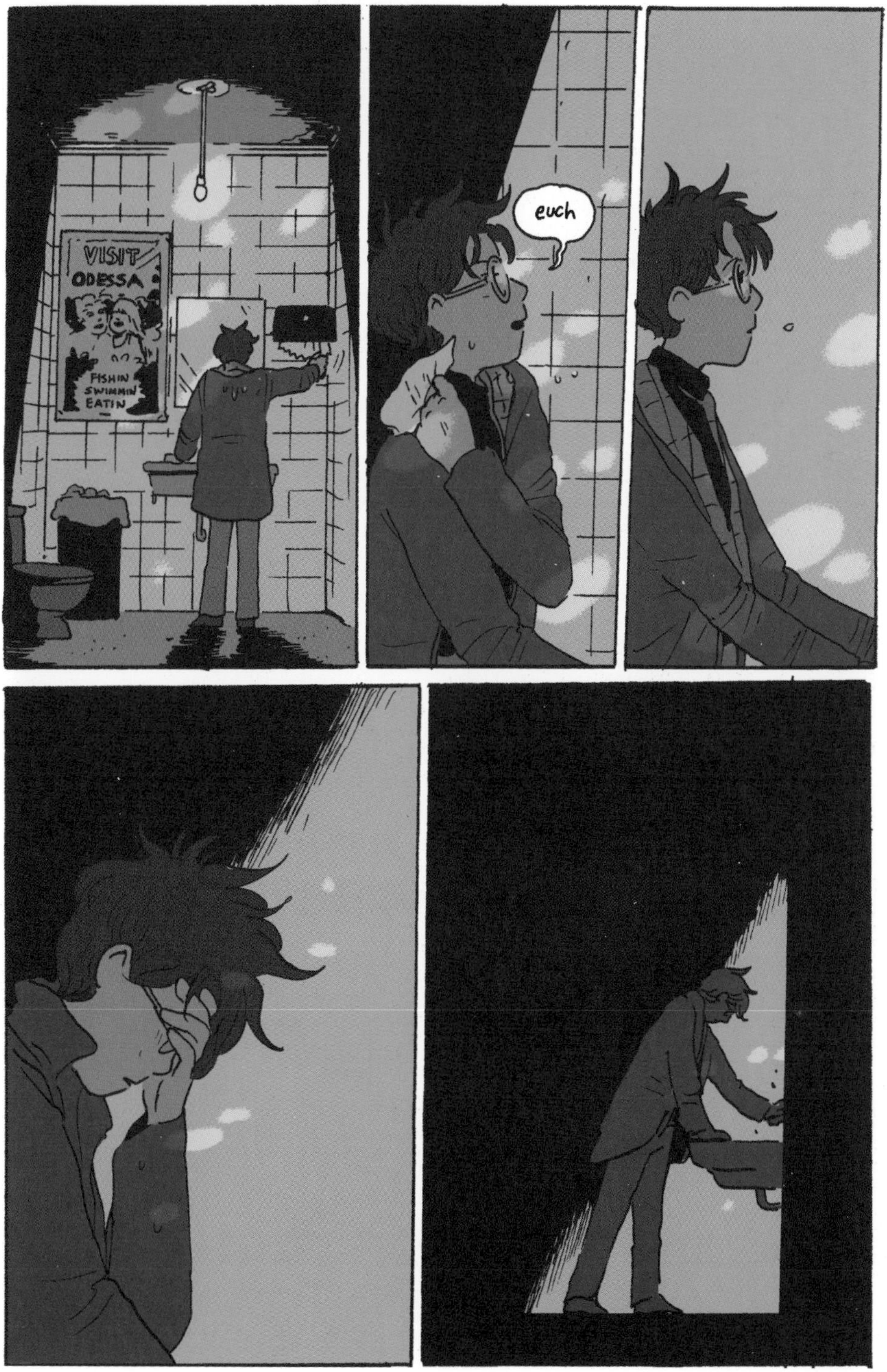
VISIT
ODESSA
FISHIN
SWIMMIN
EATIN
euch

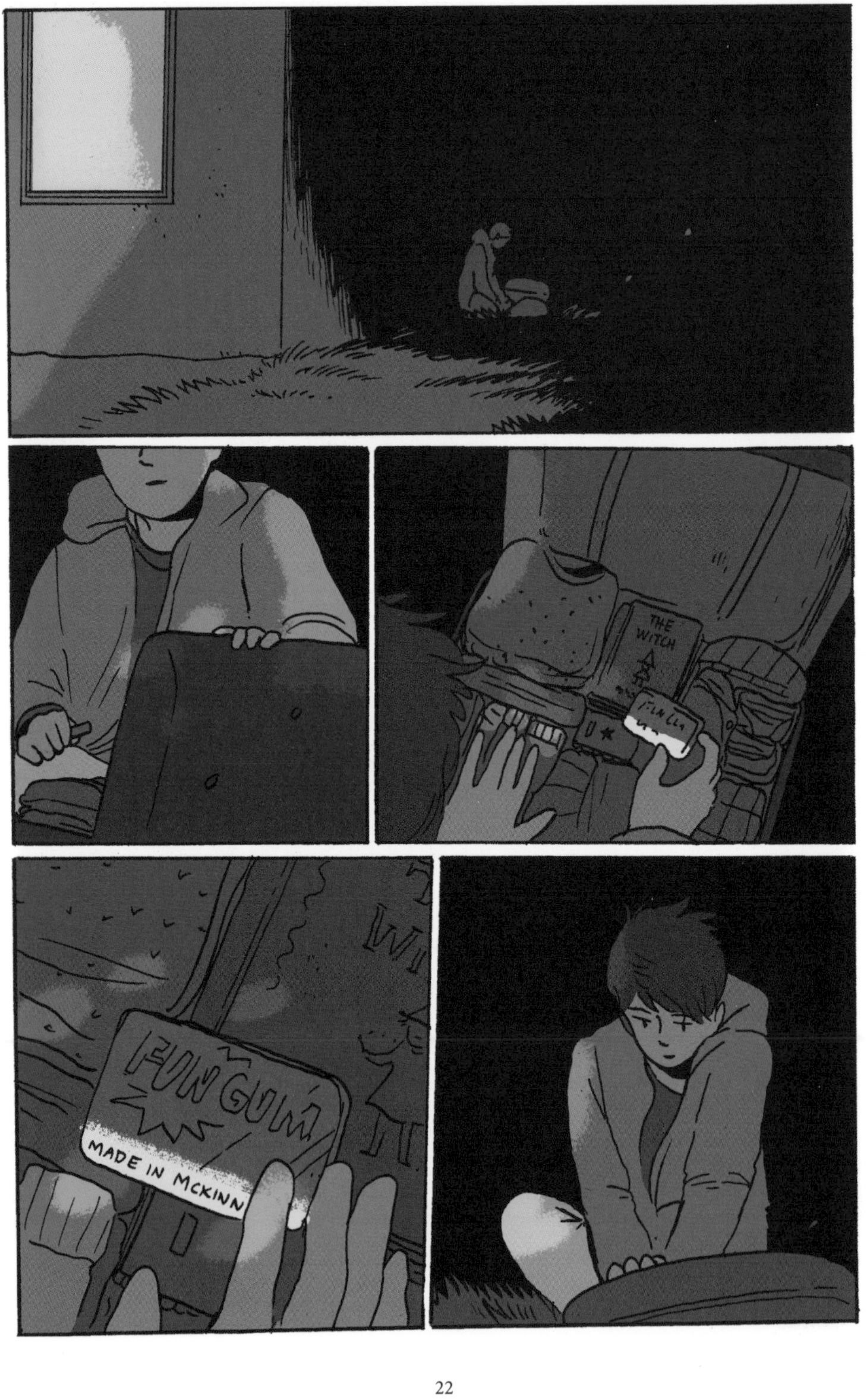
THE WITCH
FUN GUM
MADE IN MCKINN

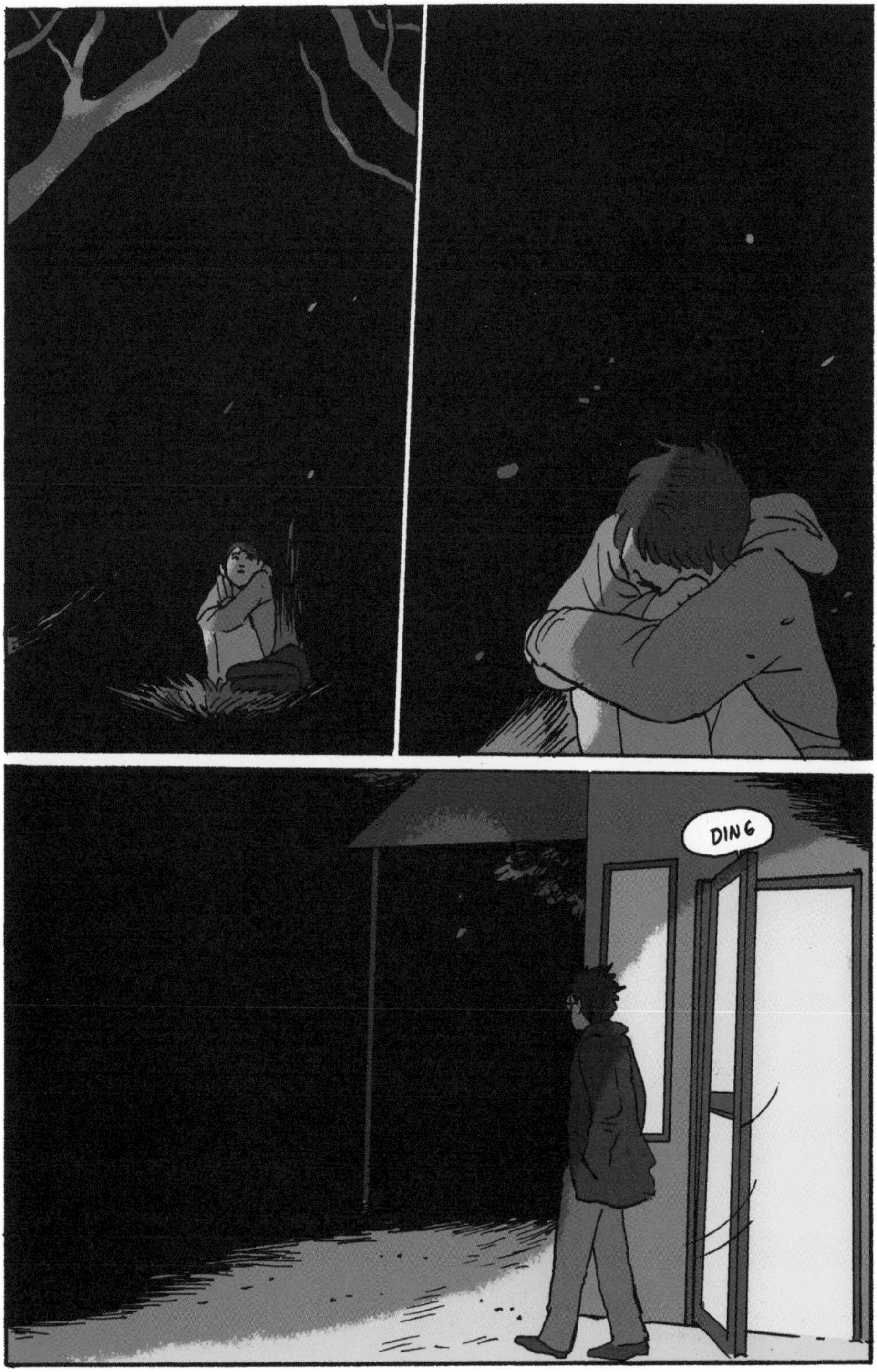
DING

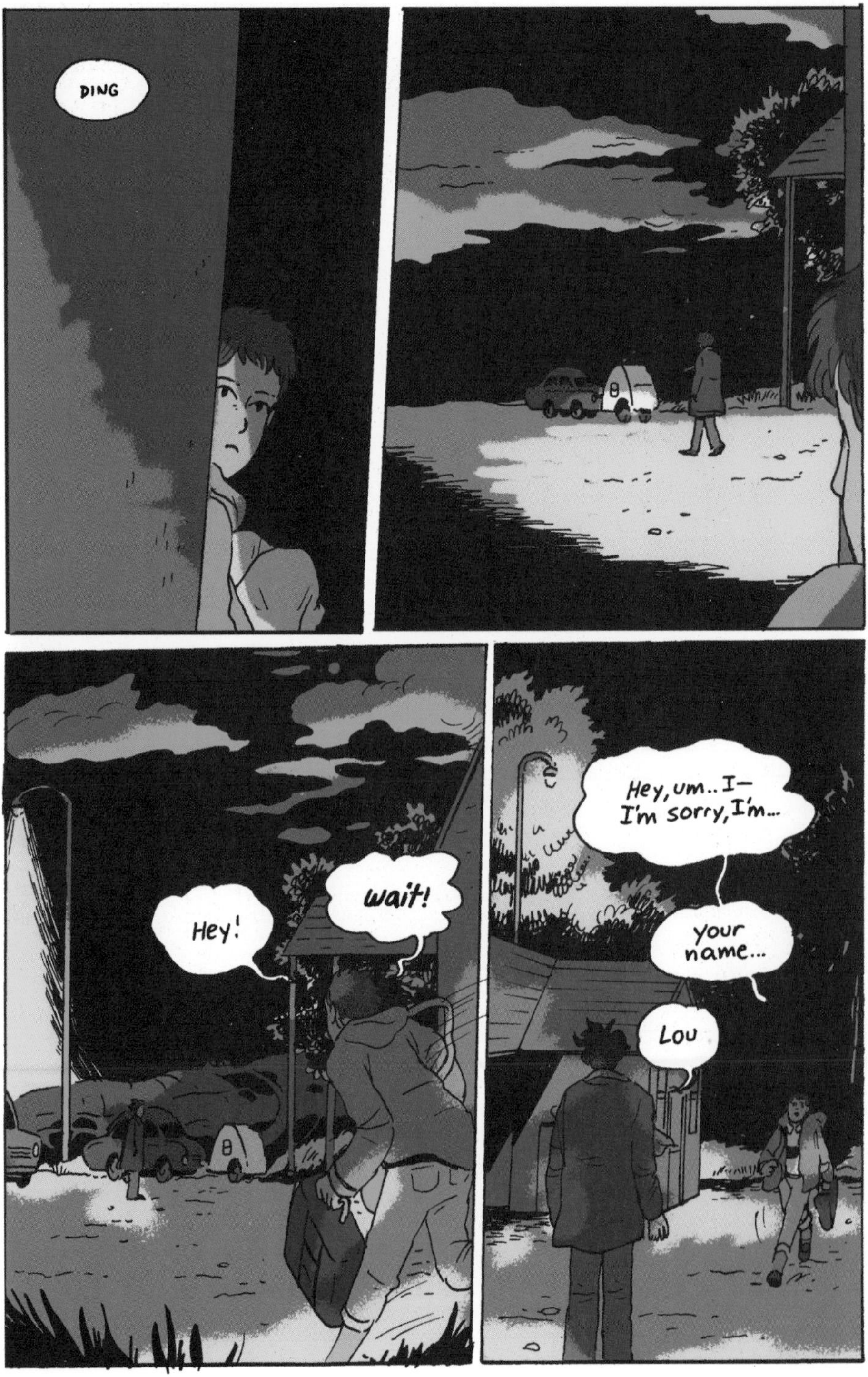
DING
Hey!
wait!
Hey, um.. I—
I'm sorry, I'm...
your name...
Lou

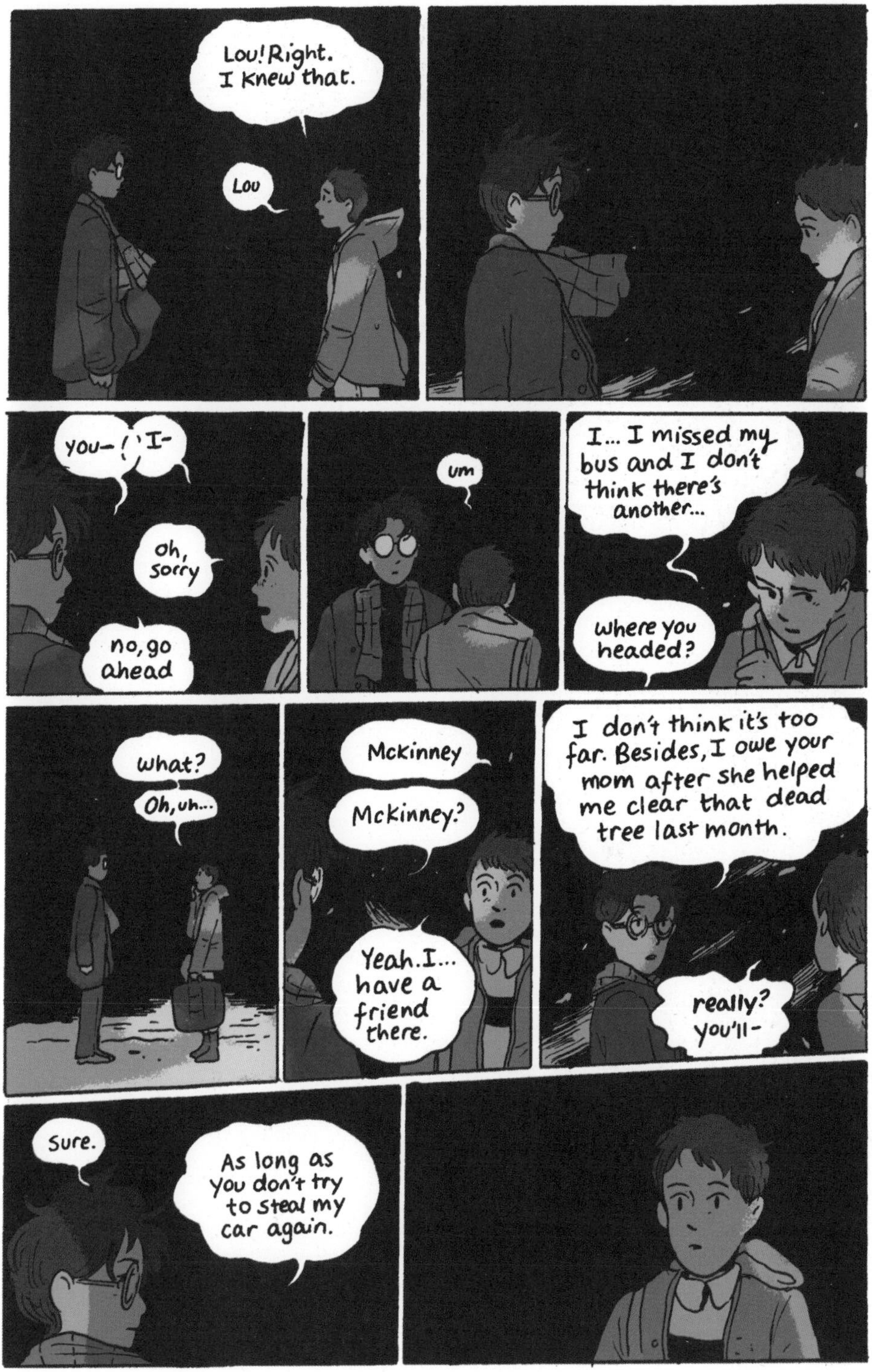
Lou! Right.
I knew that.
Lou
you-!
I-
oh, sorry
no, go ahead
um
I... I missed my bus and I don't think there's another...
where you headed?
what?
Oh, uh...
Mckinney
Mckinney?
Yeah. I... have a friend there.
I don't think it's too far. Besides, I owe your mom after she helped me clear that dead tree last month.
really? you'll-
Sure.
As long as you don't try to steal my car again.

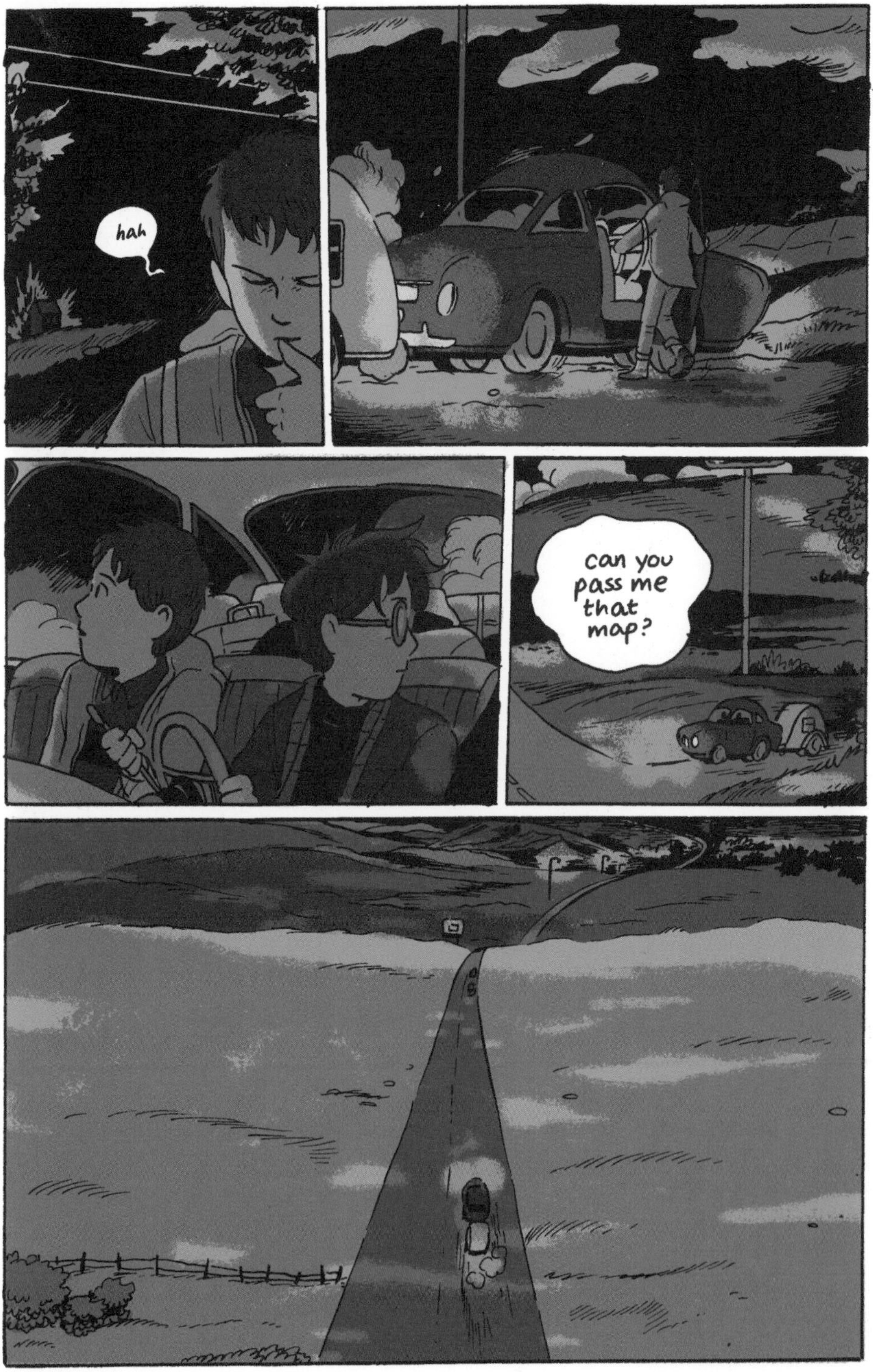
hah
can you pass me that map?

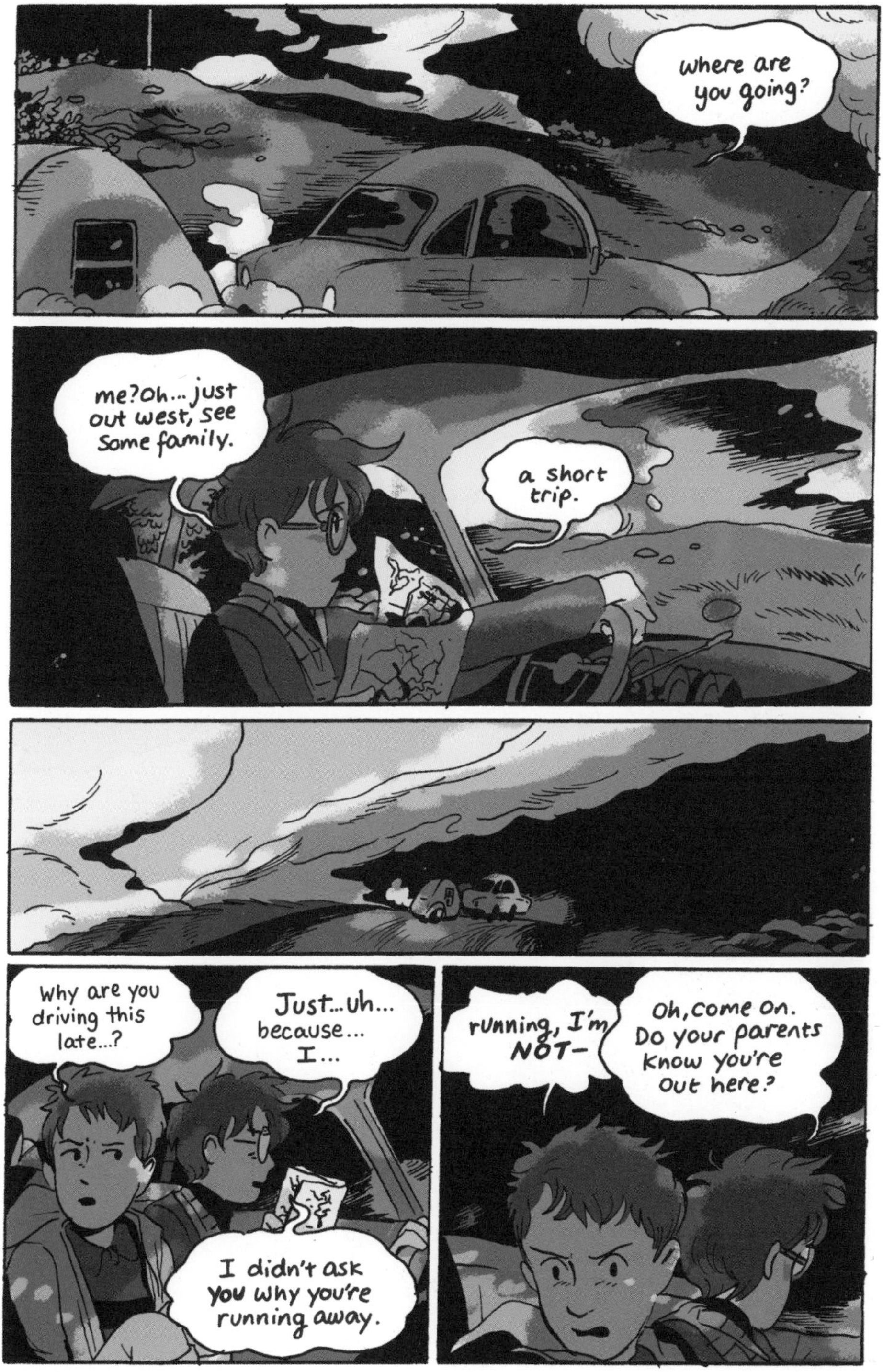
where are you going?
me? Oh... just out west, see some family.
a short trip.
why are you driving this late...?
Just... uh... because... I...
I didn't ask you why you're running away.
running, I'm NOT-
Oh, come on. Do your parents know you're out here?

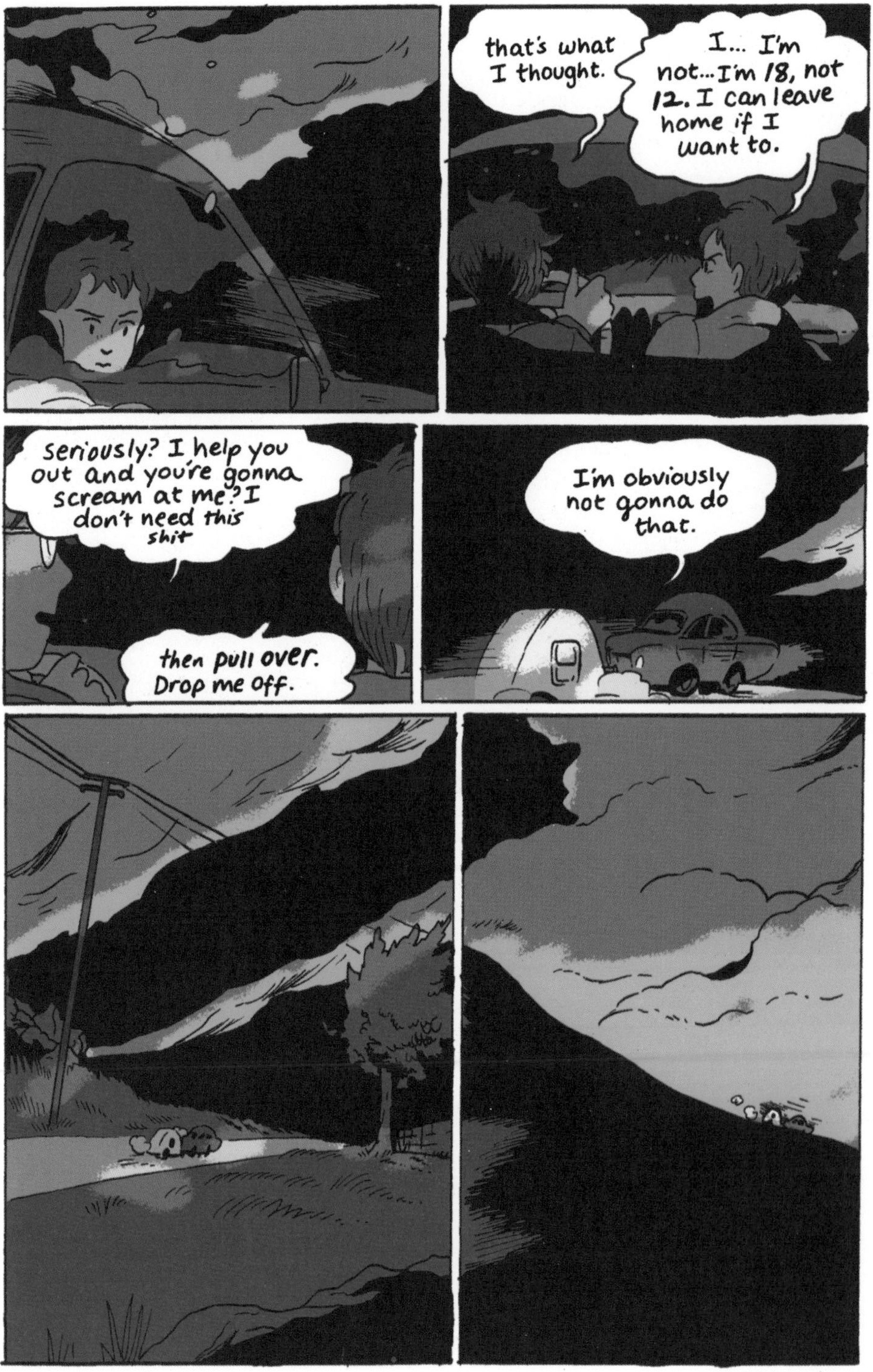
that's what I thought.
I... I'm not...I'm 18, not 12. I can leave home if I want to.
seriously? I help you out and you're gonna scream at me? I don't need this shit
then pull over. Drop me off.
I'm obviously not gonna do that.

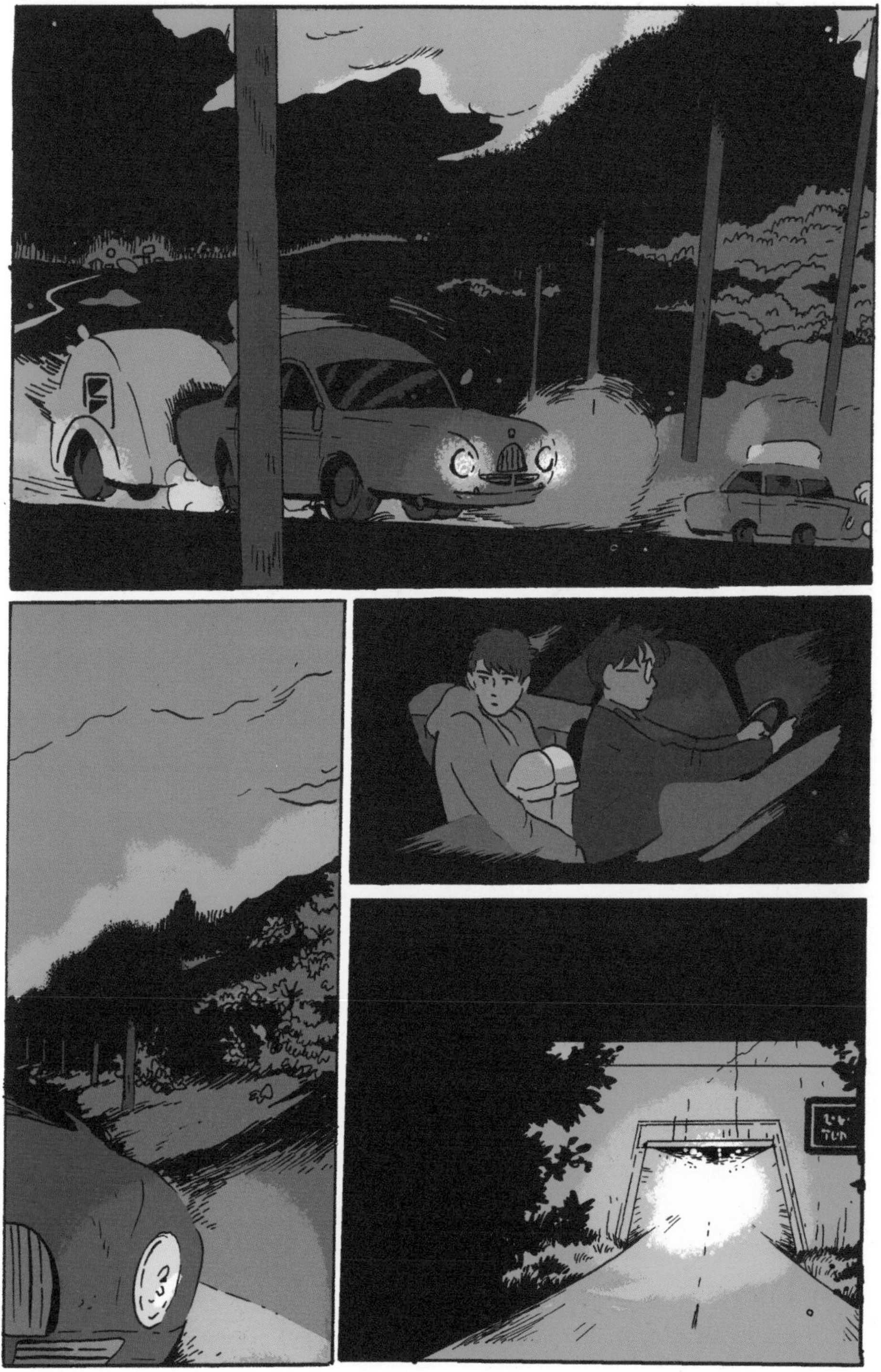

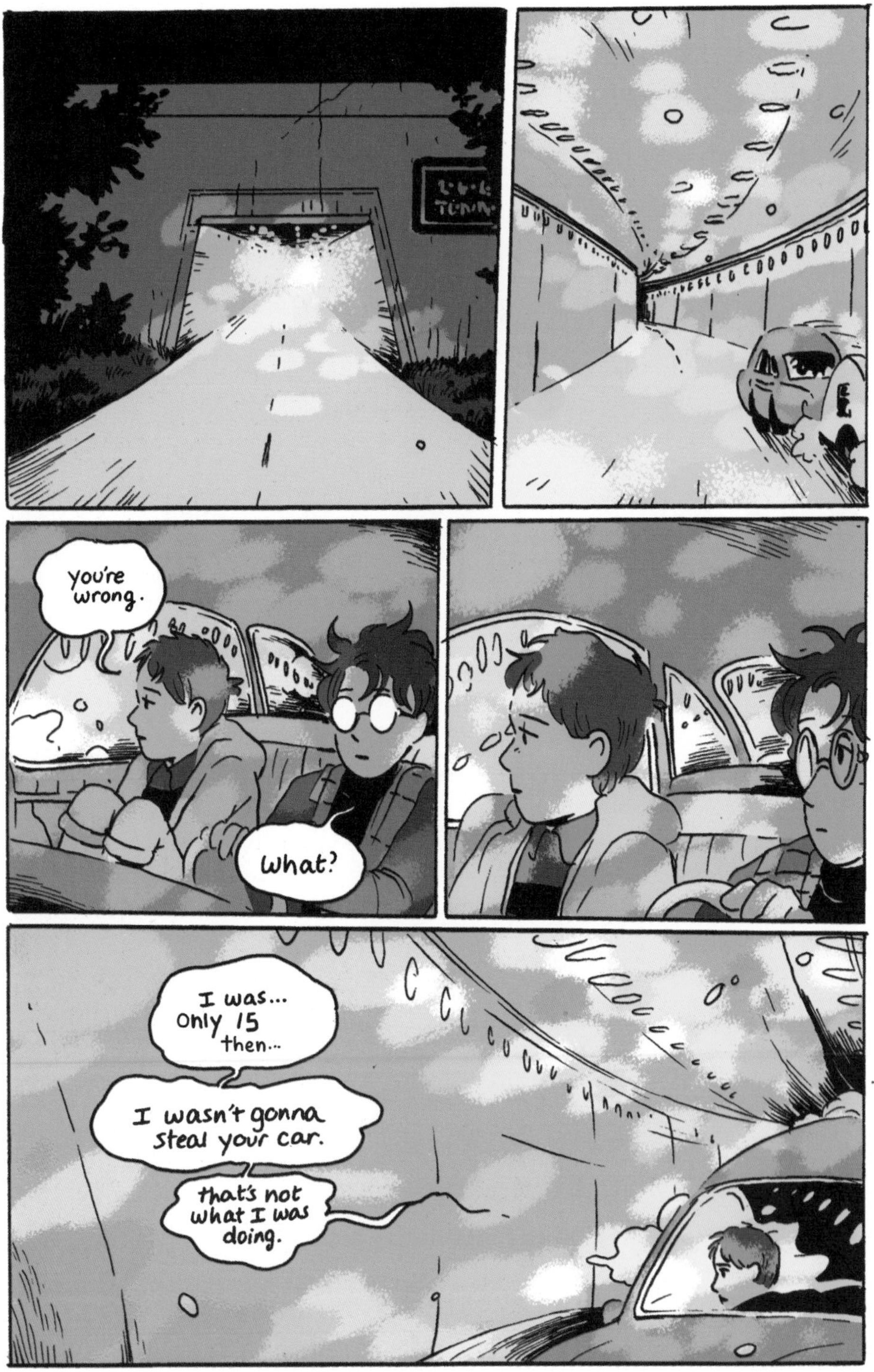
you're wrong.
What?
I was... only 15 then...
I wasn't gonna steal your car.
that's not what I was doing.

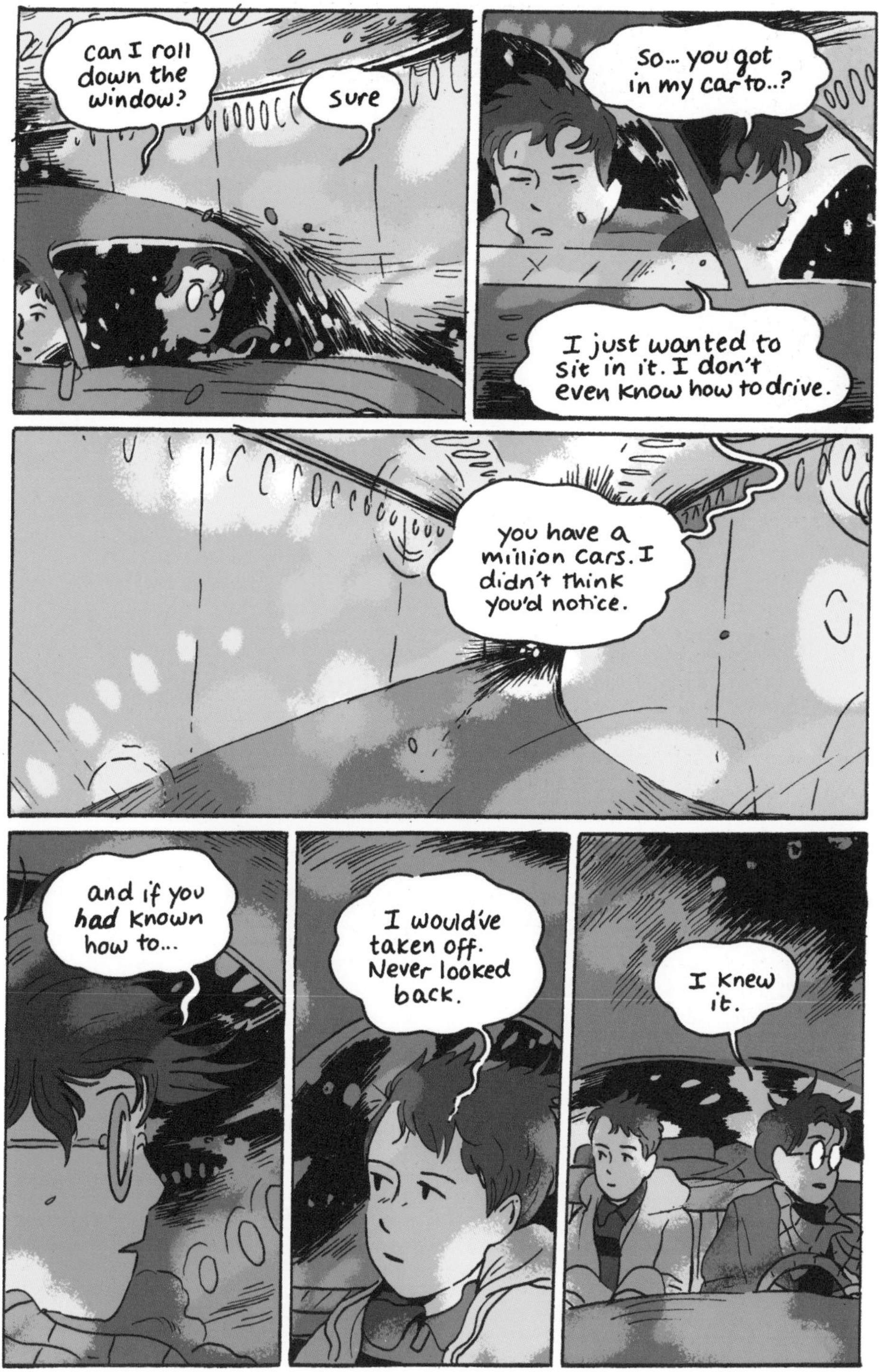
can I roll down the window?
sure
So... you got in my car to..?
I just wanted to sit in it. I don't even know how to drive.
you have a million cars. I didn't think you'd notice.
and if you had known how to...
I would've taken off. Never looked back.
I knew it.

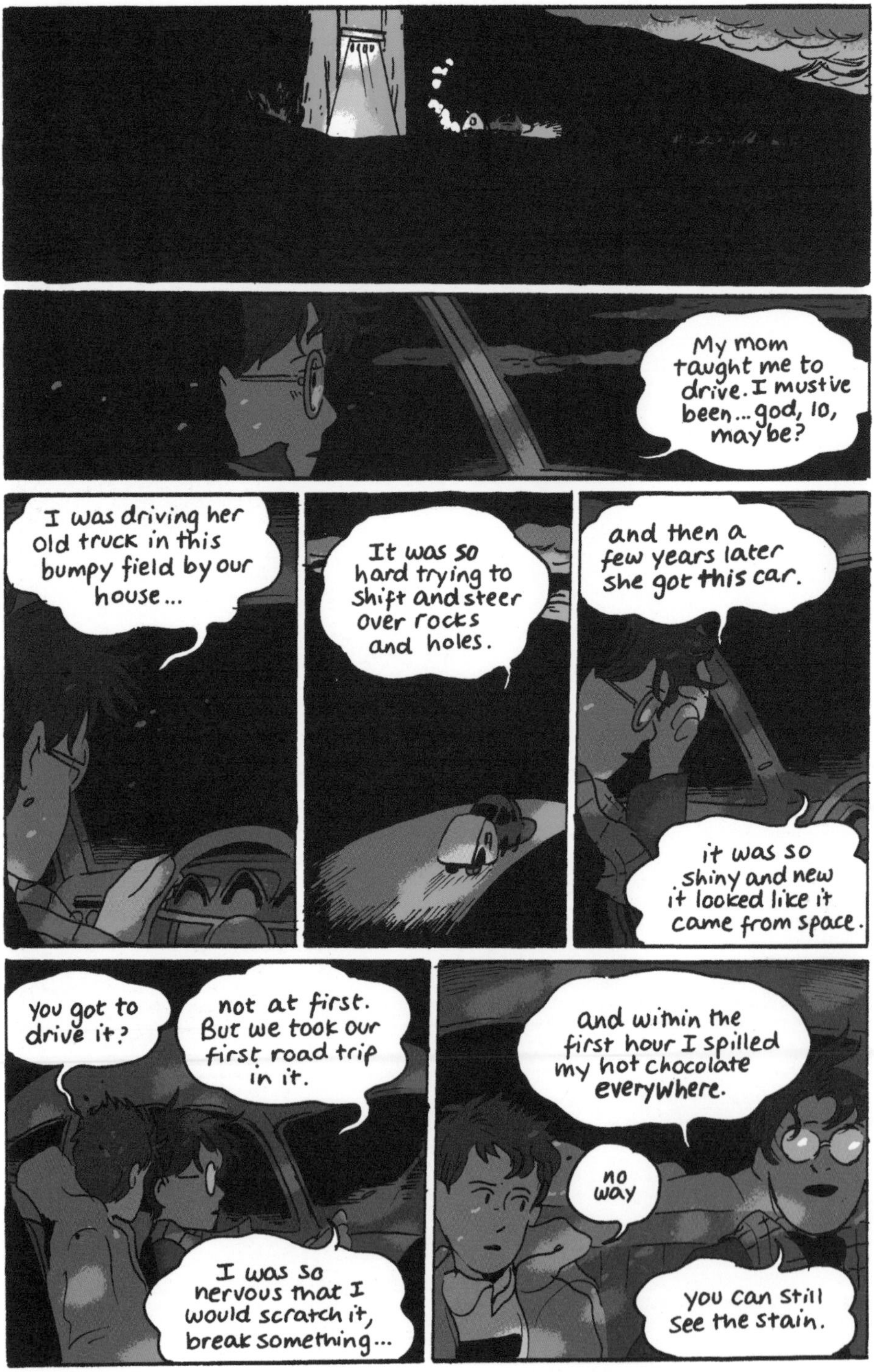
My mom taught me to drive. I mustve been...god, 10, maybe?
I was driving her old truck in this bumpy field by our house...
It was so hard trying to shift and steer over rocks and holes.
and then a few years later she got this car.
it was so shiny and new it looked like it came from space.
you got to drive it?
not at first. But we took our first road trip in it.
I was so nervous that I would scratch it, break something...
and within the first hour I spilled my hot chocolate everywhere.
no way
you can still see the stain.

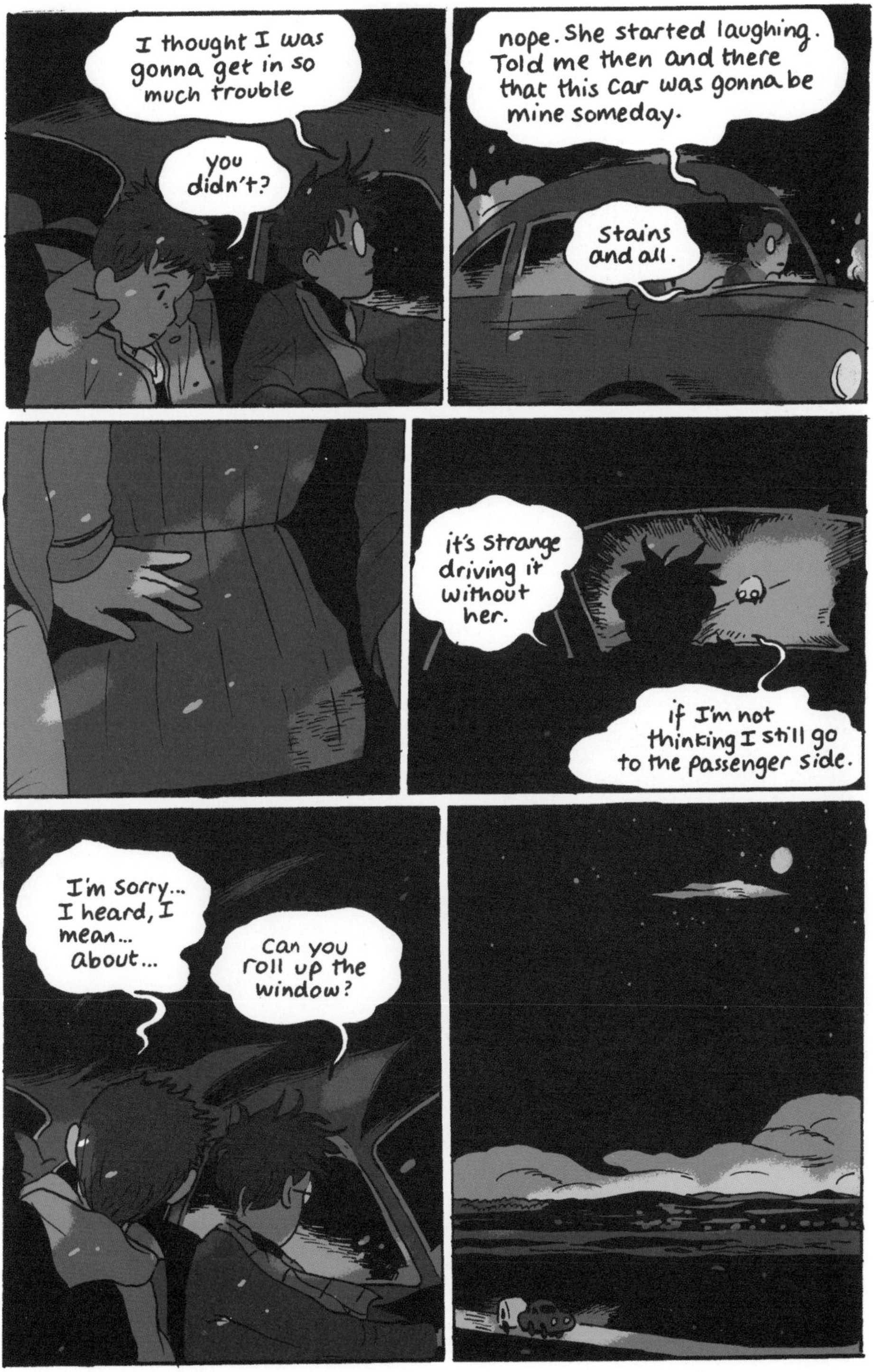

I thought I was gonna get in so much trouble
you didn't?
nope. She started laughing. Told me then and there that this car was gonna be mine someday.
Stains and all.
it's strange driving it without her.
if I'm not thinking I still go to the passenger side.
I'm sorry... I heard, I mean... about...
Can you roll up the window?

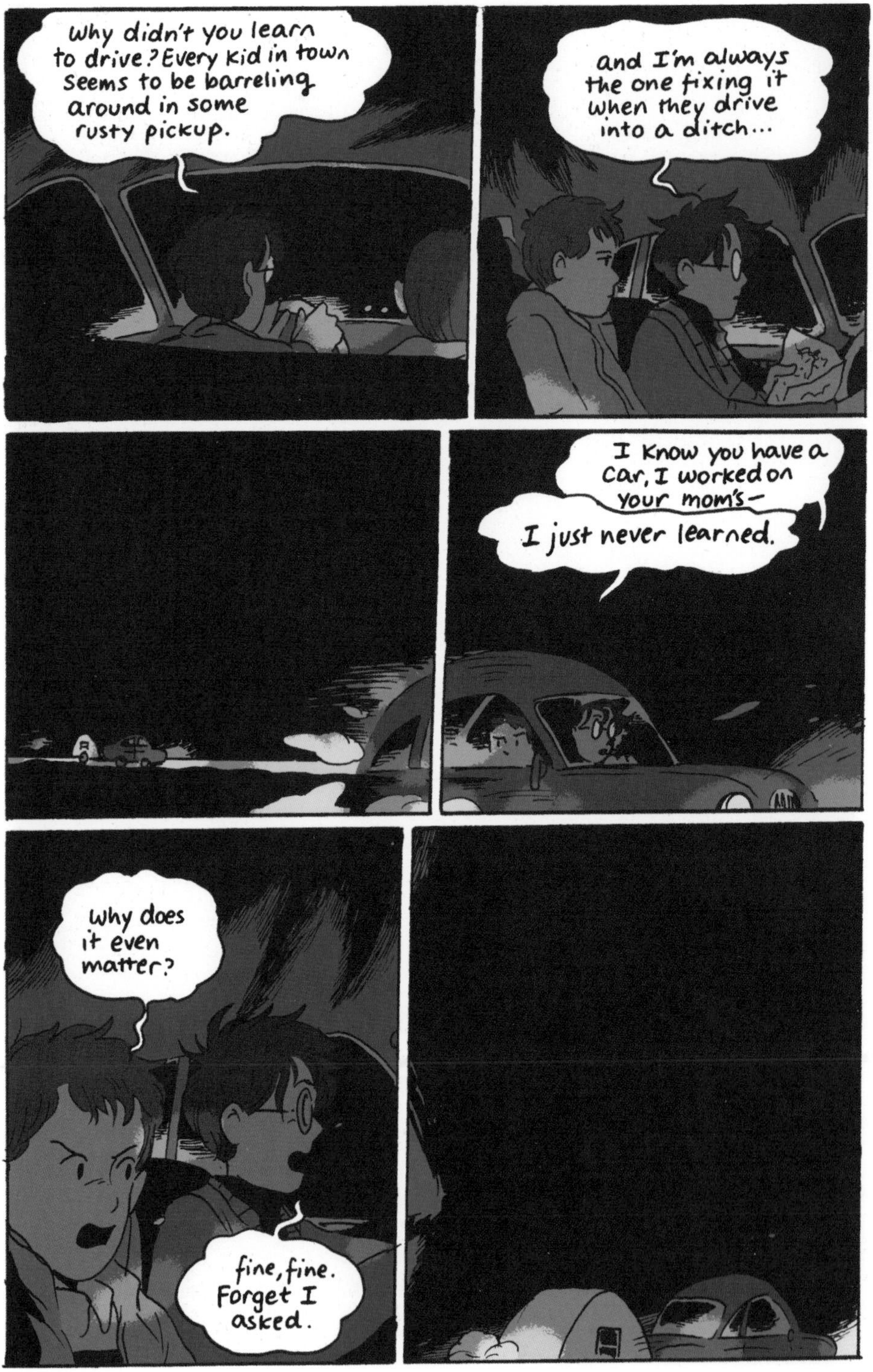
Why didn't you learn to drive? Every kid in town seems to be barreling around in some rusty pickup.
and I'm always the one fixing it when they drive into a ditch...
I know you have a car, I worked on your mom's—
I just never learned.
Why does it even matter?
fine, fine. Forget I asked.

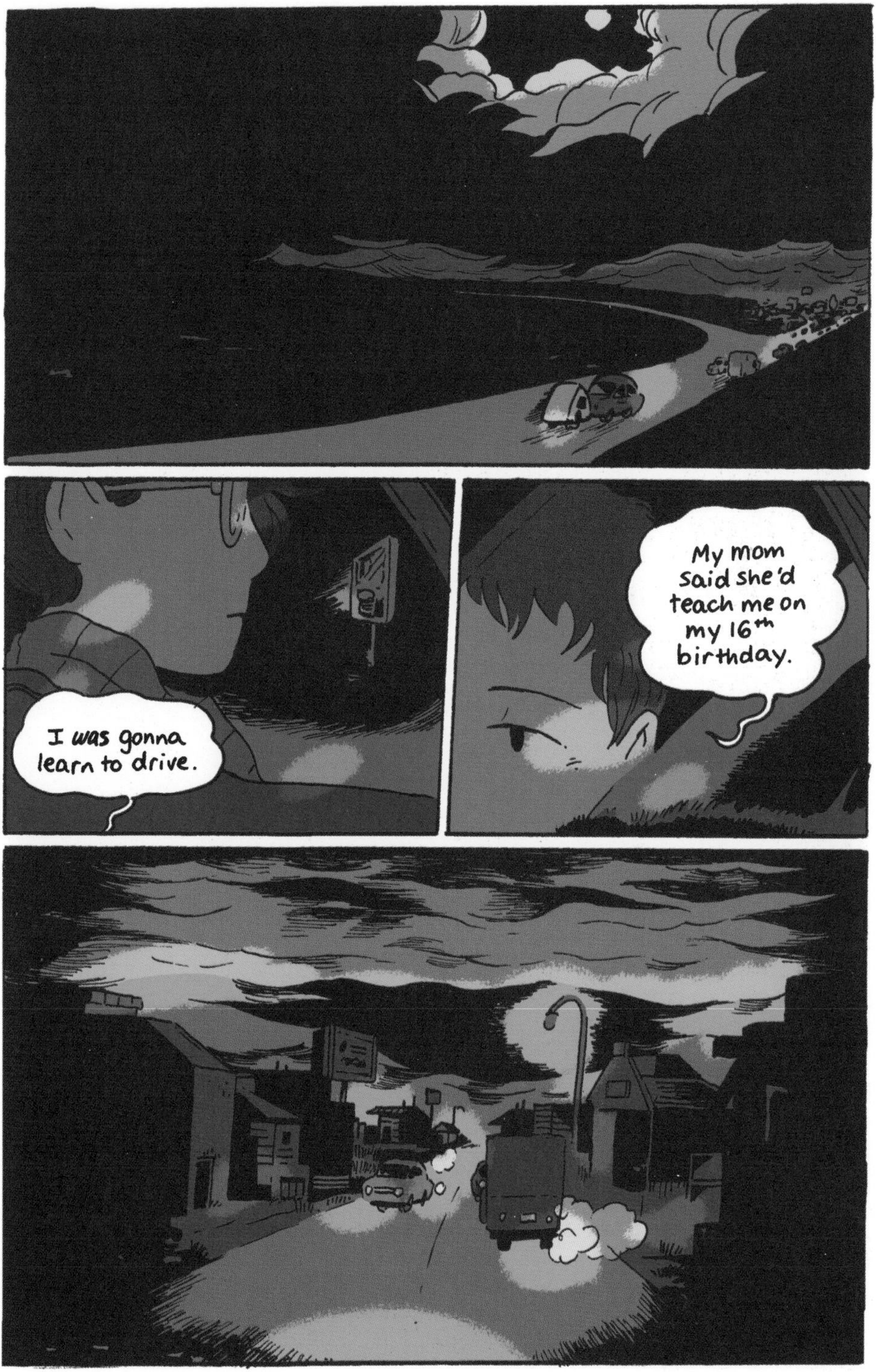
I was gonna learn to drive.
My mom said she'd teach me on my 16th birthday.

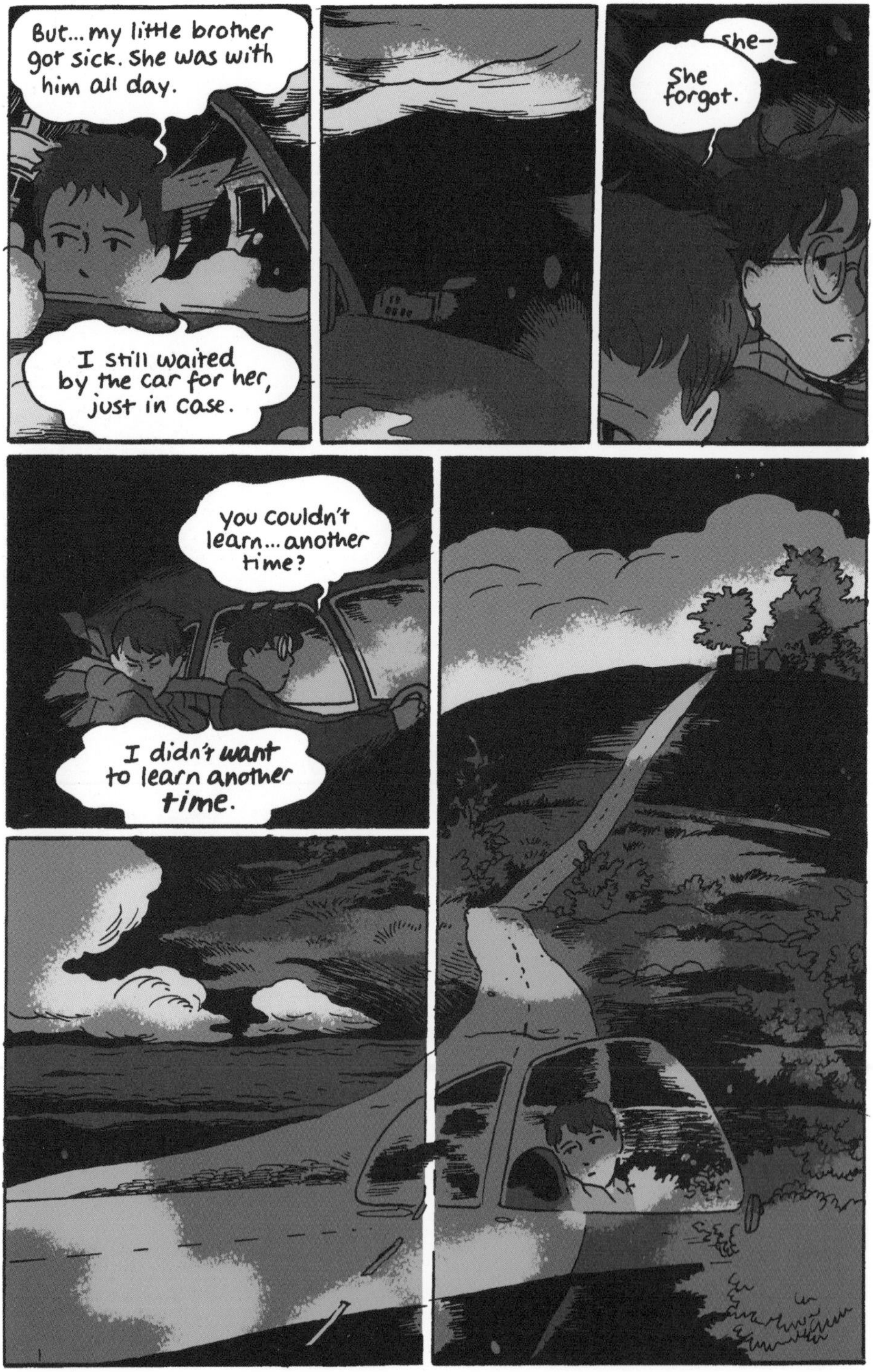
But... my little brother got sick. She was with him all day.
I still waited by the car for her, just in case.
she-
She forgot.
you couldn't learn... another time?
I didn't want to learn another time.

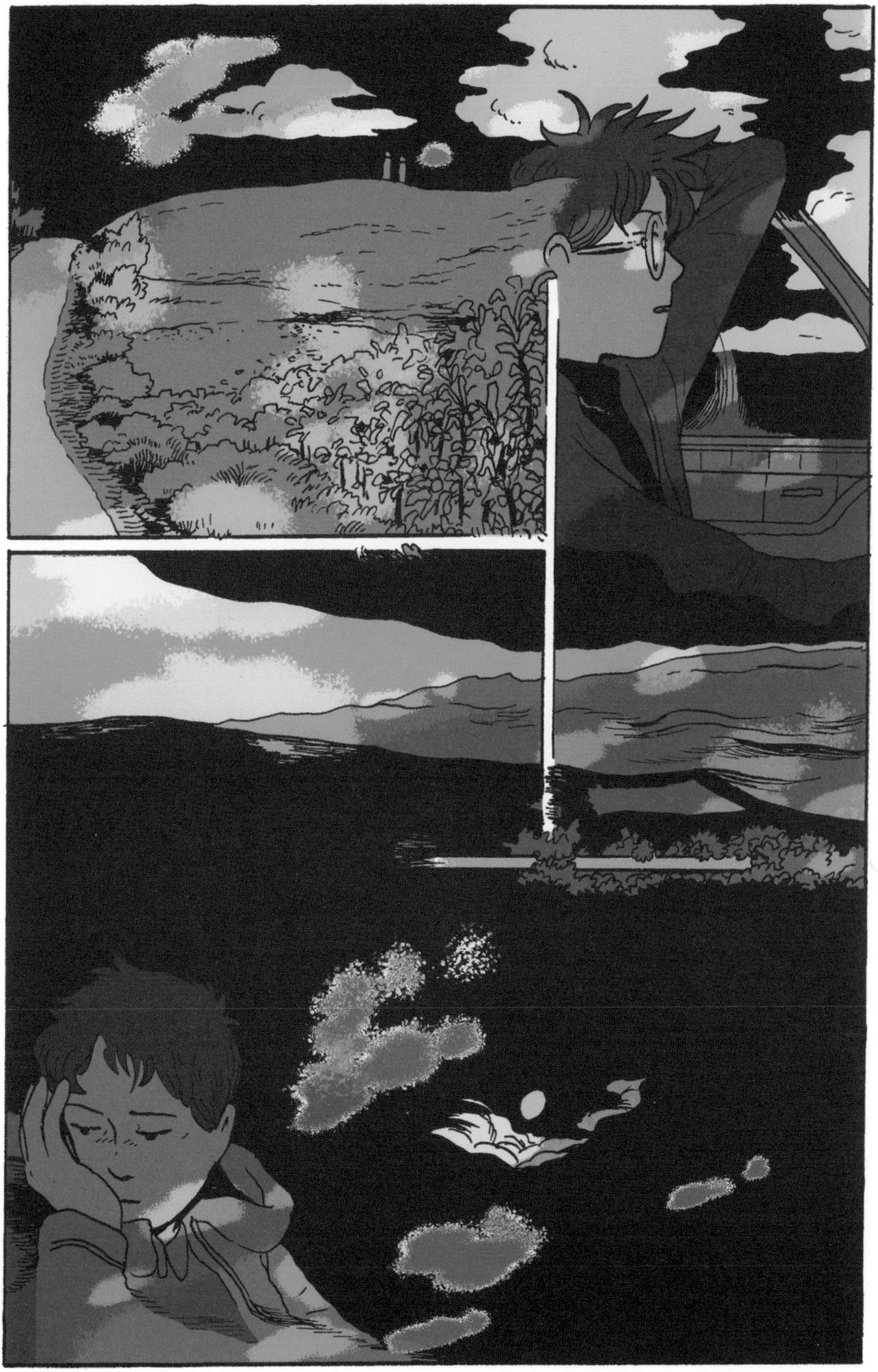

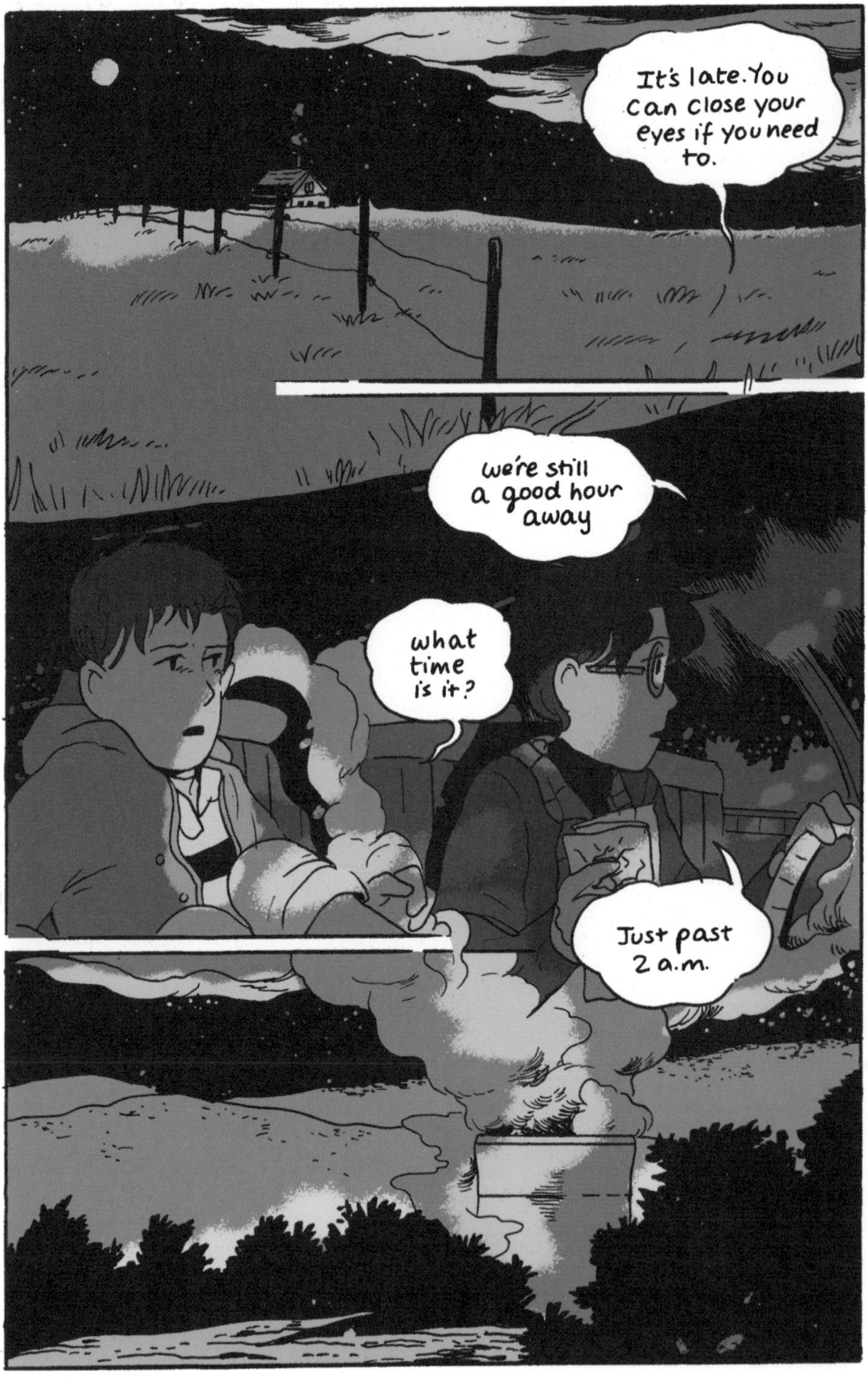
It's late. You can close your eyes if you need to.
we're still a good hour away
what time is it?
Just past 2 a.m.

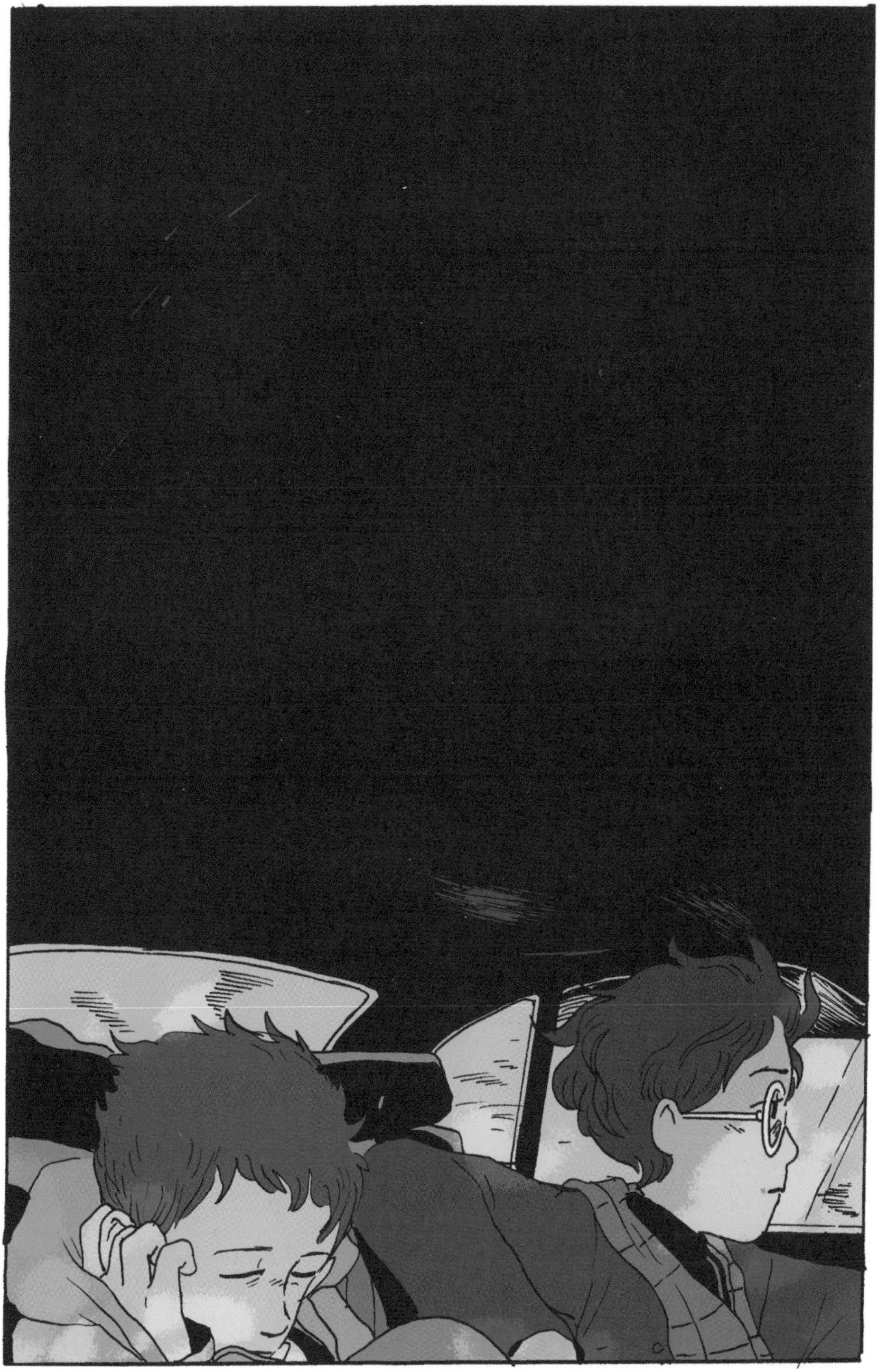

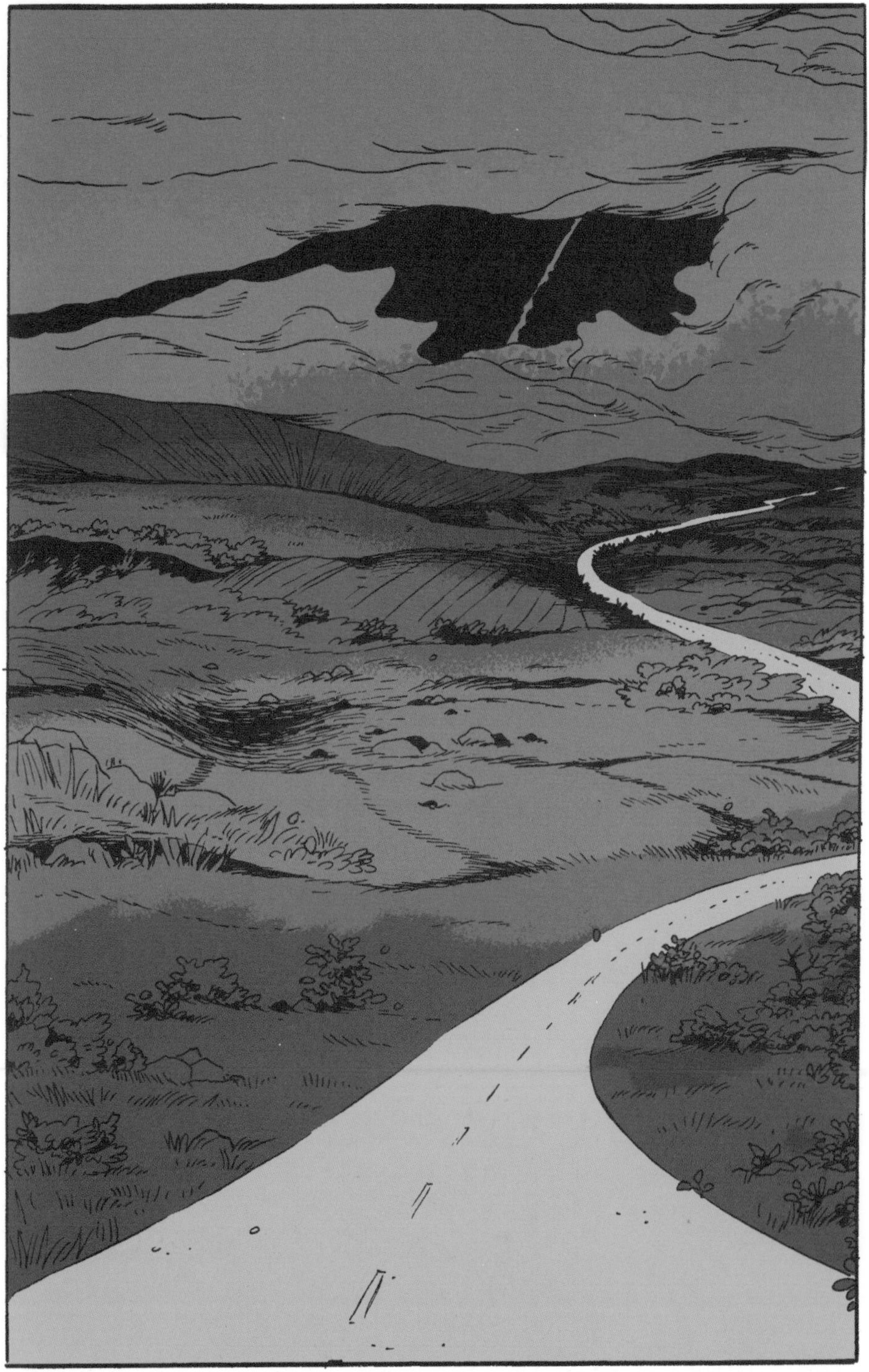

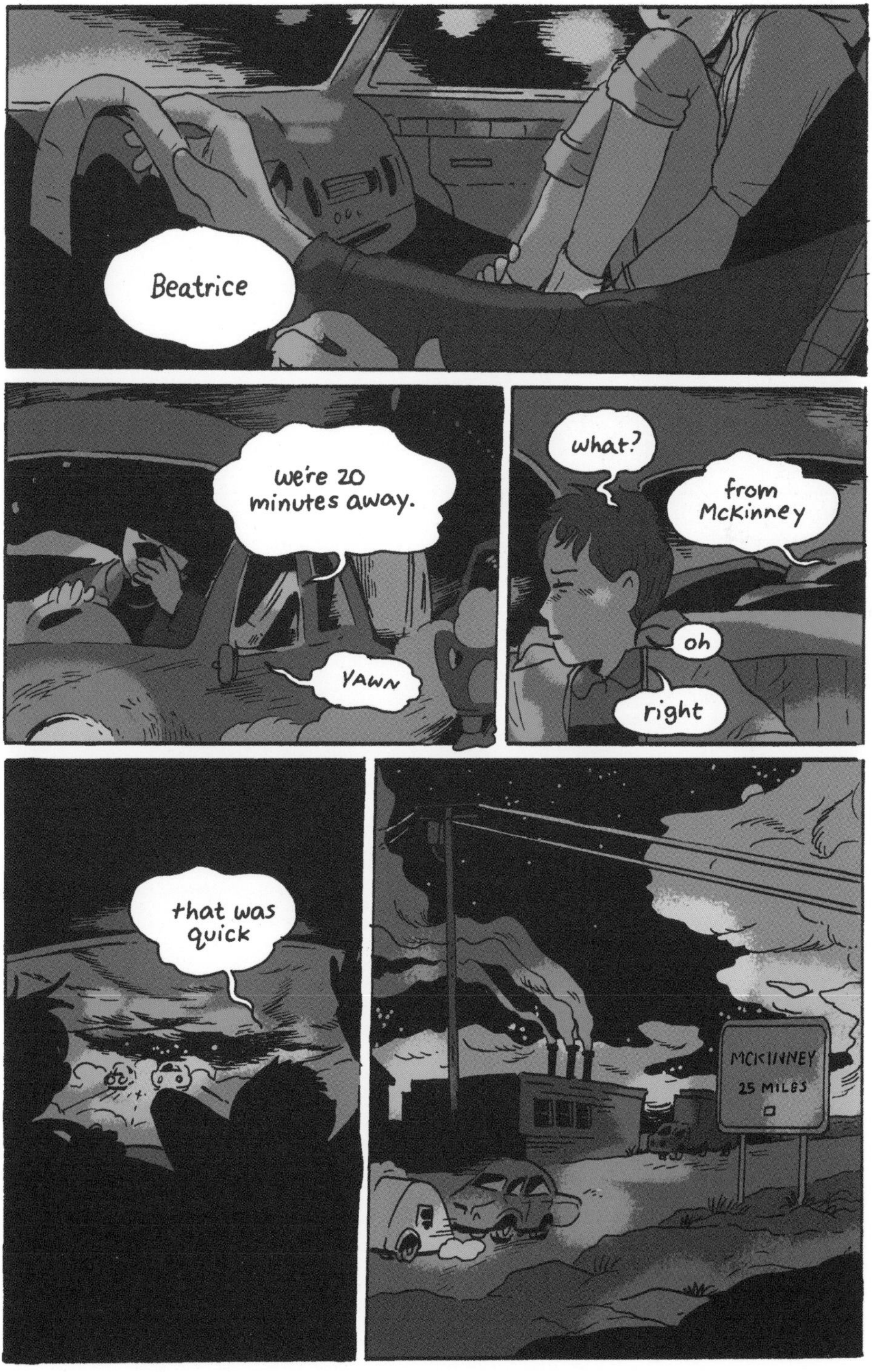
Beatrice
we're 20 minutes away.
YAWN
what?
from McKinney
oh
right
that was quick
MCKINNEY
25 MILES

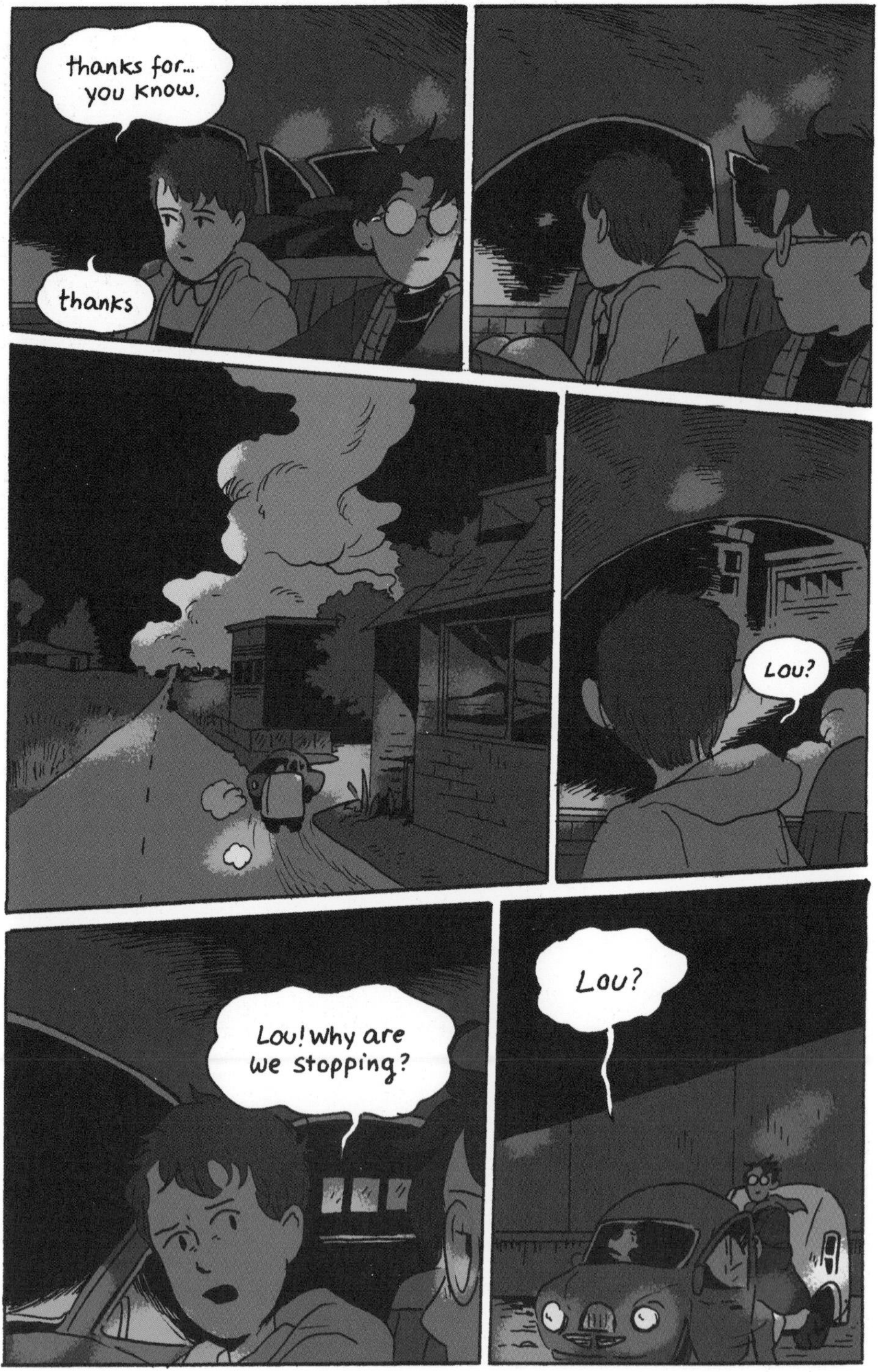
thanks for... you know.
thanks
Lou?
Lou! Why are we stopping?
Lou?

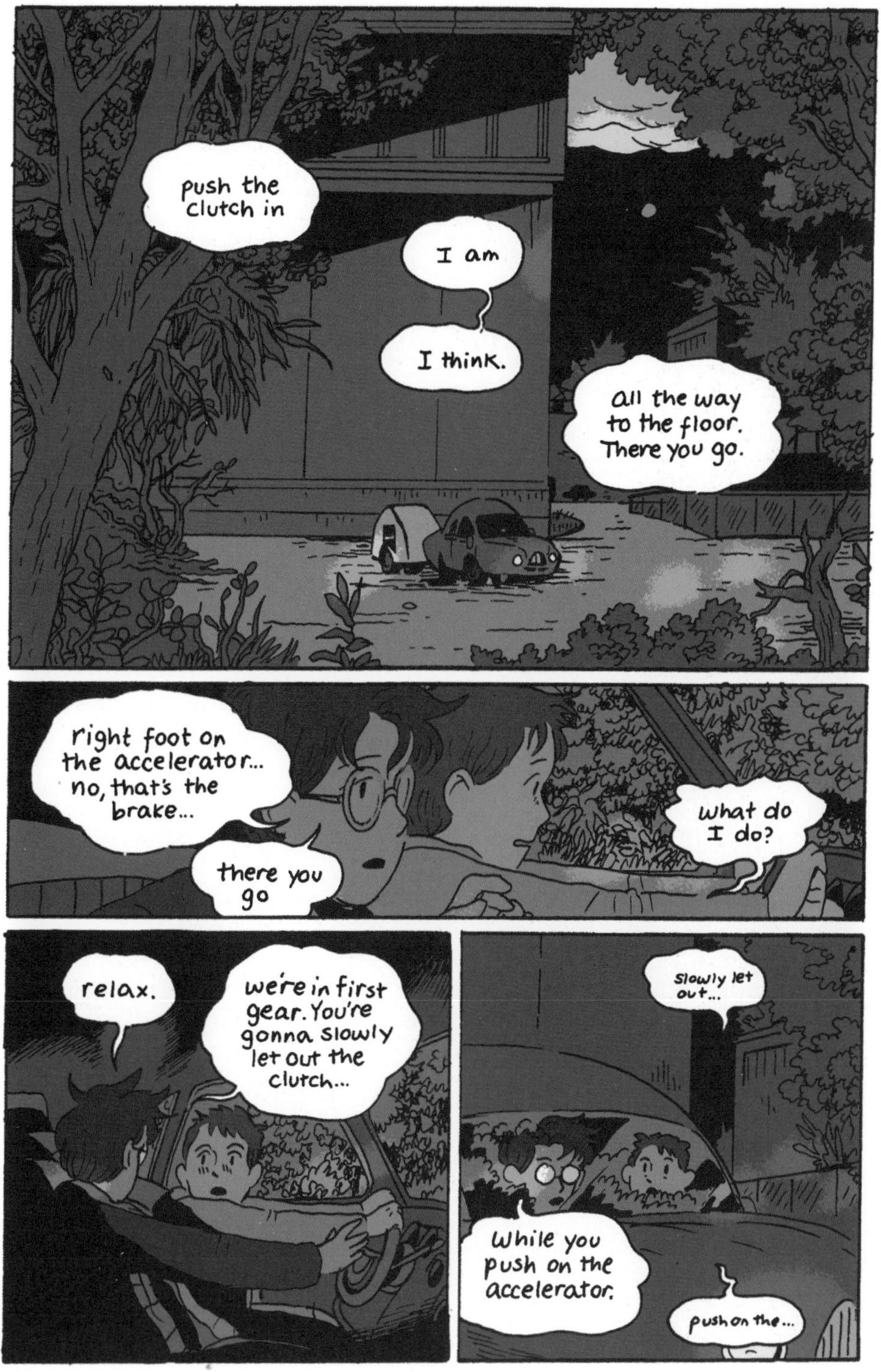
push the clutch in
I am
I think.
all the way to the floor. There you go.
right foot on the accelerator... no, that's the brake...
there you go
what do I do?
relax.
we're in first gear. You're gonna slowly let out the clutch...
slowly let out...
While you push on the accelerator.
push on the...

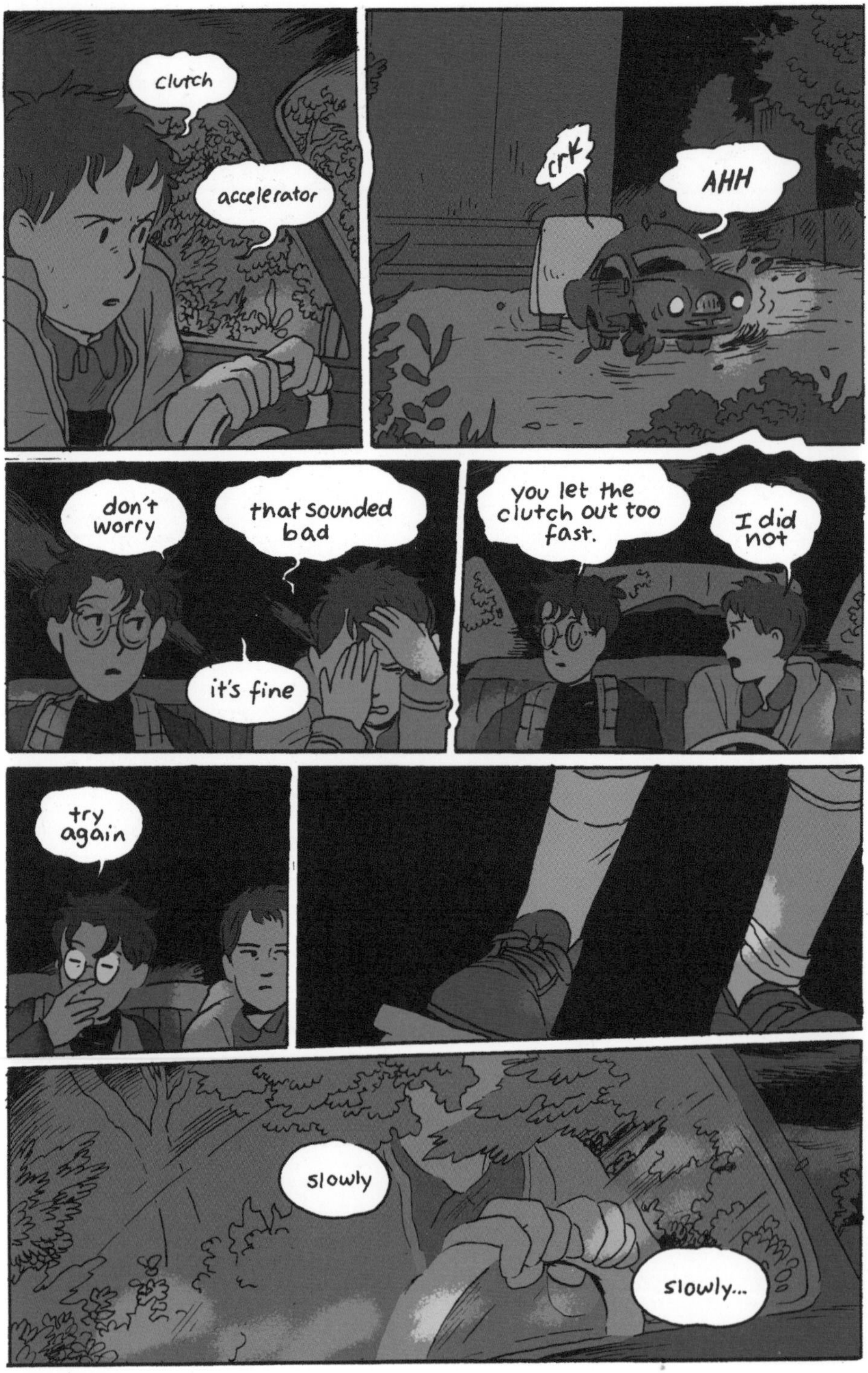
clutch
accelerator
crk
AHH
don't worry
that sounded bad
it's fine
you let the clutch out too fast.
I did not
try again
slowly
slowly...

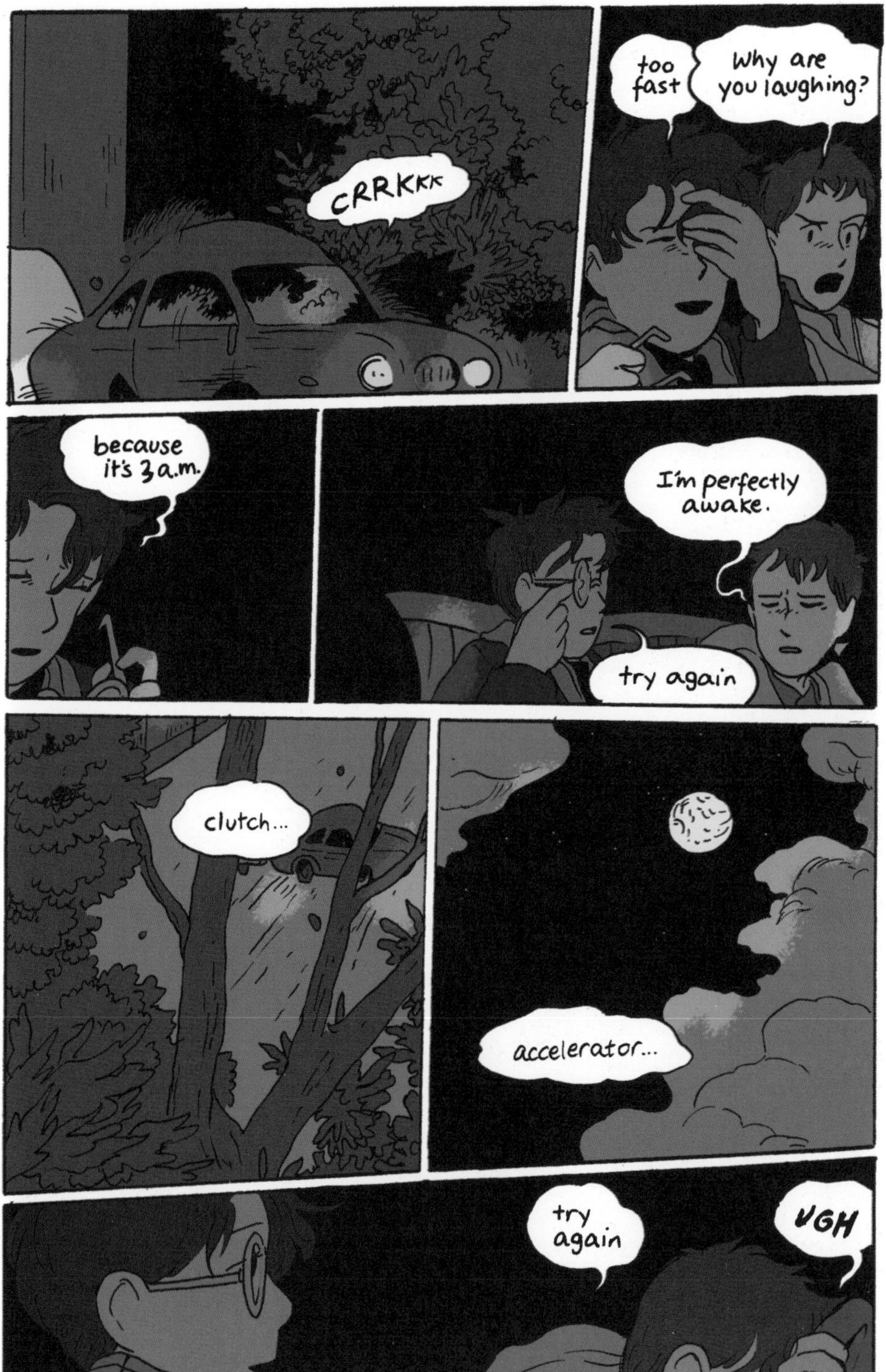
CRRKKK
too fast
Why are you laughing?
because it's 3 a.m.
I'm perfectly awake.
try again
clutch...
accelerator...
try again
UGH

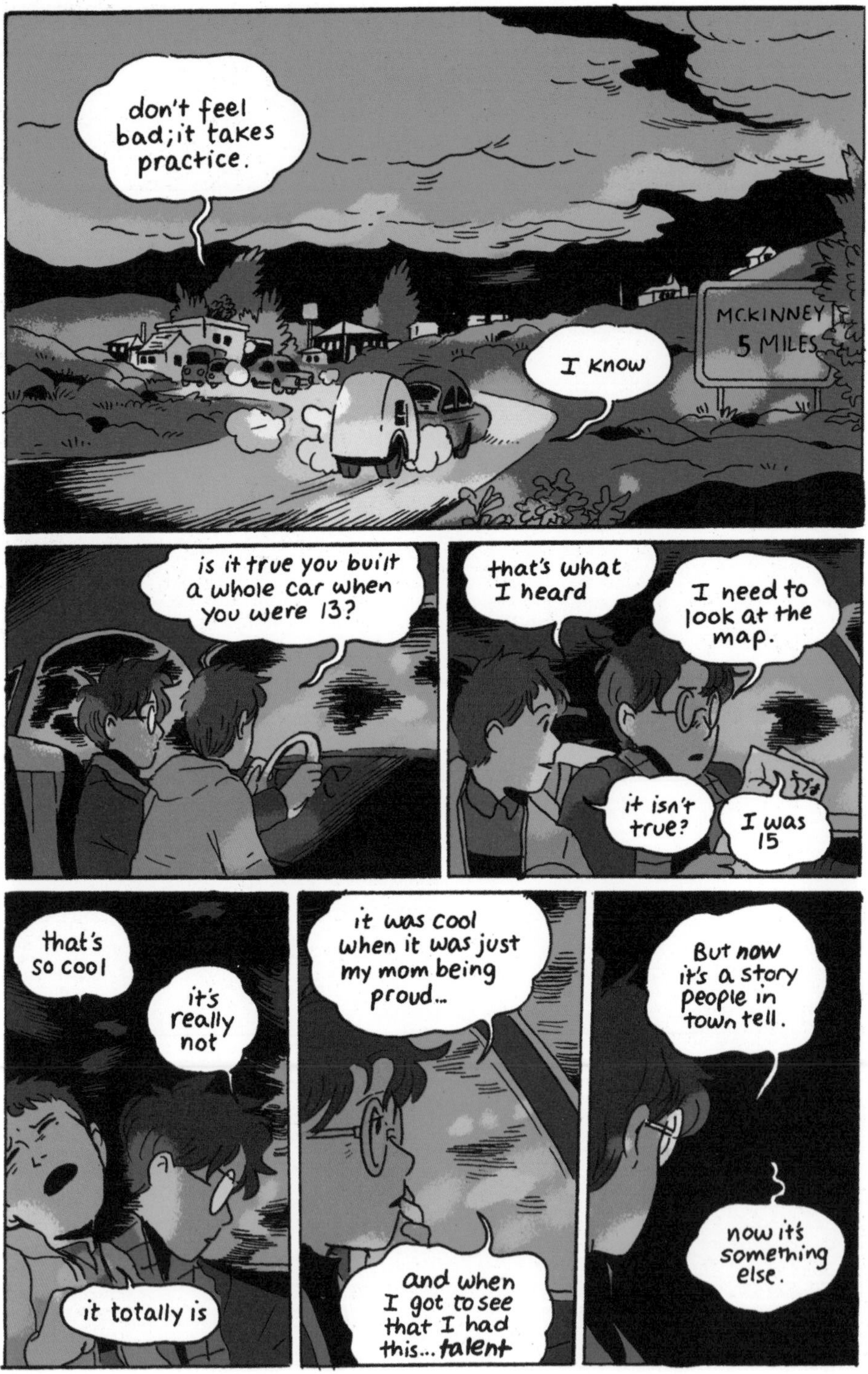
don't feel bad; it takes practice.
McKINNEY 5 MILES
I know
is it true you built a whole car when you were 13?
that's what I heard
I need to look at the map.
it isn't true?
I was 15
that's so cool
it's really not
it totally is
it was cool when it was just my mom being proud...
and when I got to see that I had this... *talent*
But *now* it's a story people in town tell.
now it's something else.

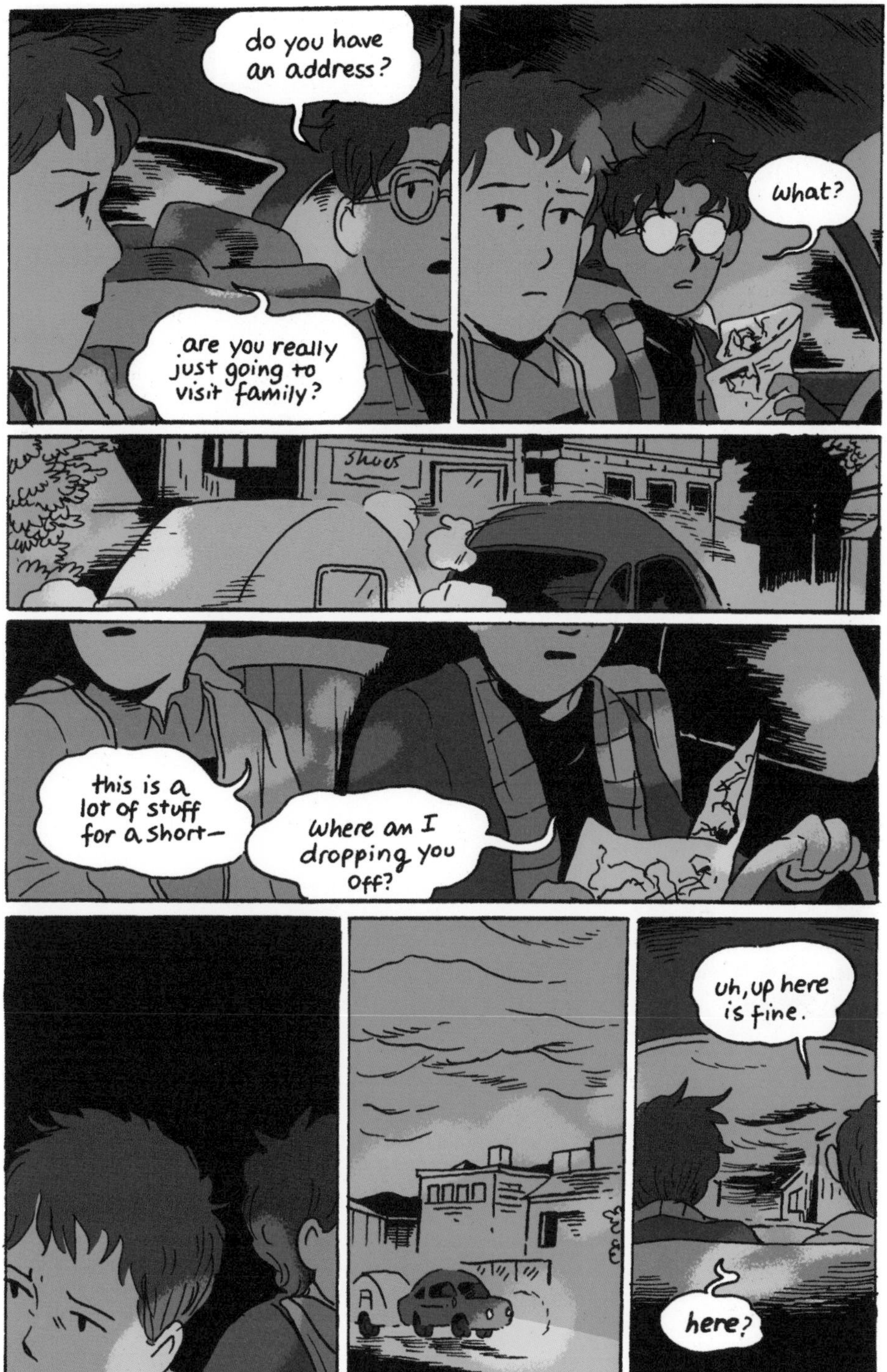
do you have an address?
are you really just going to visit family?
what?
shoes
this is a lot of stuff for a short—
where am I dropping you off?
uh, up here is fine.
here?

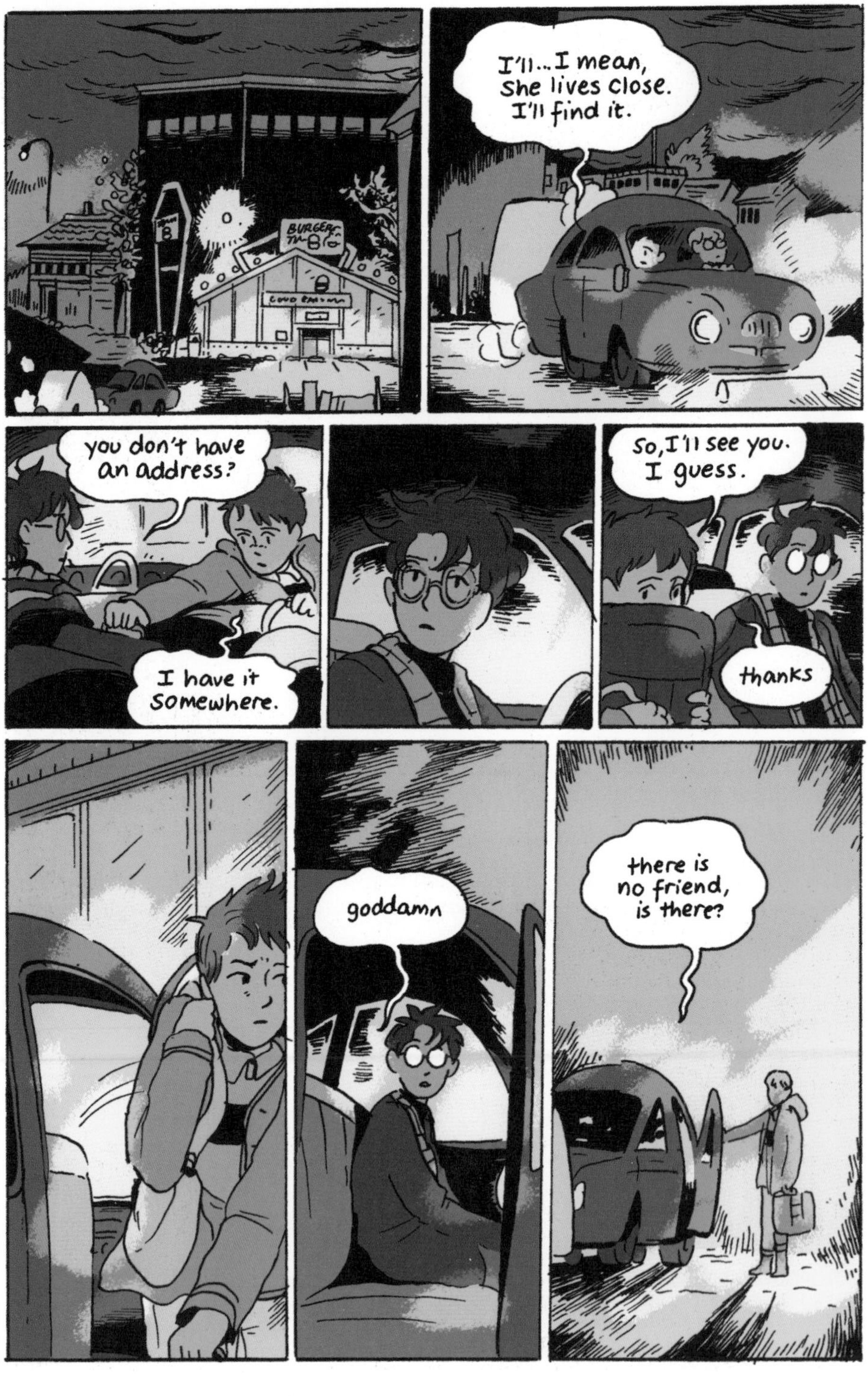
I'll... I mean, she lives close. I'll find it.
you don't have an address?
I have it somewhere.
So, I'll see you. I guess.
thanks
goddamn
there is no friend, is there?

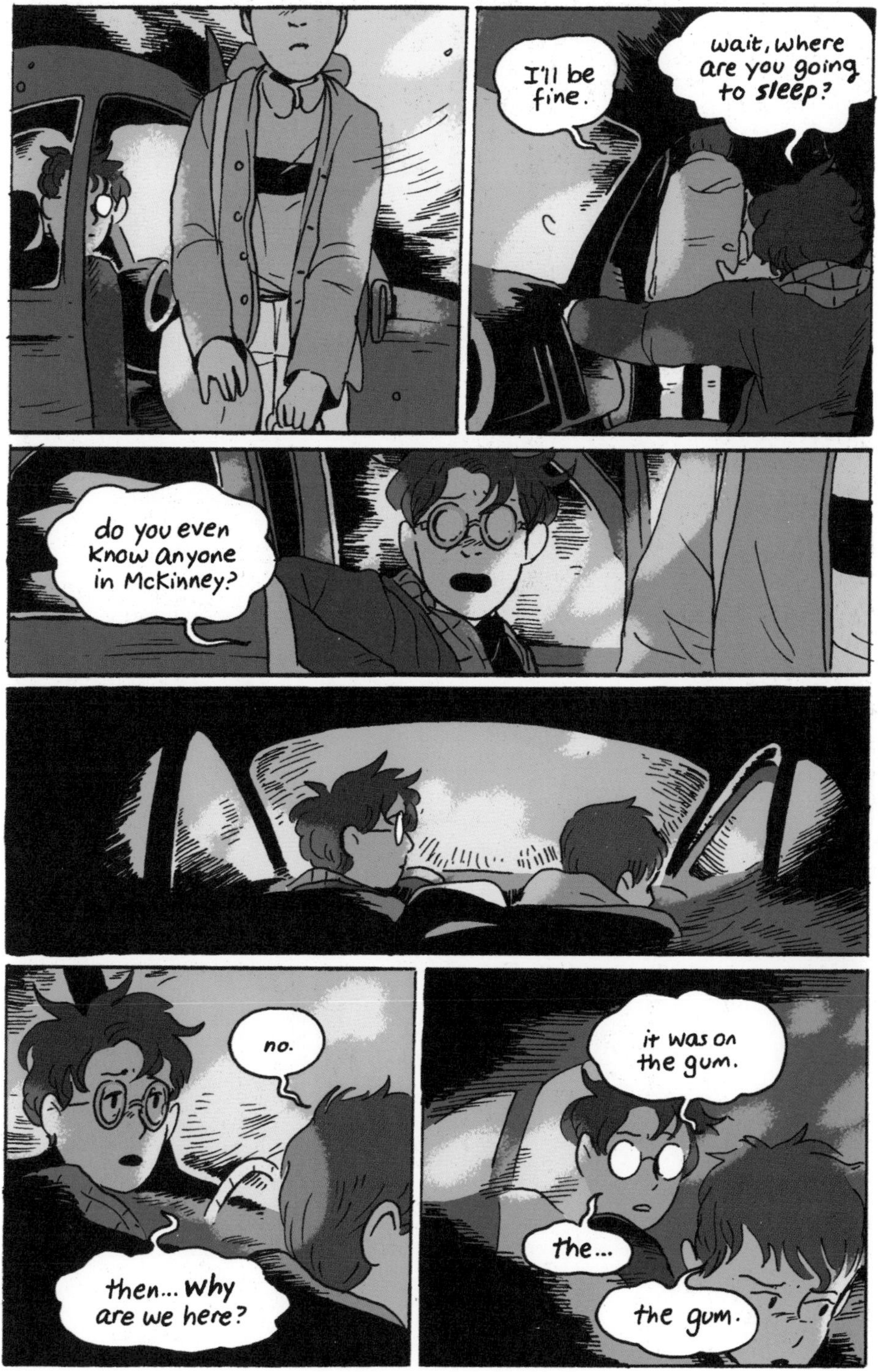
I'll be fine.
wait, where are you going to sleep?
do you even know anyone in McKinney?
no.
then... why are we here?
it was on the gum.
the...
the gum.

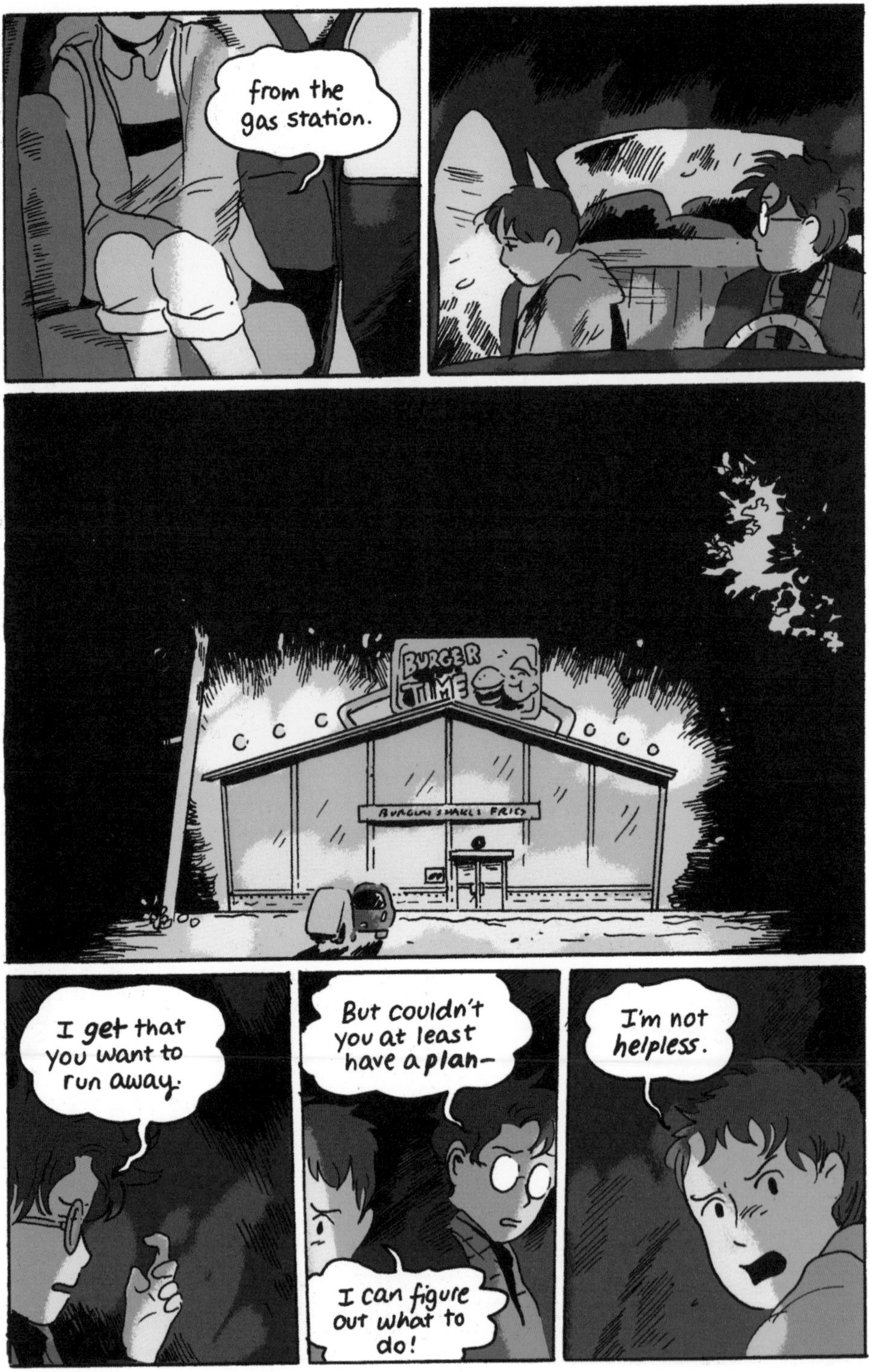
from the gas station.
BURGER TIME
I get that you want to run away.
But couldn't you at least have a plan—
I can figure out what to do!
I'm not helpless.

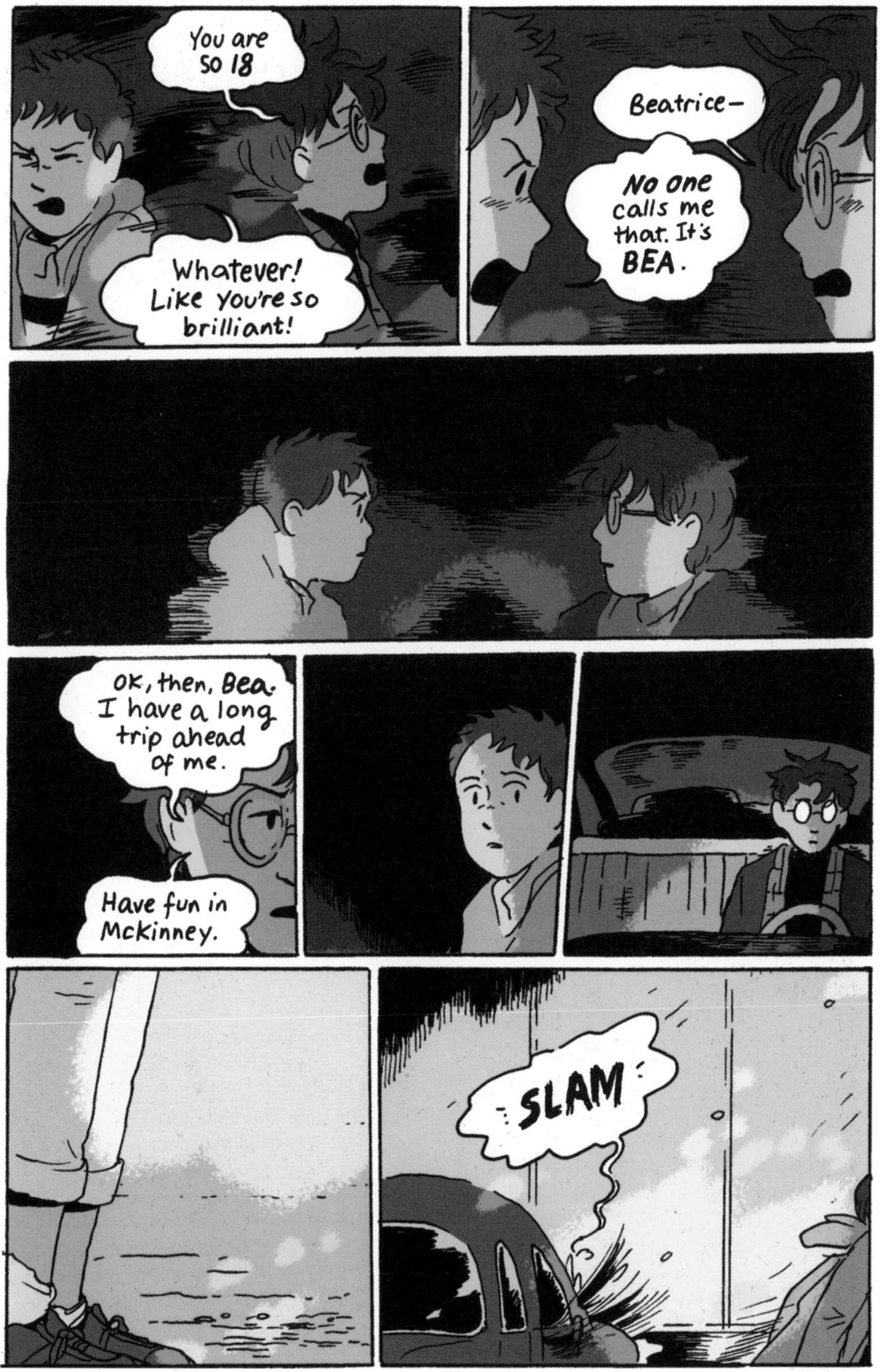
You are so 18
Whatever! Like you're so brilliant!
Beatrice-
No one calls me that. It's BEA.
OK, then, Bea. I have a long trip ahead of me.
Have fun in McKinney.
SLAM

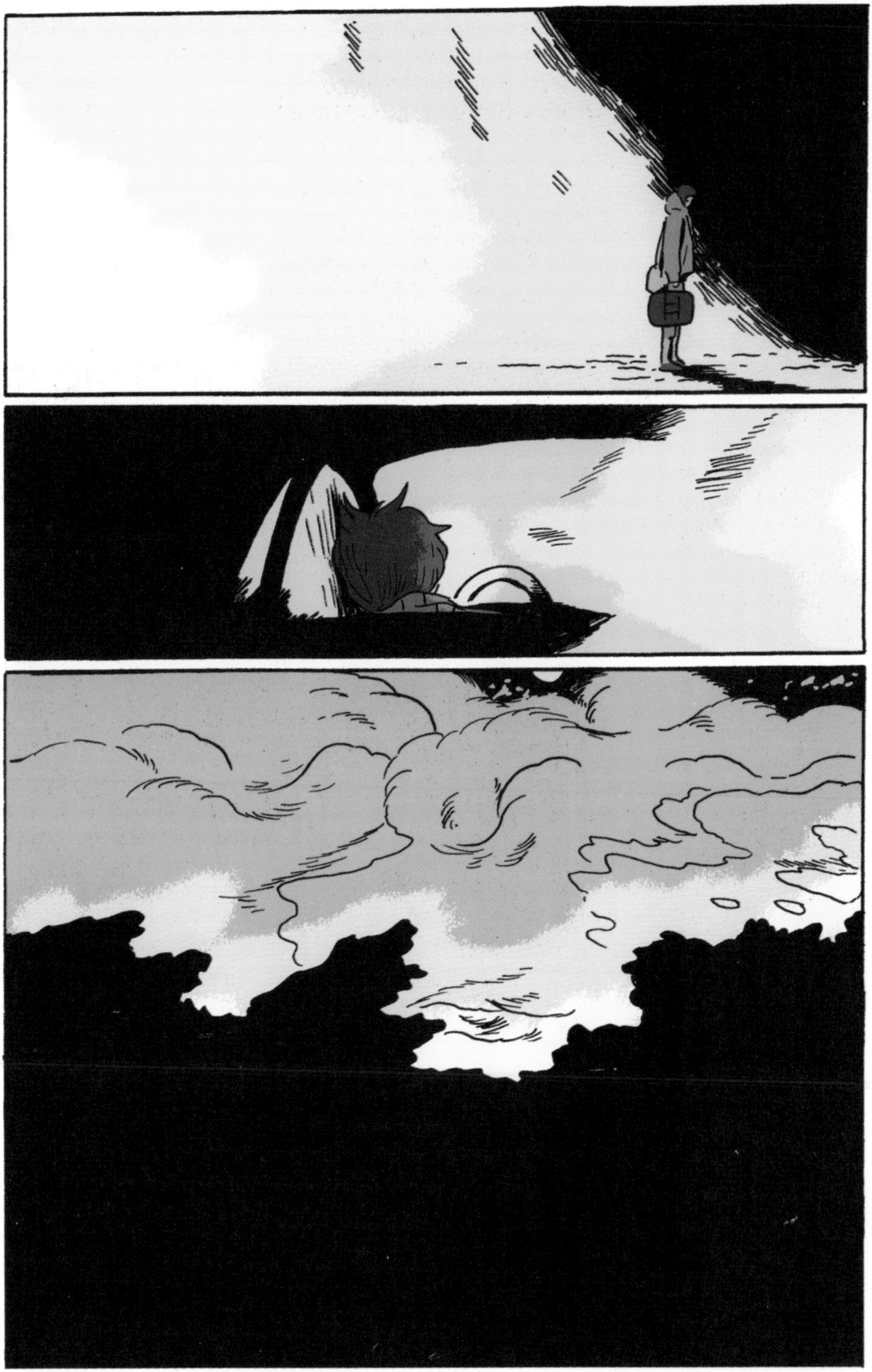

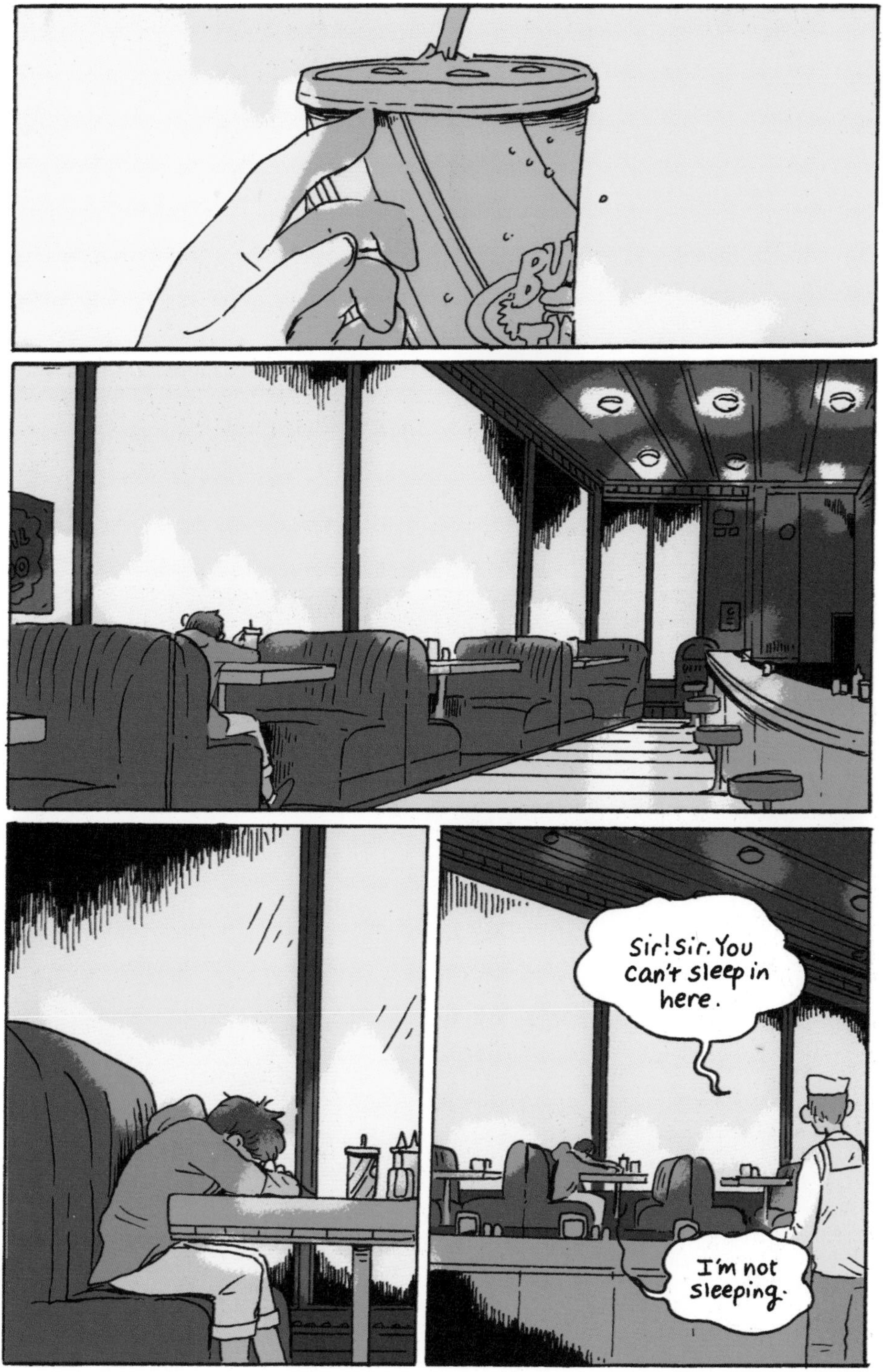
Sir! Sir. You can't sleep in here.
I'm not sleeping.

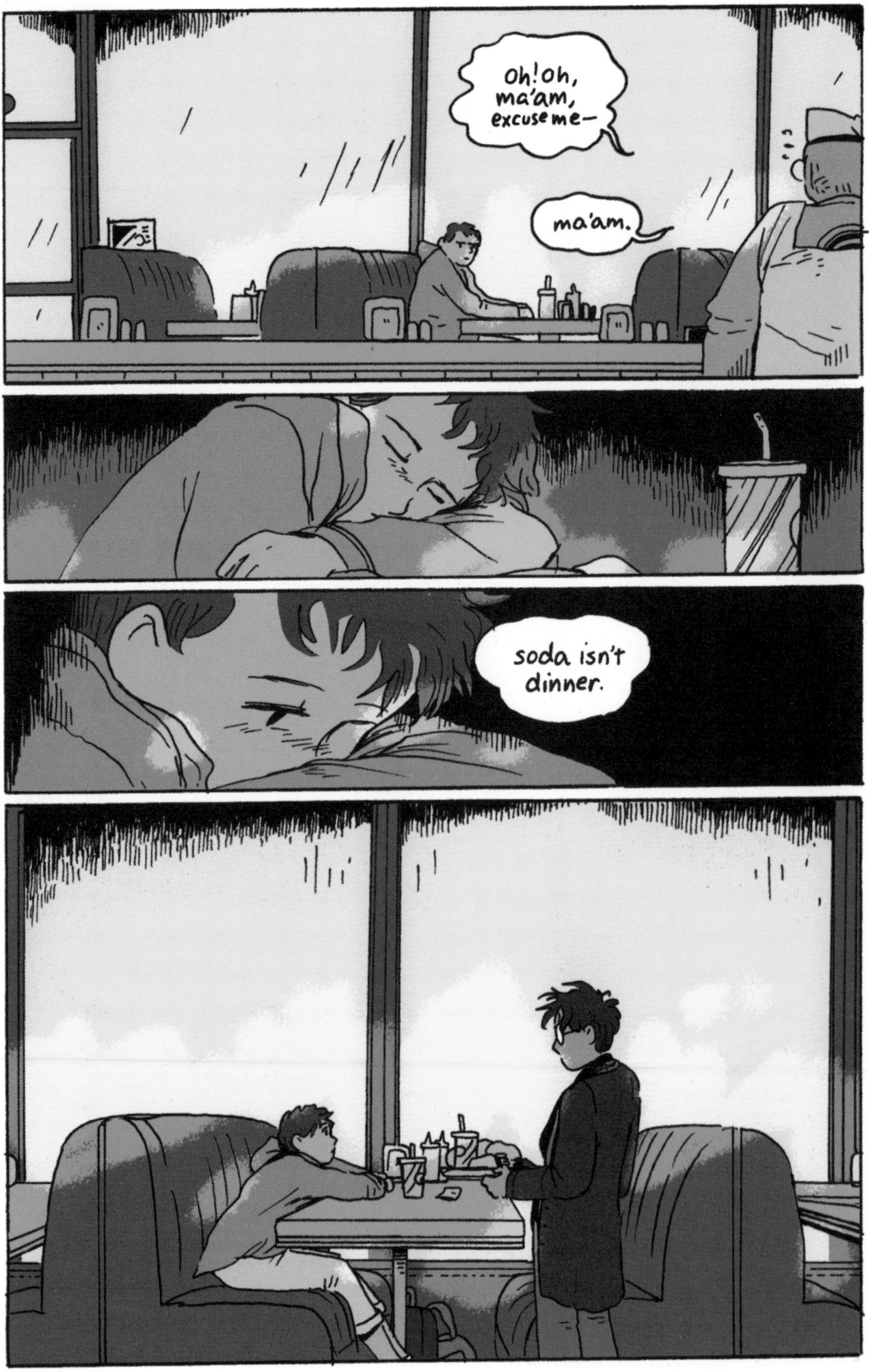
Oh! oh, ma'am, excuse me—
ma'am.
soda isn't dinner.

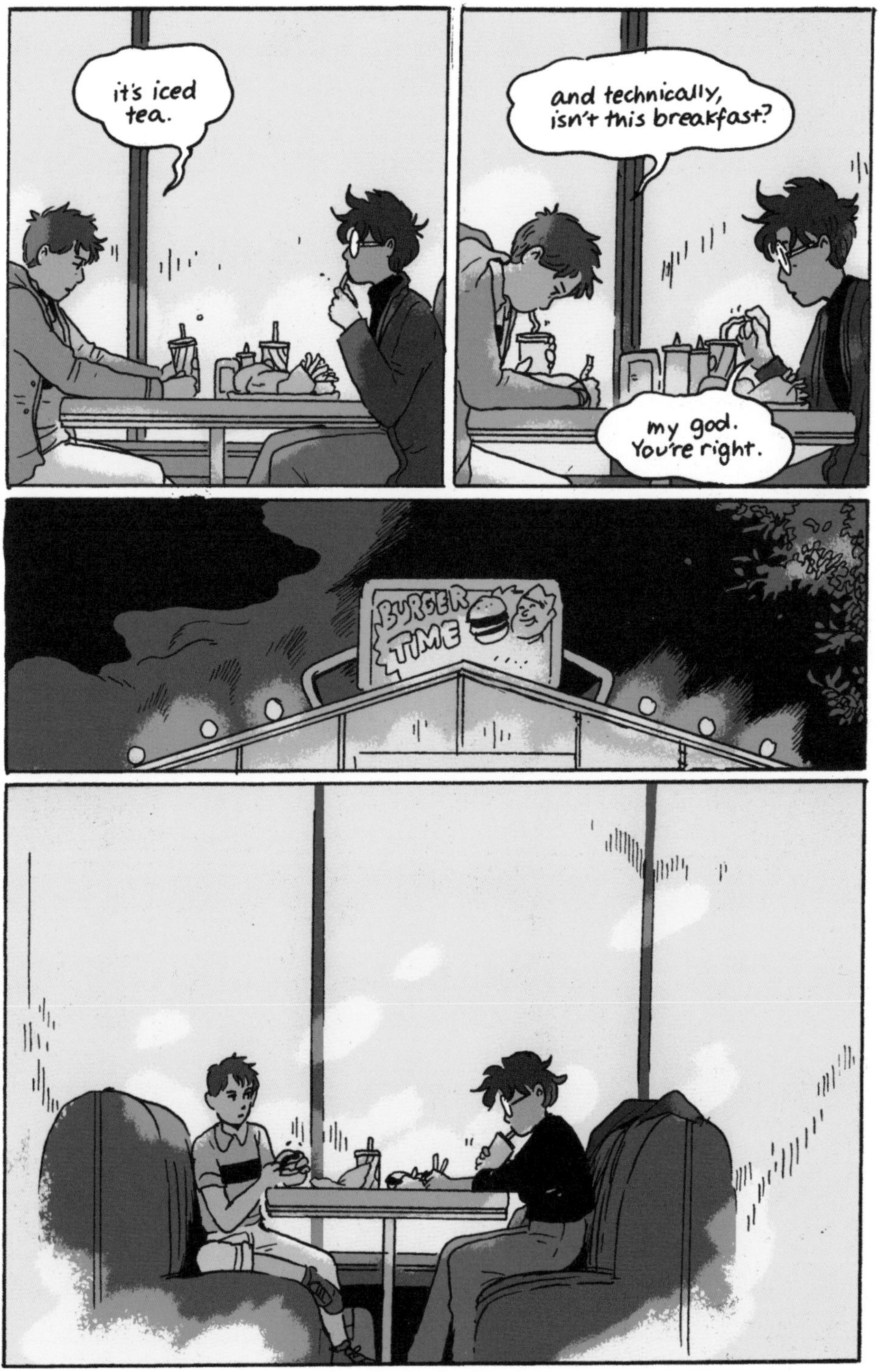
it's iced tea.
and technically, isn't this breakfast?
my god. You're right.
BURGER TIME

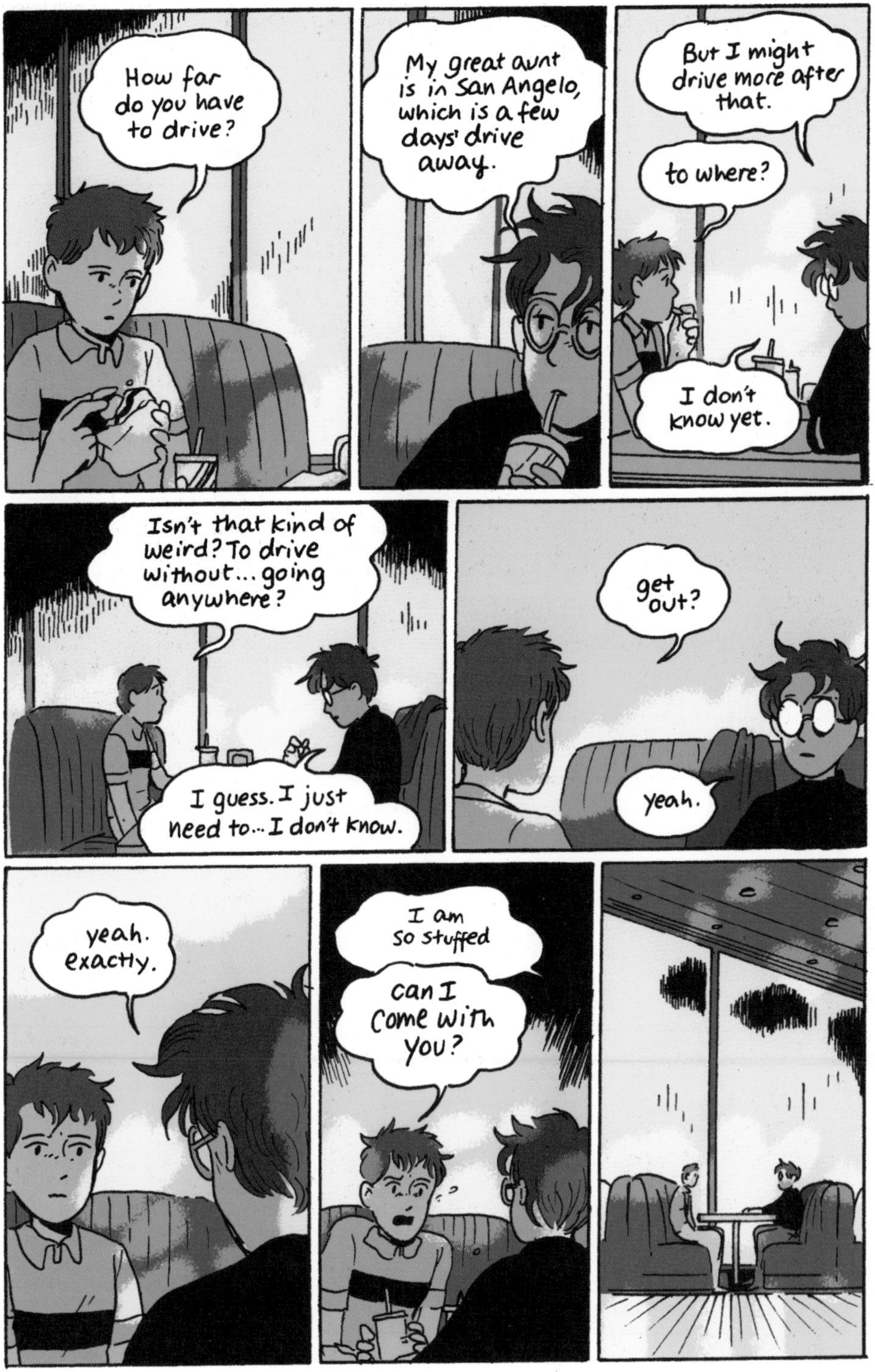
How far do you have to drive?
My great aunt is in San Angelo, which is a few days' drive away.
But I might drive more after that.
to where?
I don't know yet.
Isn't that kind of weird? To drive without... going anywhere?
I guess. I just need to... I don't know.
get out?
yeah.
yeah. exactly.
I am so stuffed
can I come with you?

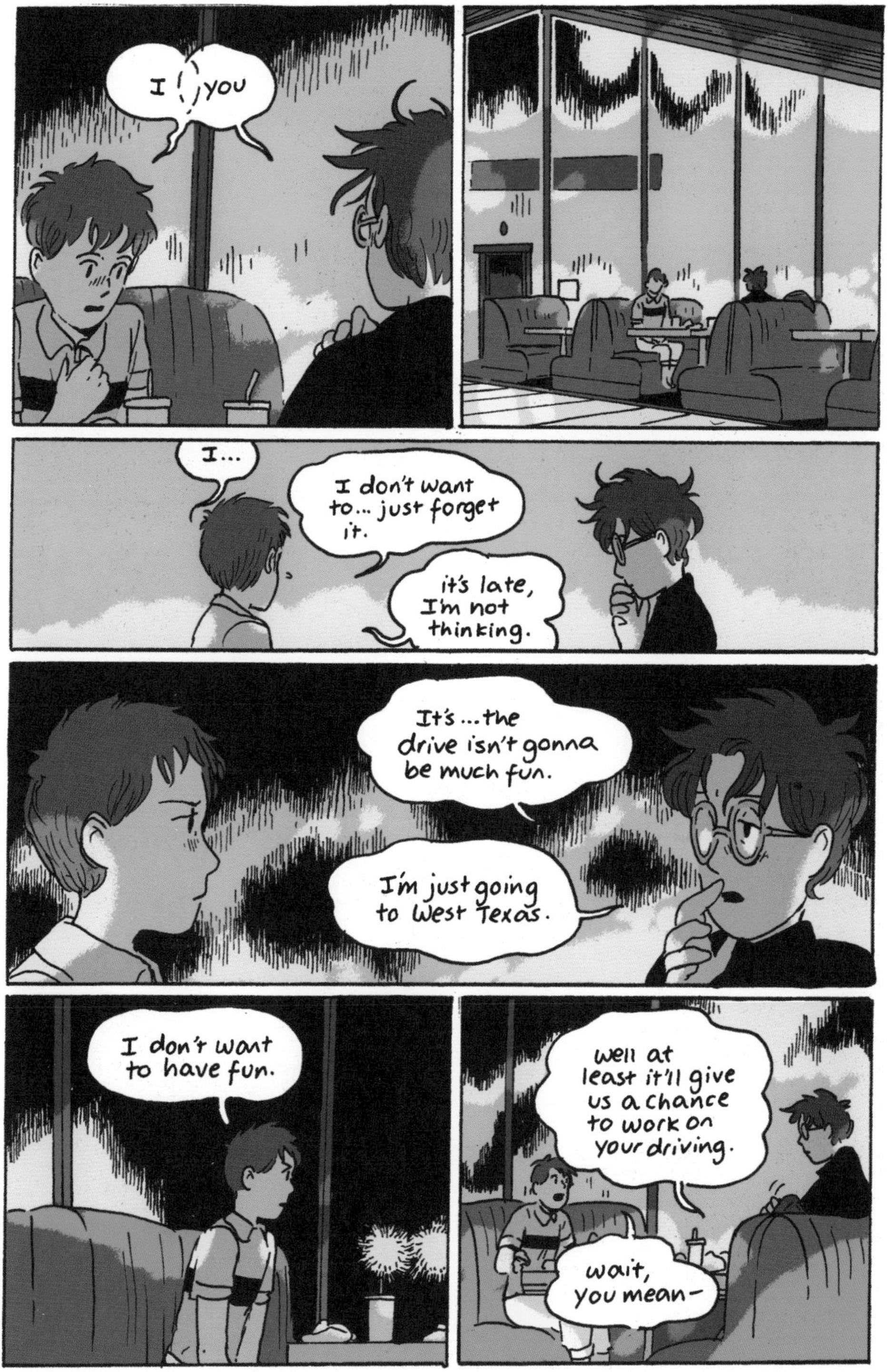
I ( ) you
I...
I don't want to... just forget it.
it's late, I'm not thinking.
It's... the drive isn't gonna be much fun.
I'm just going to West Texas.
I don't want to have fun.
well at least it'll give us a chance to work on your driving.
wait, you mean-

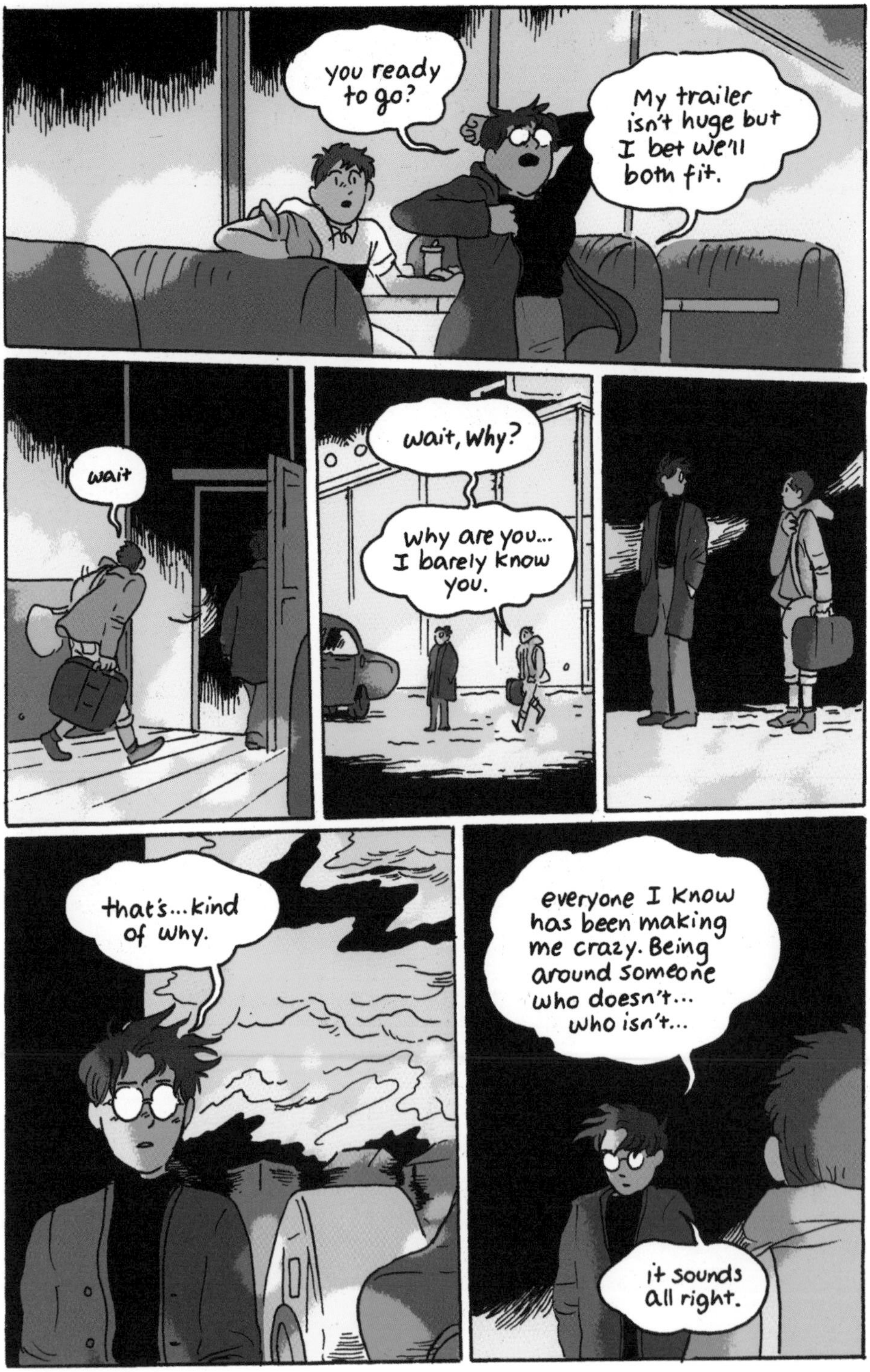
you ready to go?
My trailer isn't huge but I bet we'll both fit.
wait
wait, Why?
Why are you... I barely know you.
that's...kind of why.
everyone I know has been making me crazy. Being around someone who doesn't... who isn't...
it sounds all right.

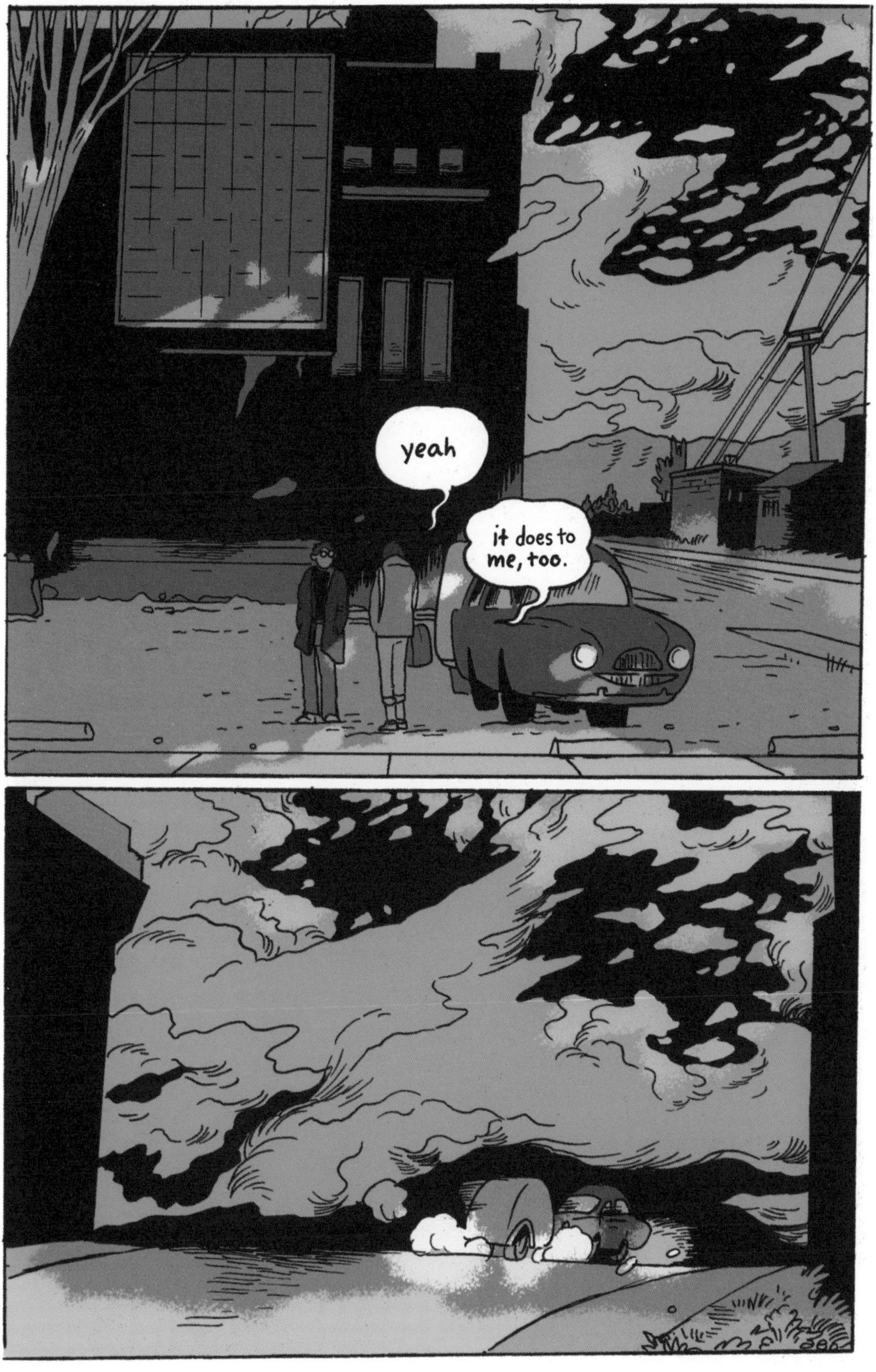
yeah
it does to me, too.

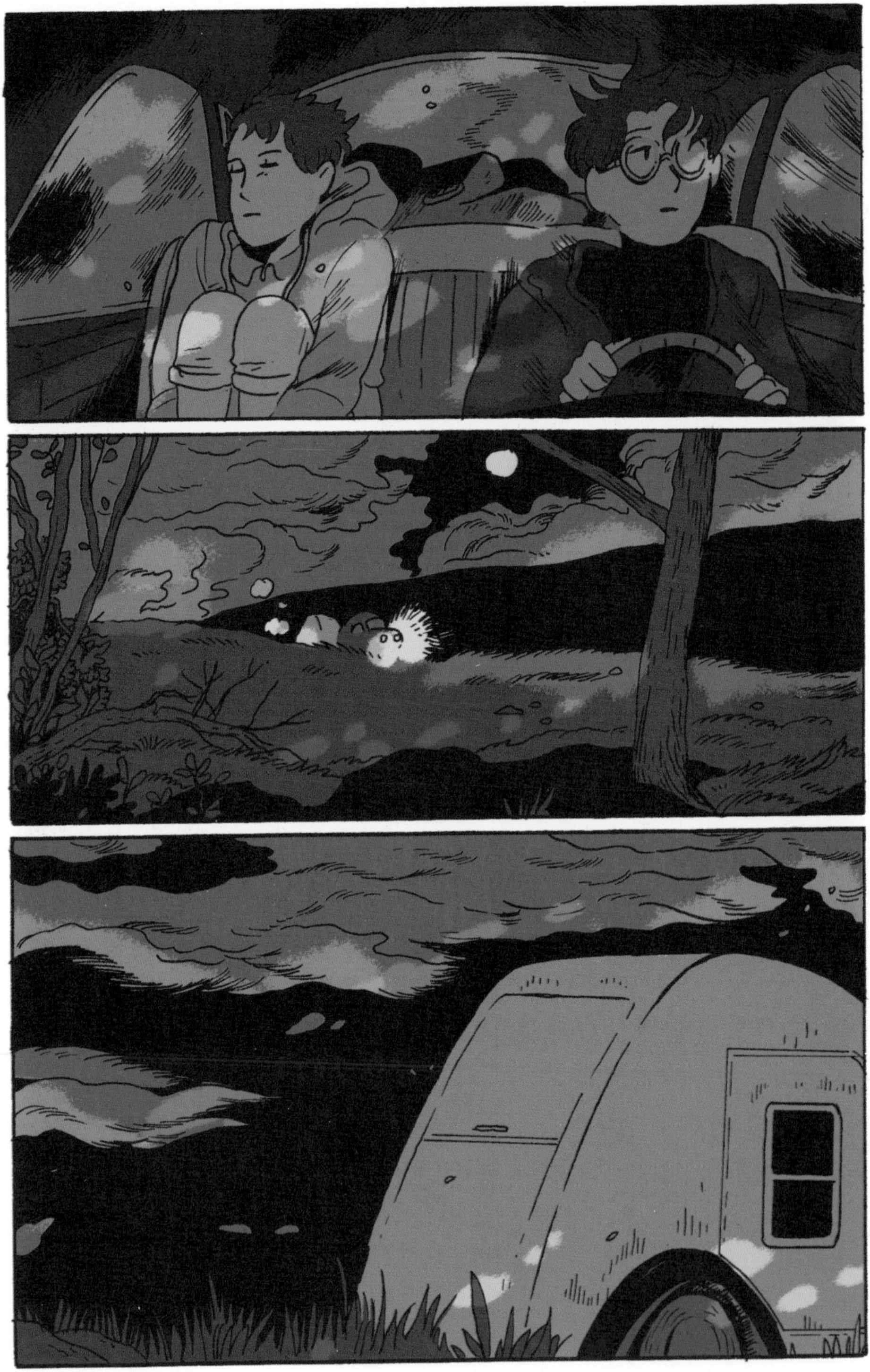

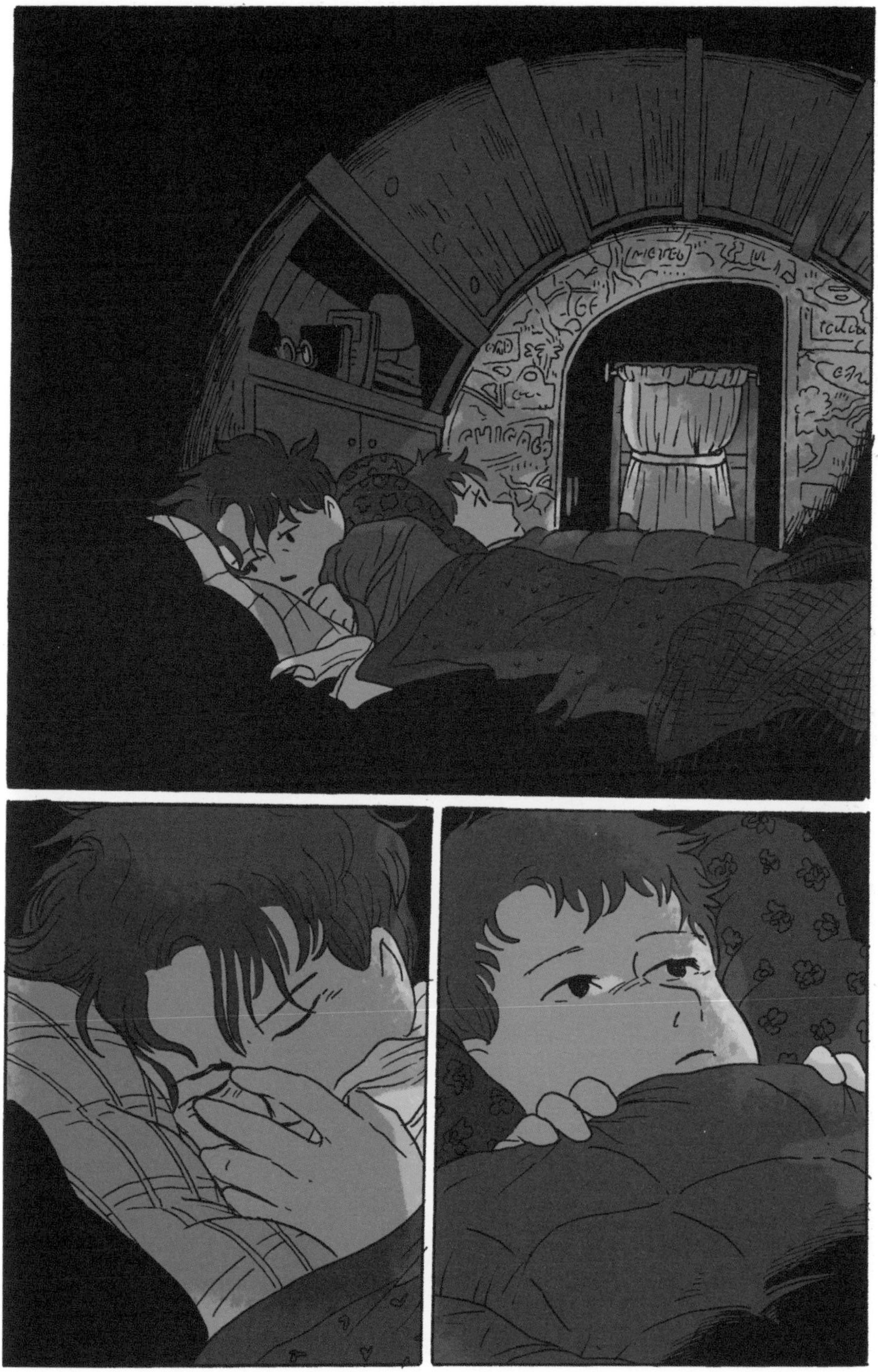

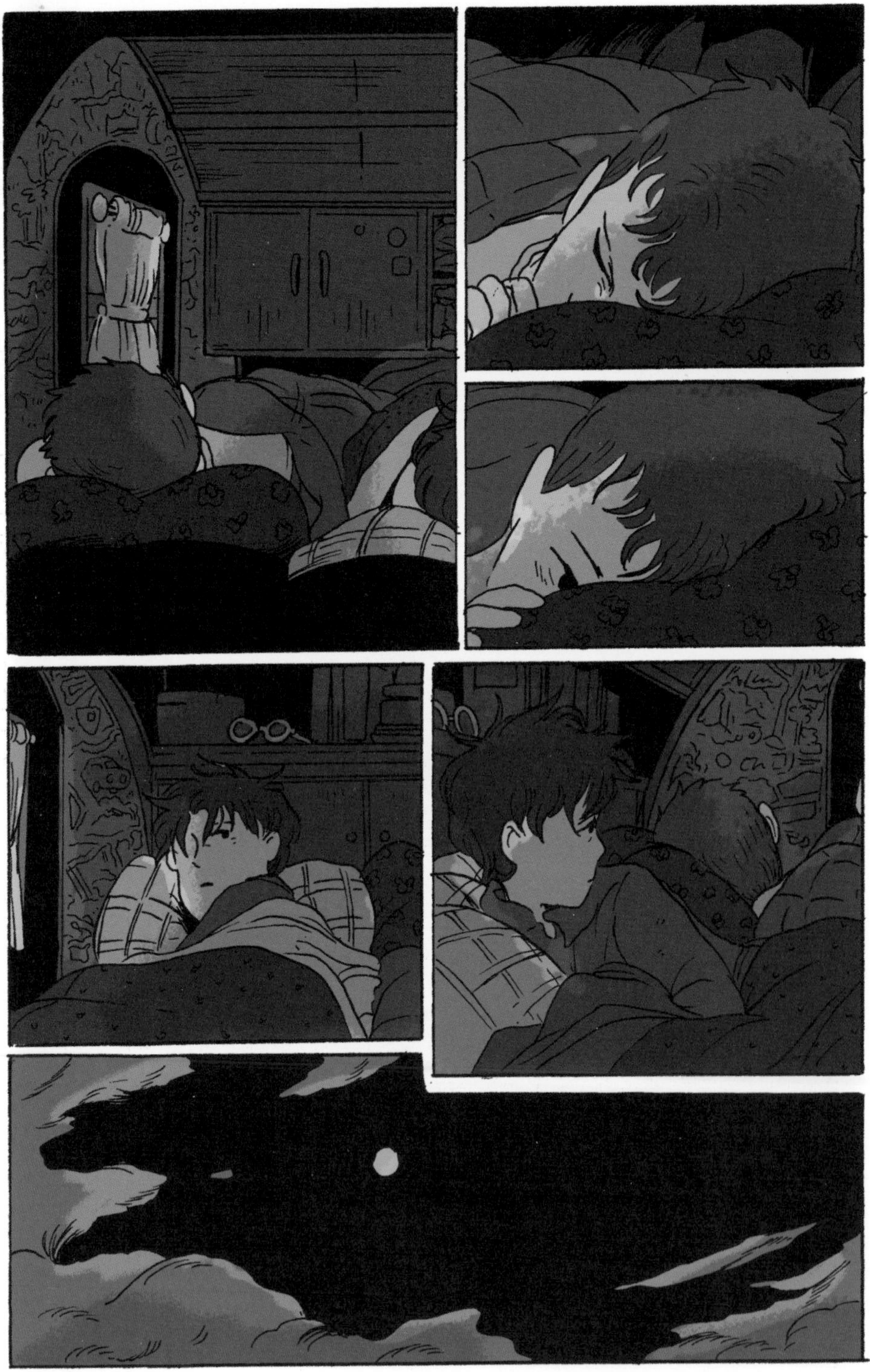

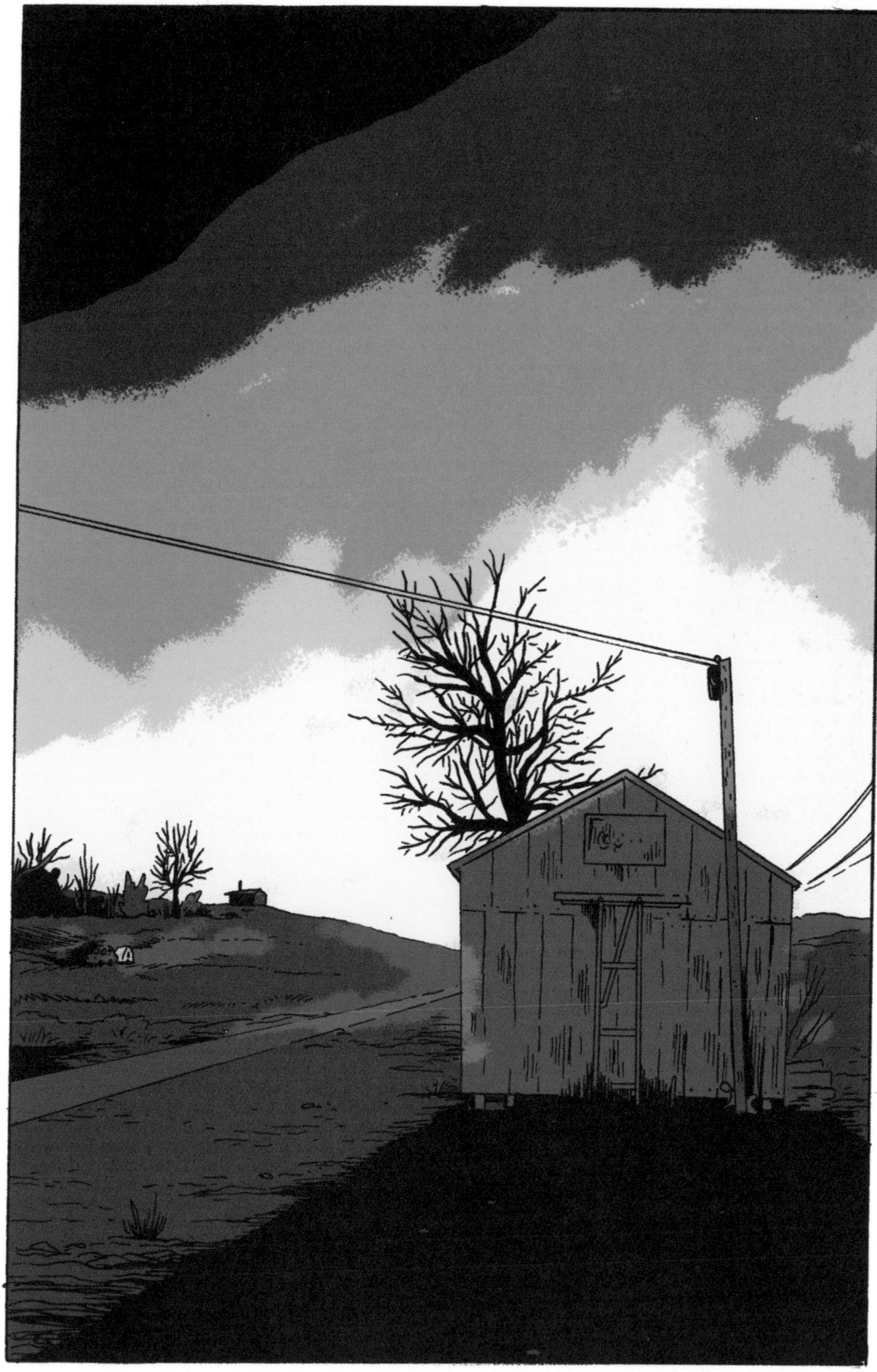

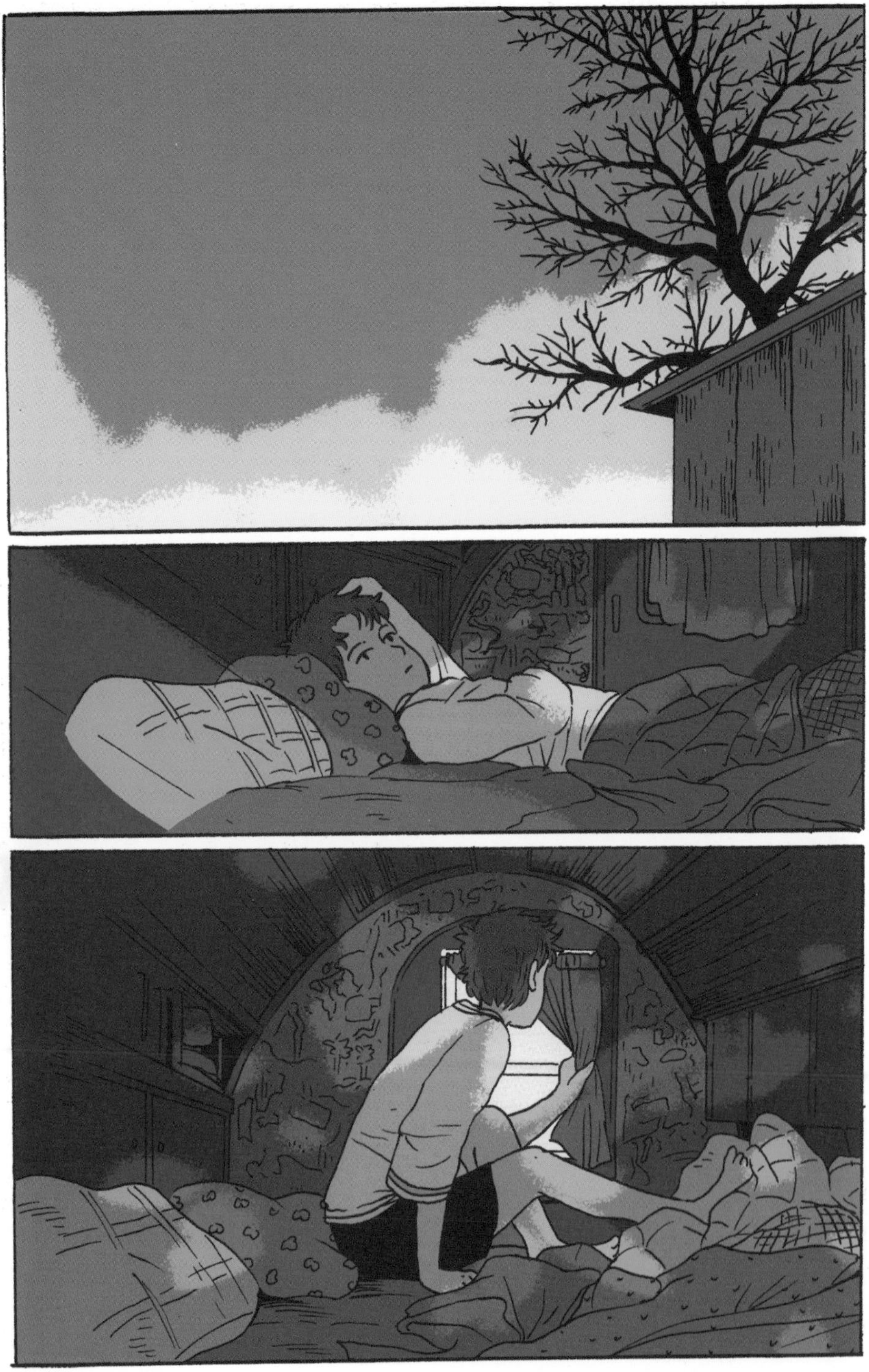

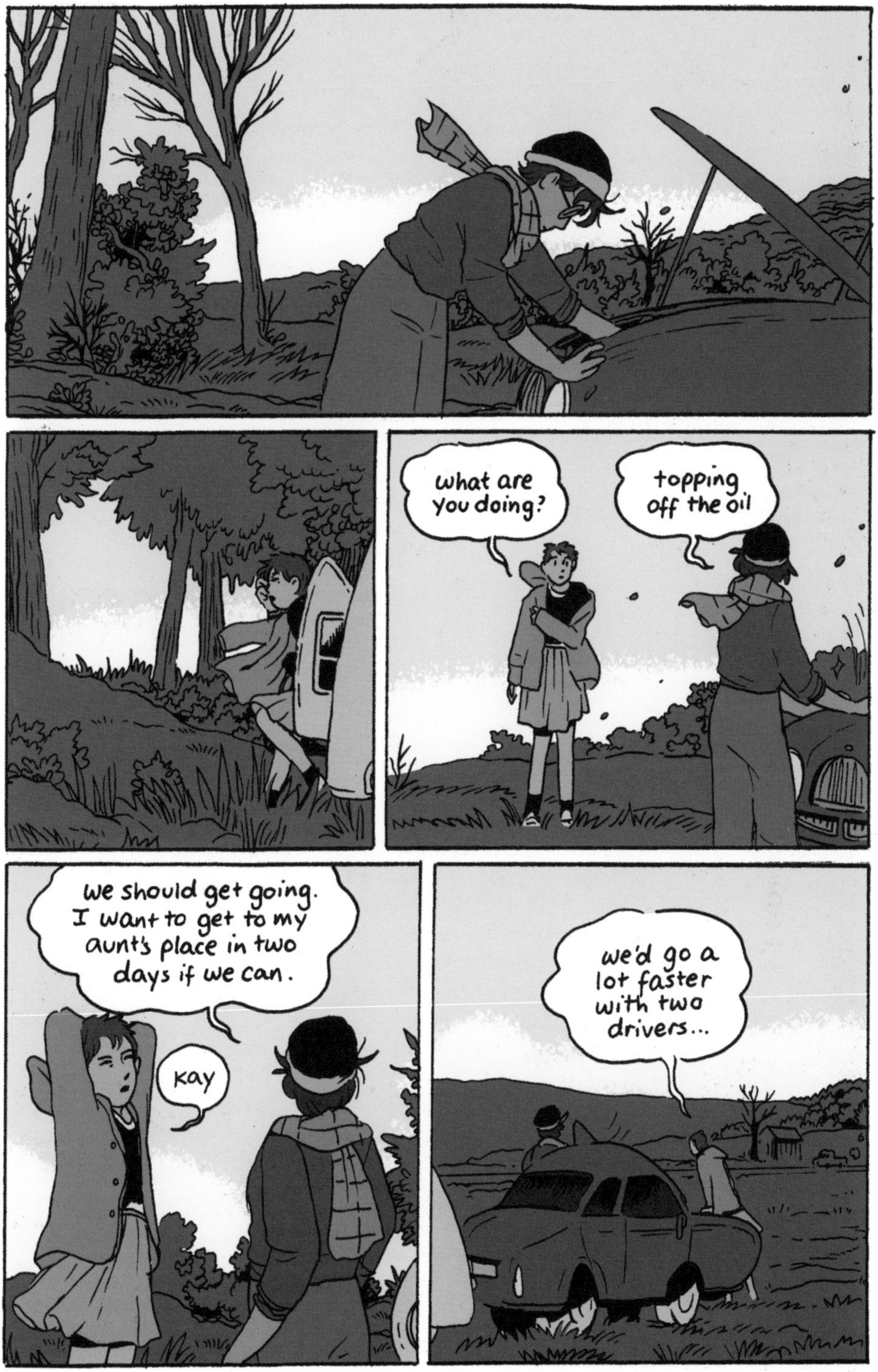
what are you doing?
topping off the oil
we should get going. I want to get to my aunt's place in two days if we can.
kay
we'd go a lot faster with two drivers...

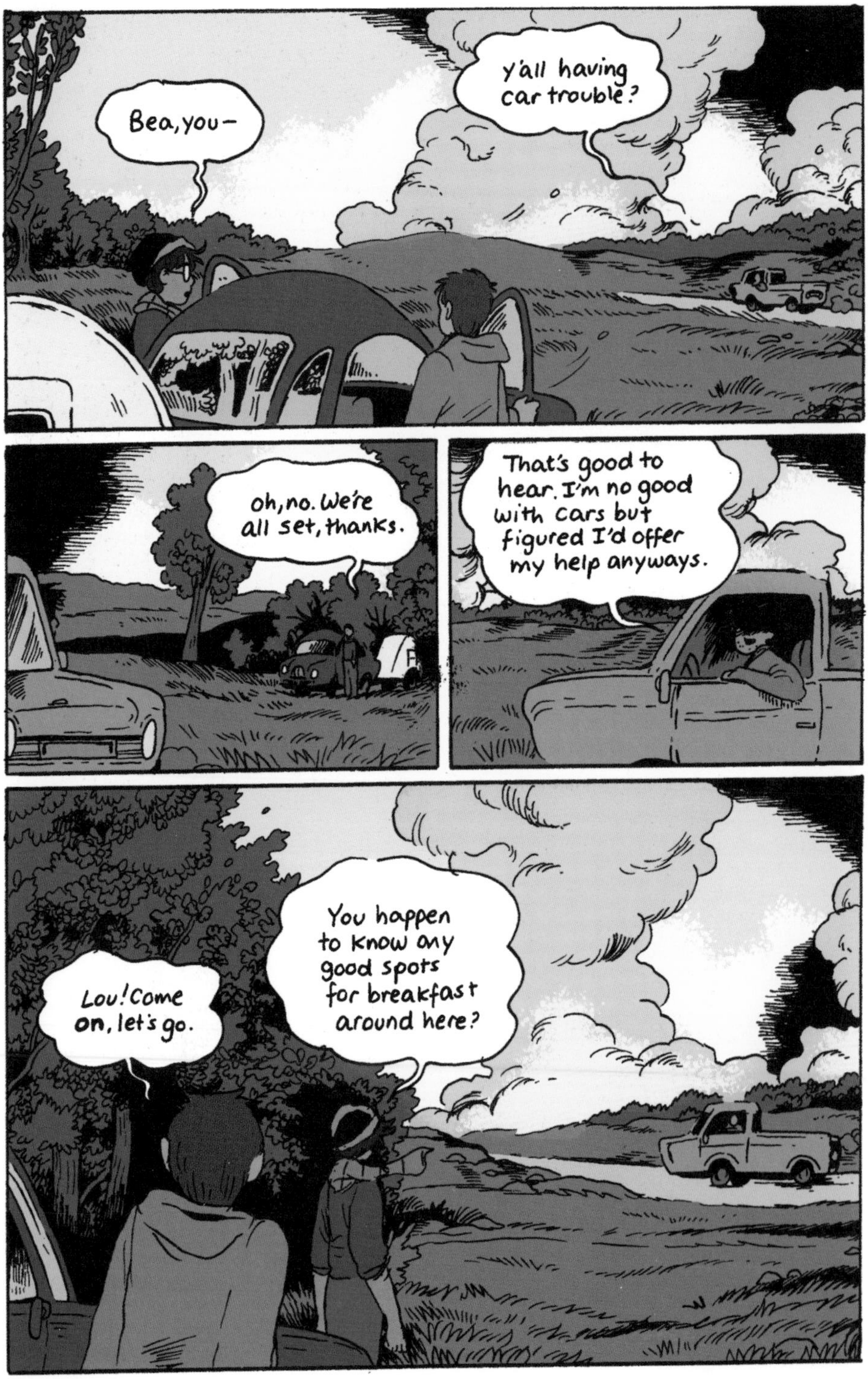
Bea, you-
y'all having car trouble?
oh, no. We're all set, thanks.
That's good to hear. I'm no good with cars but figured I'd offer my help anyways.
Lou! Come on, let's go.
You happen to know any good spots for breakfast around here?

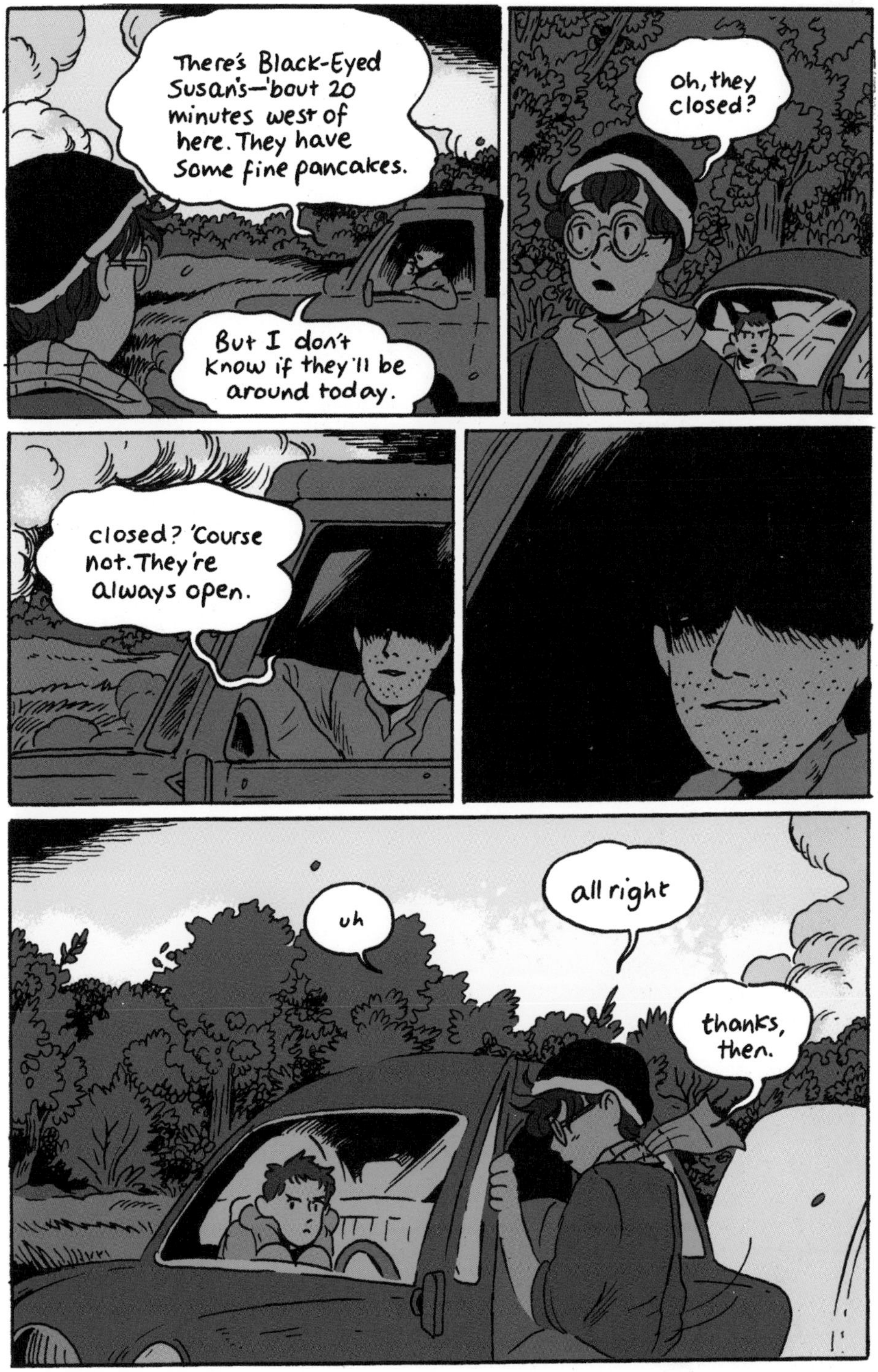
There's Black-Eyed Susan's—'bout 20 minutes west of here. They have some fine pancakes.
But I don't know if they'll be around today.
Oh, they closed?
closed? 'Course not. They're always open.
uh
all right
thanks, then.

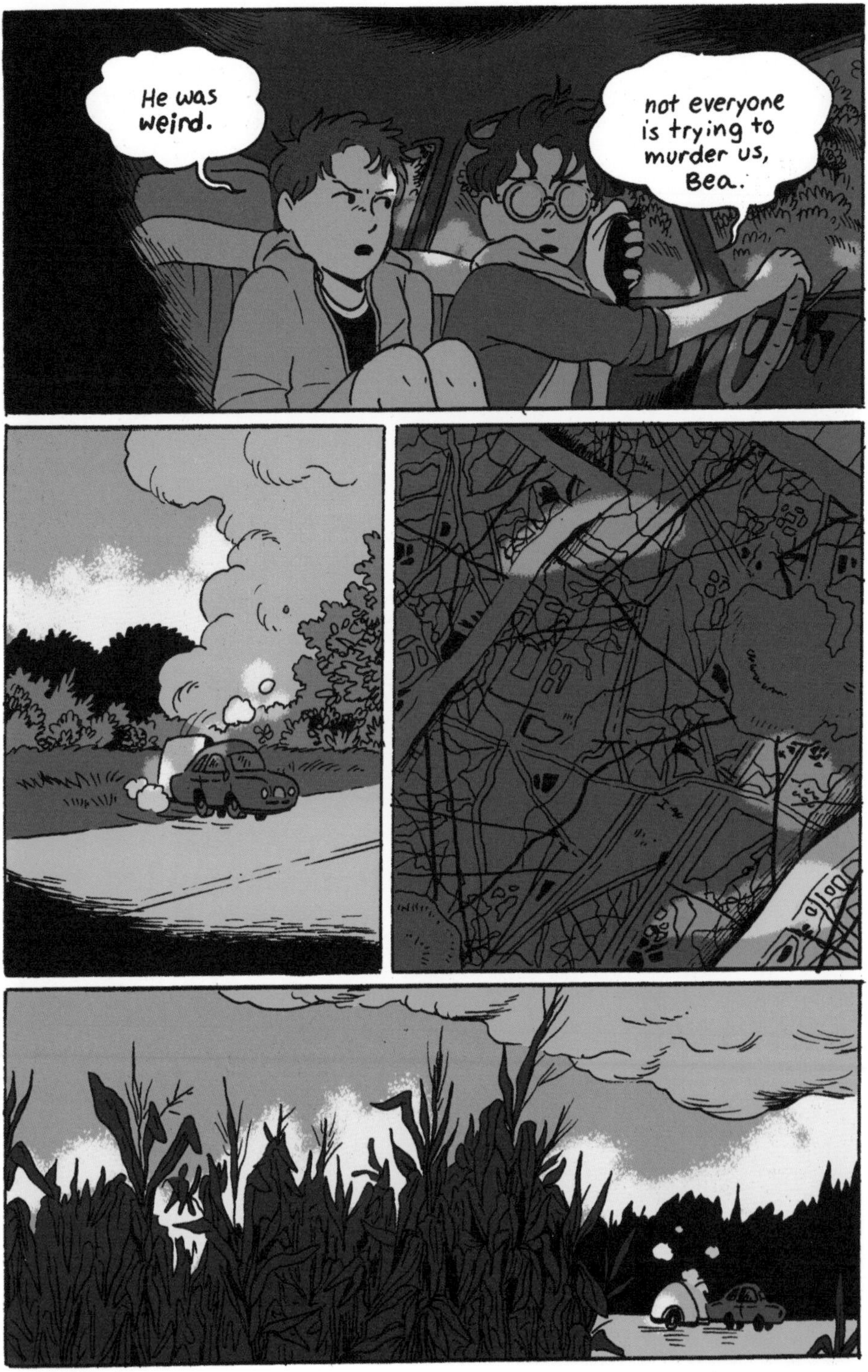
He was weird.
not everyone is trying to murder us, Bea.

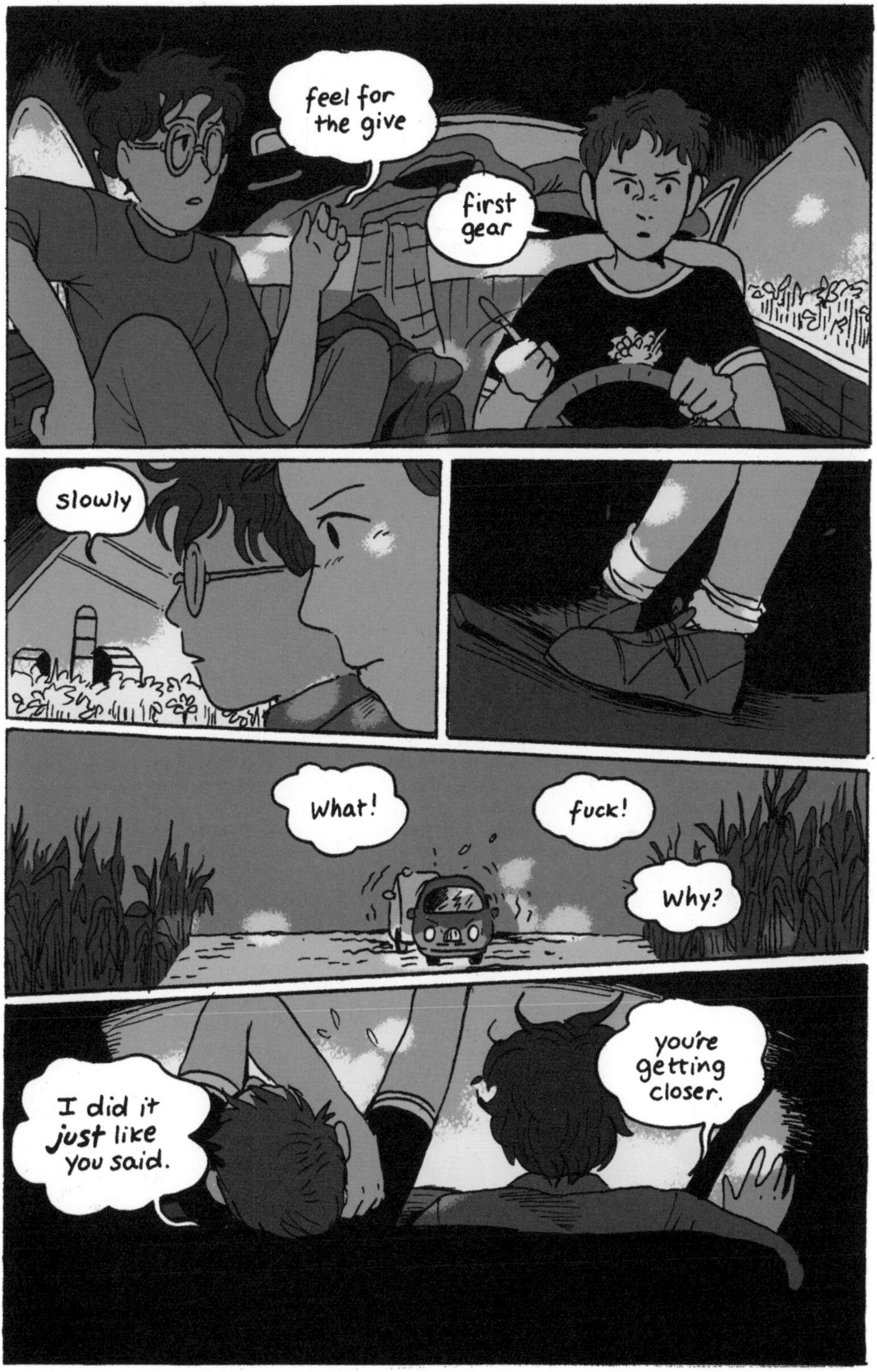
feel for the give
first gear
slowly
What!
fuck!
Why?
I did it just like you said.
you're getting closer.

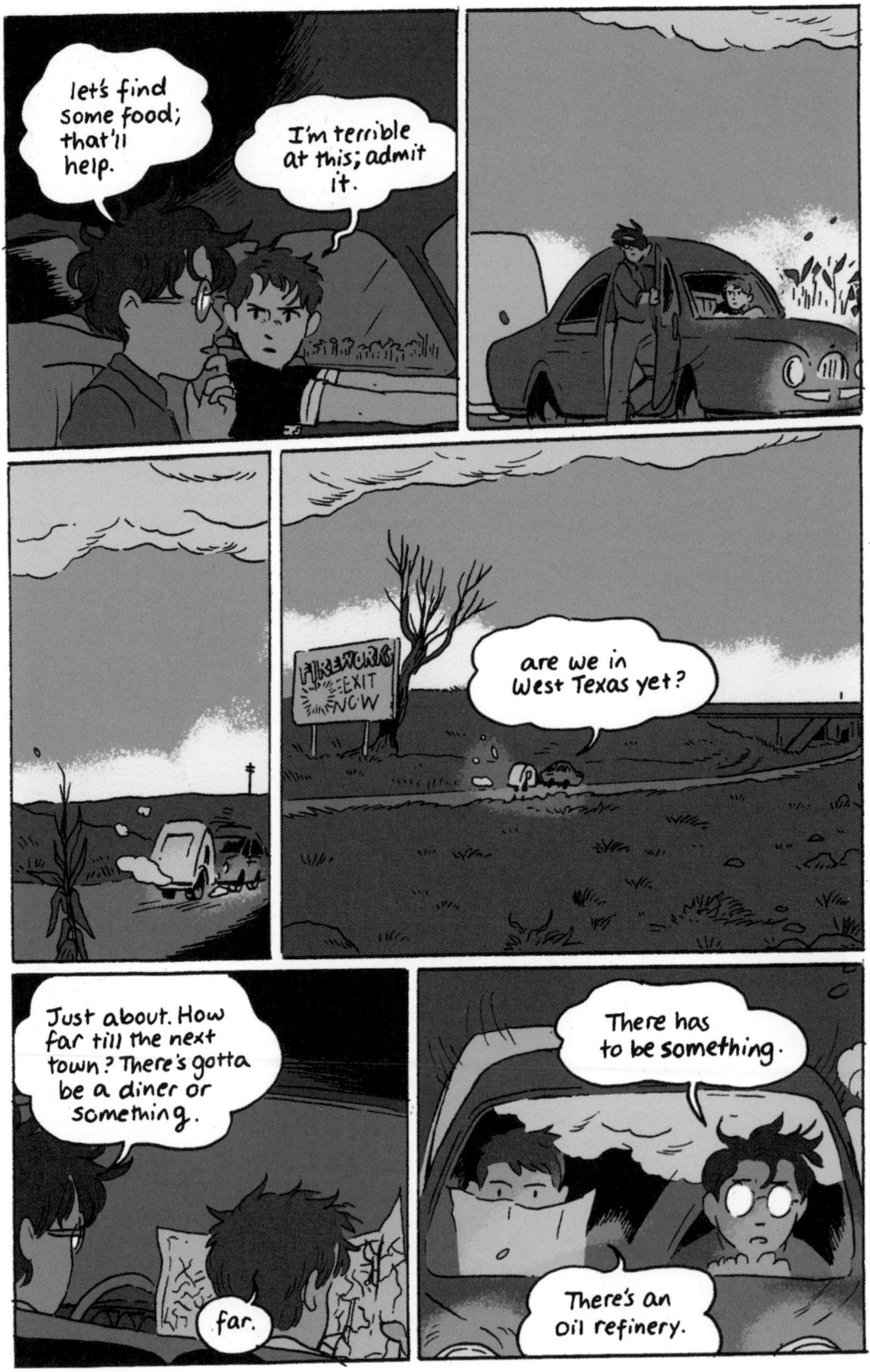
let's find some food; that'll help.
I'm terrible at this; admit it.
FIREWORKS EXIT NOW
are we in West Texas yet?
Just about. How far till the next town? There's gotta be a diner or something.
far.
There has to be something.
There's an oil refinery.

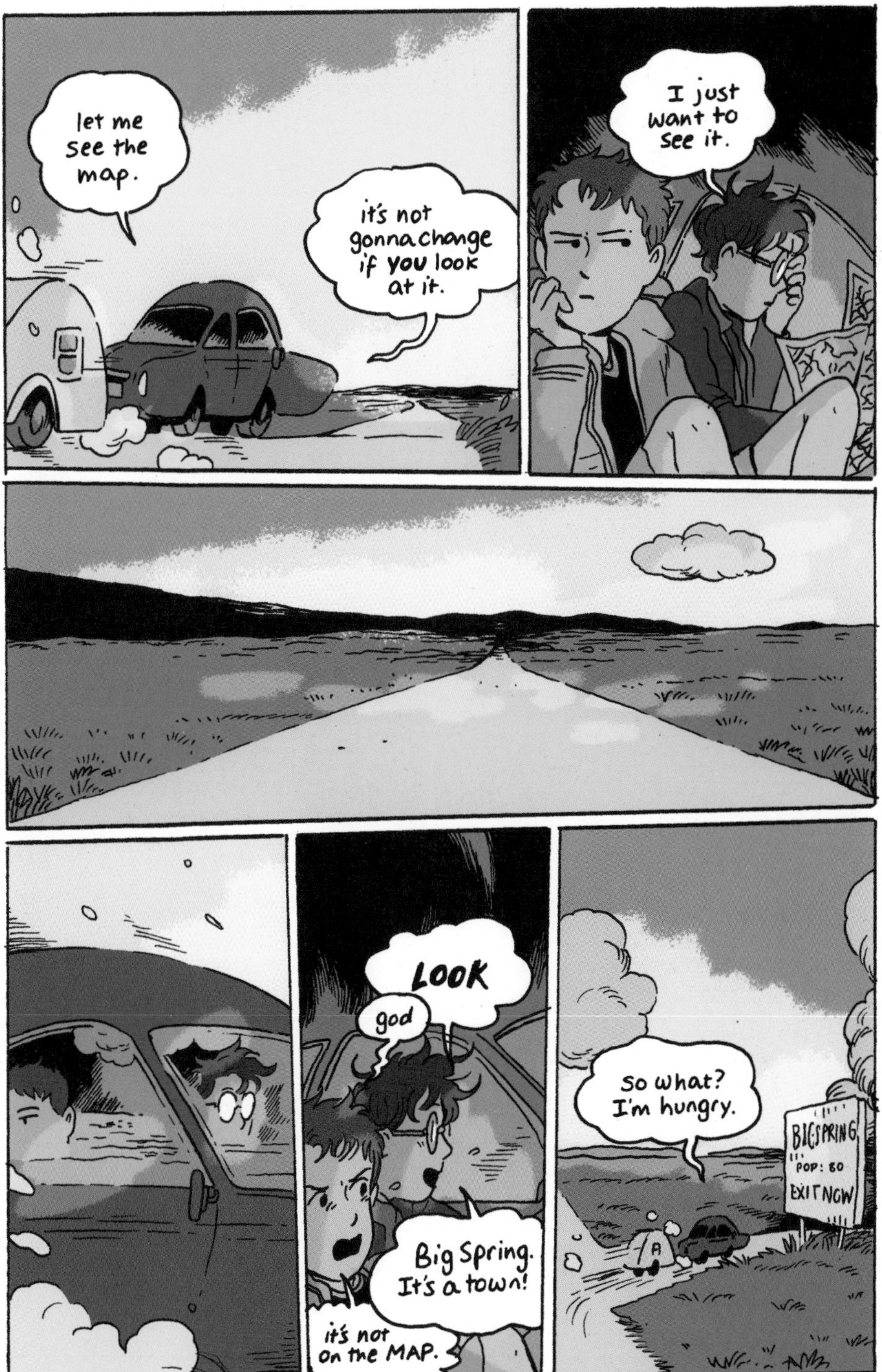
let me see the map.
it's not gonna change if you look at it.
I just want to see it.
god
LOOK
Big Spring. It's a town!
it's not on the MAP.
So what? I'm hungry.
BIG SPRING POP: 80 EXIT NOW

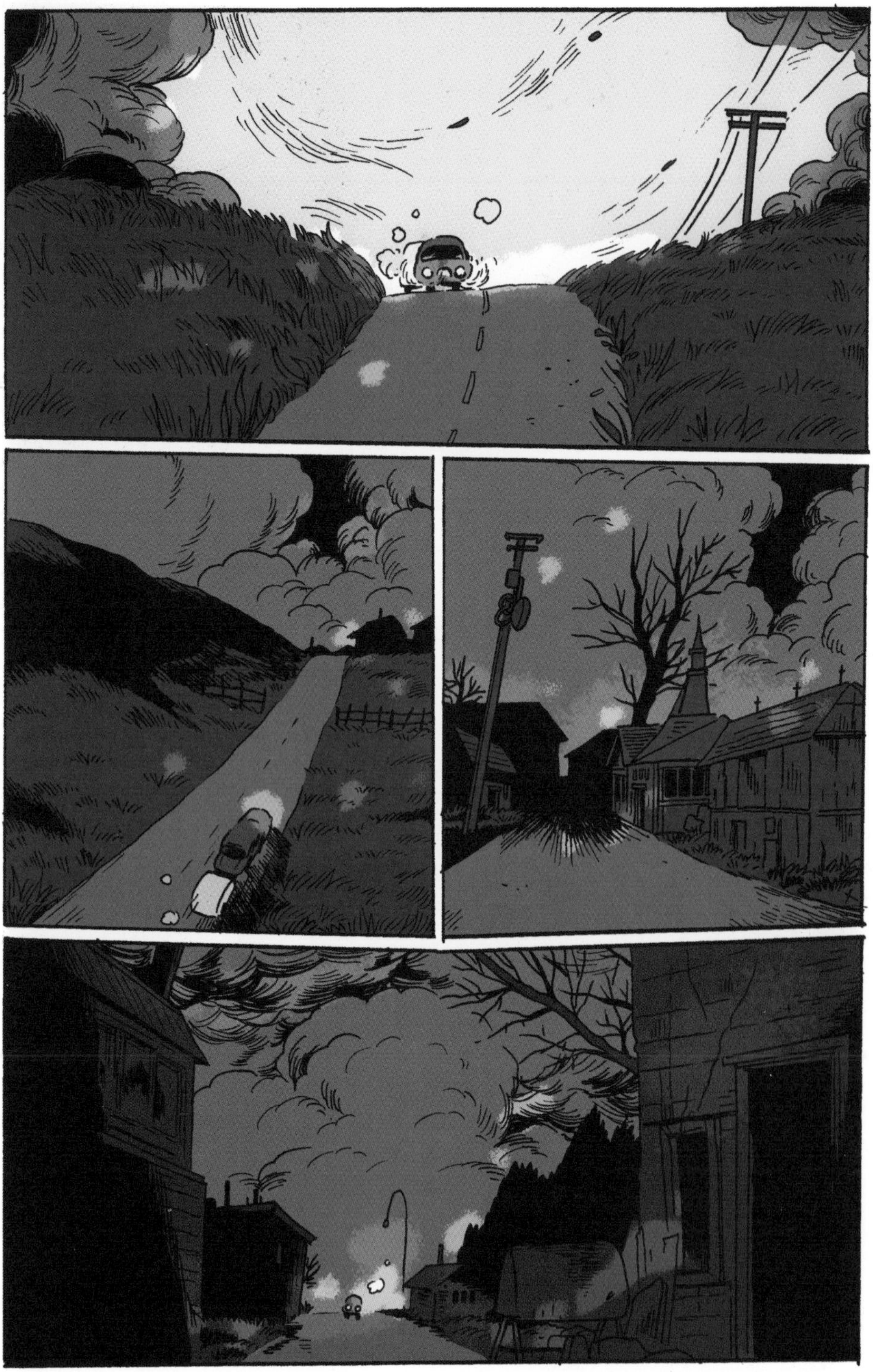

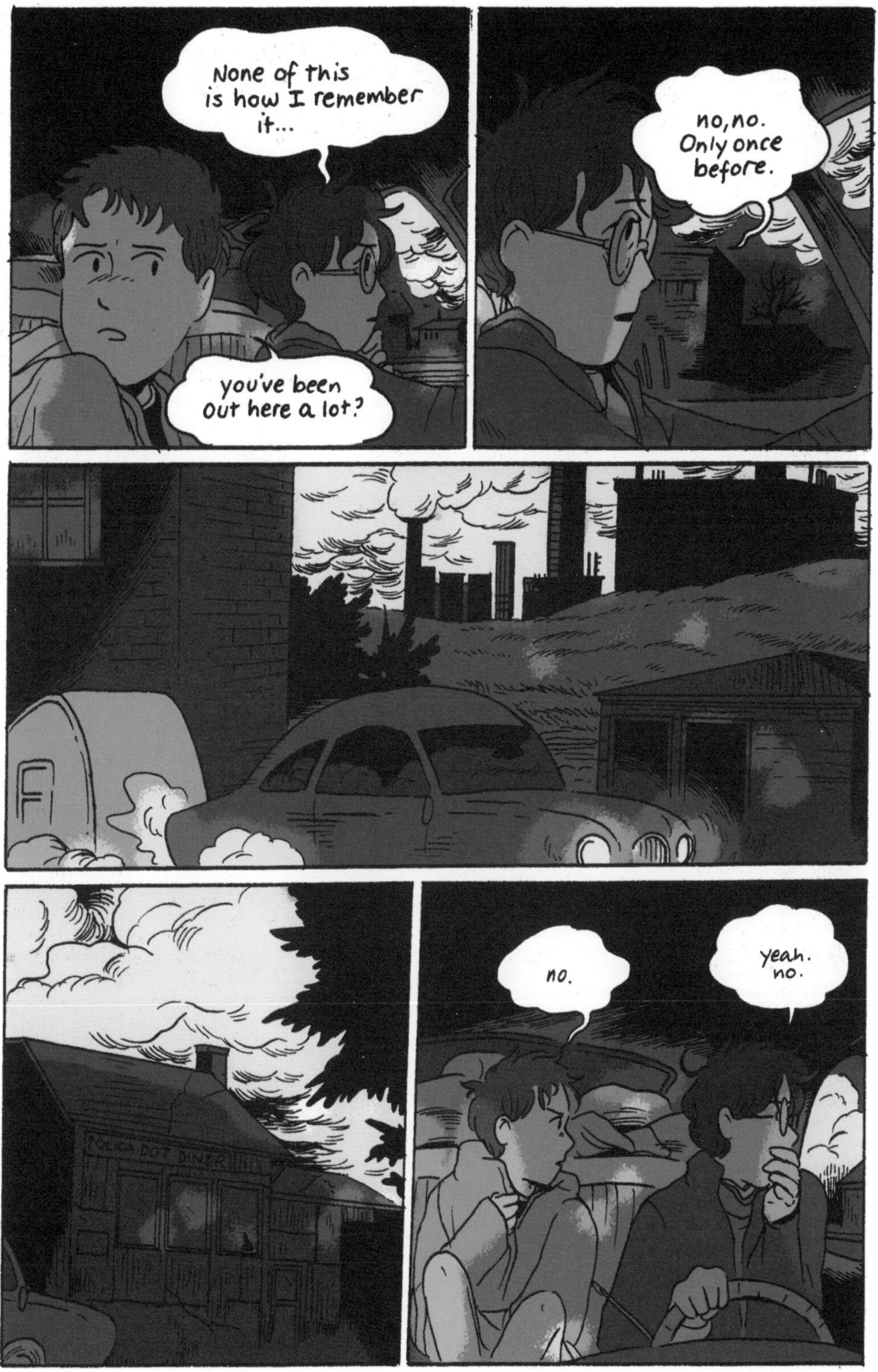
None of this is how I remember it...
you've been out here a lot?
no, no. Only once before.
POLKA DOT DINER
no.
yeah. no.

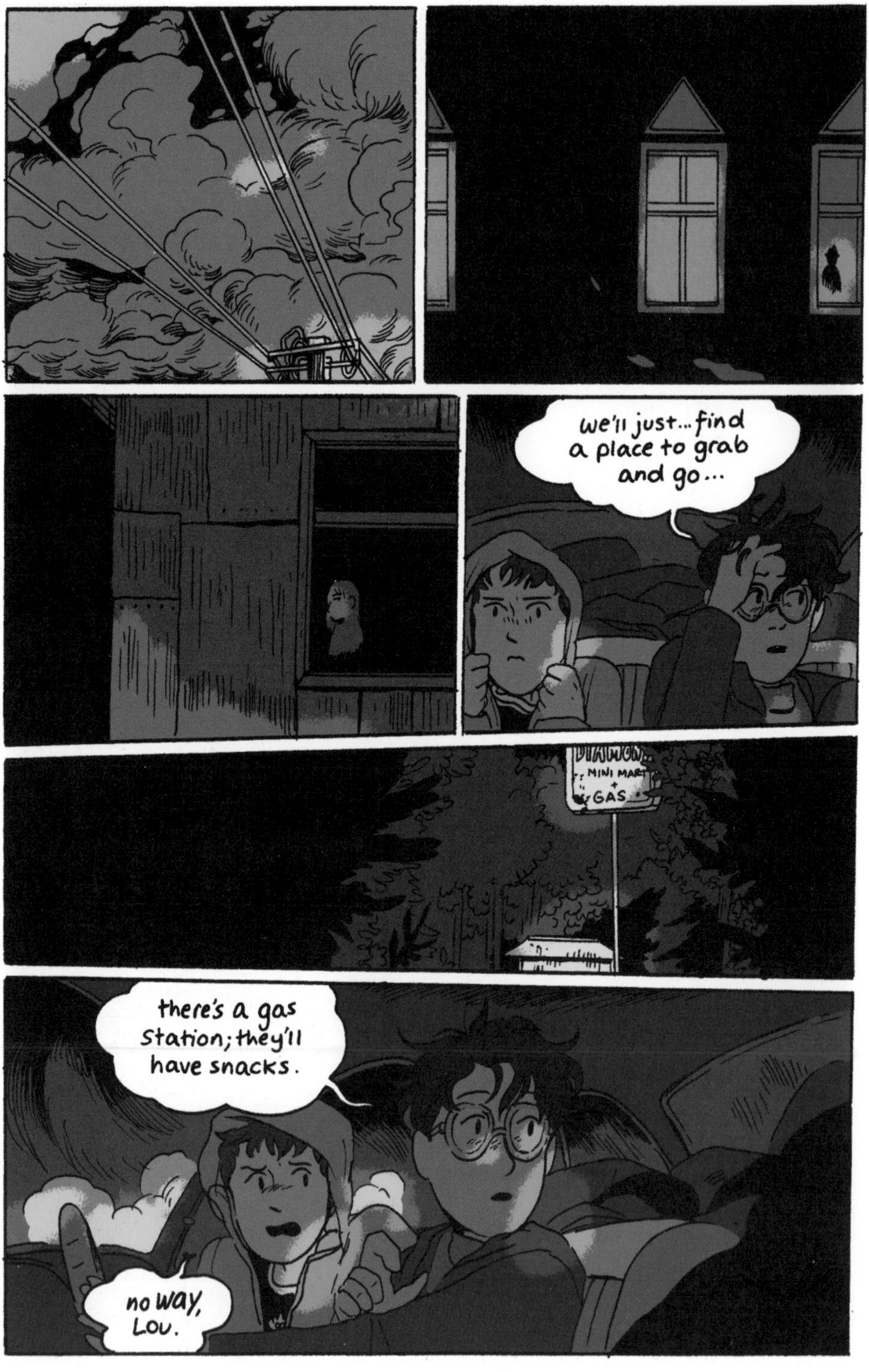
we'll just... find a place to grab and go...
MINI MART
+
GAS
there's a gas station; they'll have snacks.
no way, Lou.

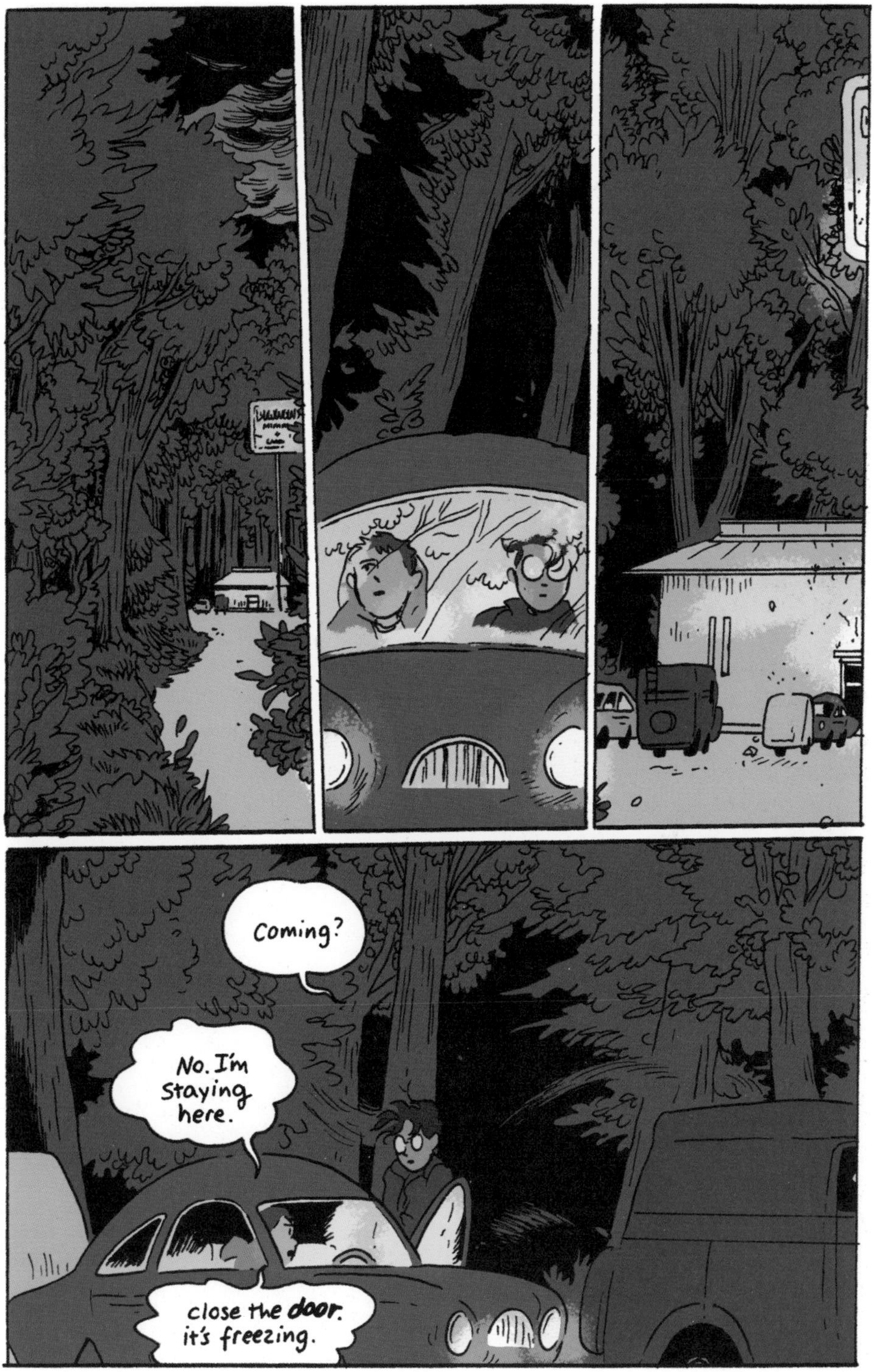
Coming?
No. I'm staying here.
close the door. it's freezing.

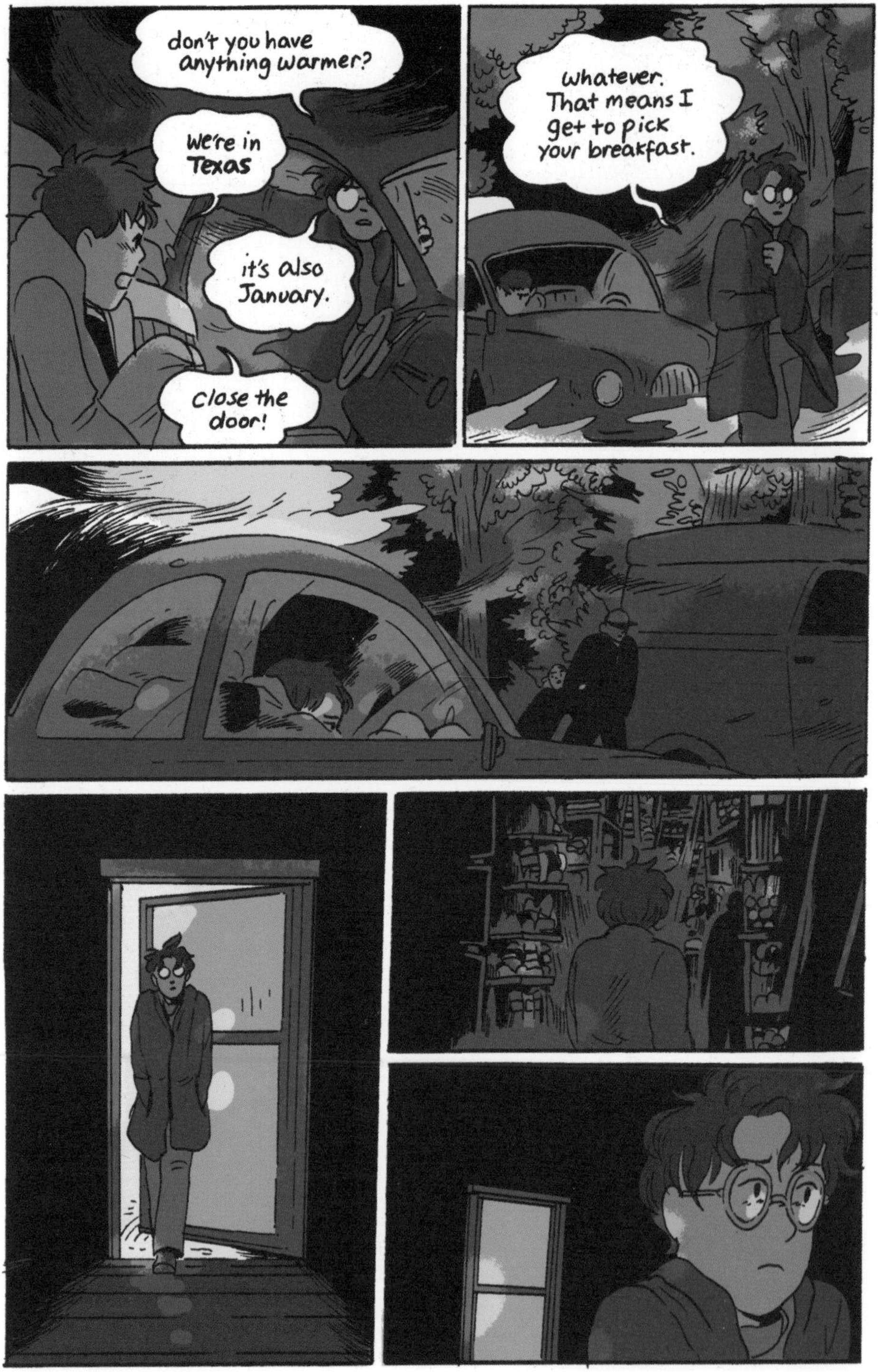

don't you have anything warmer?
We're in Texas
it's also January.
Close the door!
whatever. That means I get to pick your breakfast.

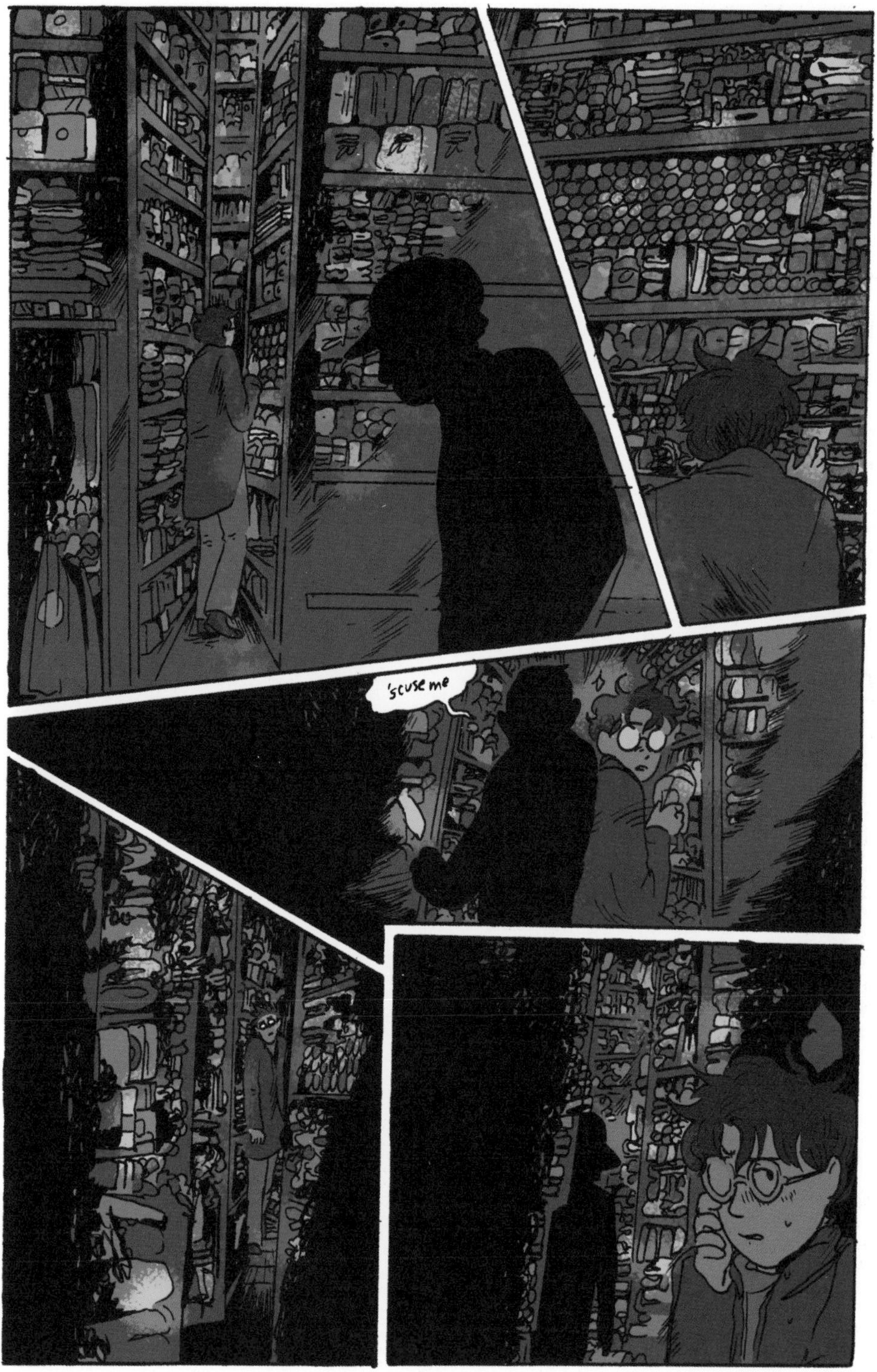
'scuse me

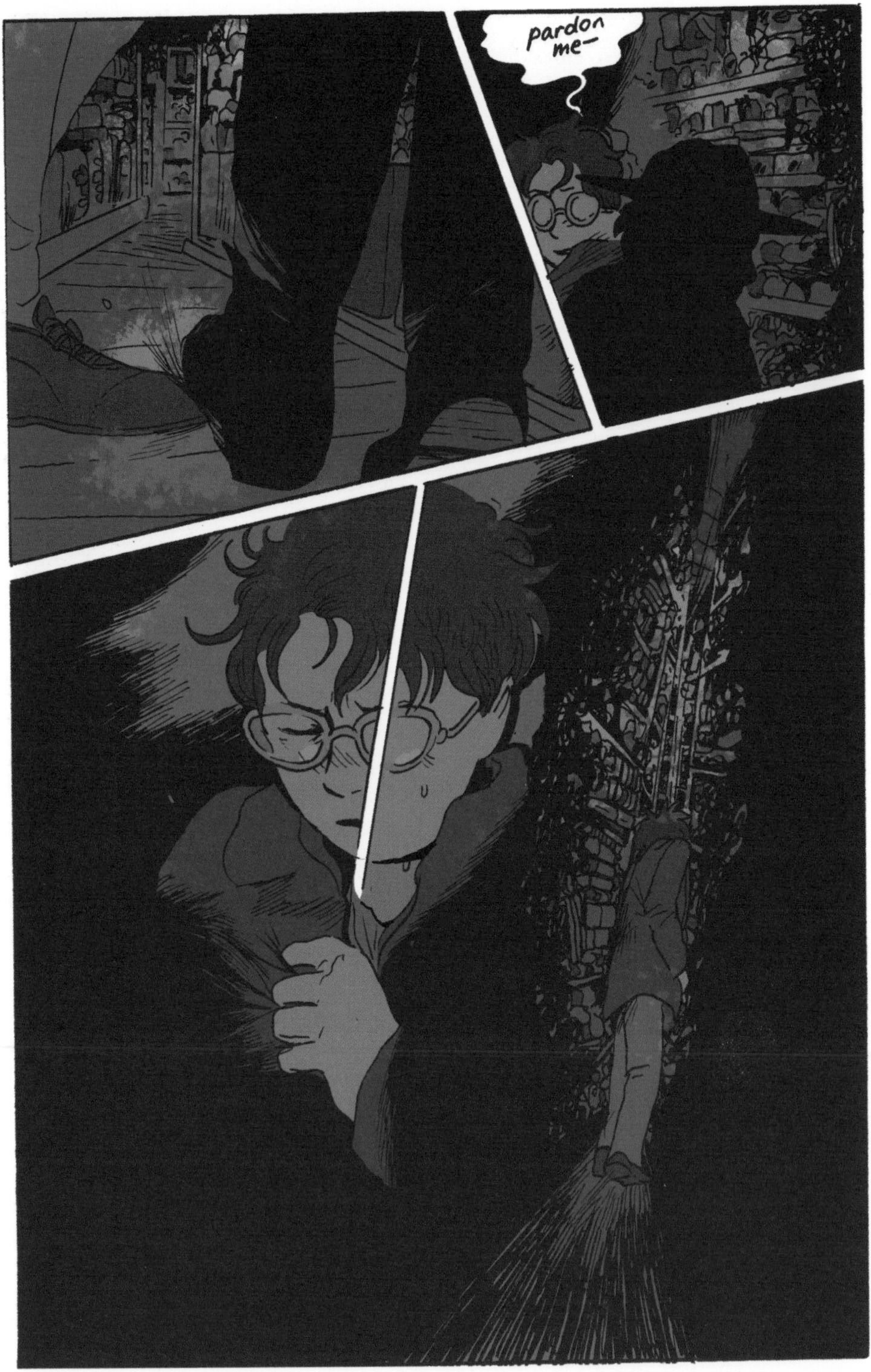
pardon me-

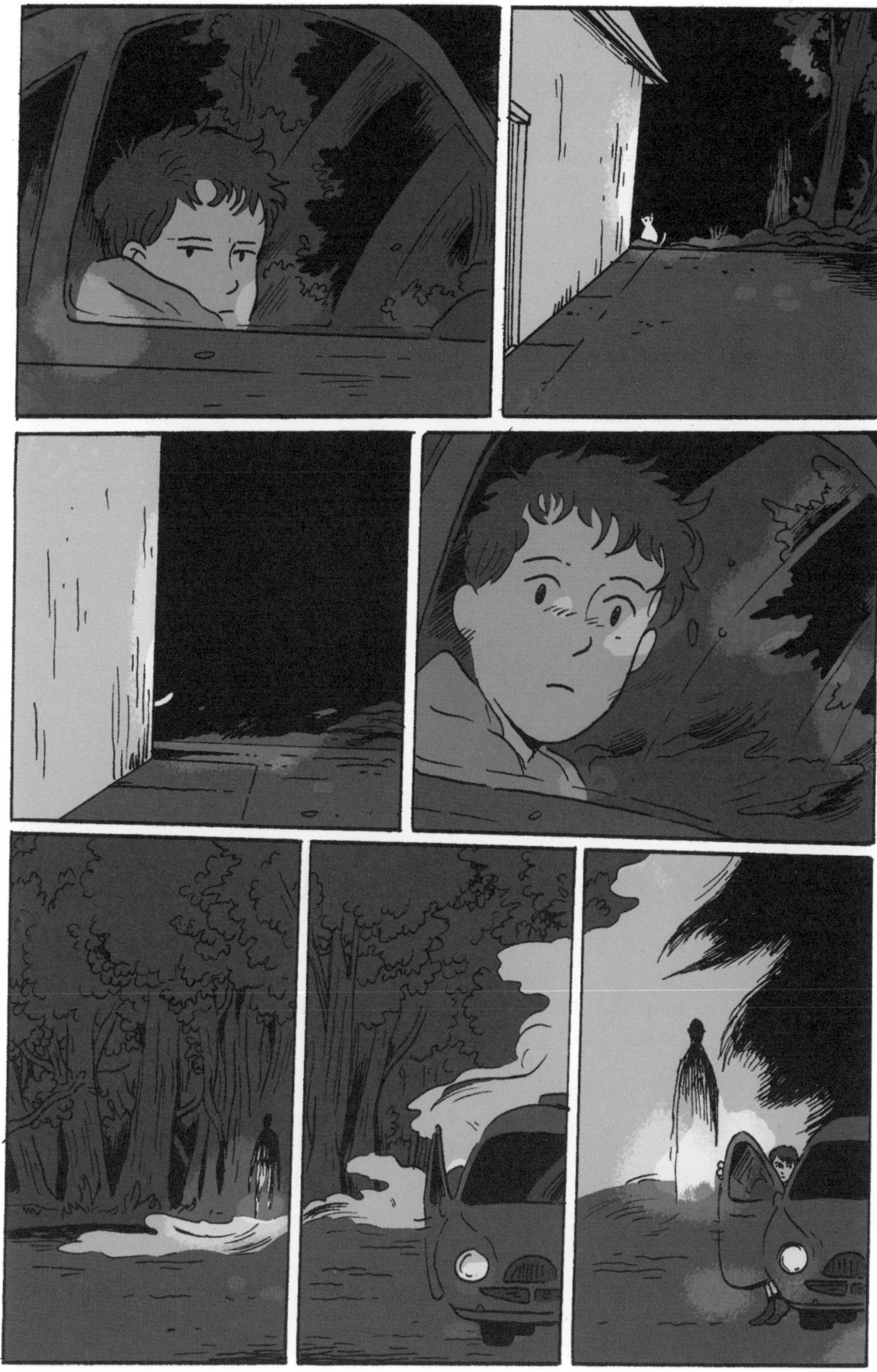

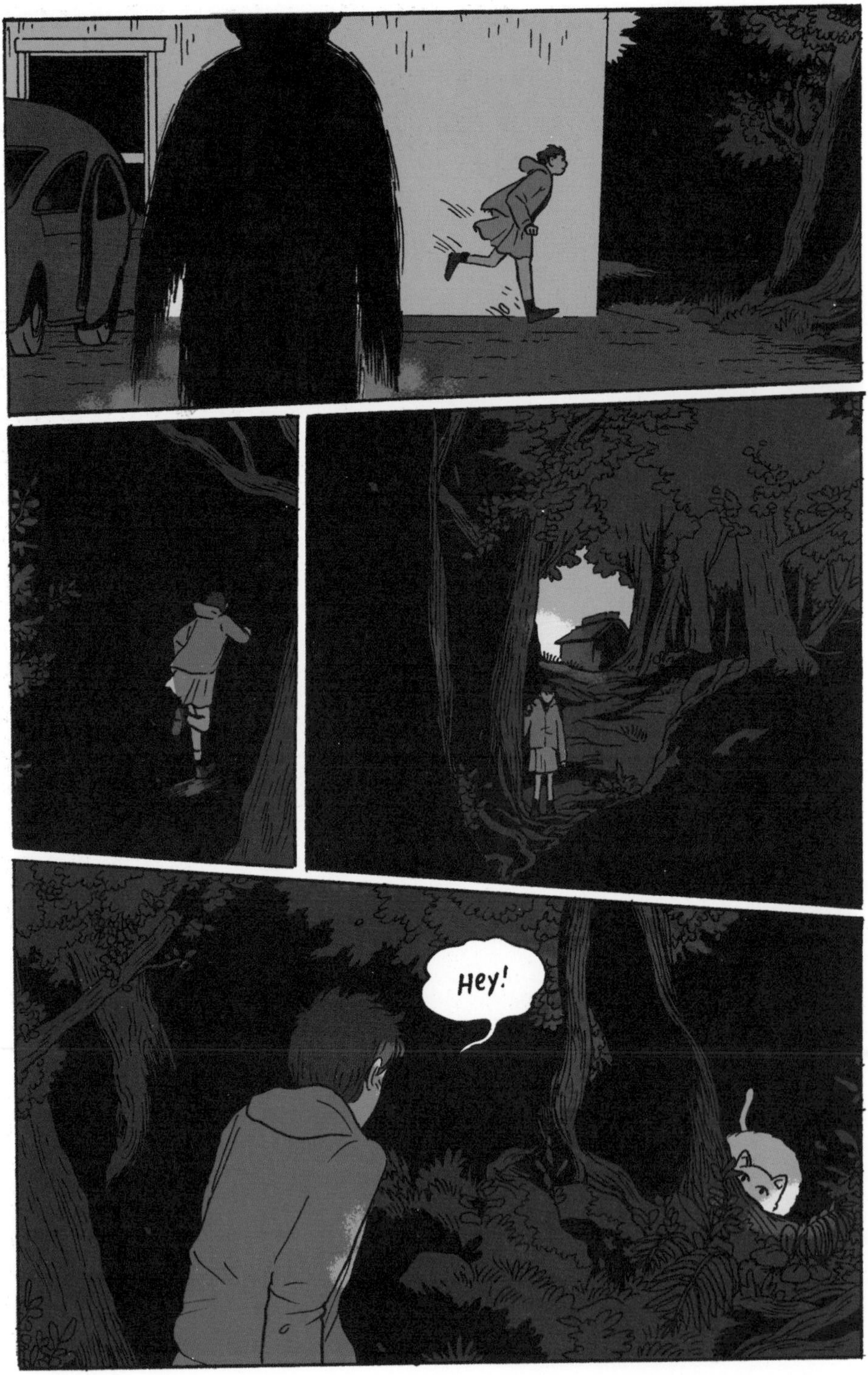
Hey!

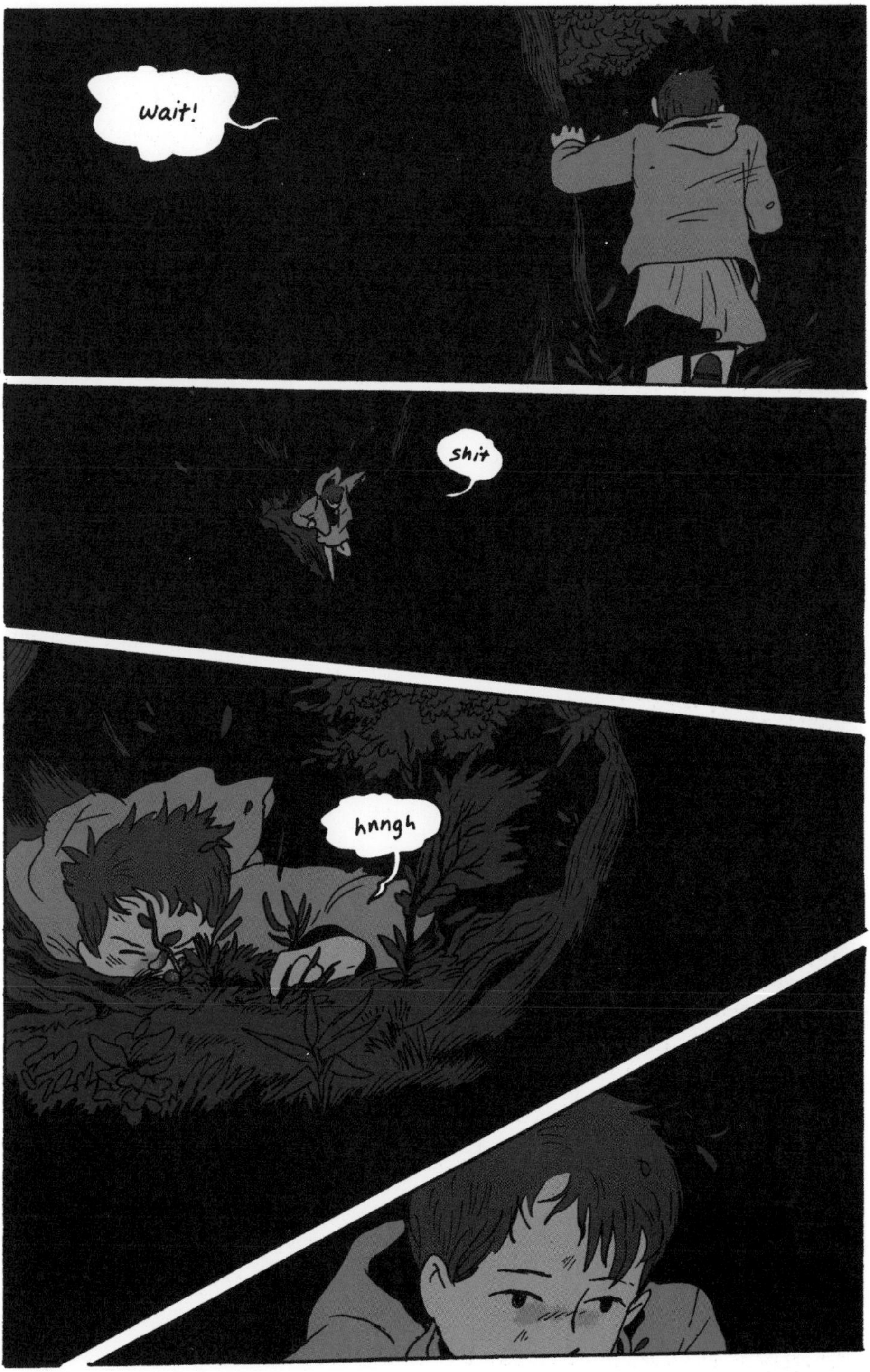
wait!
shit
hnngh

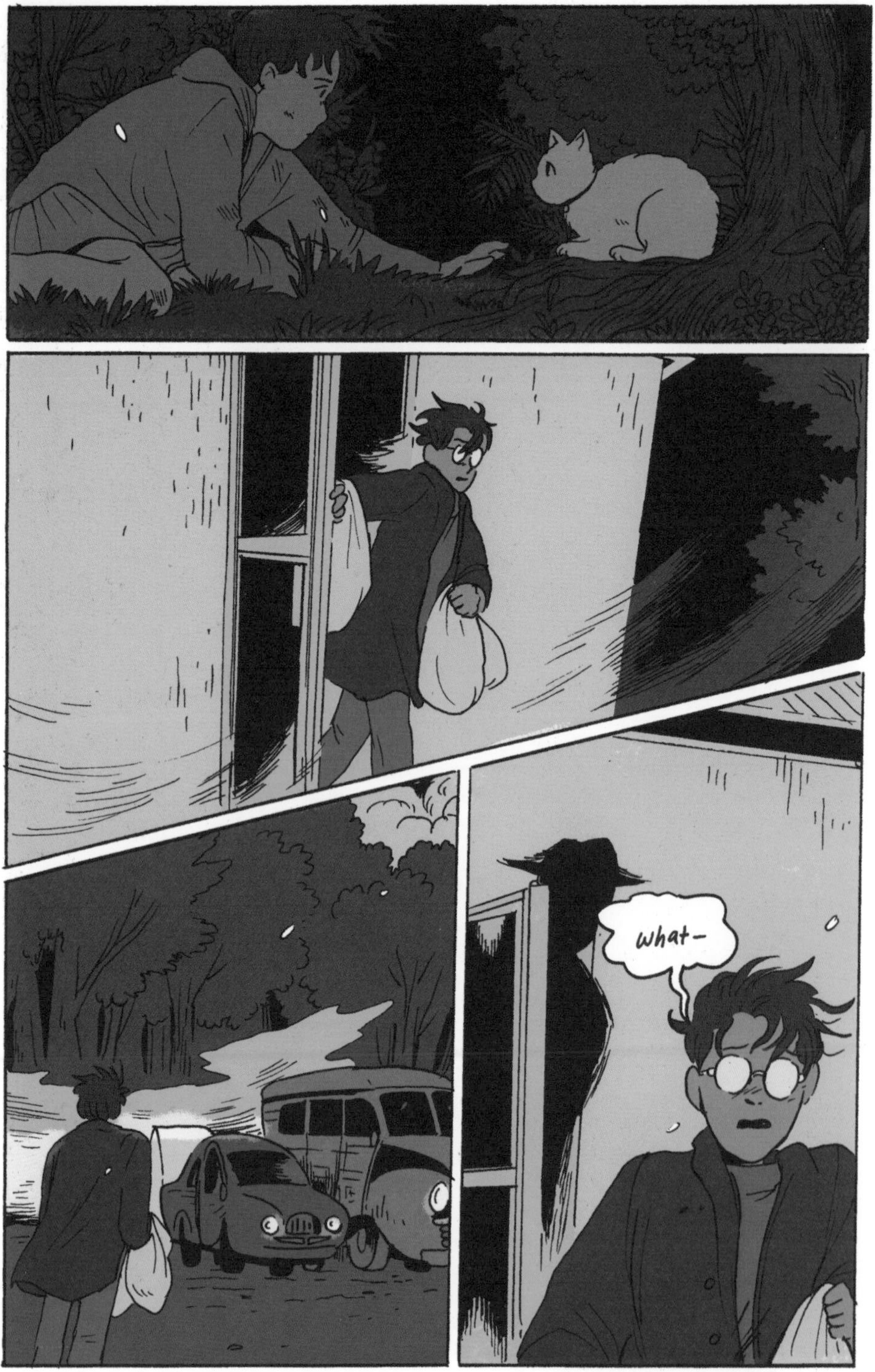
what-

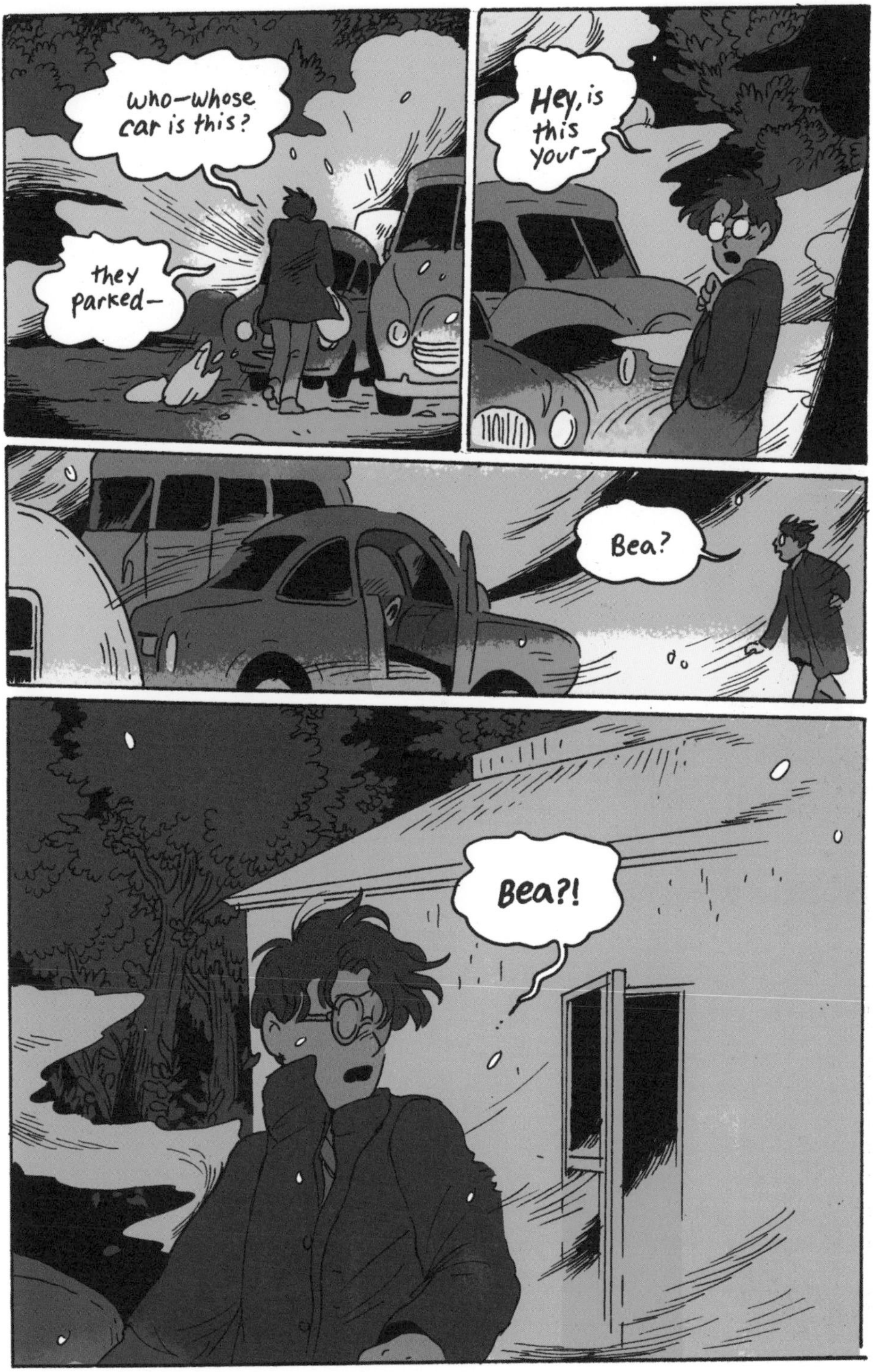
who-whose car is this?
they parked-
Hey, is this your-
Bea?
Bea?!

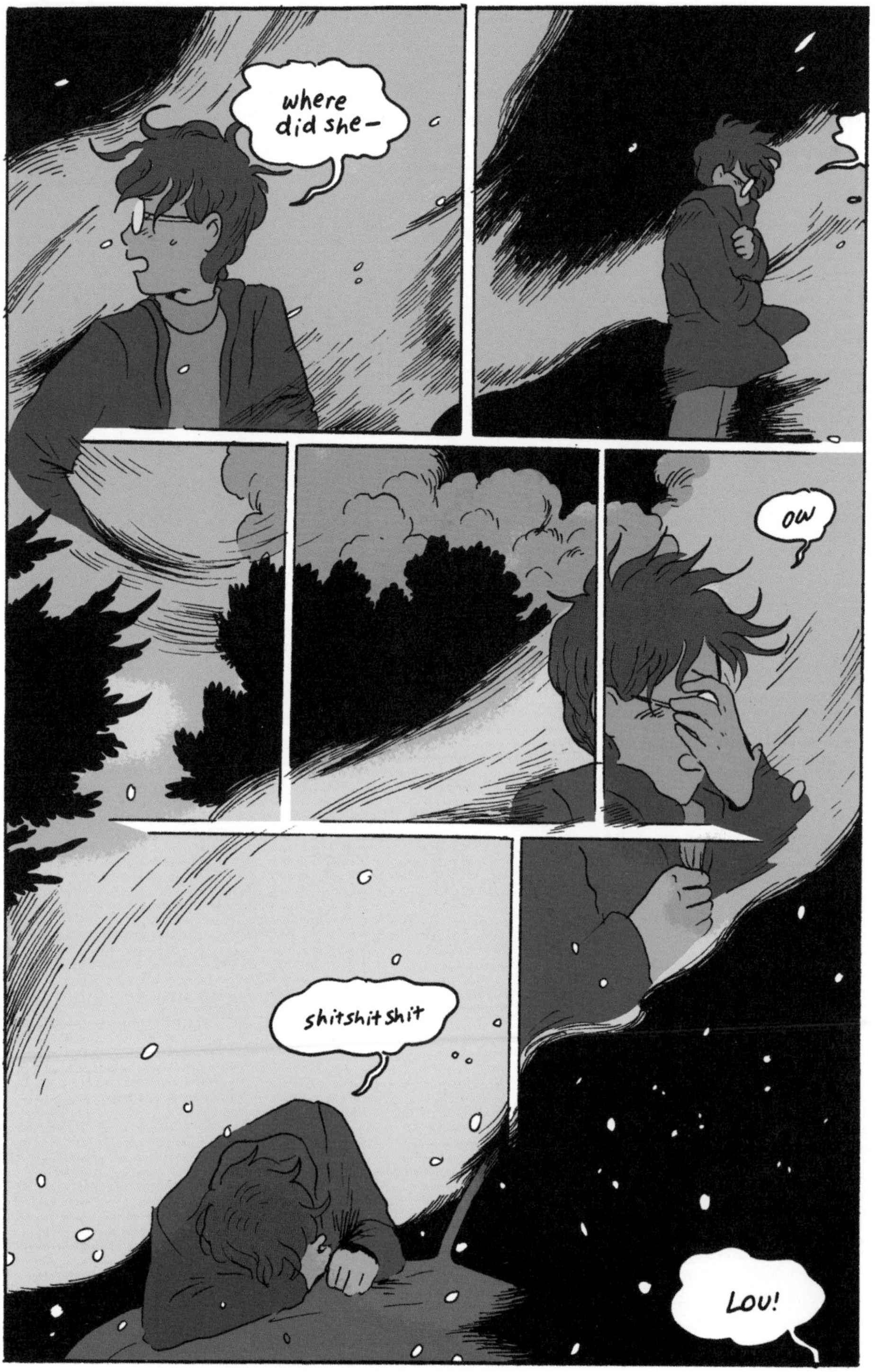
where did she-
ow
shitshitshit
LOU!

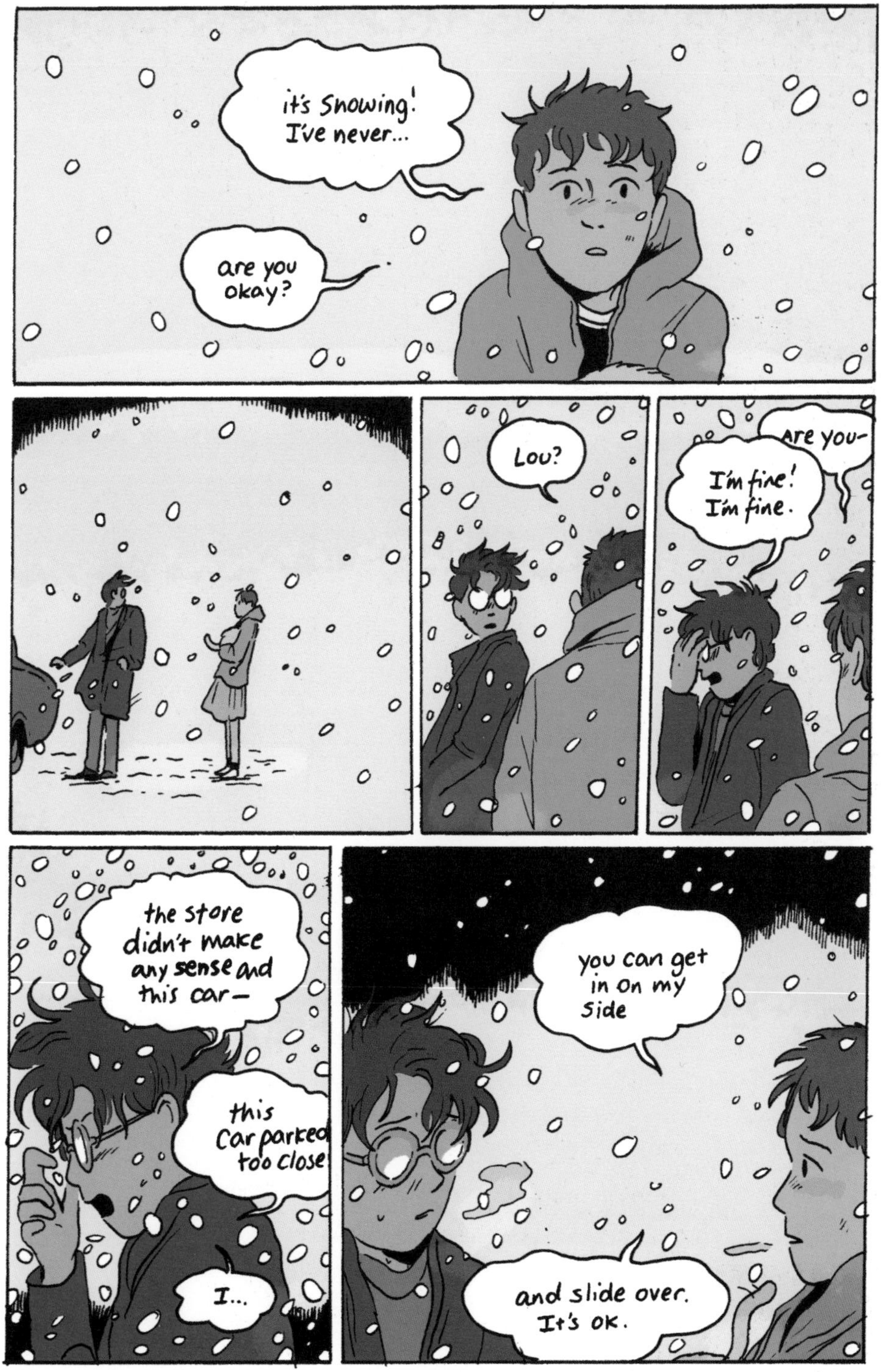
it's Snowing! I've never...
are you okay?
Lou?
Are you-
I'm fine! I'm fine.
the store didn't make any sense and this car—
this car parked too close
I...
you can get in on my side
and slide over. It's OK.

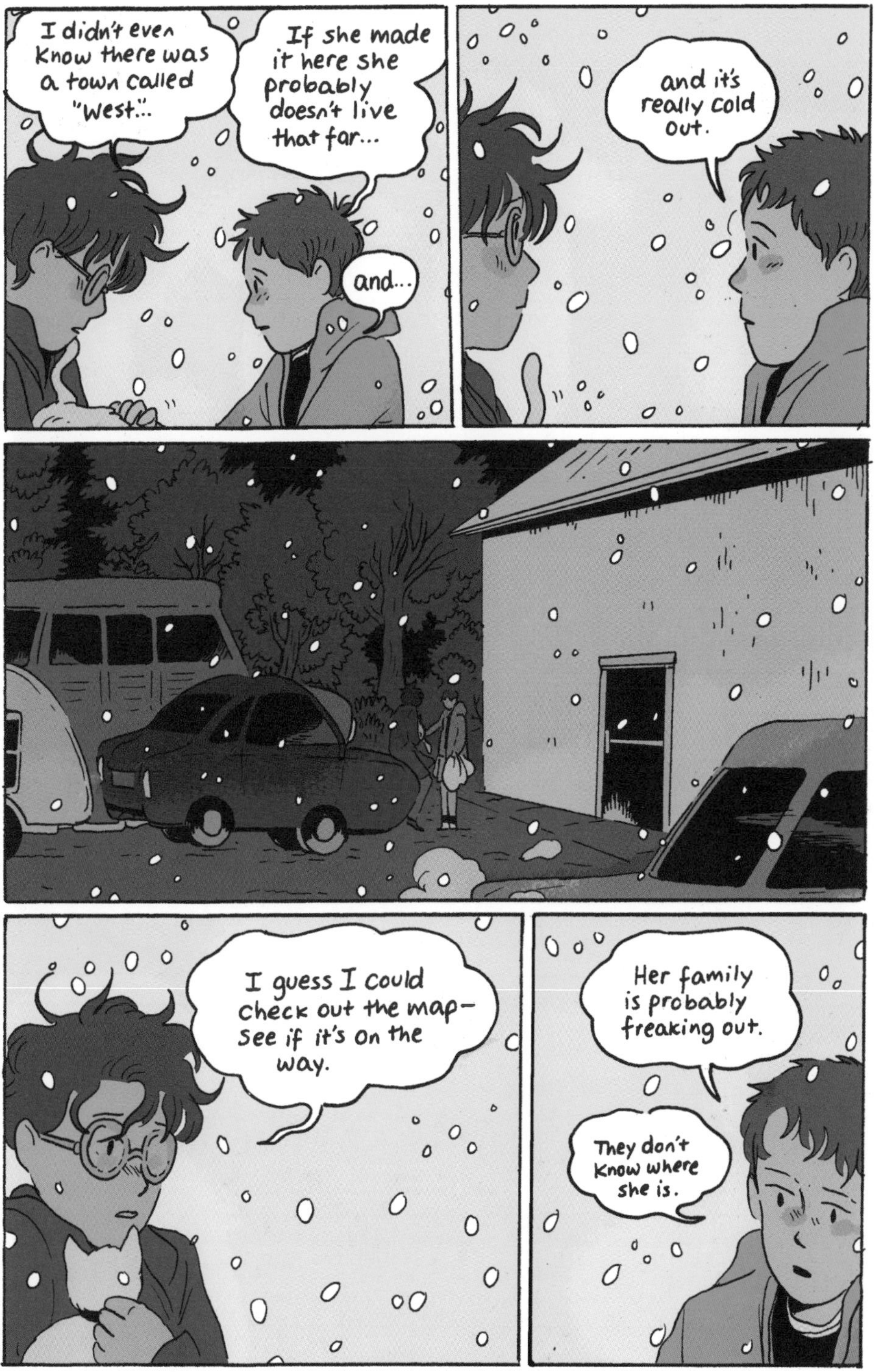
I didn't even know there was a town called "West."..
If she made it here she probably doesn't live that far...
and...
and it's really cold out.
I guess I could check out the map– see if it's on the way.
Her family is probably freaking out.
They don't know where she is.

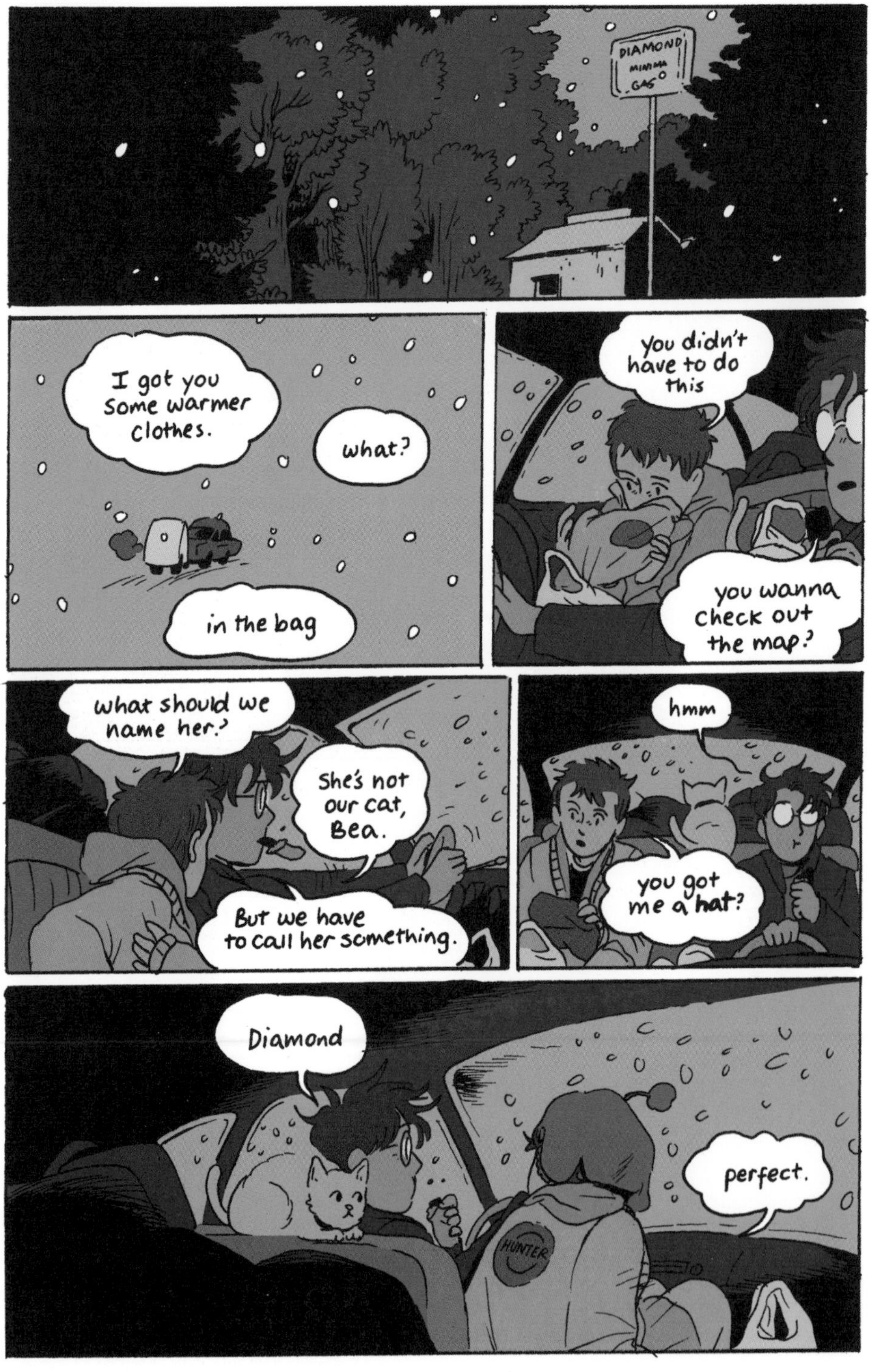
DIAMOND
GAS
I got you some warmer clothes.
what?
in the bag
you didn't have to do this
you wanna check out the map?
what should we name her?
She's not our cat, Bea.
But we have to call her something.
hmm
you got me a hat?
Diamond
HUNTER
perfect.

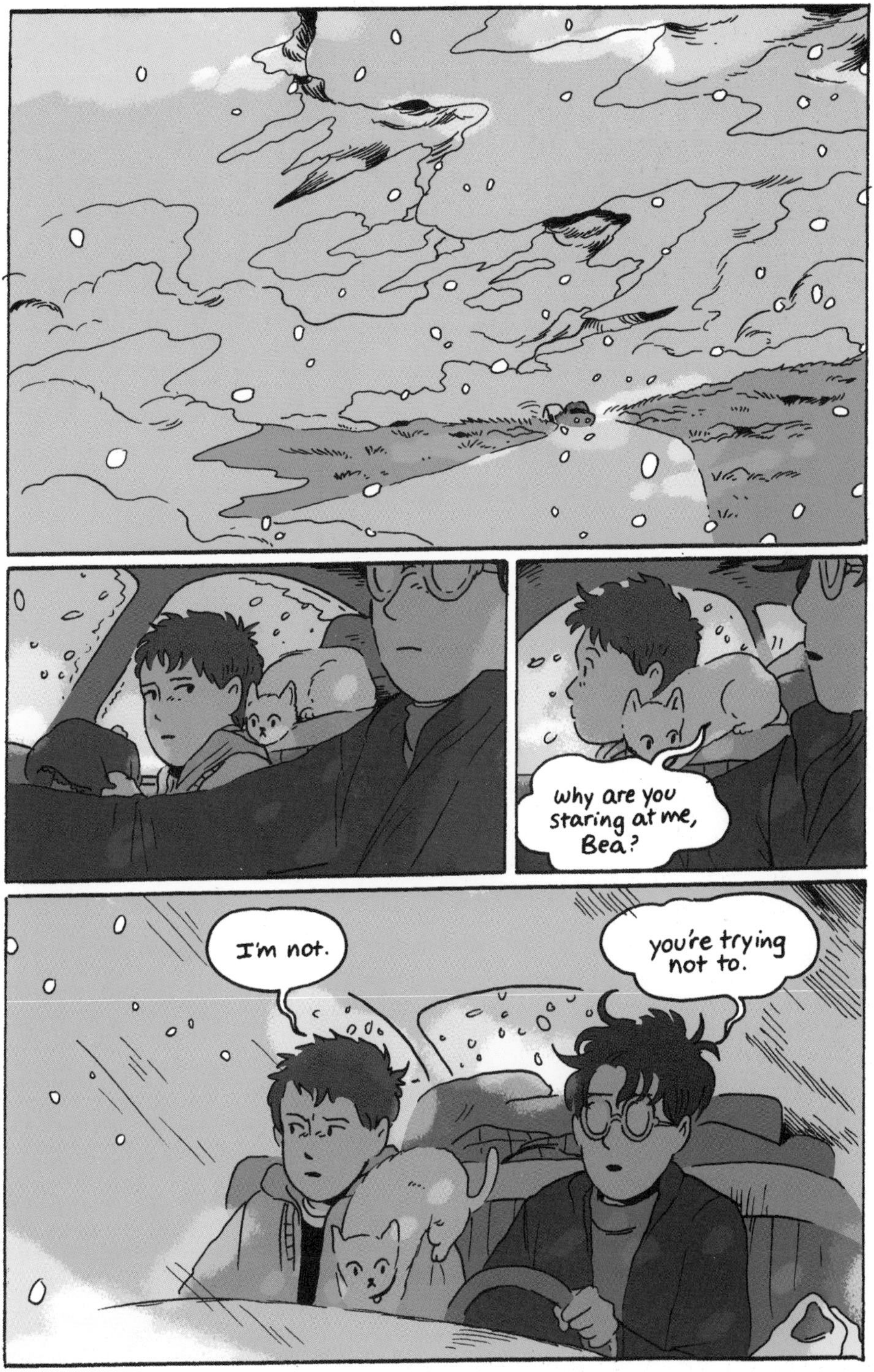
why are you staring at me, Bea?
I'm not.
you're trying not to.

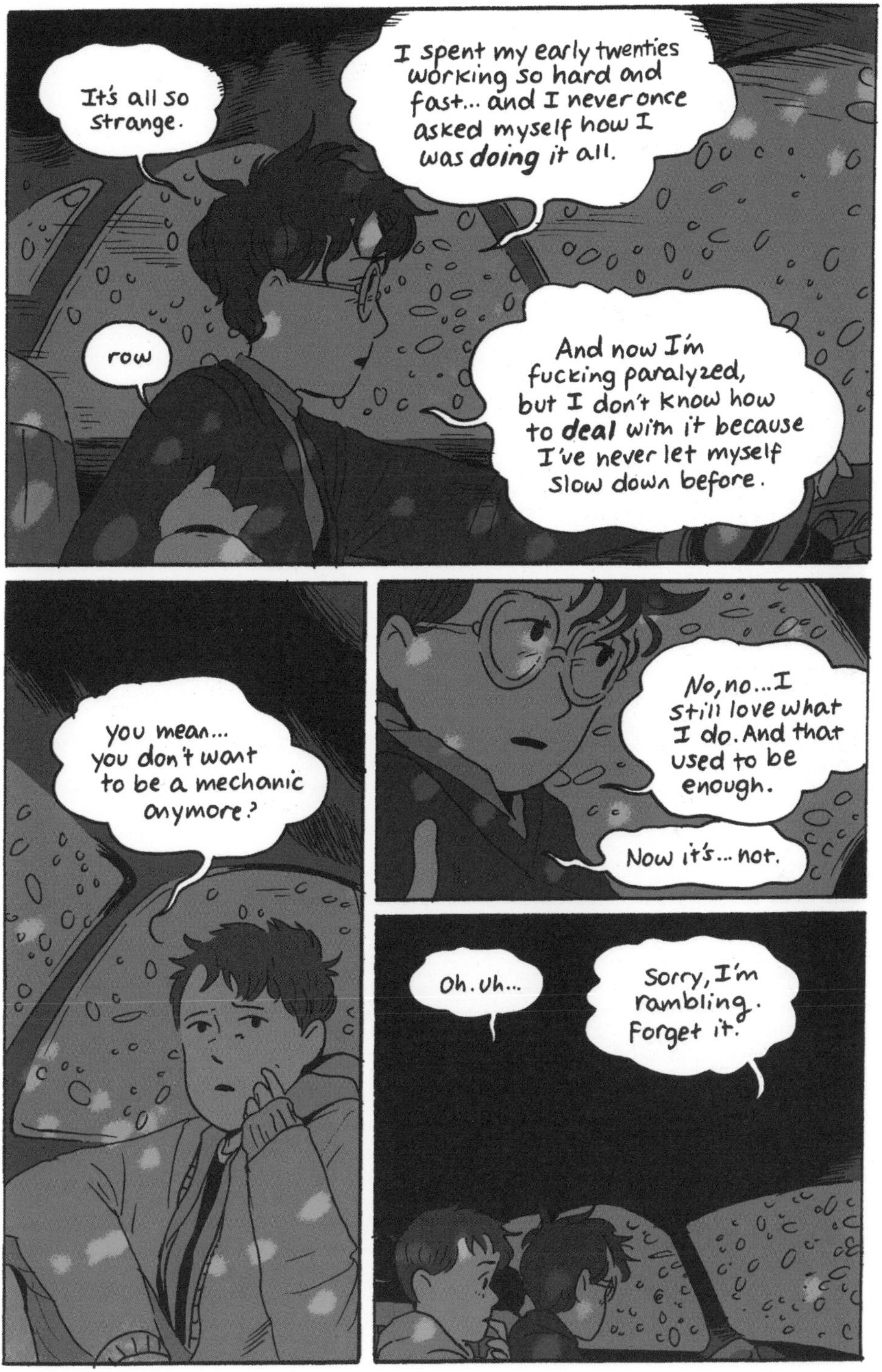
It's all so strange.
I spent my early twenties working so hard and fast... and I never once asked myself how I was *doing* it all.
row
And now I'm fucking paralyzed, but I don't know how to **deal** with it because I've never let myself slow down before.
you mean... you don't want to be a mechanic anymore?
No, no... I still love what I do. And that used to be enough.
Now it's... not.
Oh. uh...
Sorry, I'm rambling. Forget it.

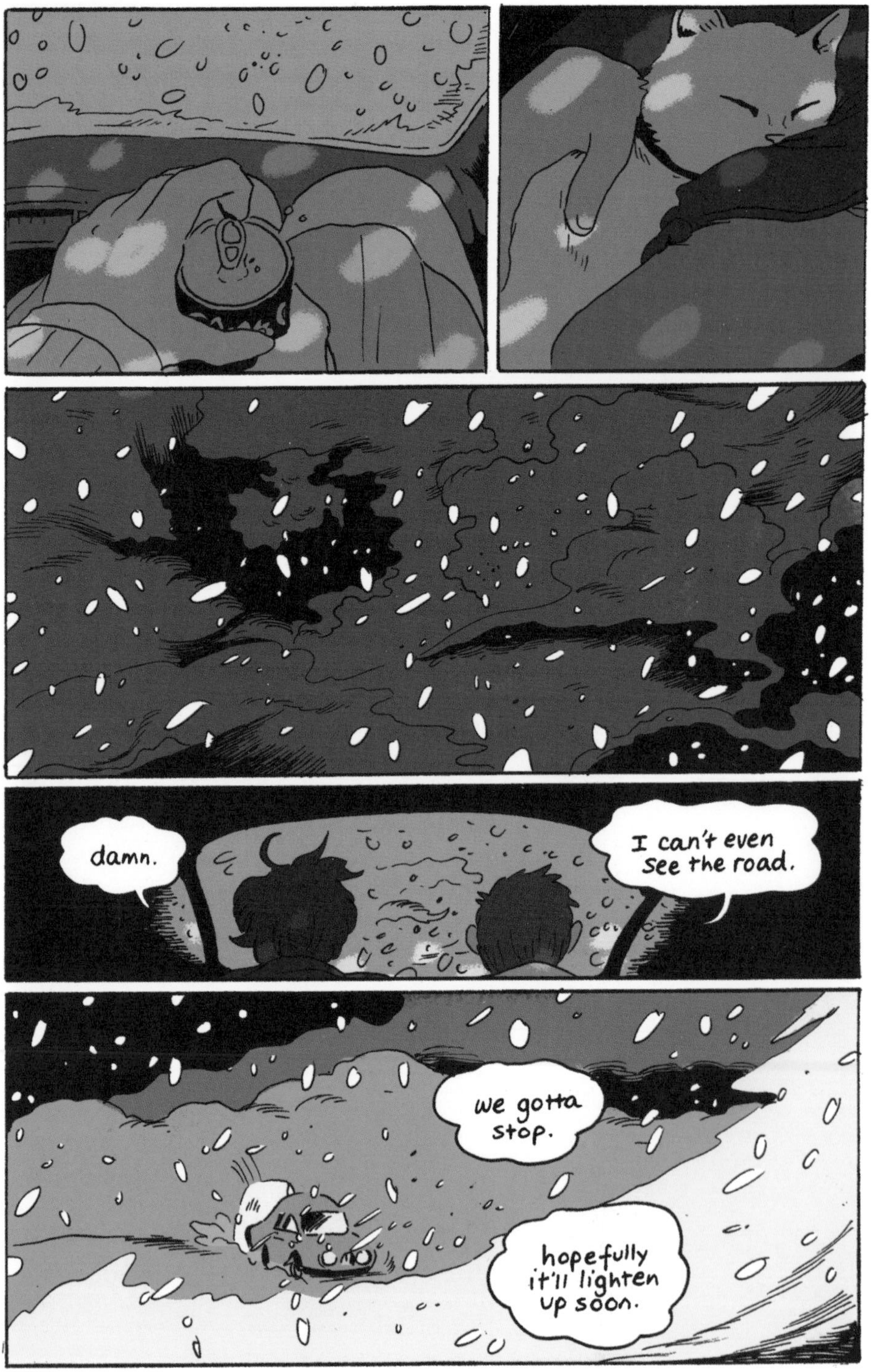
damn.
I can't even see the road.
we gotta stop.
hopefully it'll lighten up soon.

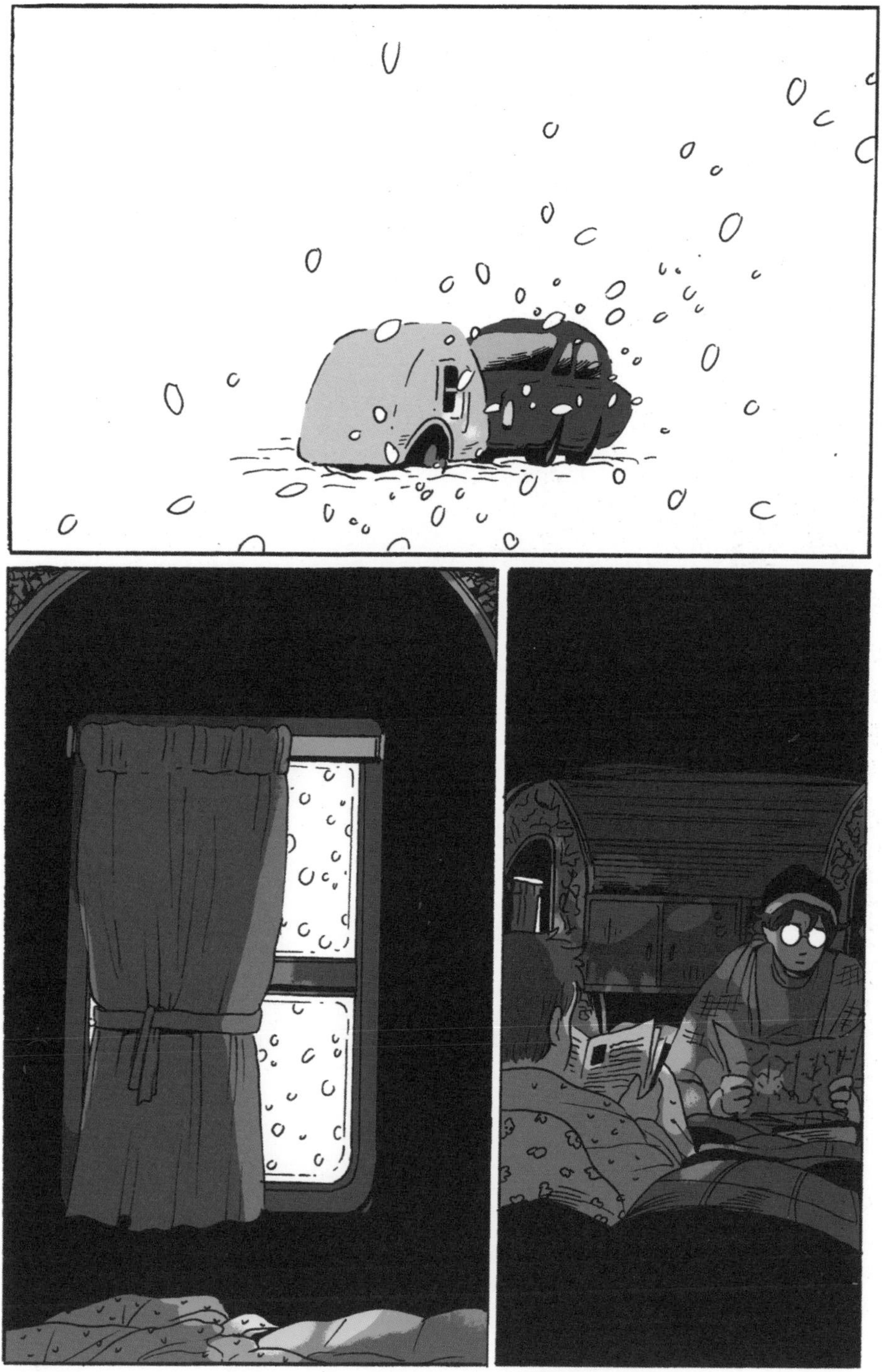

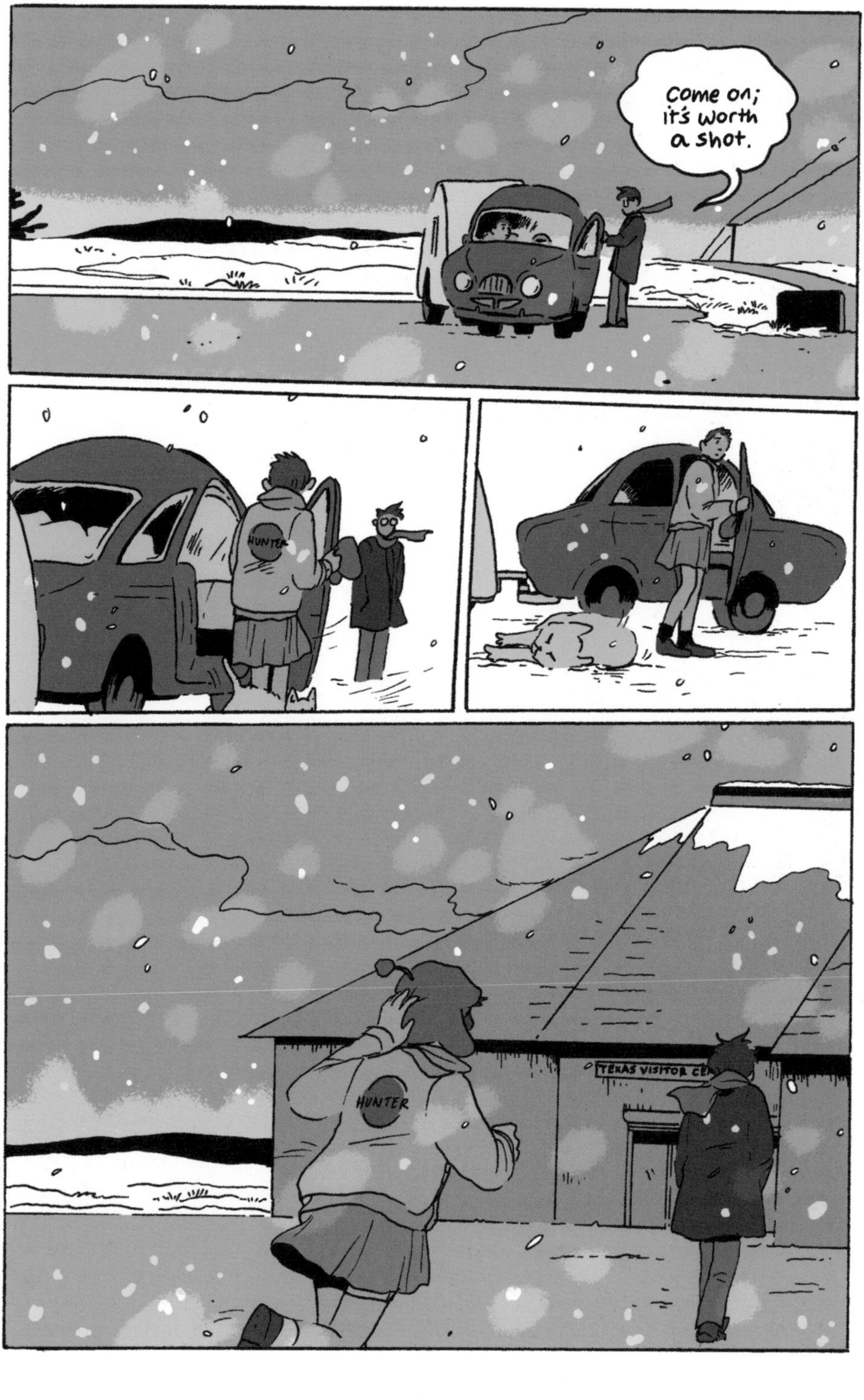
Come on;
it's worth
a shot.
HUNTER
HUNTER
HUNTER
TEXAS VISITOR

100

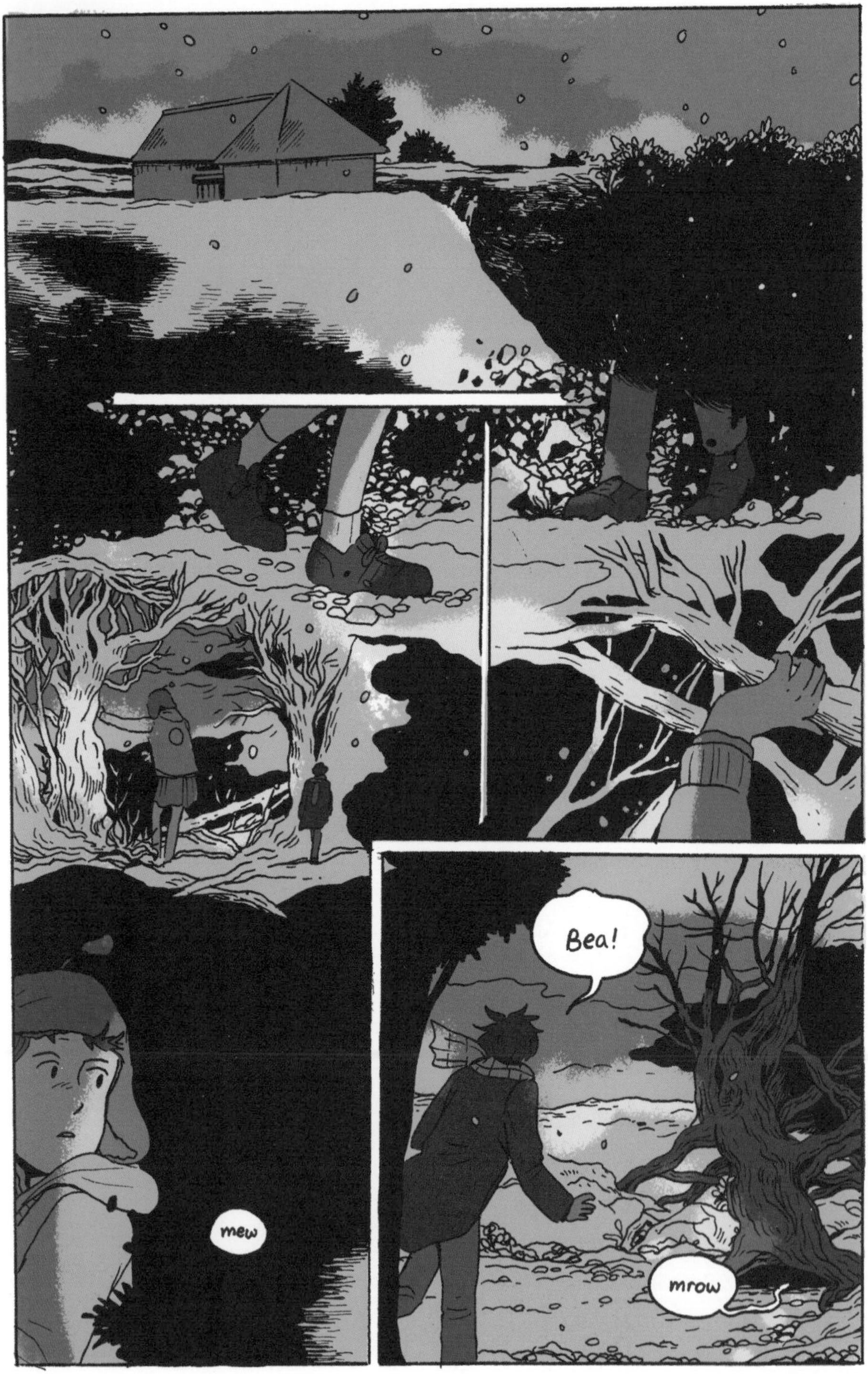
mew
Bea!
mrow

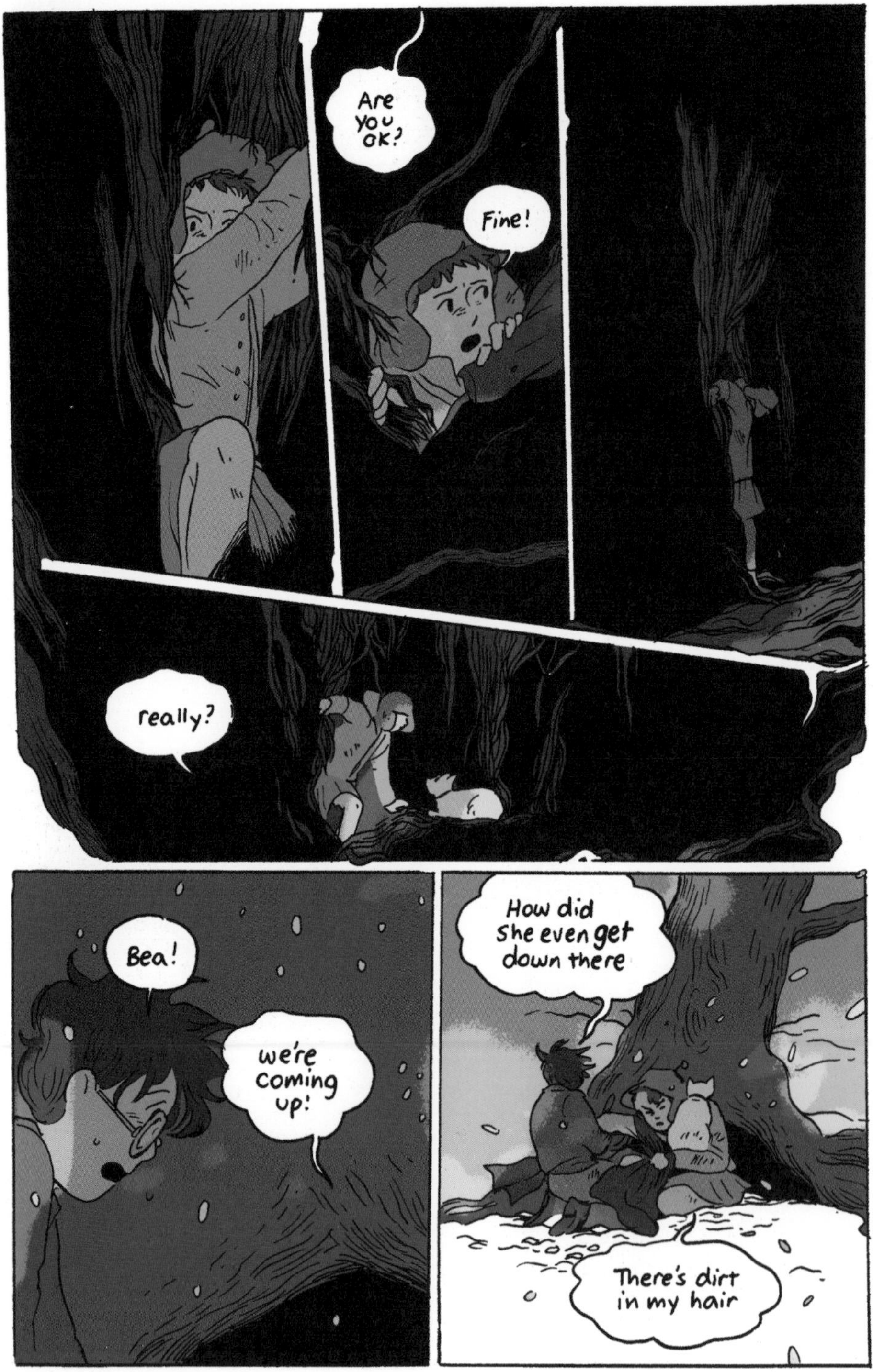
Are you ok?
Fine!
really?
Bea!
we're coming up!
How did she even get down there
There's dirt in my hair

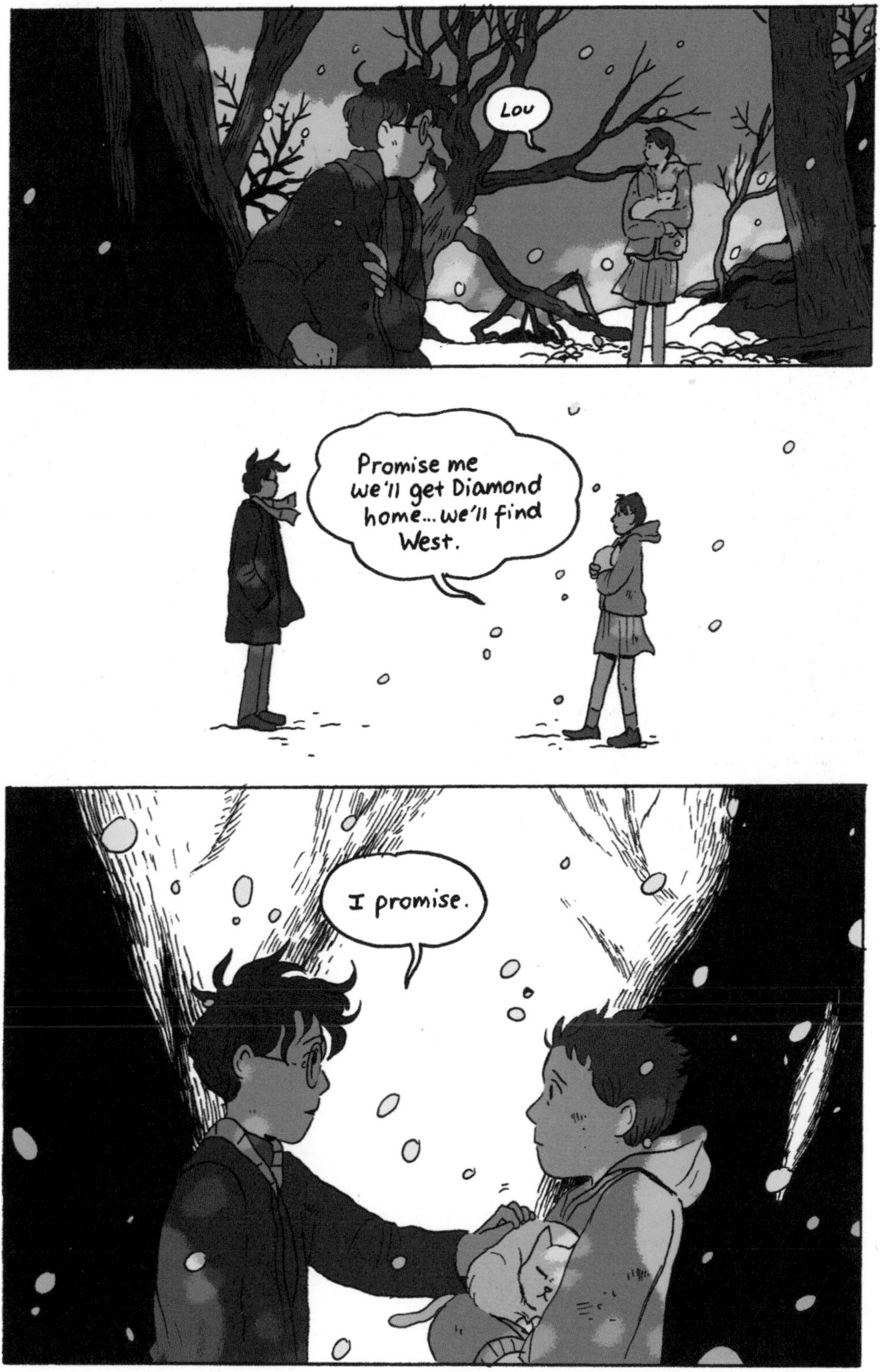
Lou
Promise me we'll get Diamond home... we'll find West.
I promise.

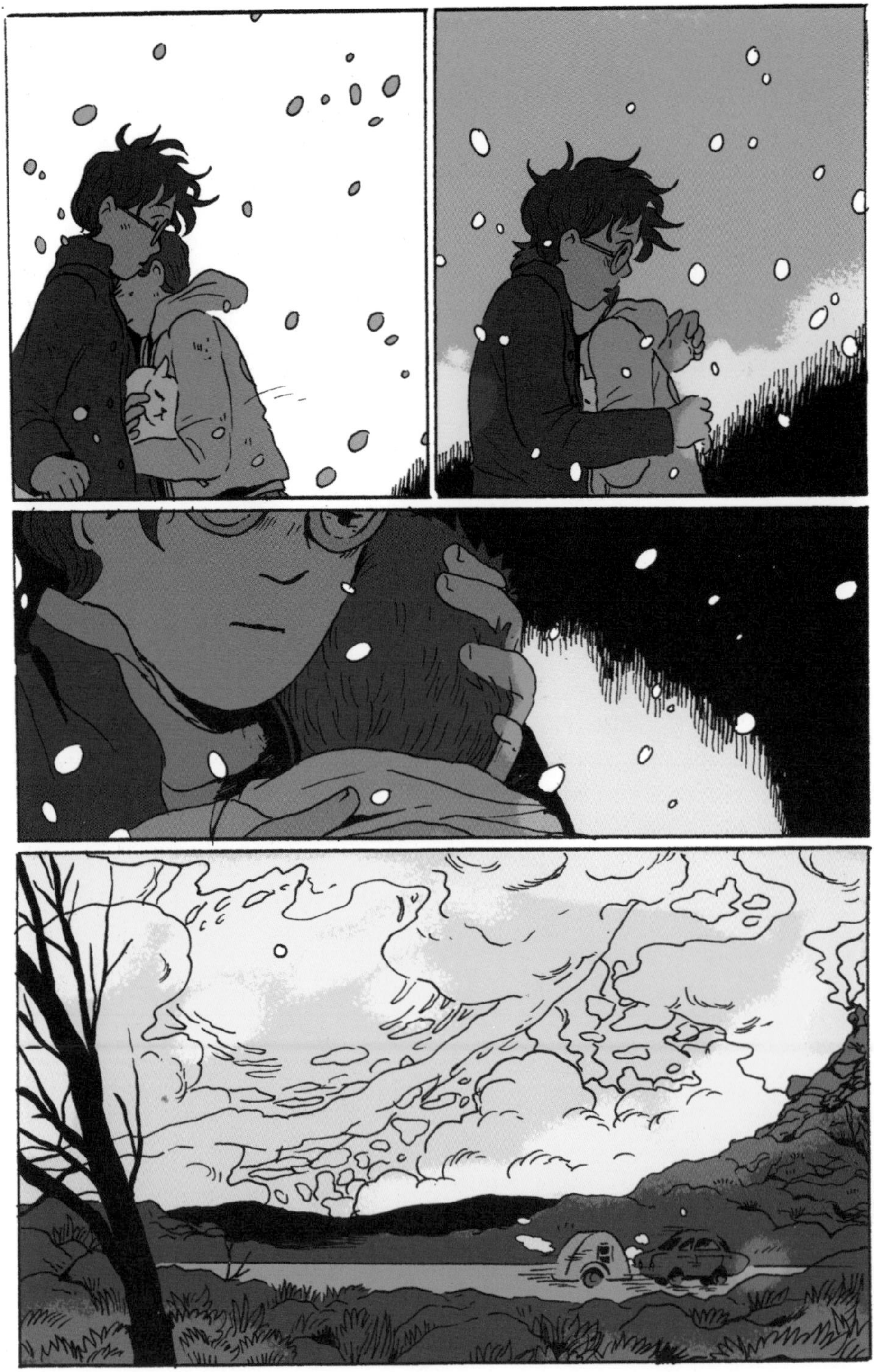

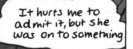

110

111

113

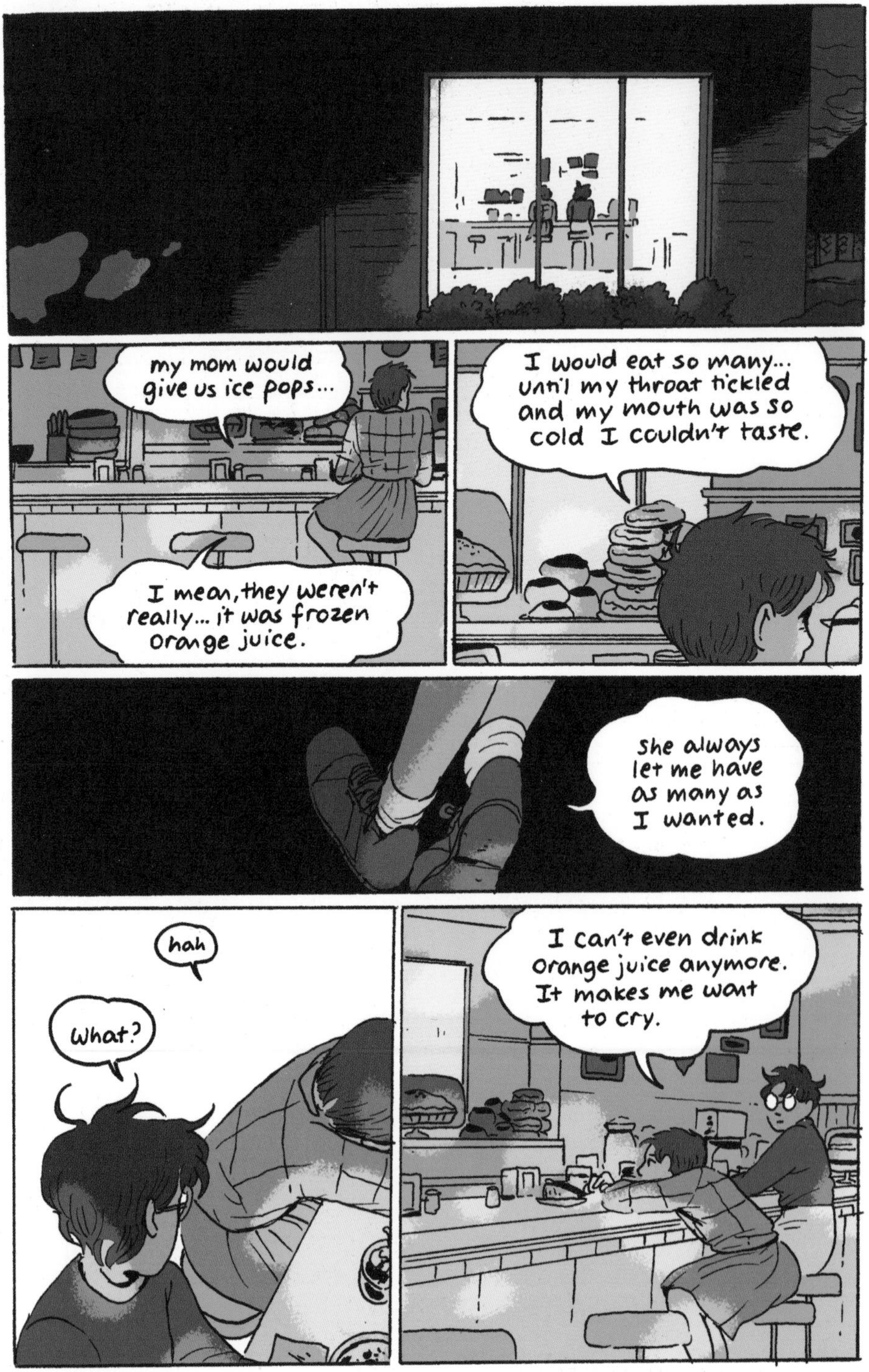
my mom would give us ice pops...
I mean, they weren't really... it was frozen orange juice.
I would eat so many... until my throat tickled and my mouth was so cold I couldn't taste.
she always let me have as many as I wanted.
hah
What?
I can't even drink orange juice anymore. It makes me want to cry.

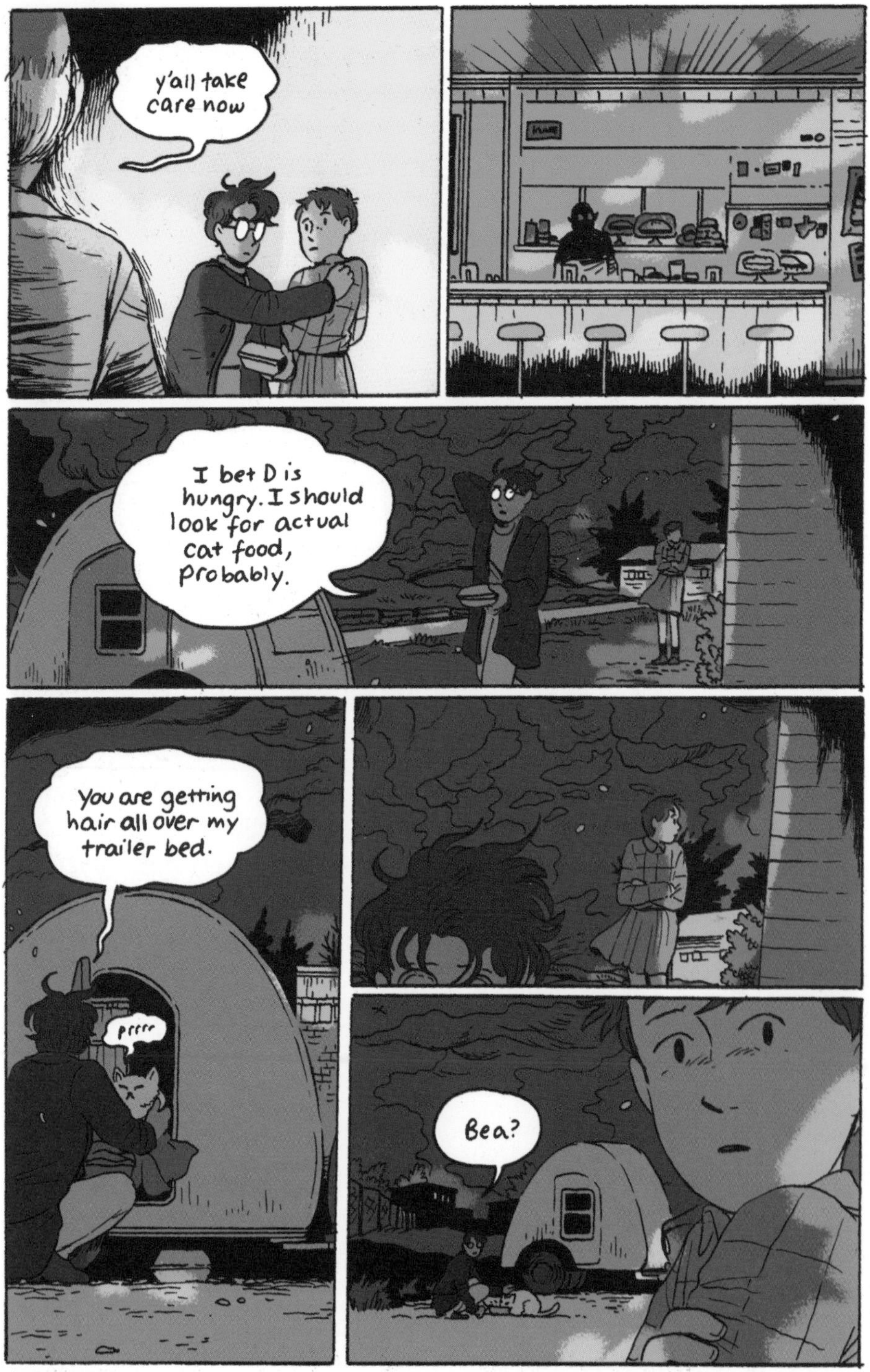
y'all take care now
I bet D is hungry. I should look for actual cat food, probably.
You are getting hair all over my trailer bed.
prrrr
Bea?

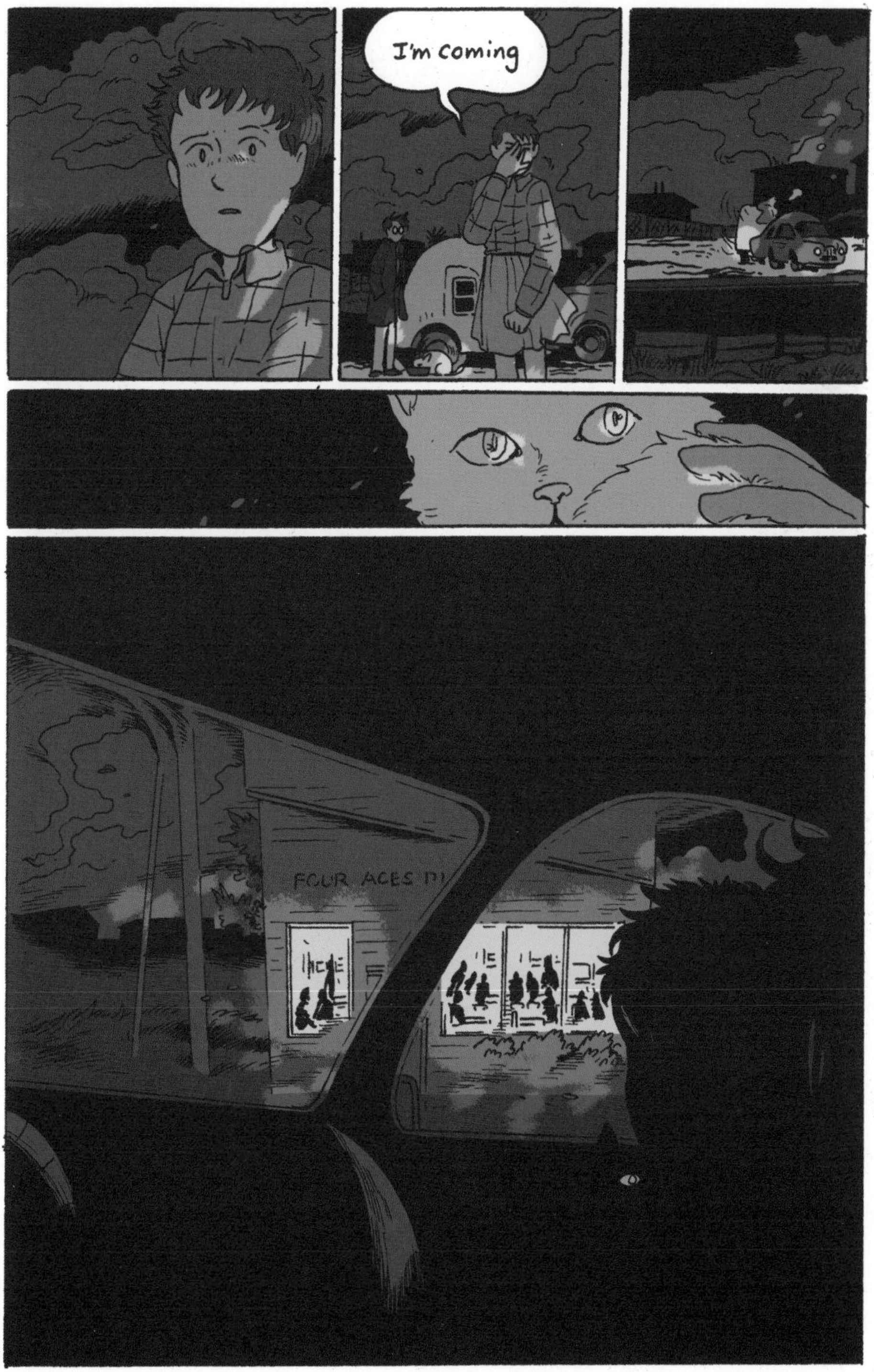
I'm coming
FOUR ACES

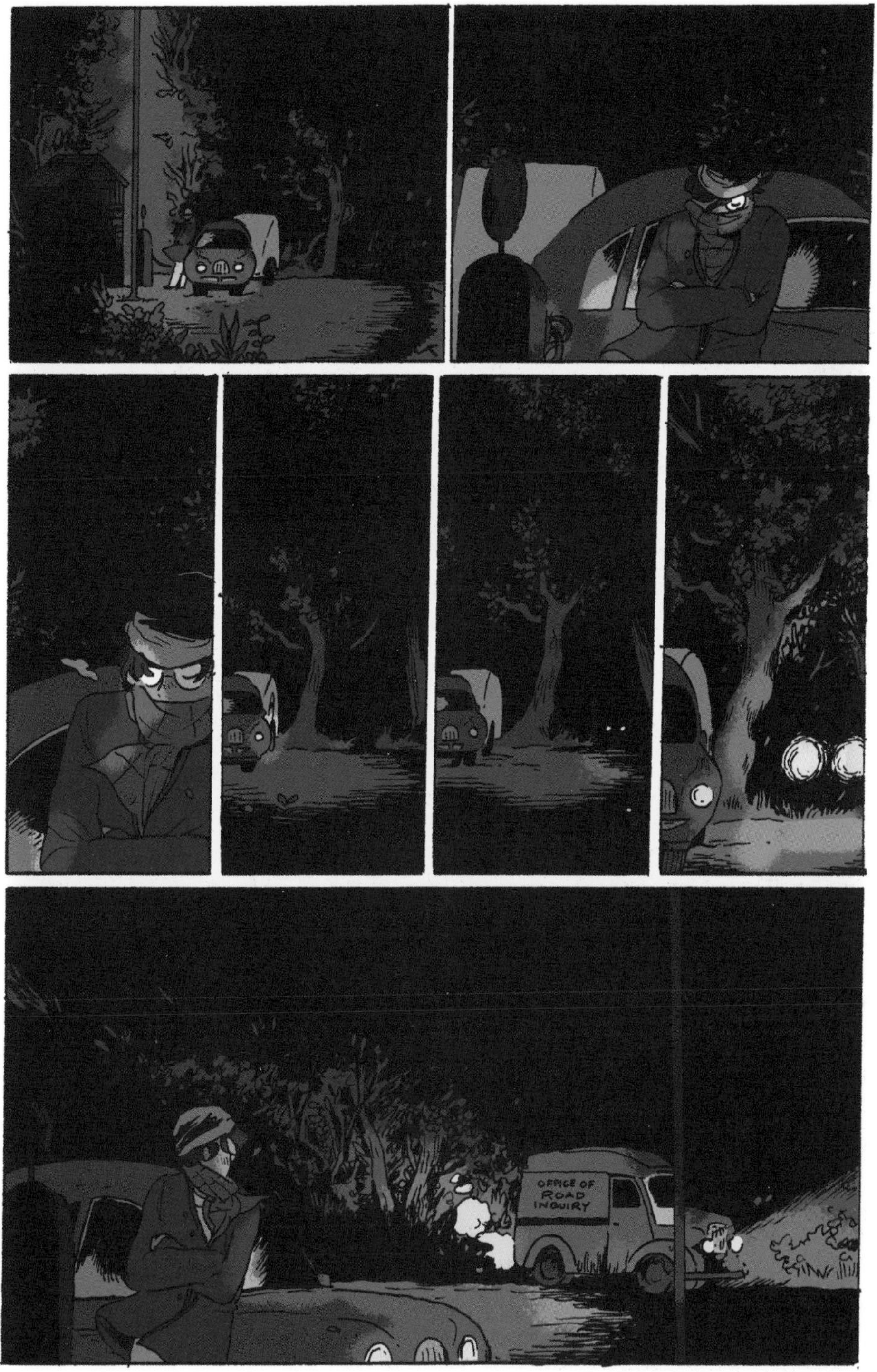
OFFICE OF
ROAD
INQUIRY

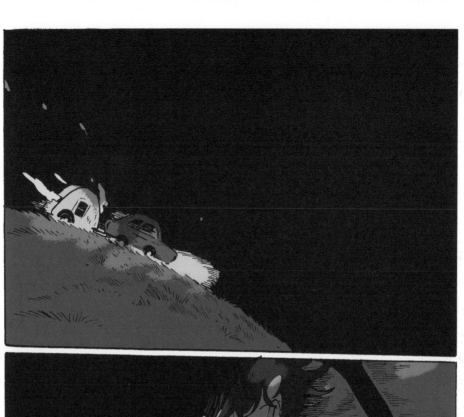

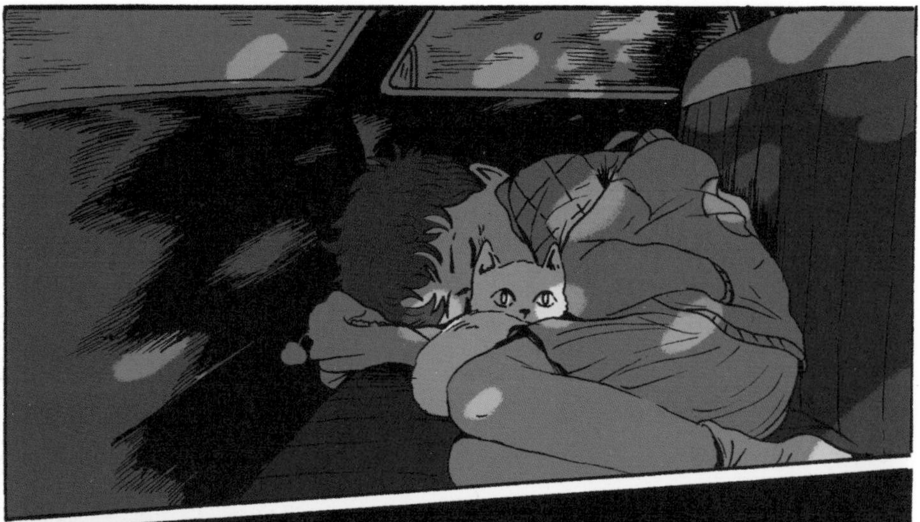

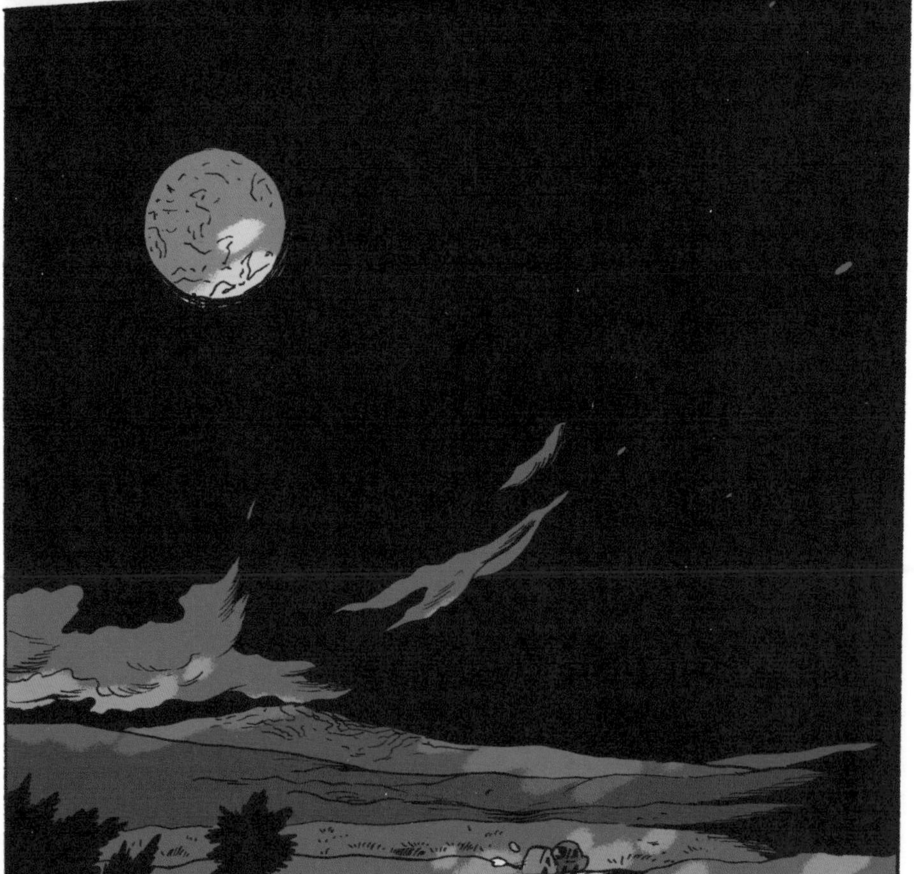

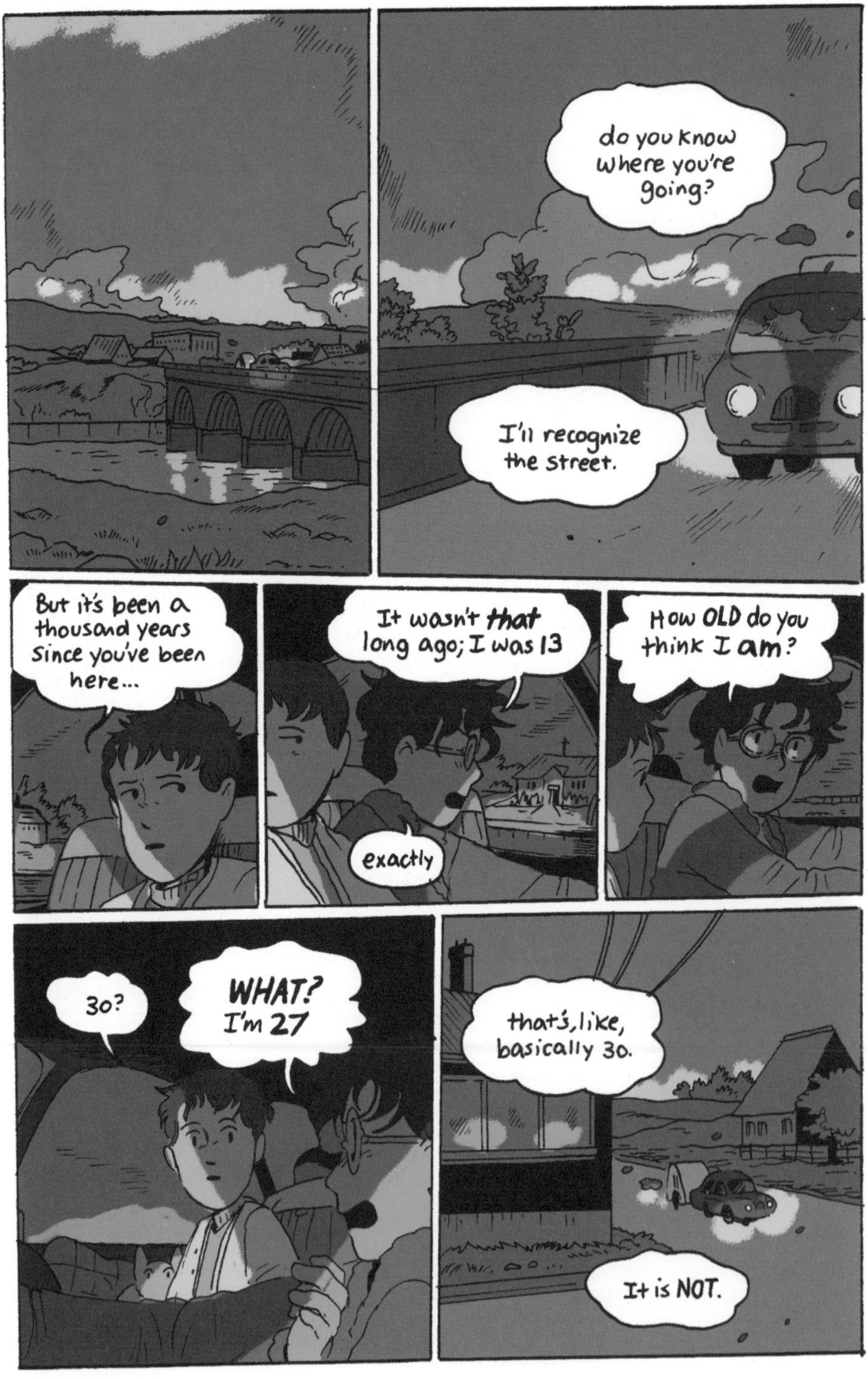
do you know where you're going?
I'll recognize the street.
But it's been a thousand years since you've been here...
It wasn't that long ago; I was 13
exactly
How OLD do you think I am?
30?
WHAT? I'm 27
that's, like, basically 30.
It is NOT.

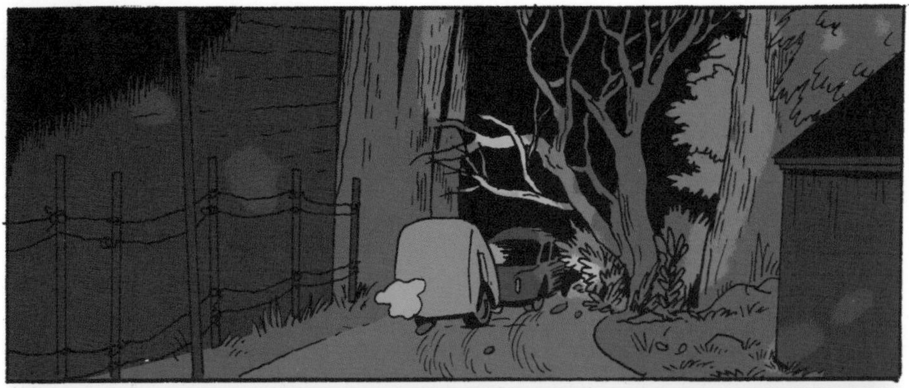

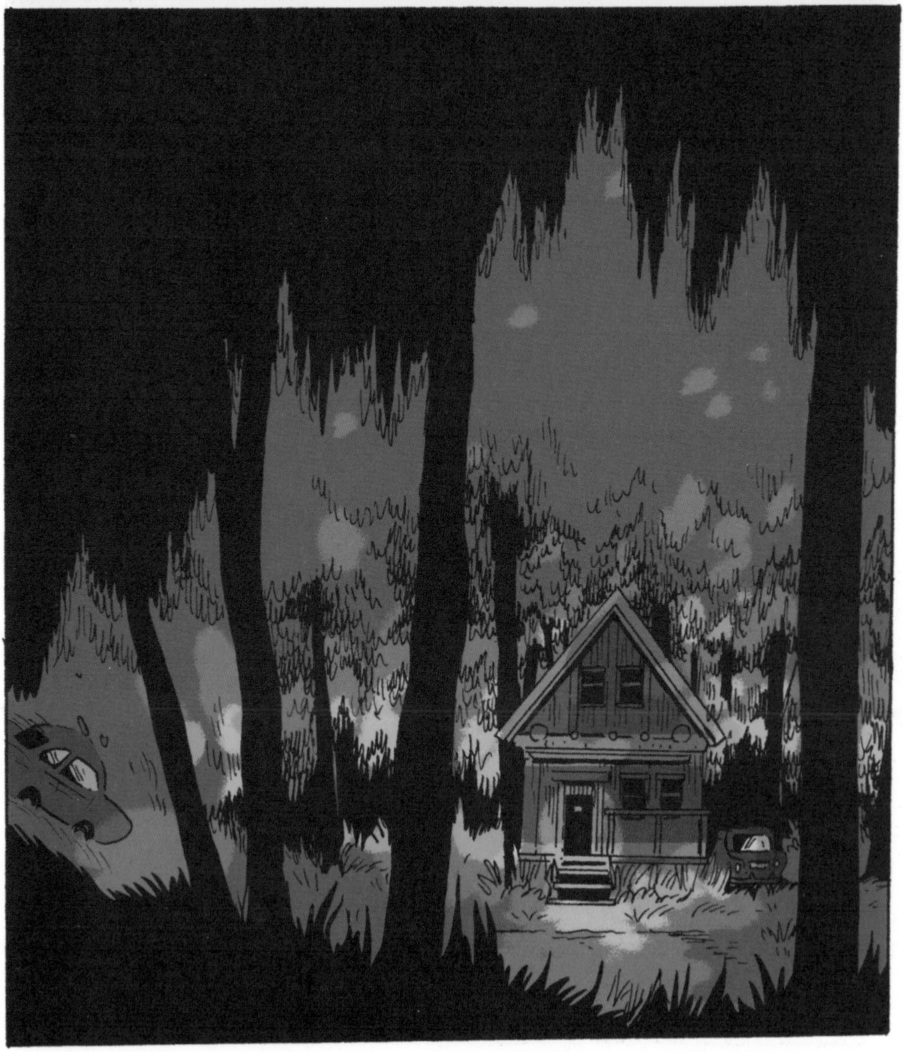

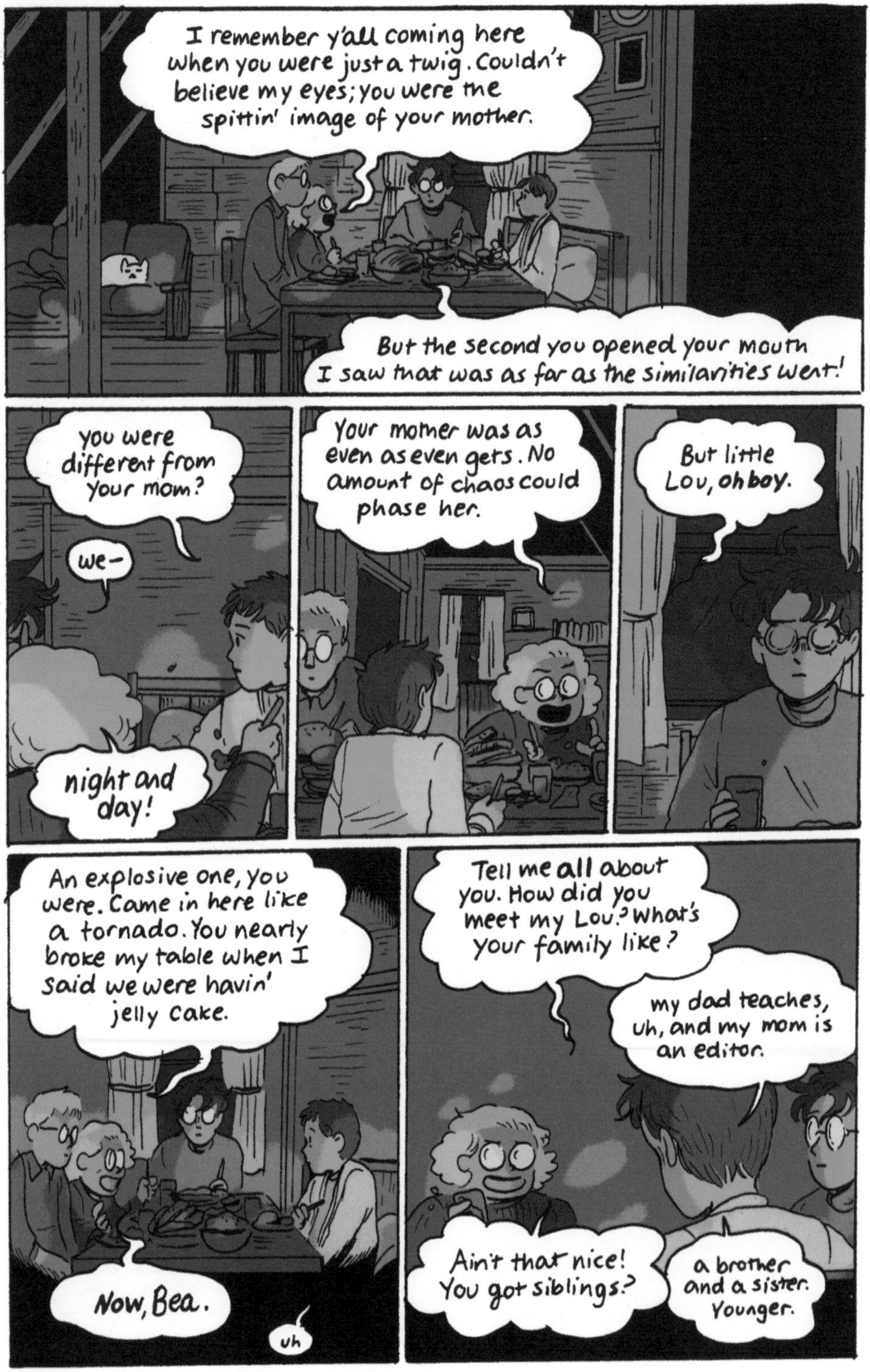
I remember y'all coming here when you were just a twig. Couldn't believe my eyes; you were the spittin' image of your mother.
But the second you opened your mouth I saw that was as far as the similarities went!
you were different from your mom?
we-
night and day!
Your mother was as even as even gets. No amount of chaos could phase her.
But little Lou, oh boy.
An explosive one, you were. Came in here like a tornado. You nearly broke my table when I said we were havin' jelly cake.
Now, Bea.
uh
Tell me all about you. How did you meet my Lou? What's your family like?
my dad teaches, uh, and my mom is an editor.
Ain't that nice! You got siblings?
a brother and a sister. Younger.

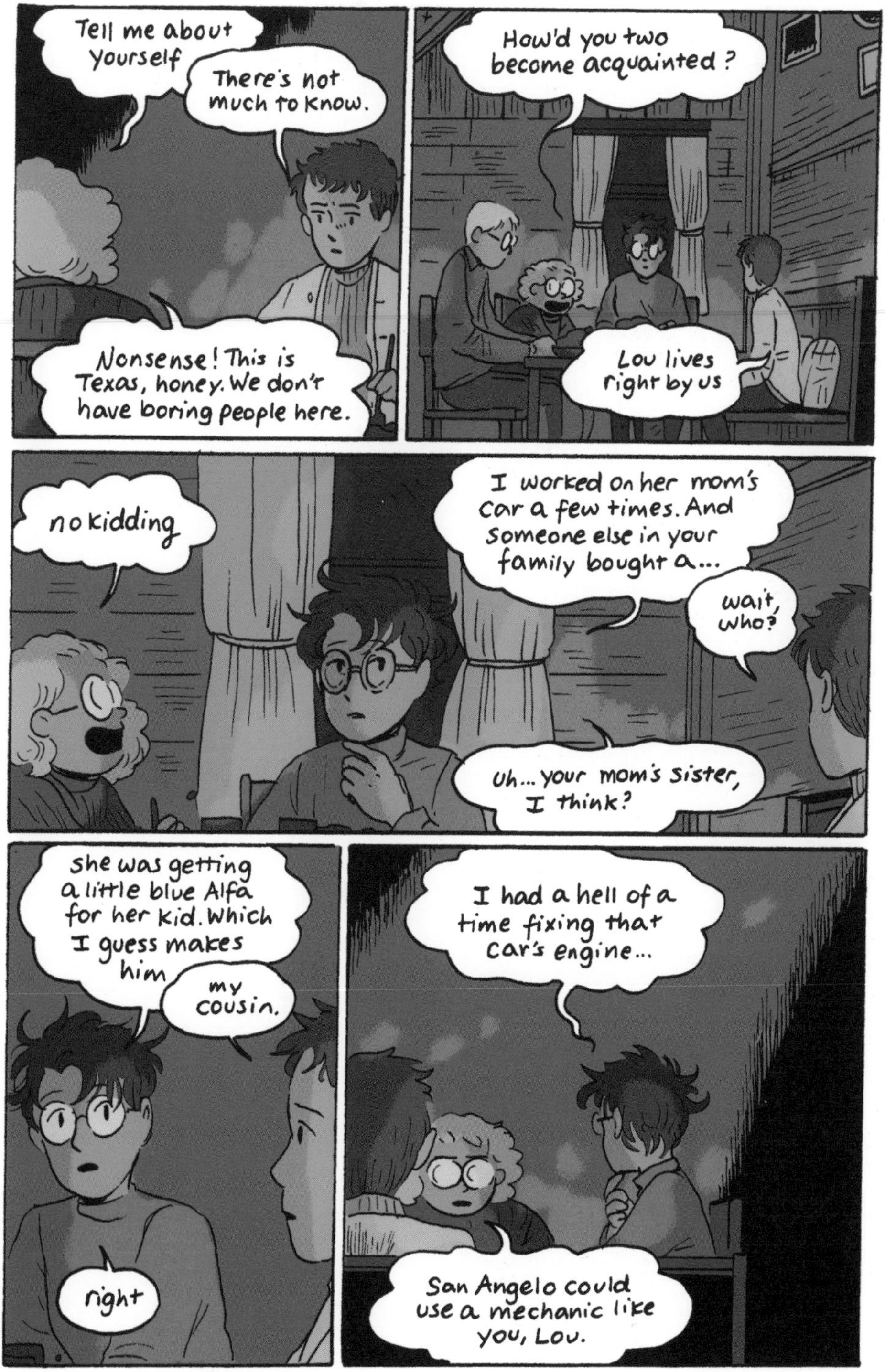
Tell me about yourself
There's not much to know.
Nonsense! This is Texas, honey. We don't have boring people here.
How'd you two become acquainted?
Lou lives right by us
no kidding
I worked on her mom's car a few times. And someone else in your family bought a...
wait, who?
uh... your mom's sister, I think?
she was getting a little blue Alfa for her kid. Which I guess makes him
my cousin.
right
I had a hell of a time fixing that car's engine...
San Angelo could use a mechanic like you, Lou.

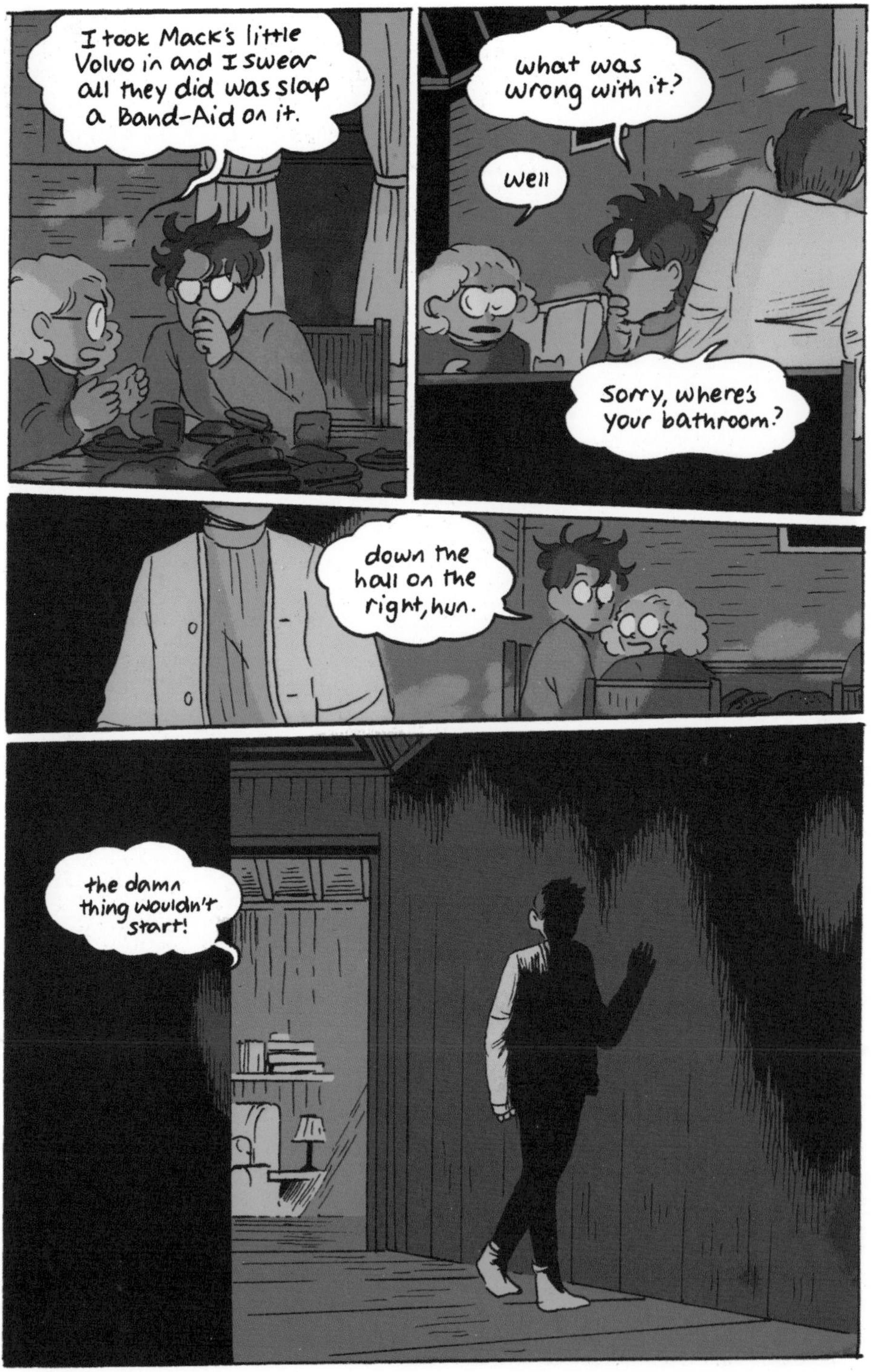
I took Mack's little Volvo in and I swear all they did was slap a Band-Aid on it.
what was wrong with it?
well
Sorry, where's your bathroom?
down the hall on the right, hun.
the damn thing wouldn't start!

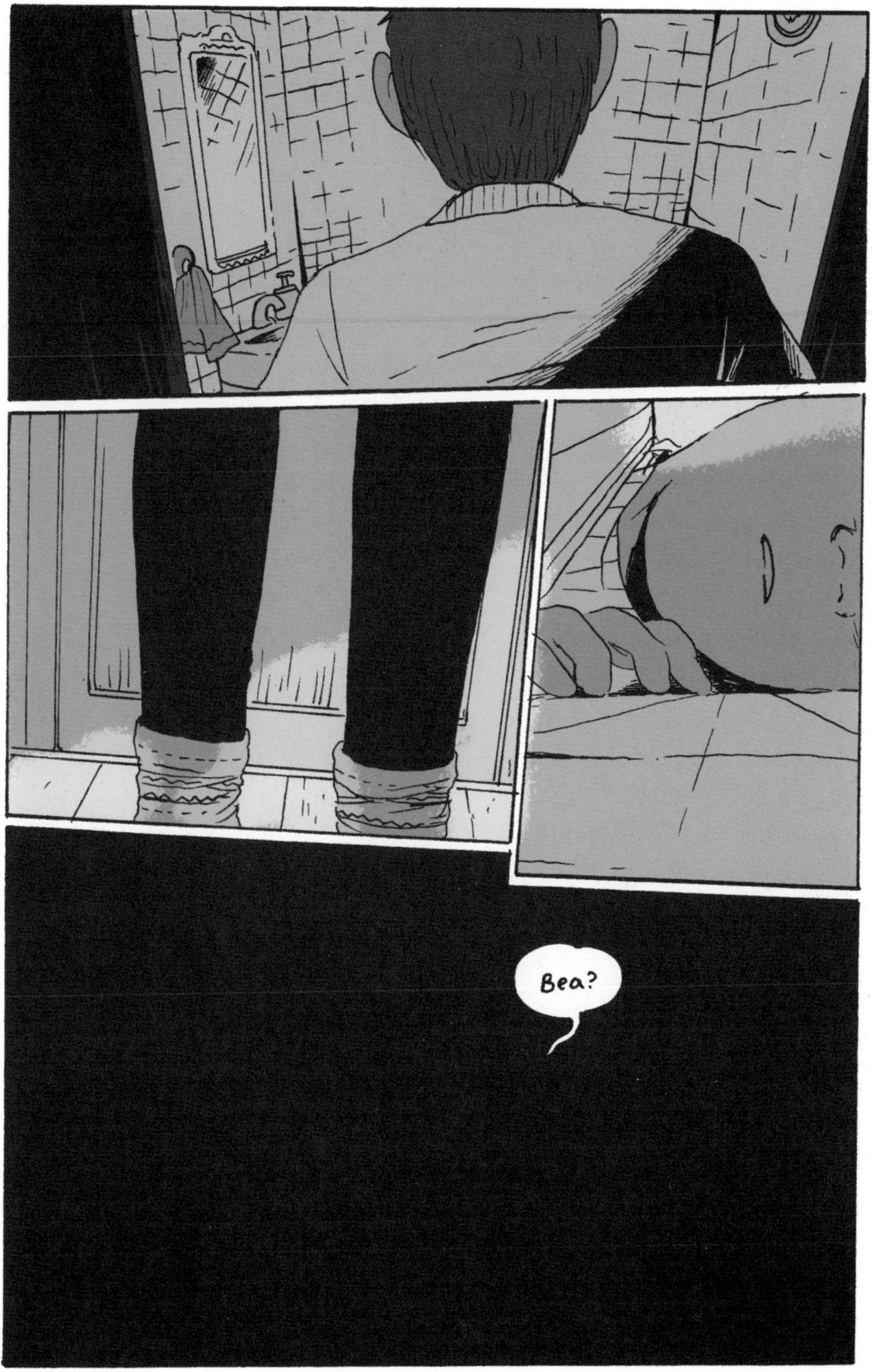
Bea?

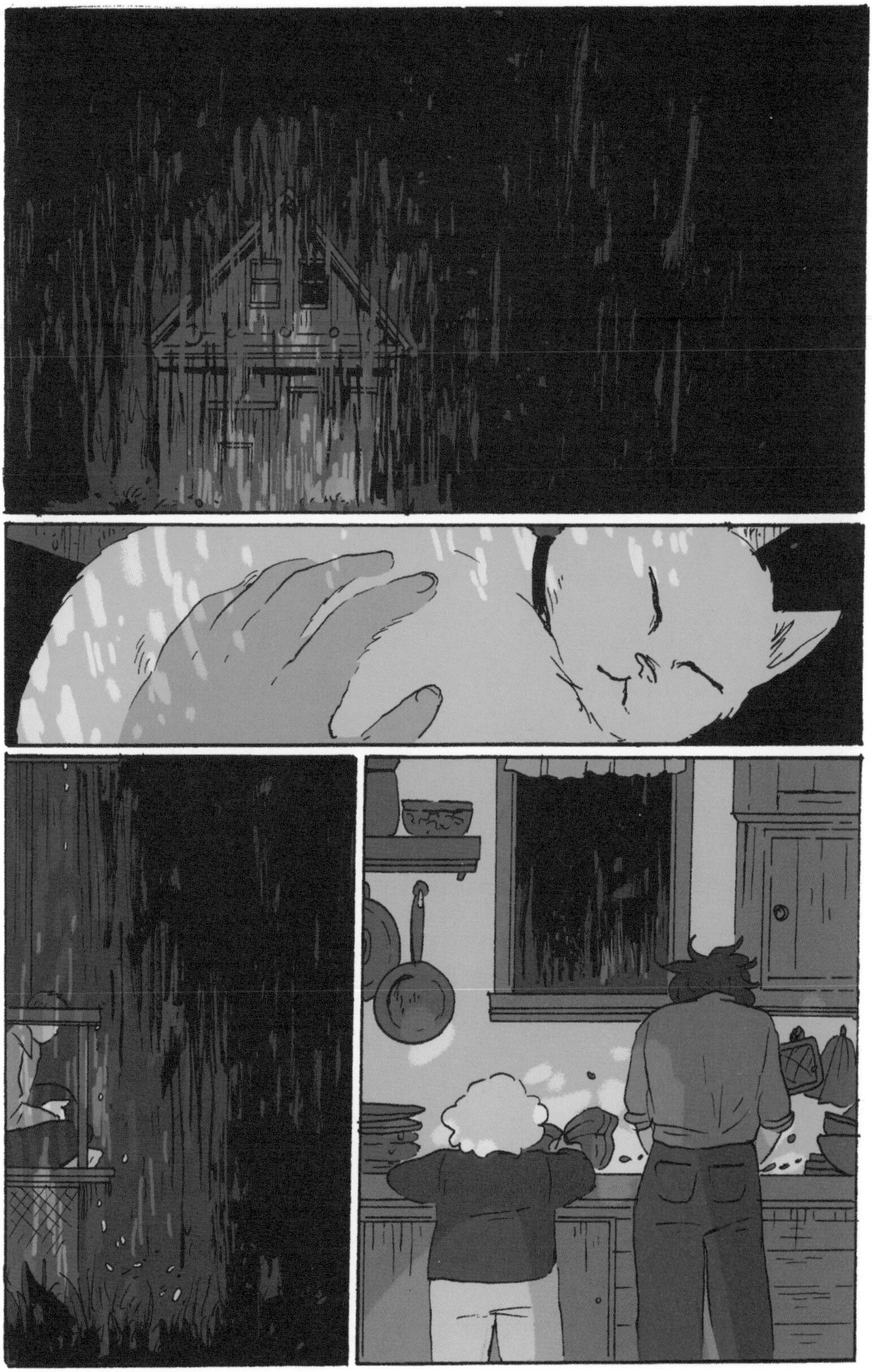

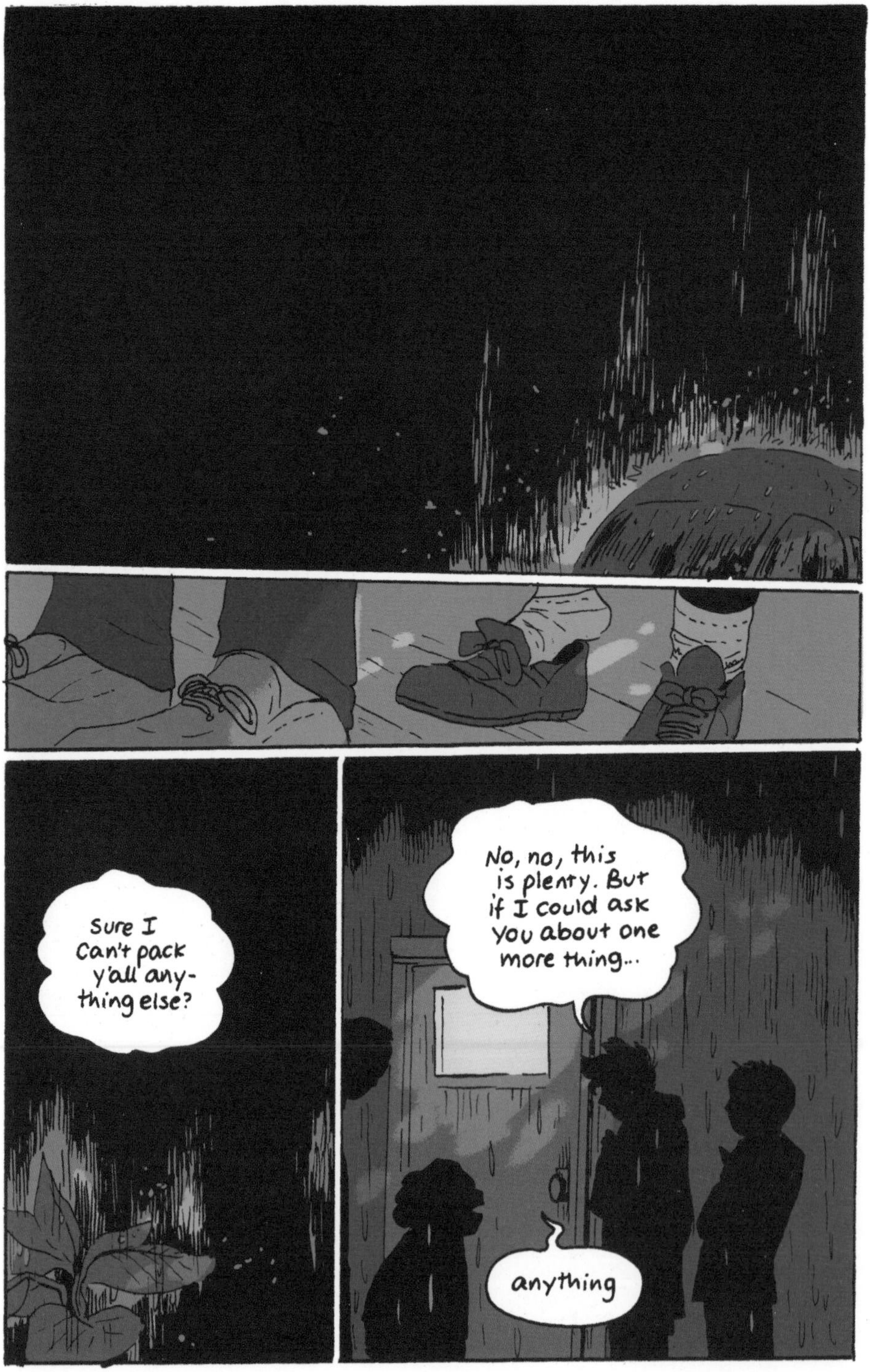
Sure I can't pack y'all any-thing else?
No, no, this is plenty. But if I could ask you about one more thing...
anything

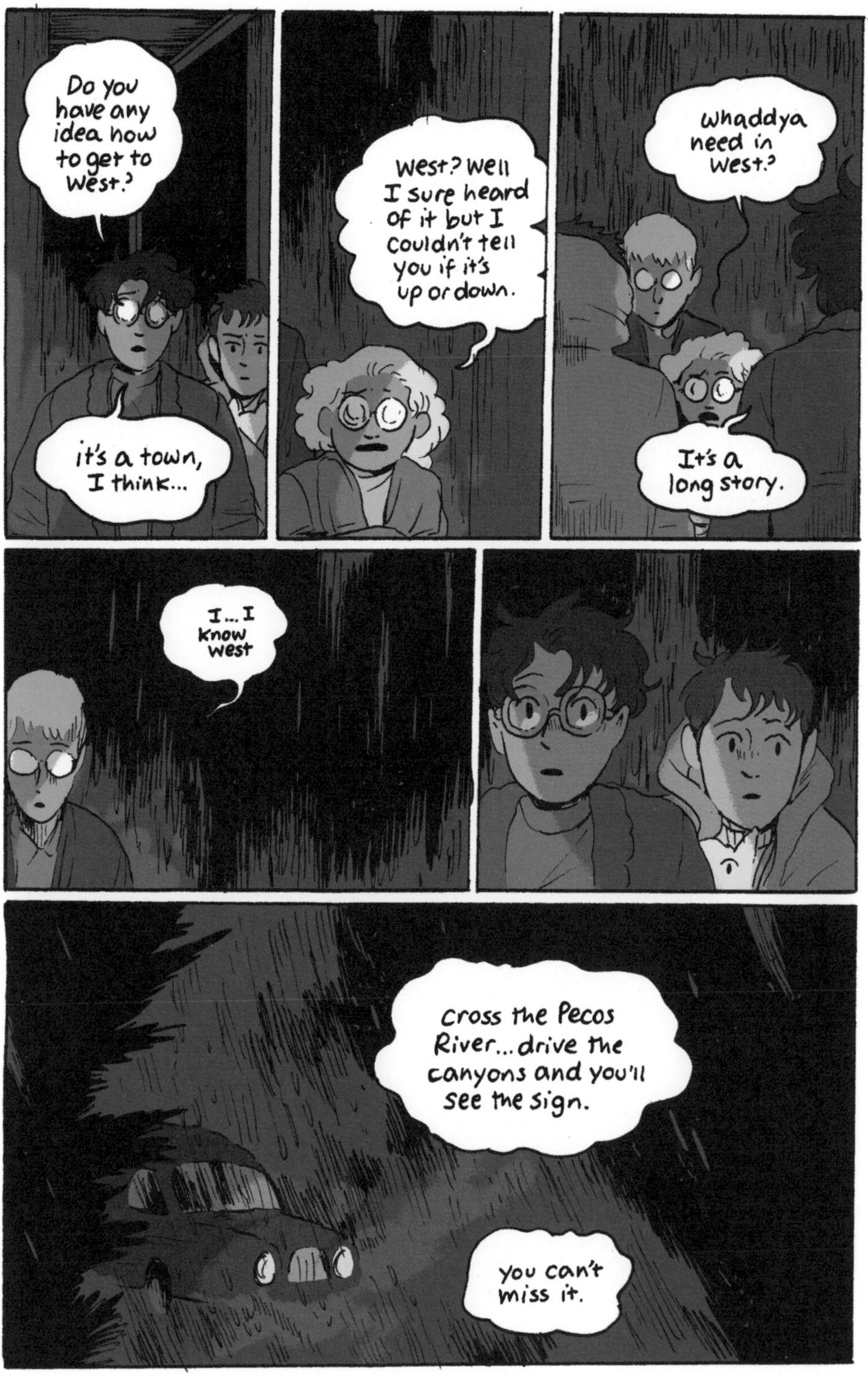
Do you have any idea how to get to West?
it's a town, I think...
West? Well I sure heard of it but I couldn't tell you if it's up or down.
Whaddya need in West?
It's a long story.
I... I know West
Cross the Pecos River... drive the canyons and you'll see the sign.
You can't miss it.

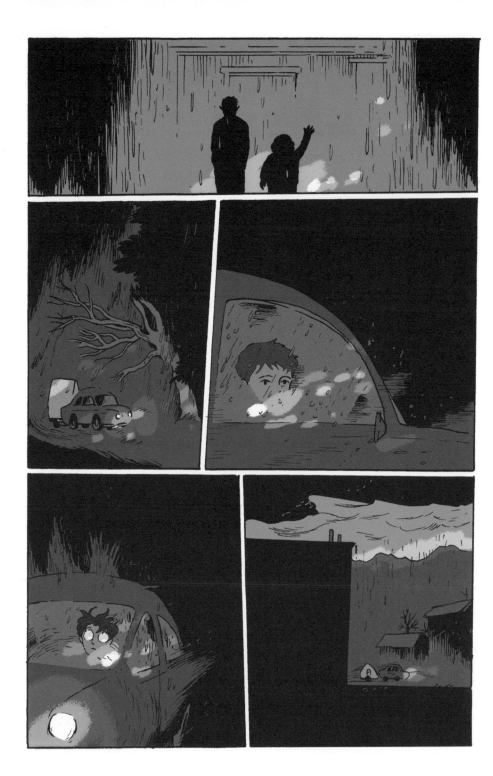

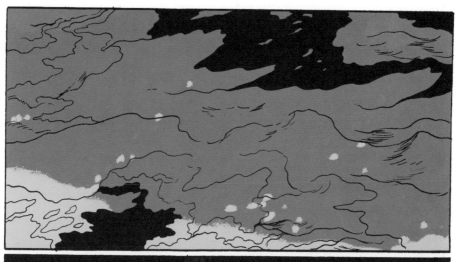

: KNOCK :
: KNOCK :

Lord, they back already? Bet the rain got to be too much.

Mack, get the door!

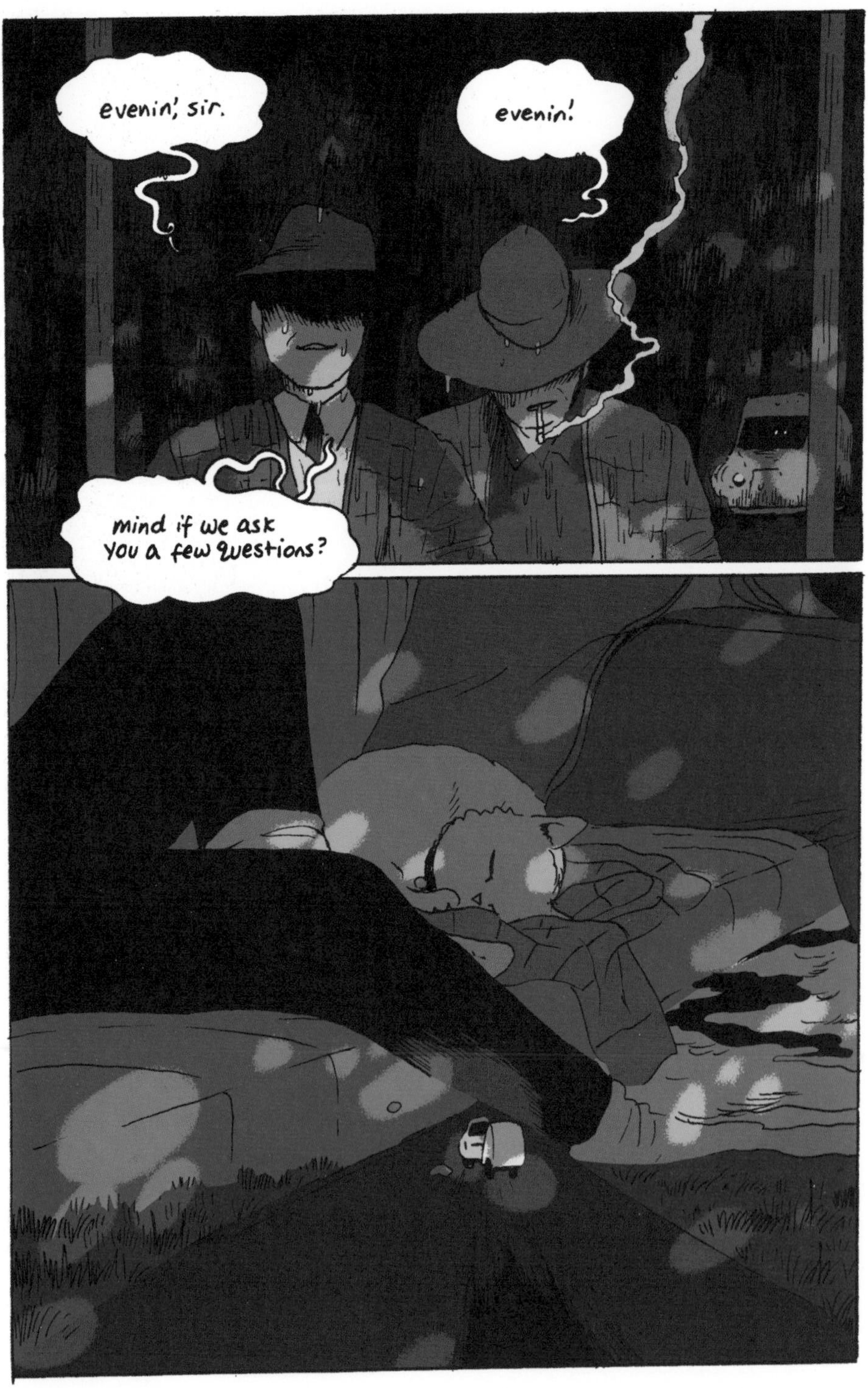
evenin', sir.
evenin'.
mind if we ask you a few questions?

148

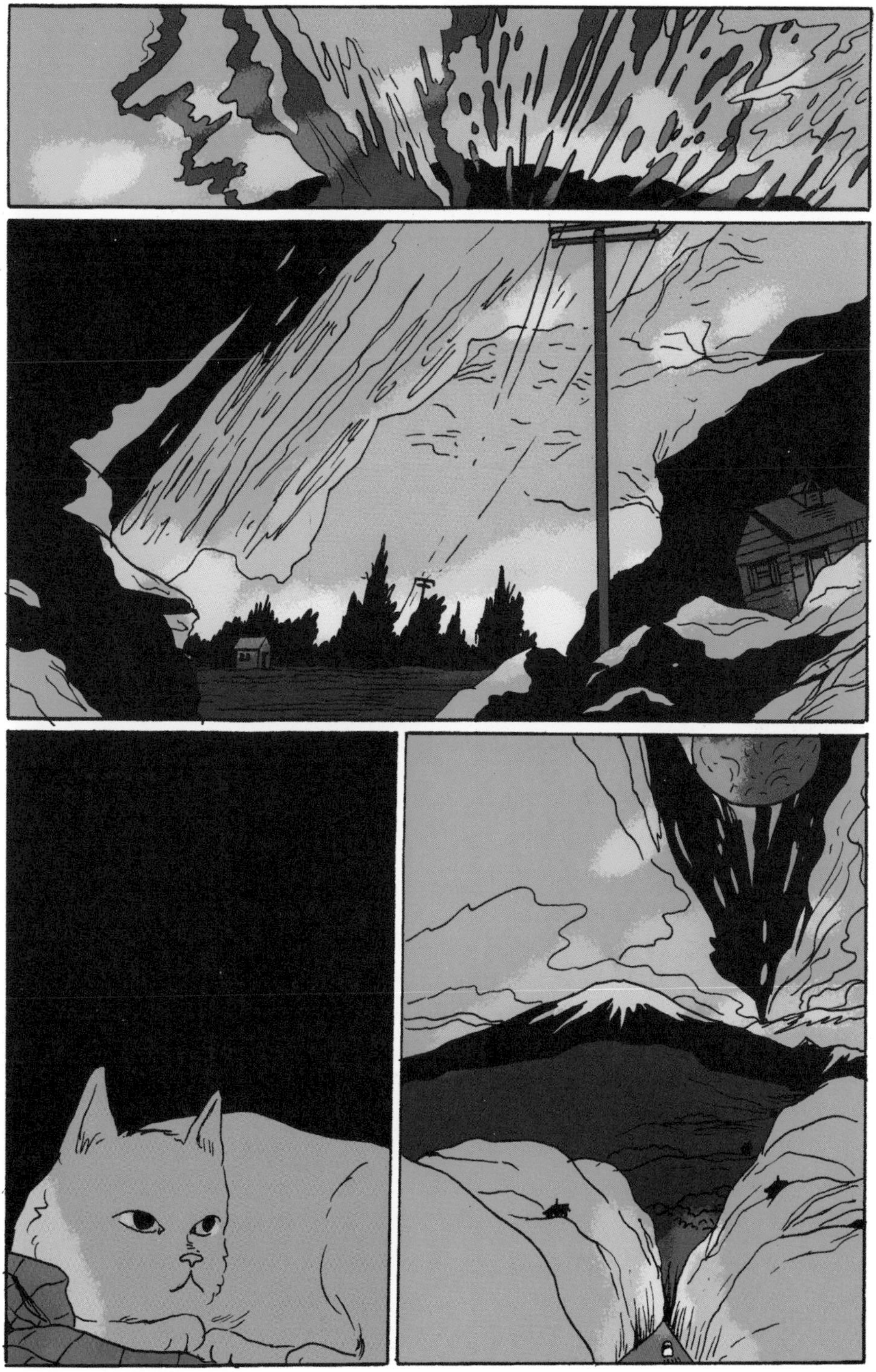

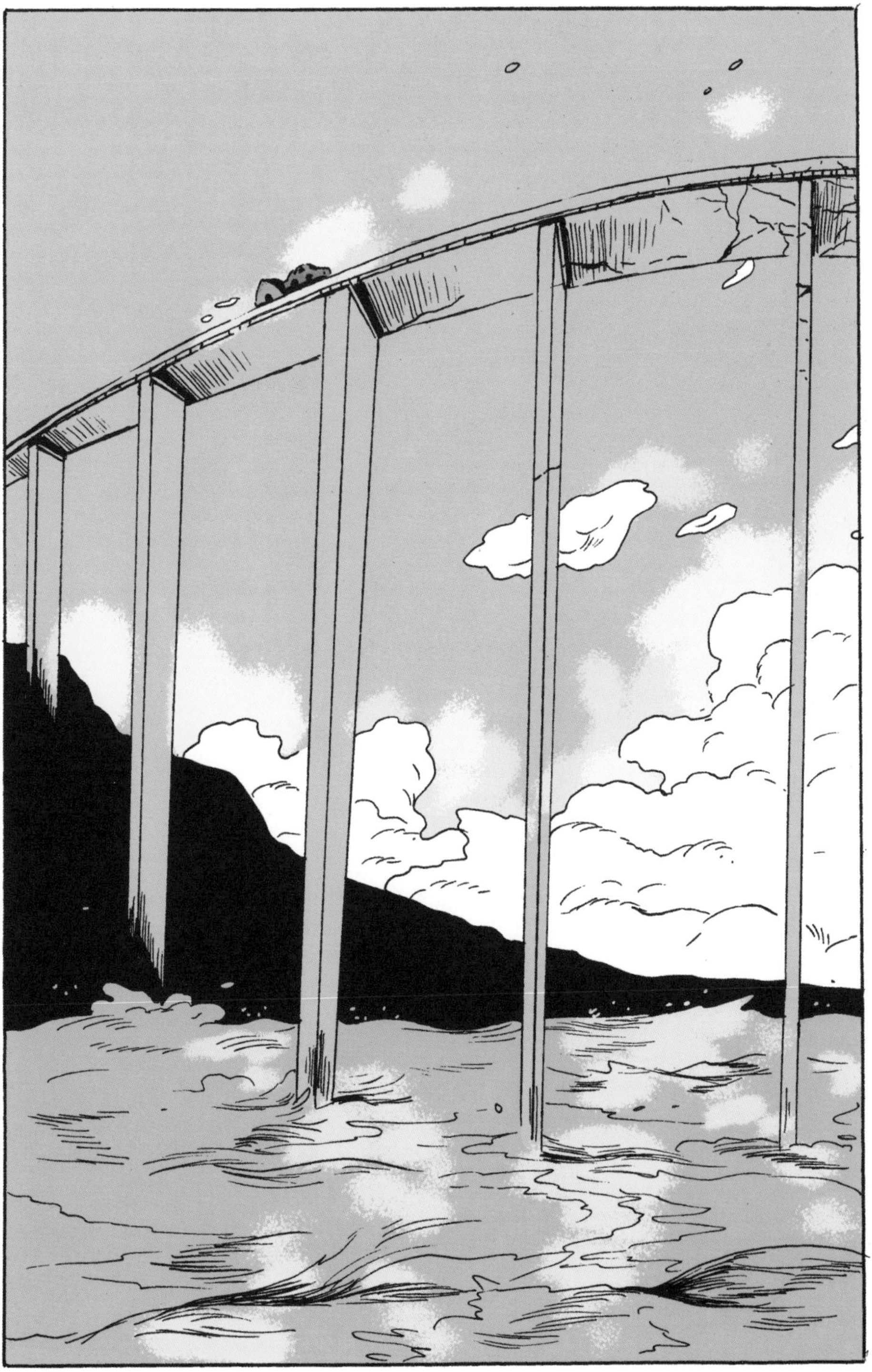

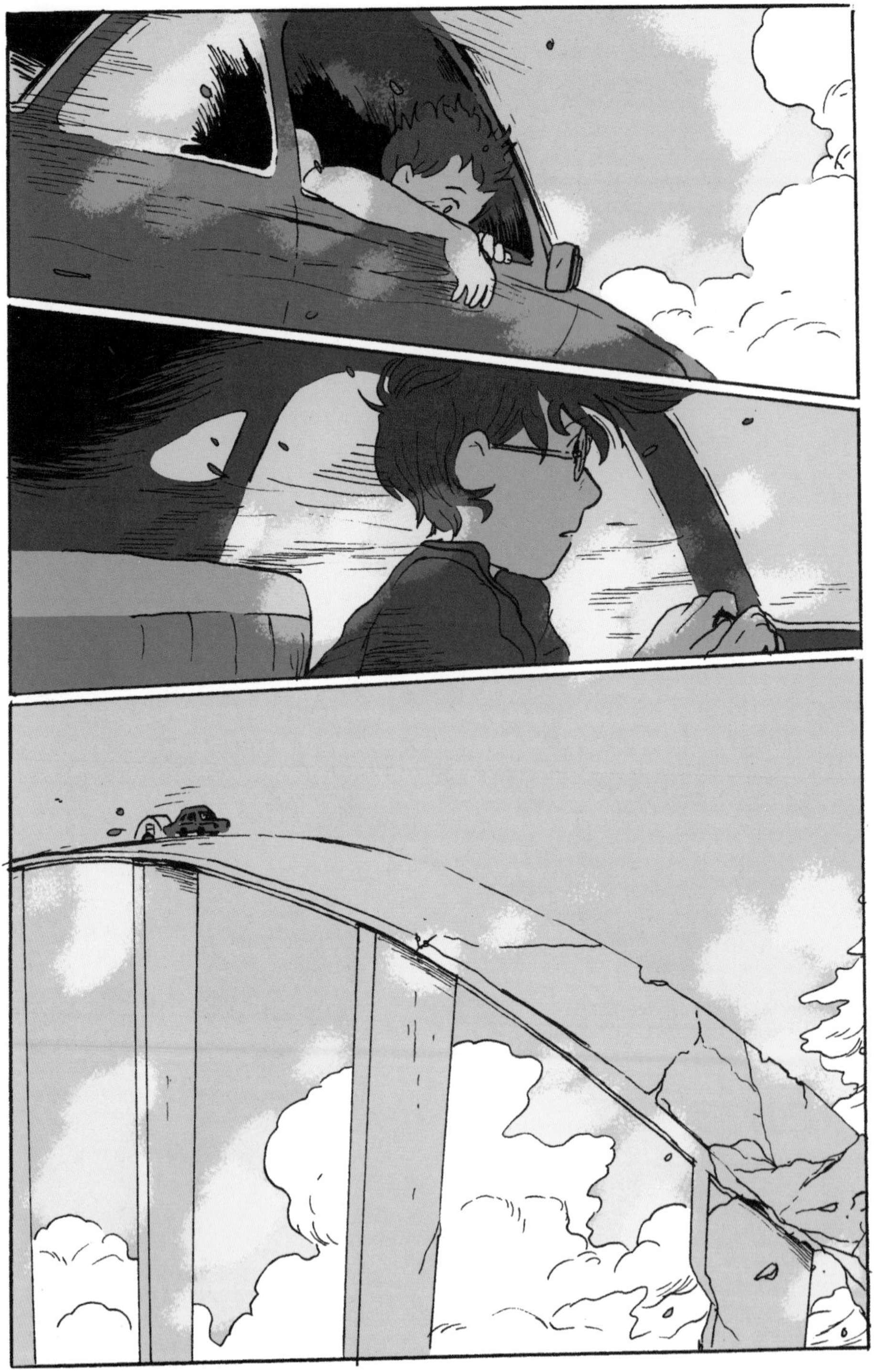

153

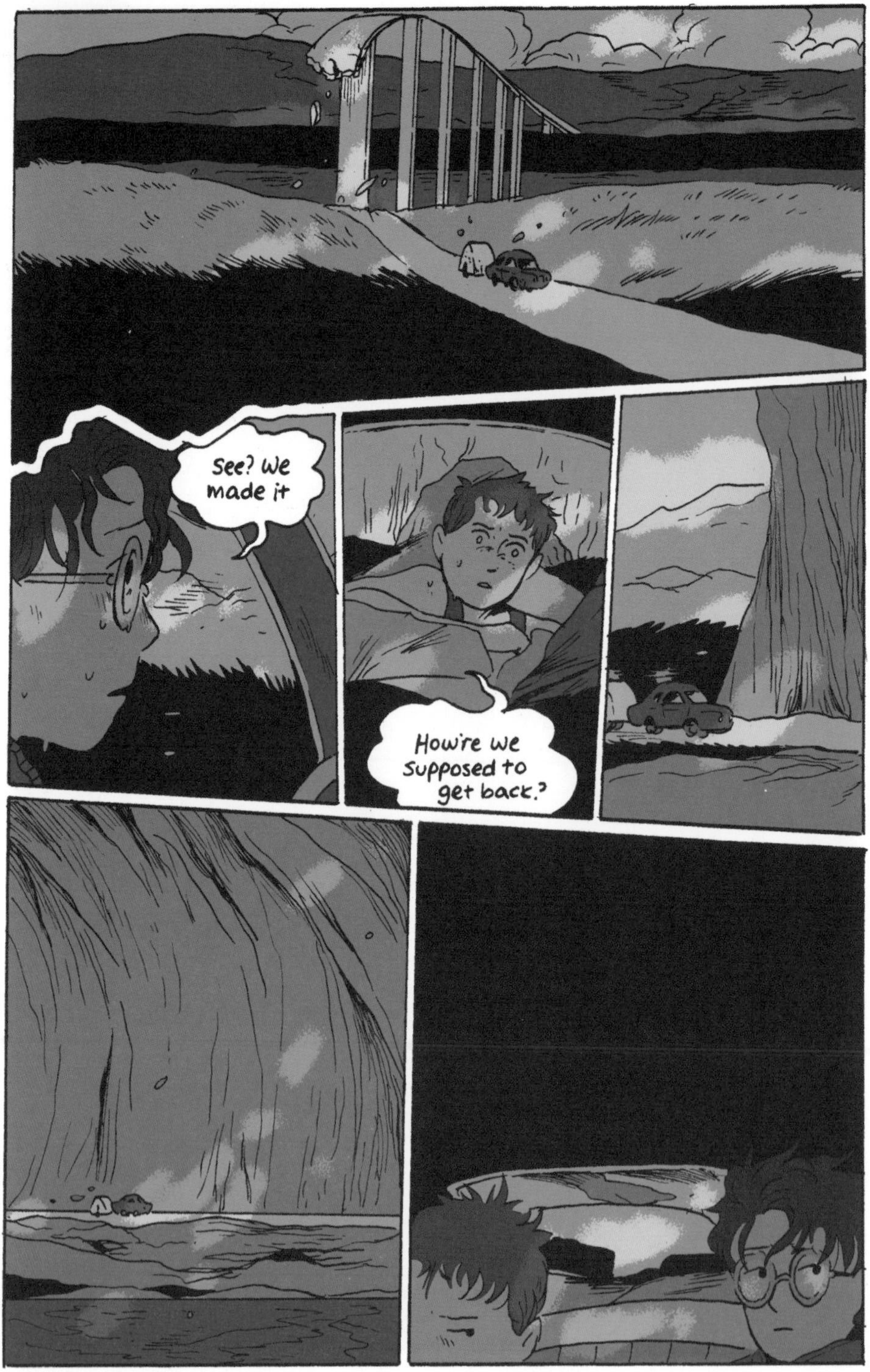

See? We made it
How're we supposed to get back?

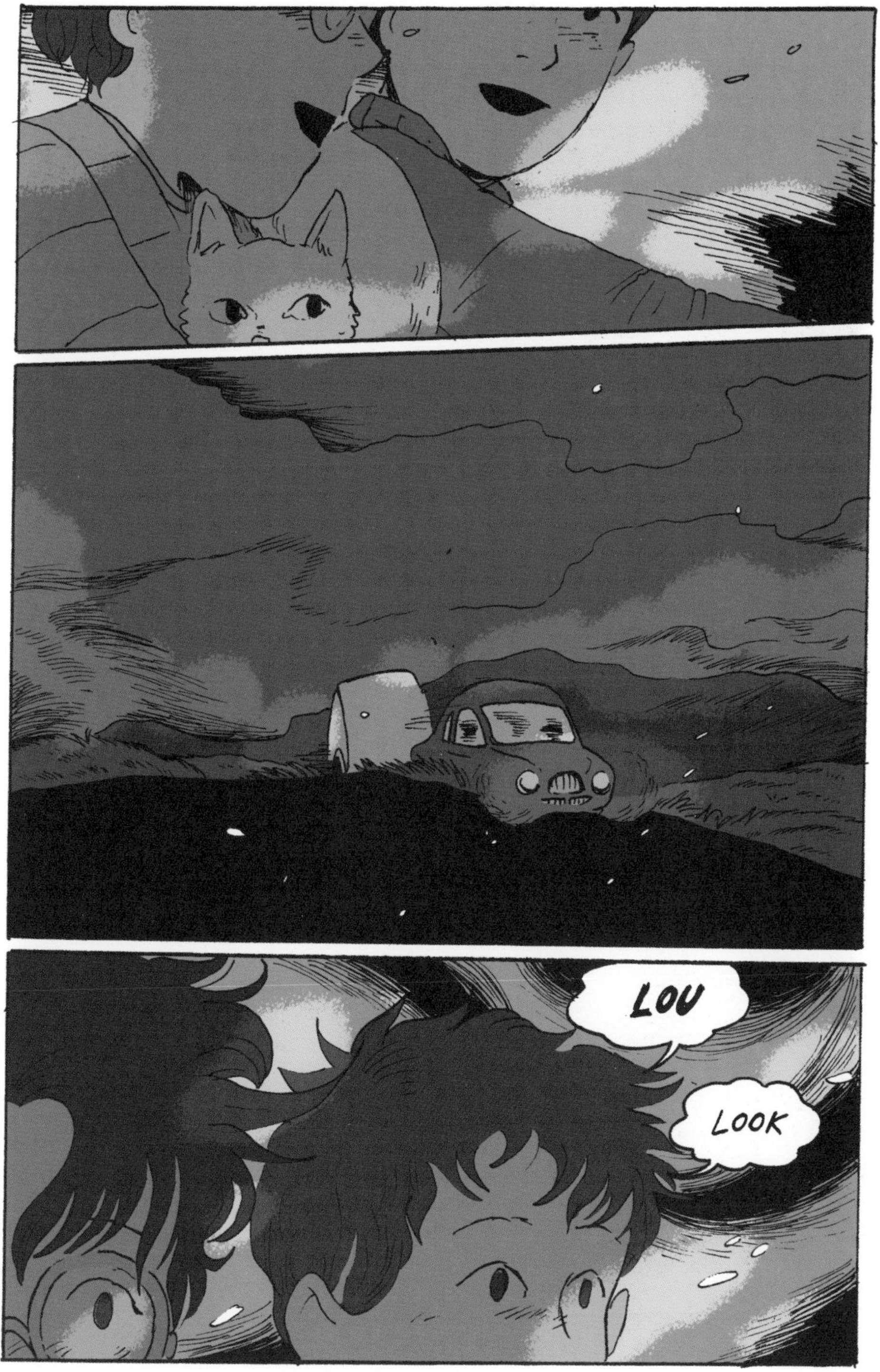
LOU
LOOK

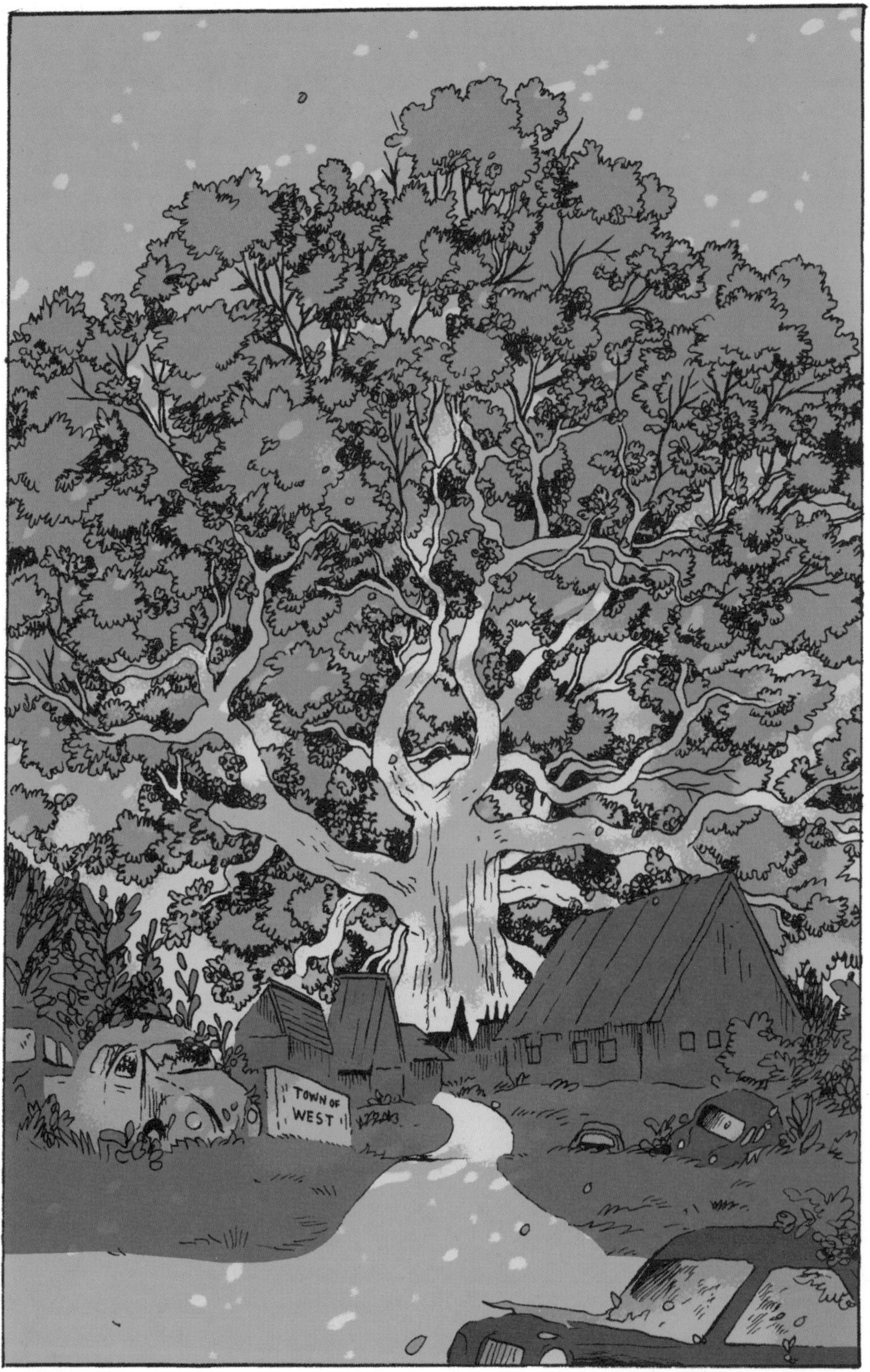
TOWN OF
WEST

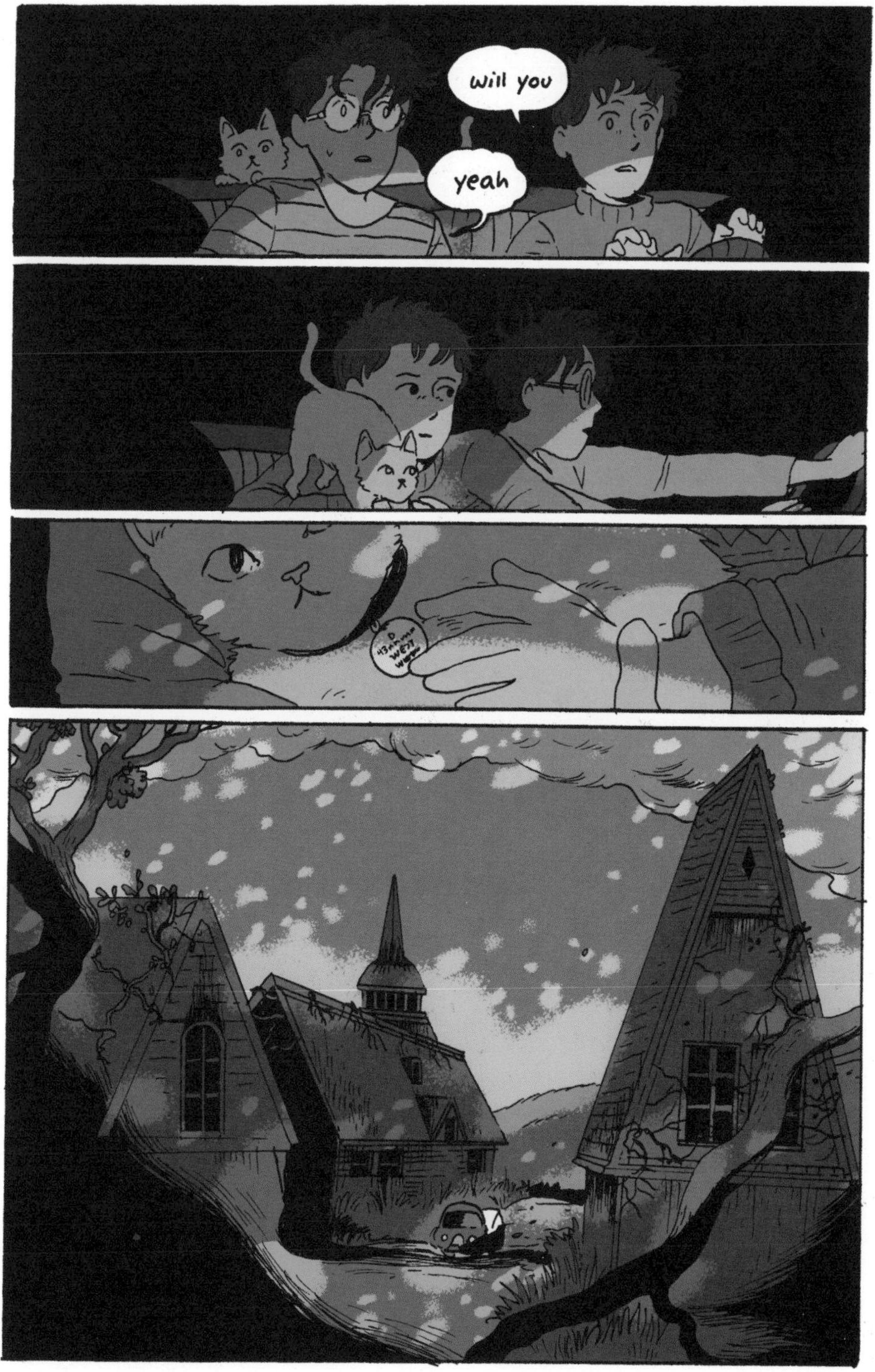
will you
yeah

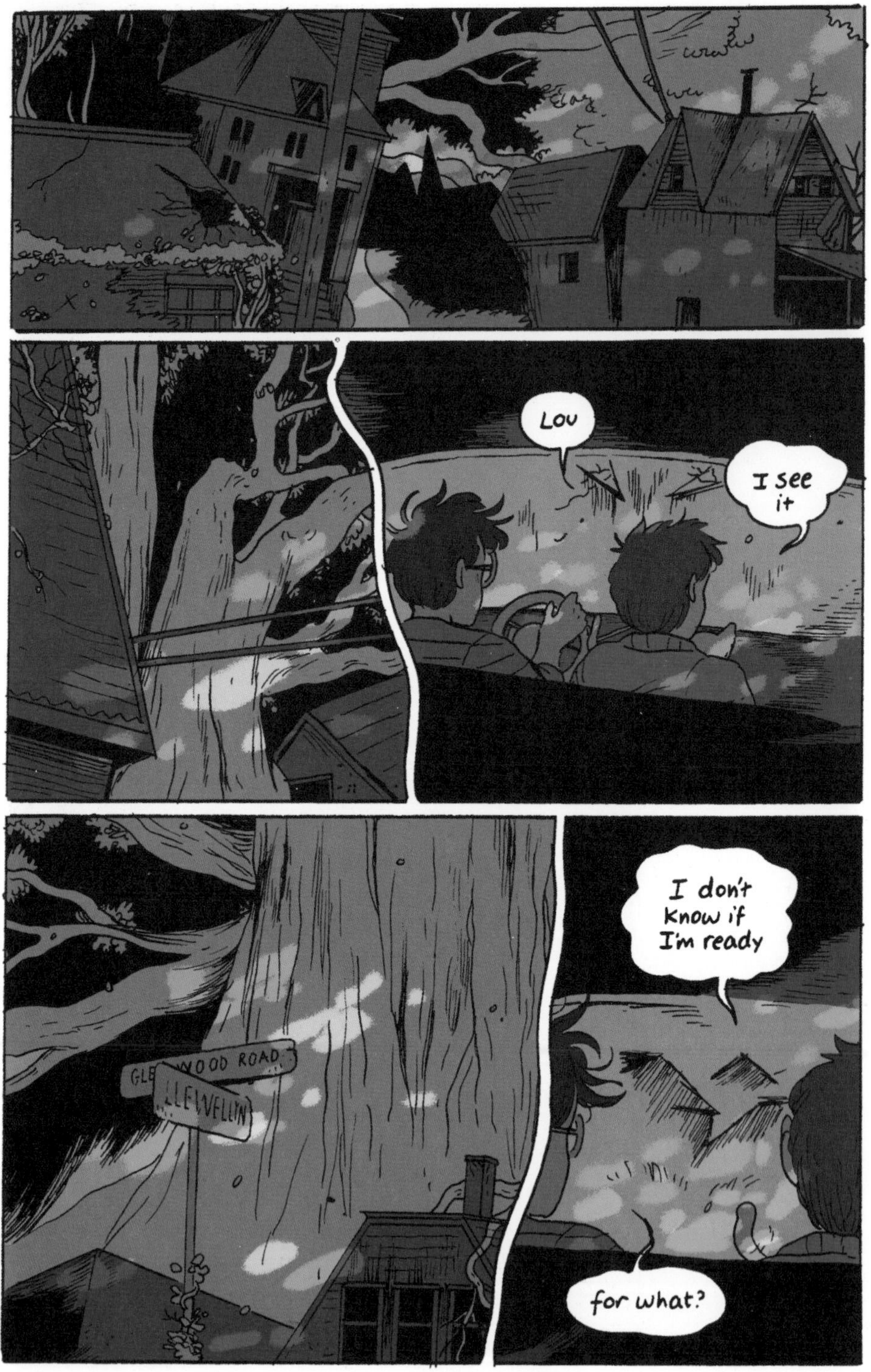
Lou
I see it
I don't know if I'm ready
for what?

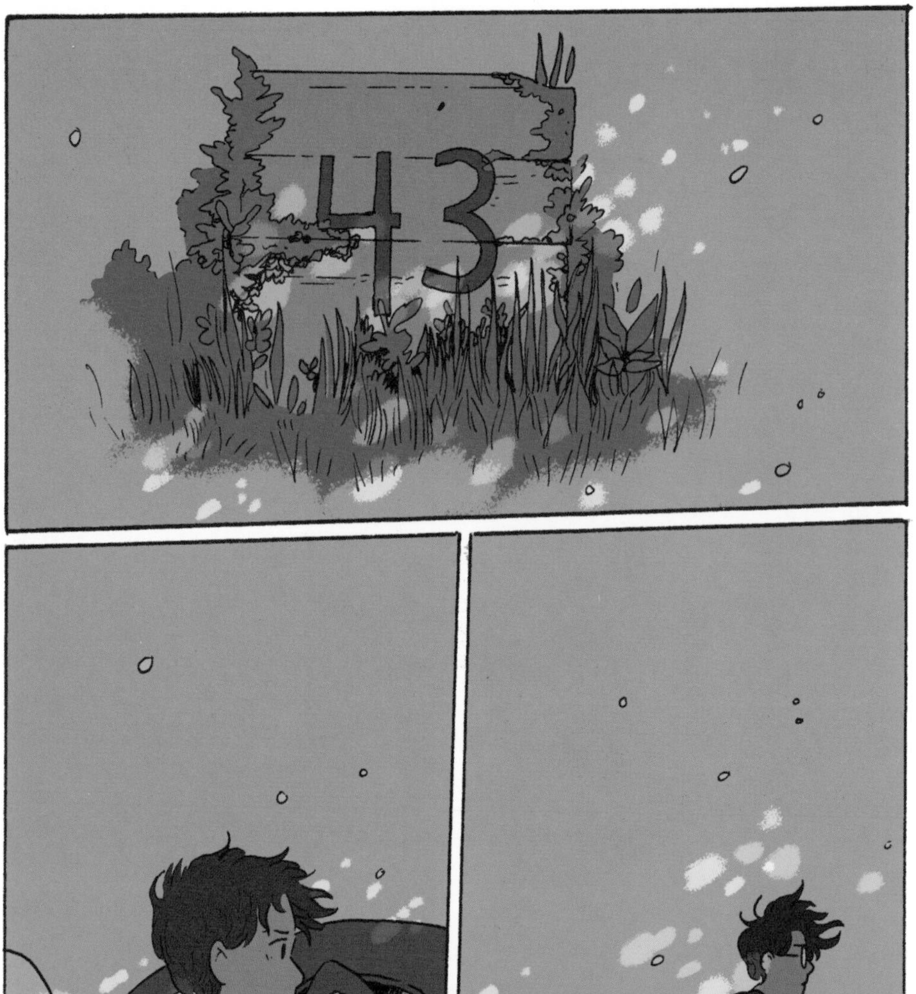
43

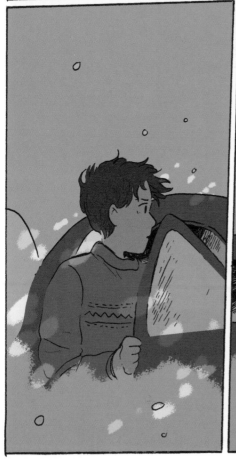

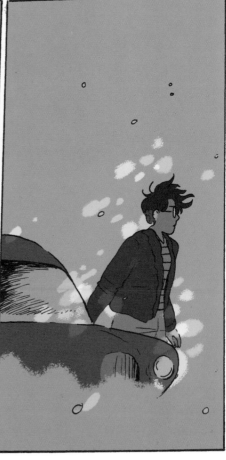

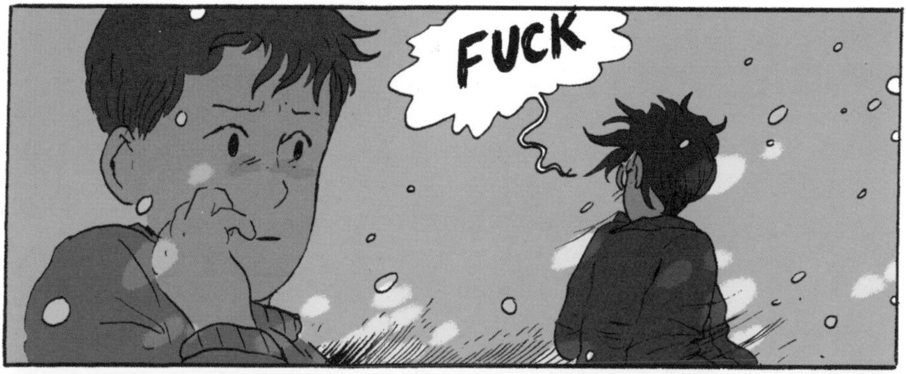
FUCK

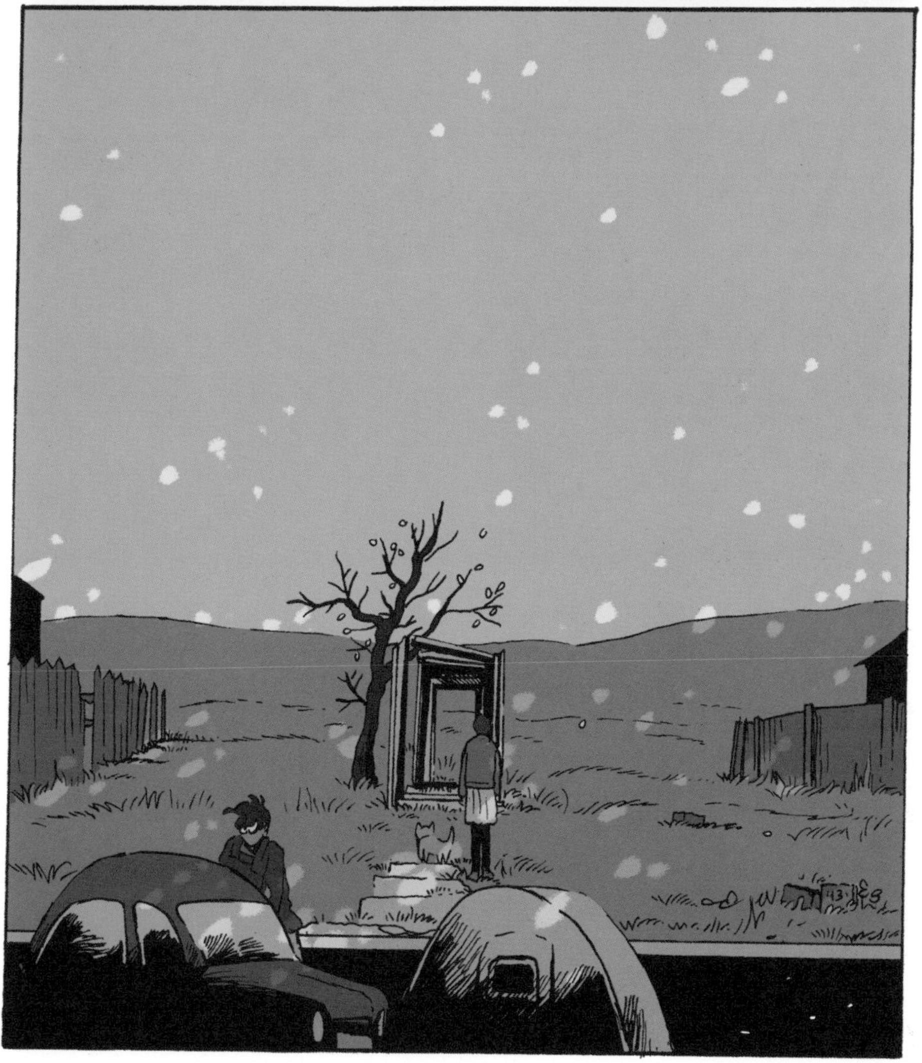

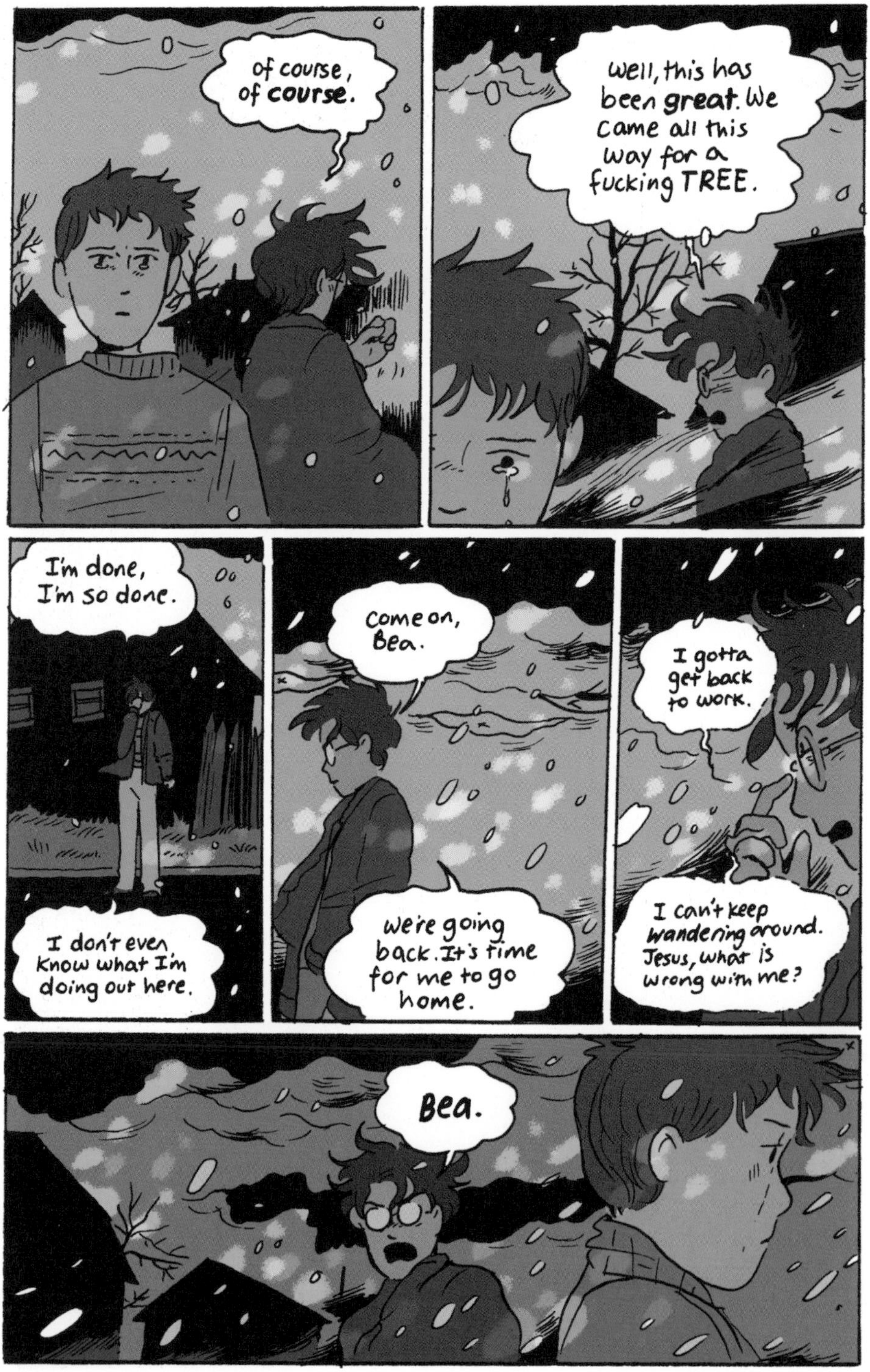
of course, of course.
well, this has been great. We came all this way for a fucking TREE.
I'm done, I'm so done.
I don't even know what I'm doing out here.
come on, Bea.
we're going back. It's time for me to go home.
I gotta get back to work.
I can't keep wandering around. Jesus, what is wrong with me?
Bea.

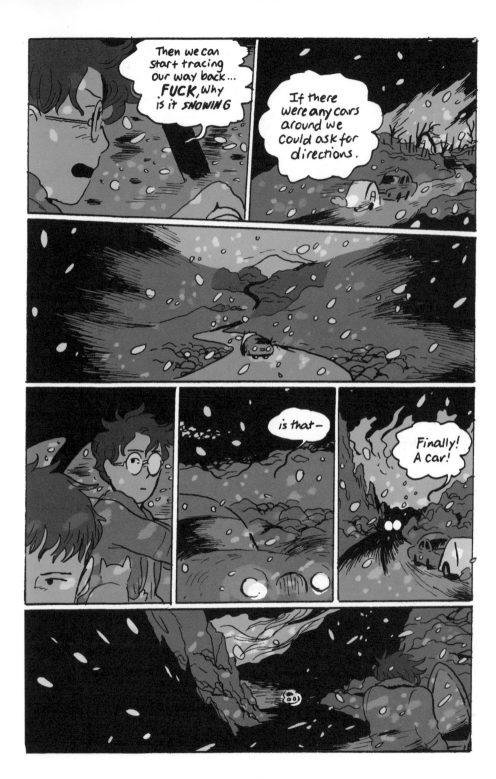

171

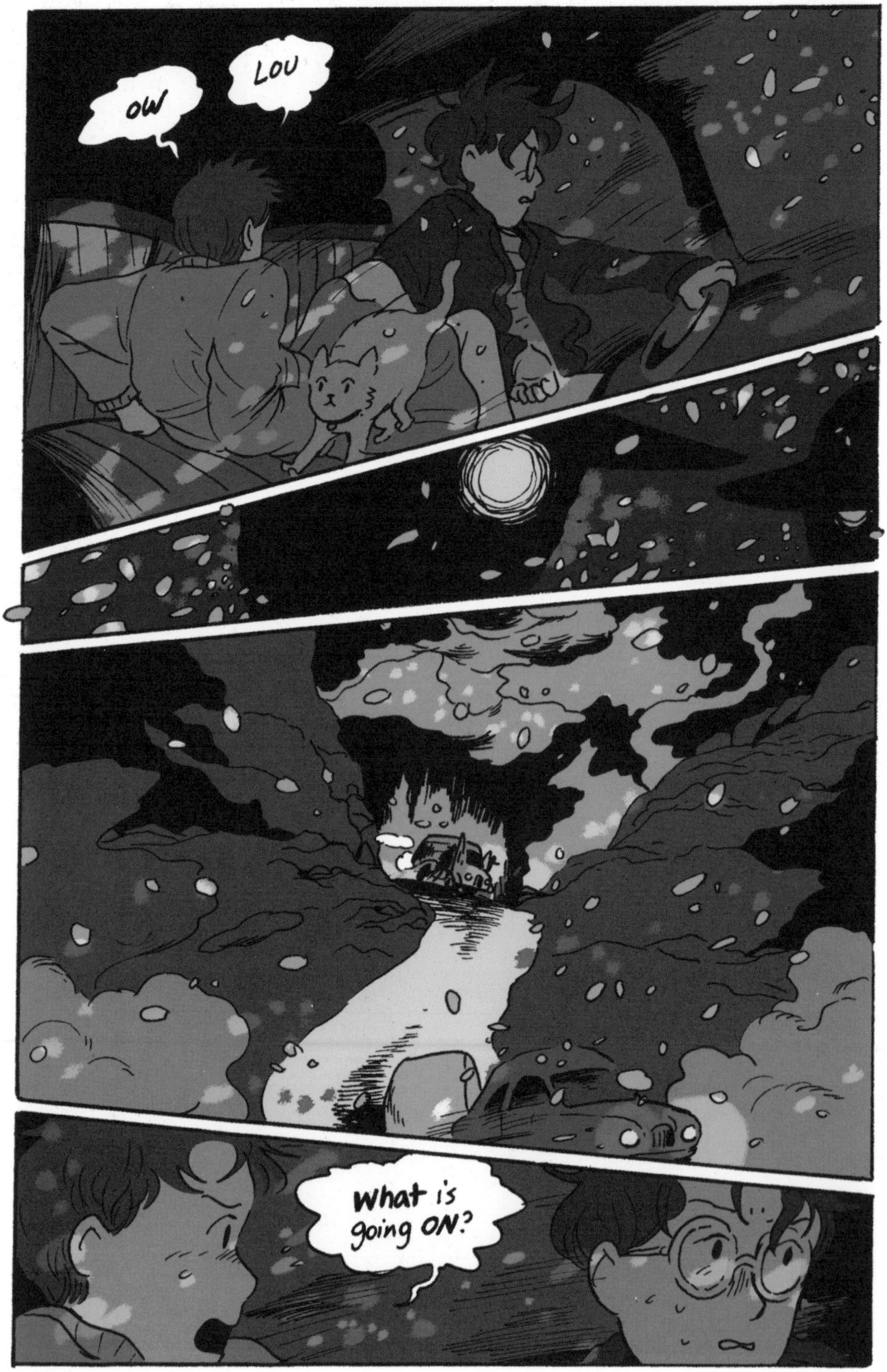
OW
LOU
What is going ON?

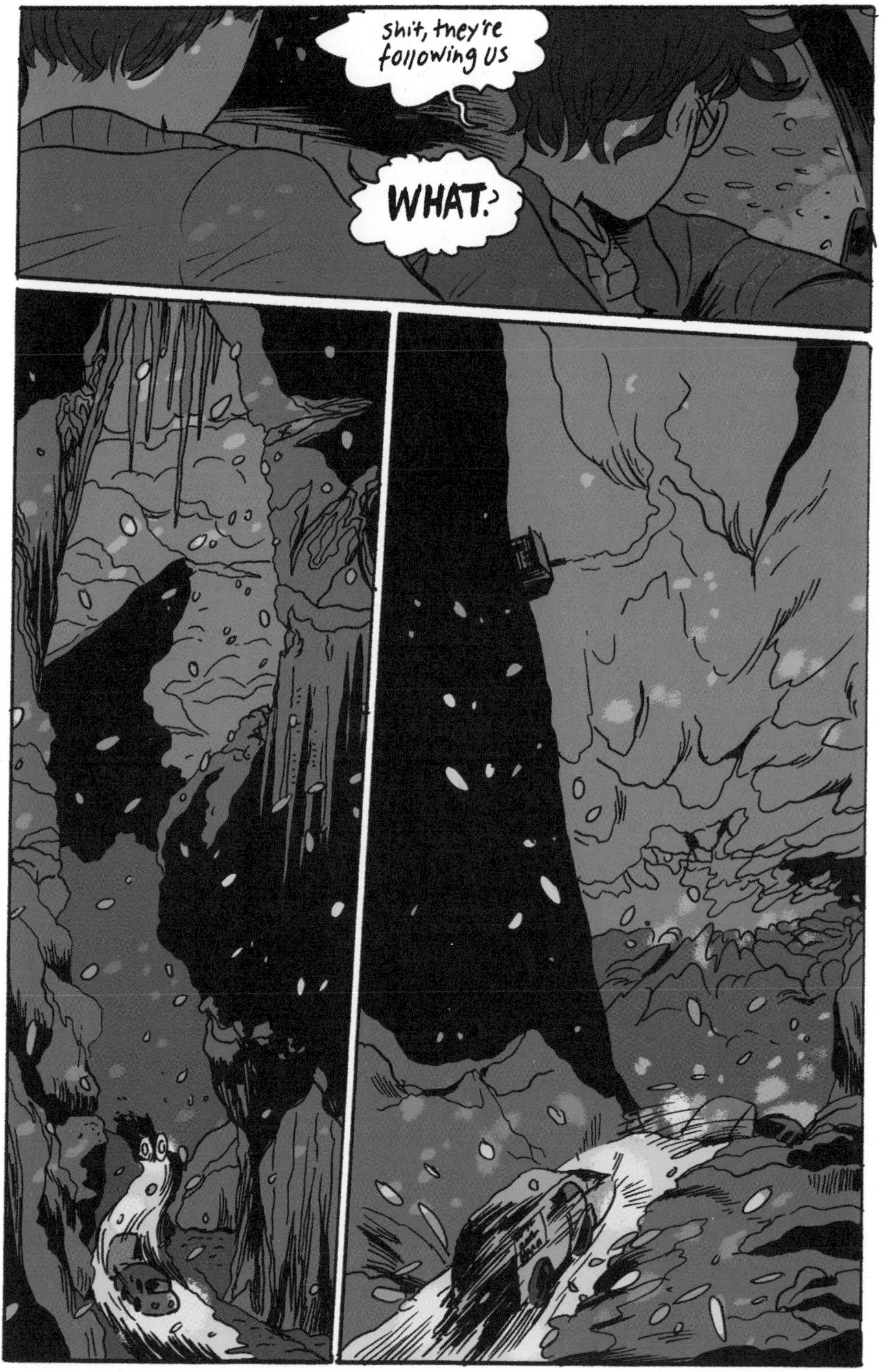

shit, they're following us
WHAT?

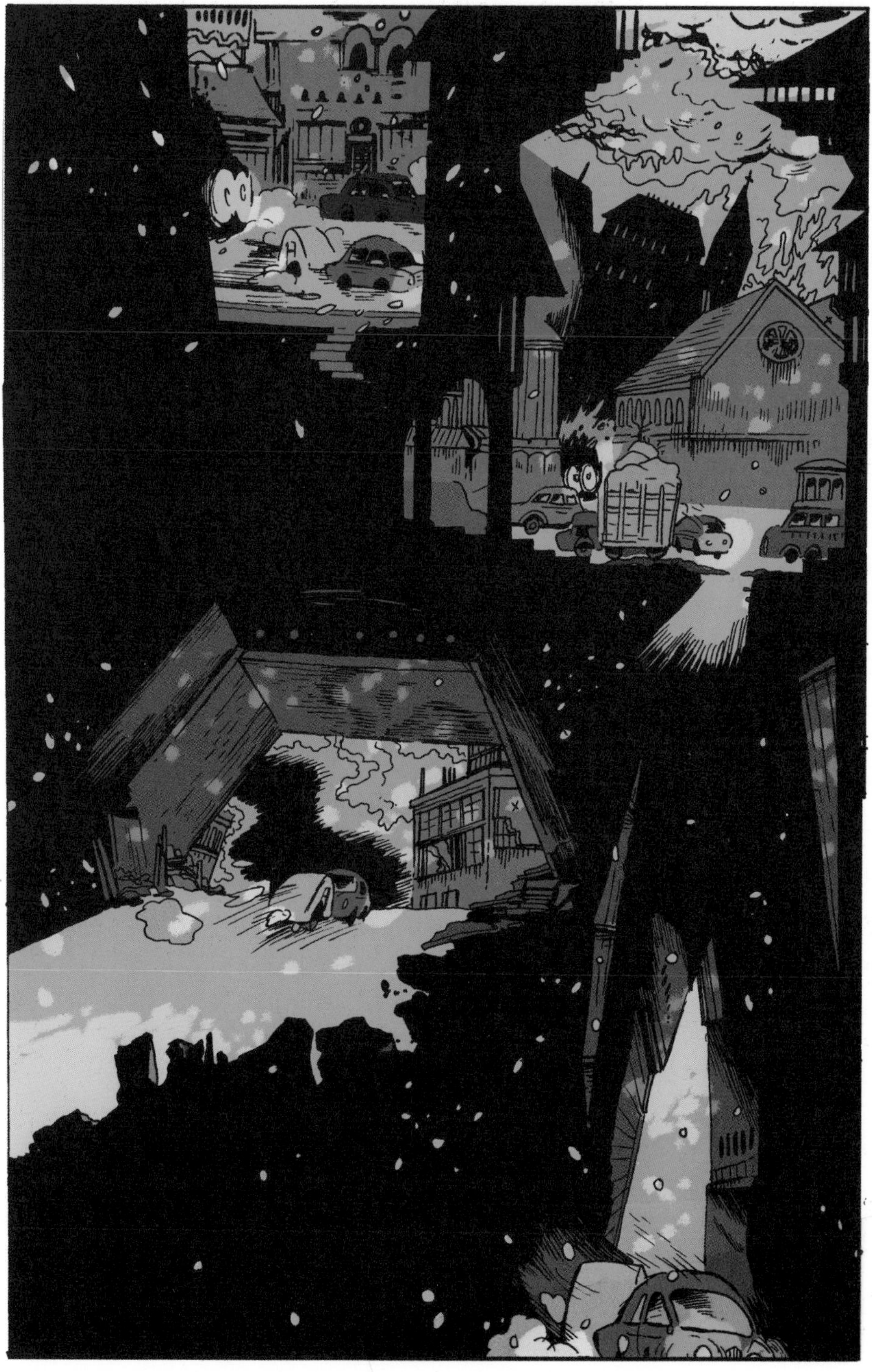

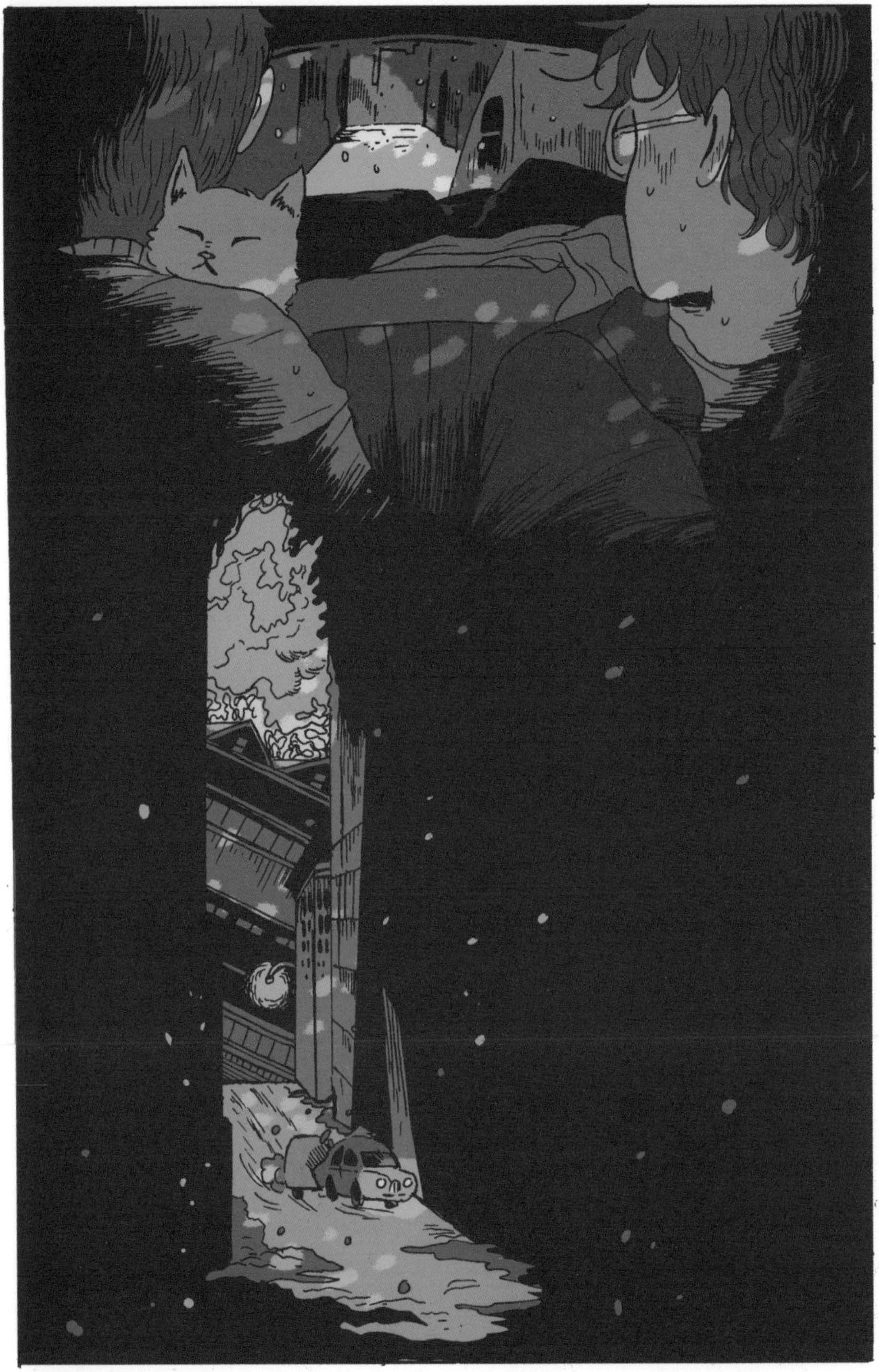

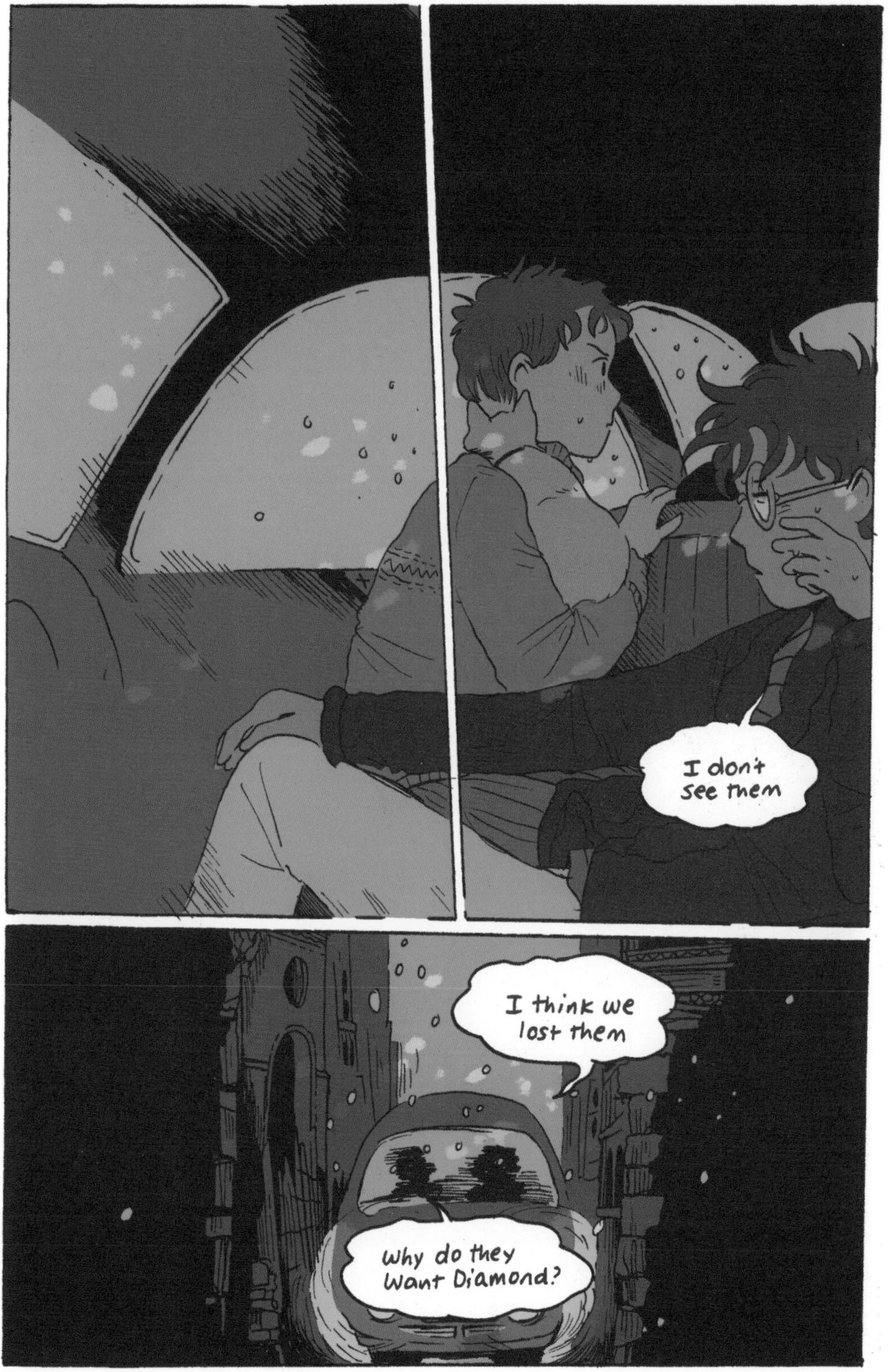
I don't see them
I think we lost them
Why do they want Diamond?

I have no idea.

they're not gonna get her.

no, they're fucking not.

Any sign of them?

no.

When I was a kid, we used to play this game...

Well, it wasn't really much of a game, now that I think about it.

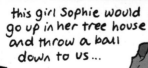

this girl Sophie would go up in her tree house and throw a ball down to us...

...whoever caught it won and got to go up to the tree house with her.

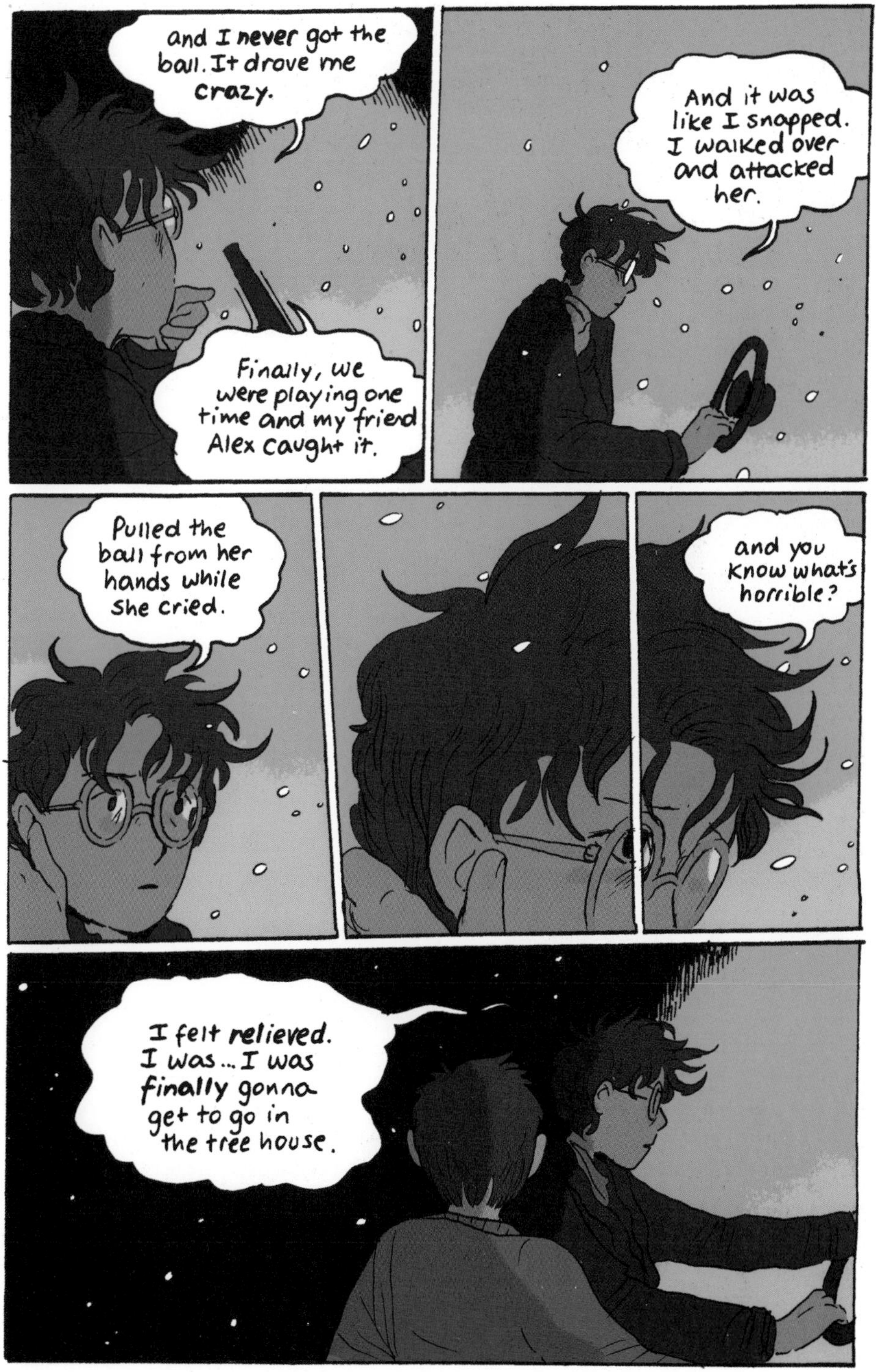
and I never got the ball. It drove me crazy.
Finally, we were playing one time and my friend Alex caught it.
And it was like I snapped. I walked over and attacked her.
Pulled the ball from her hands while she cried.
and you know what's horrible?
I felt relieved. I was... I was finally gonna get to go in the tree house.

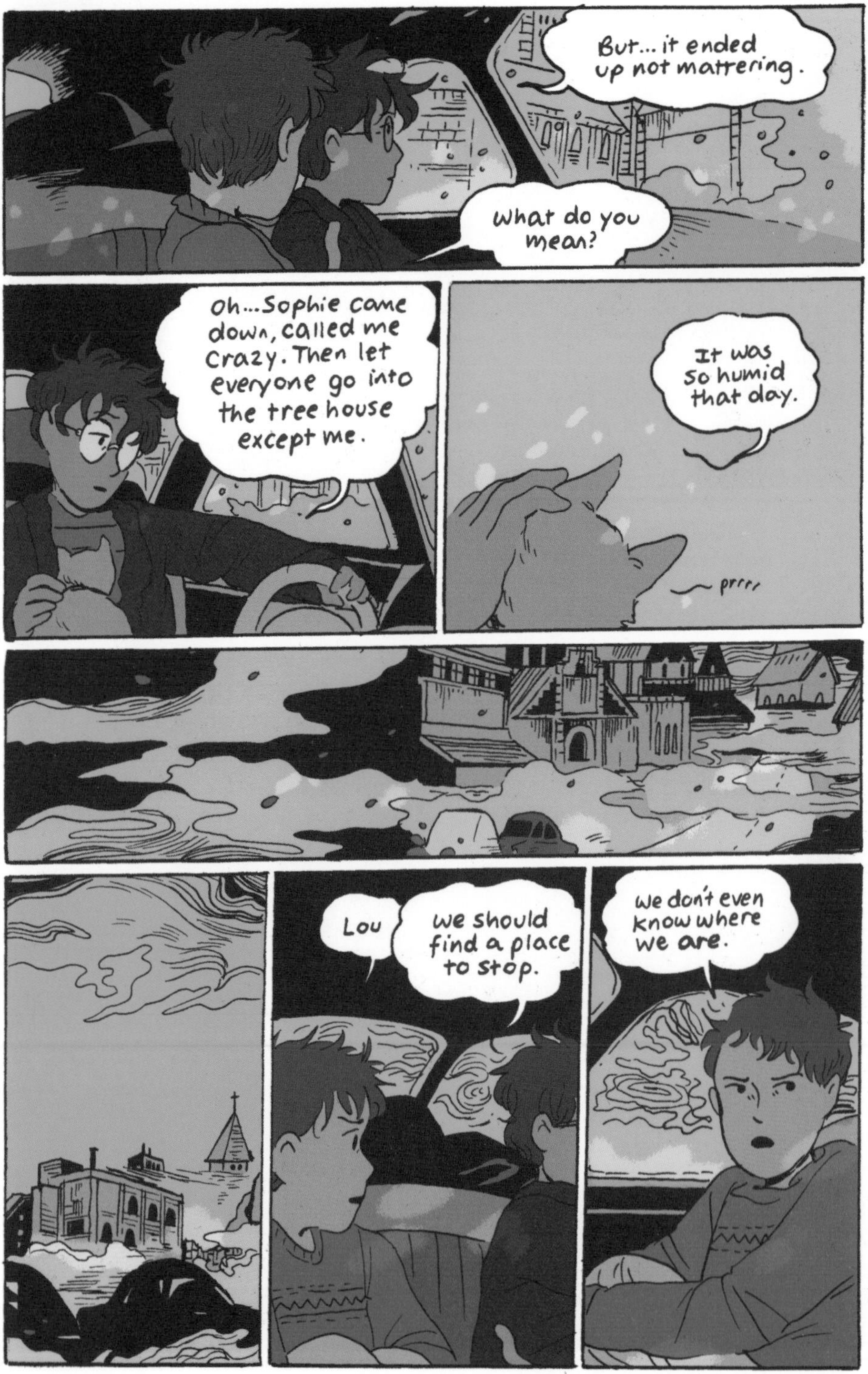

But... it ended up not mattering.
What do you mean?
Oh...Sophie came down, called me crazy. Then let everyone go into the tree house except me.
It was so humid that day.
prrrr
Lou
we should find a place to stop.
we don't even know where we are.

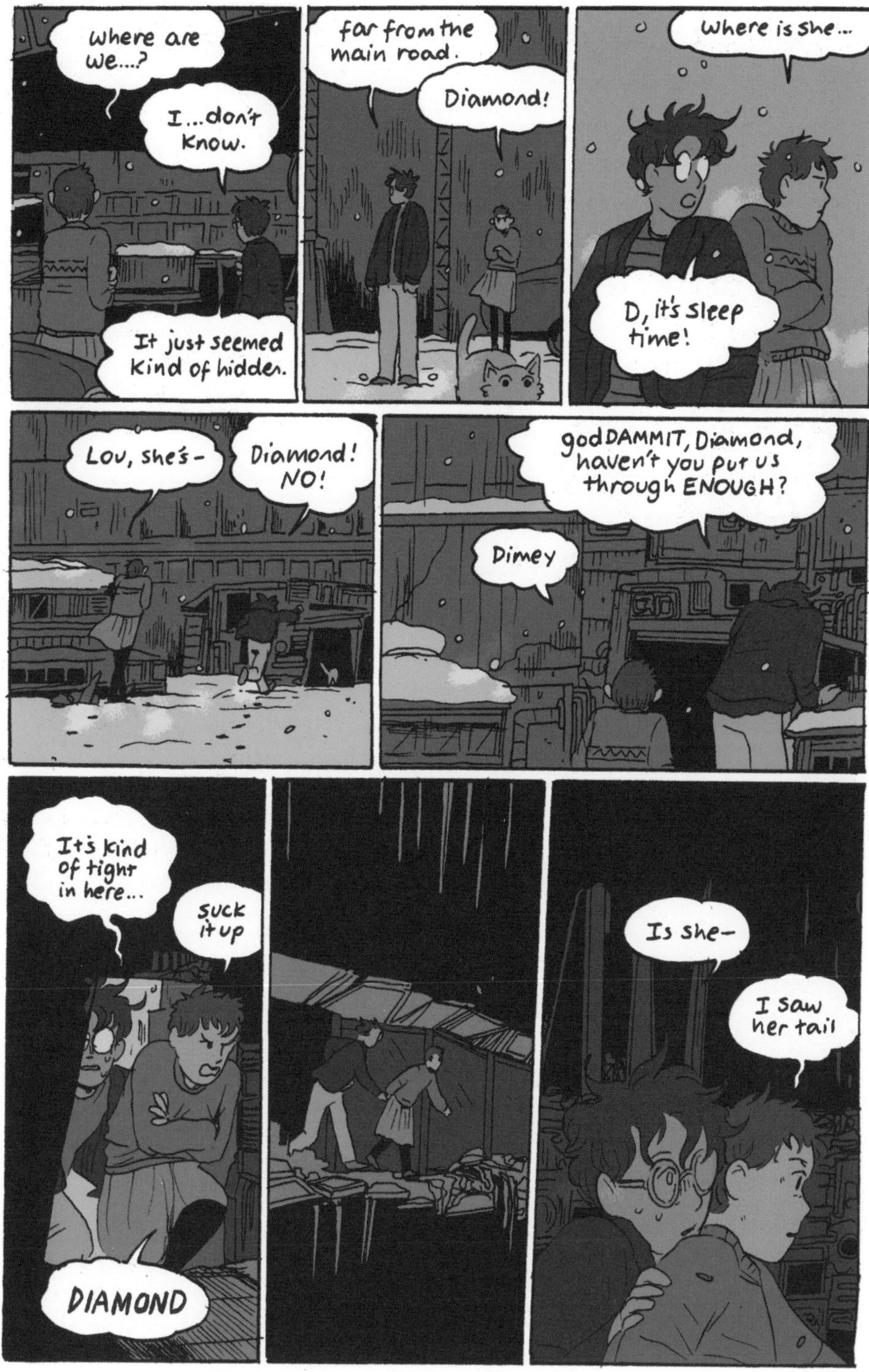
where are we...?
I...don't know.
It just seemed kind of hidden.
far from the main road.
Diamond!
Where is she...
D, it's sleep time!
Lou, she's-
Diamond! NO!
godDAMMIT, Diamond, haven't you put us through ENOUGH?
Dimey
It's kind of tight in here...
suck it up
DIAMOND
Is she-
I saw her tail

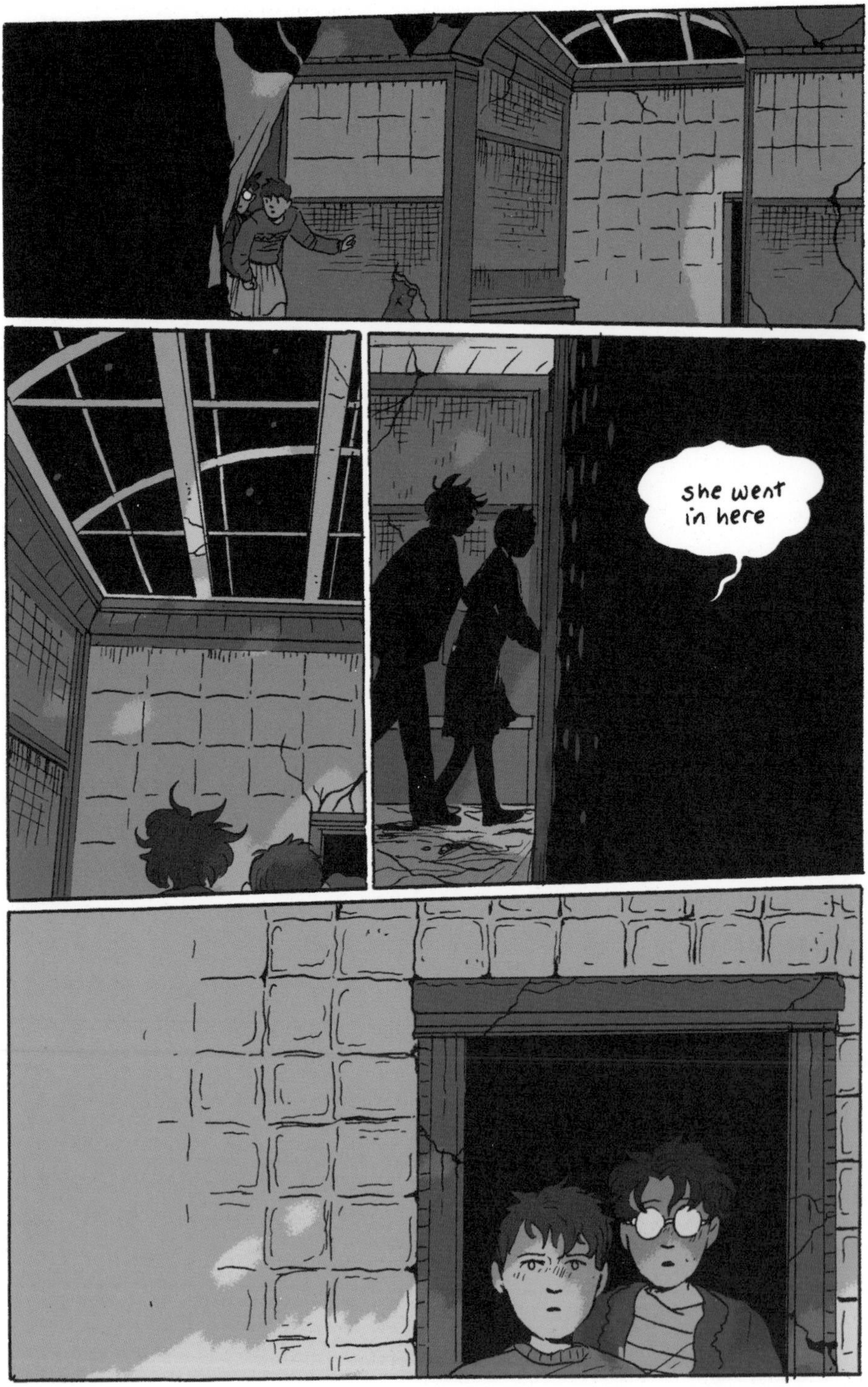
she went in here

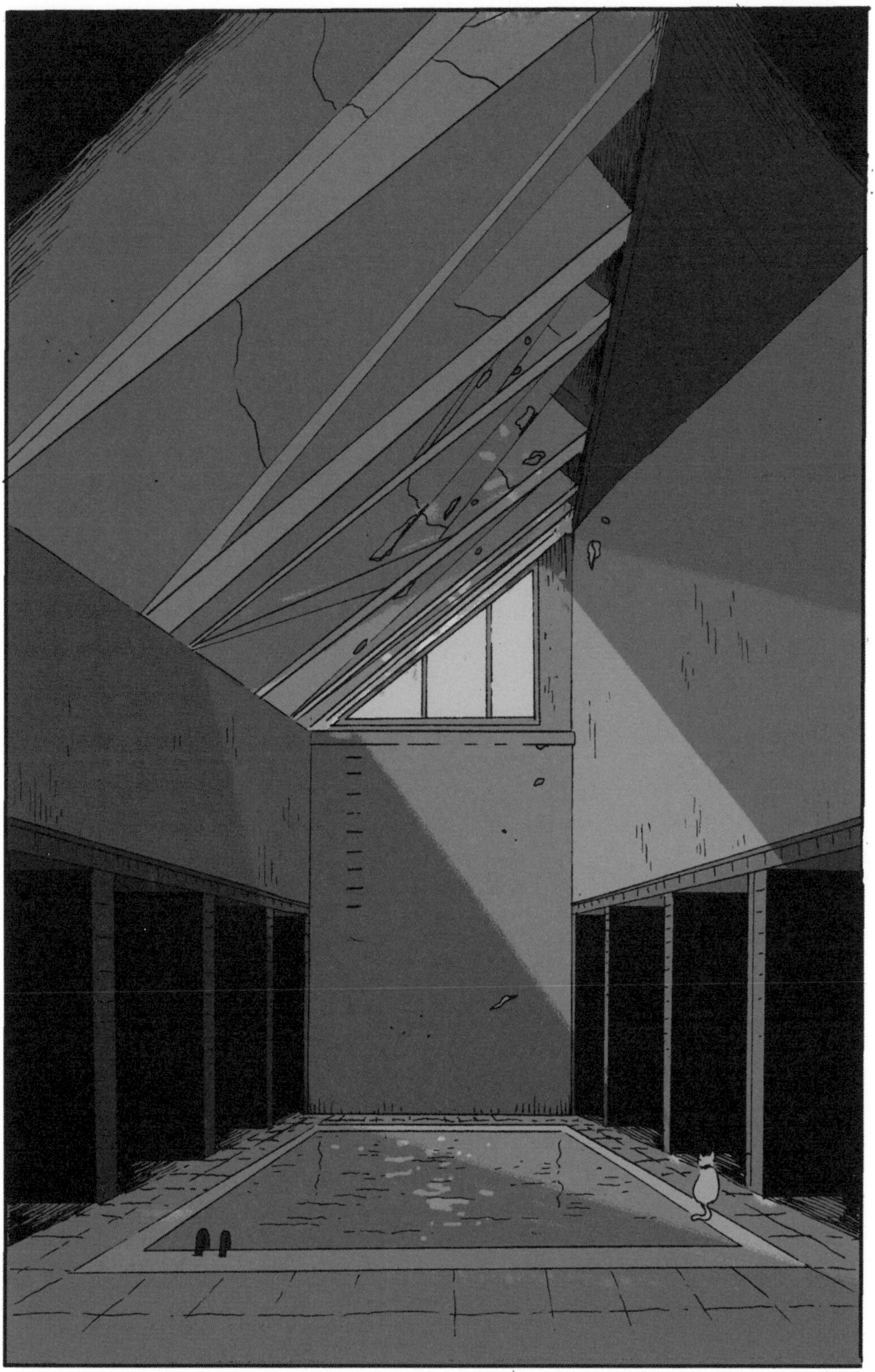

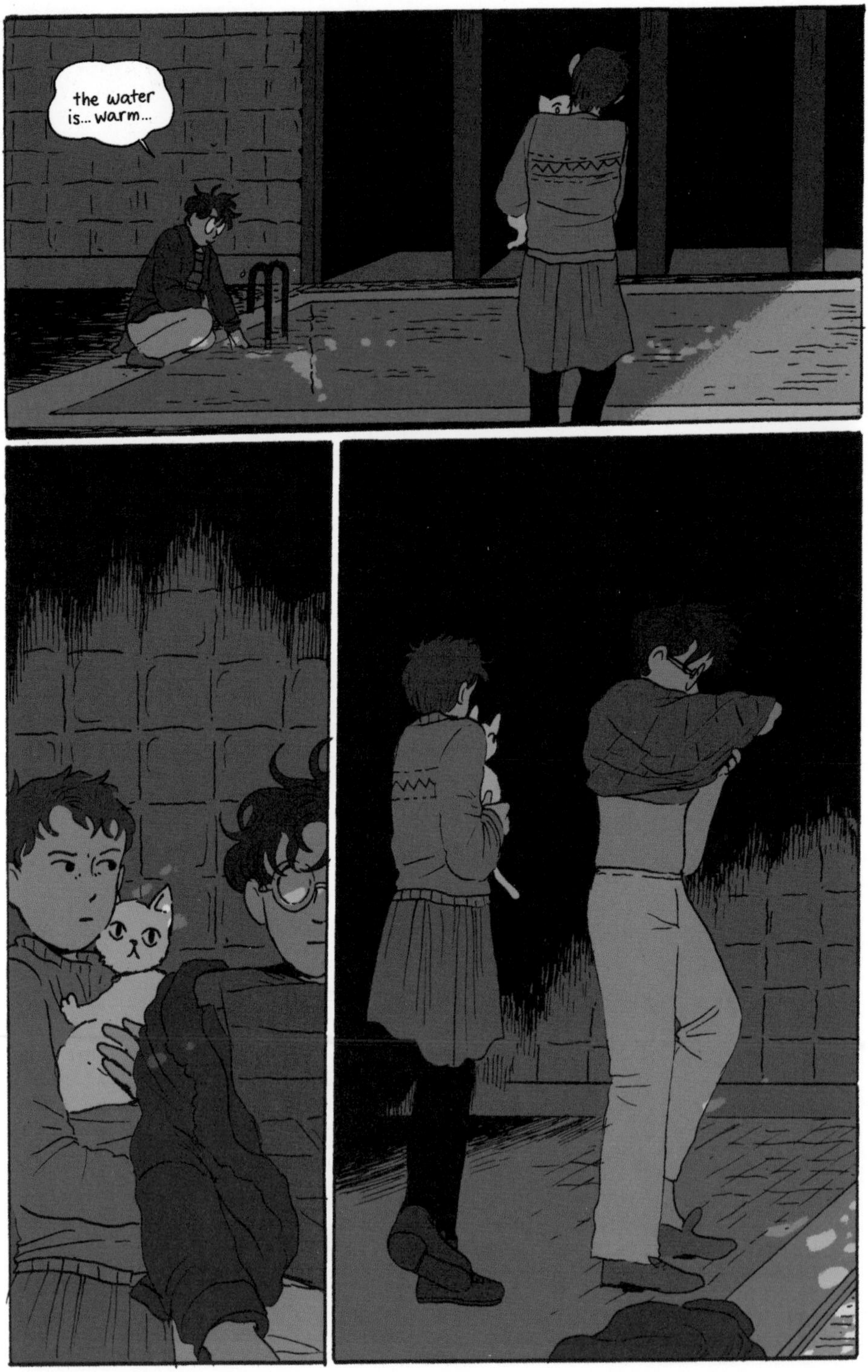
the water is... warm...

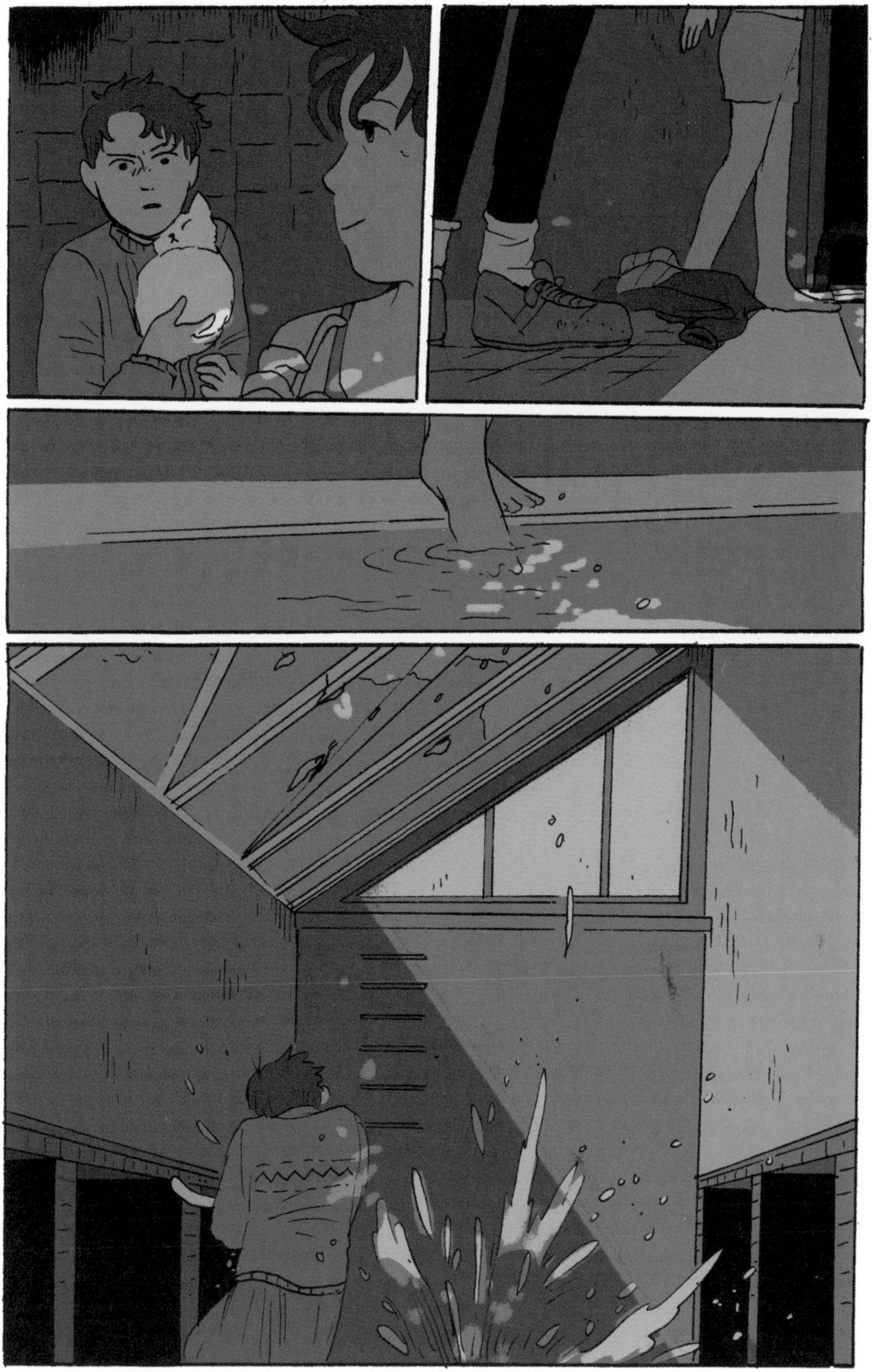

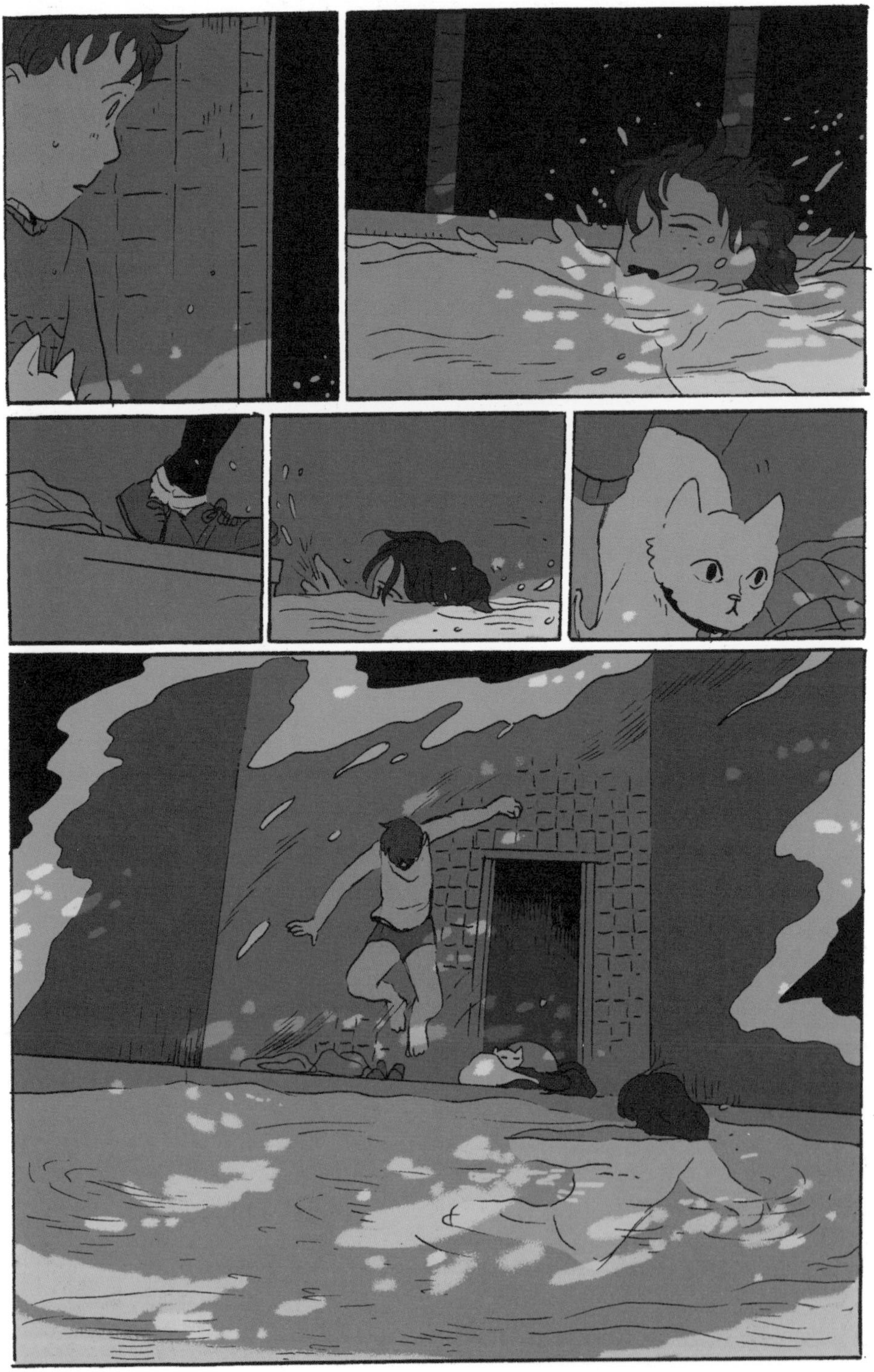

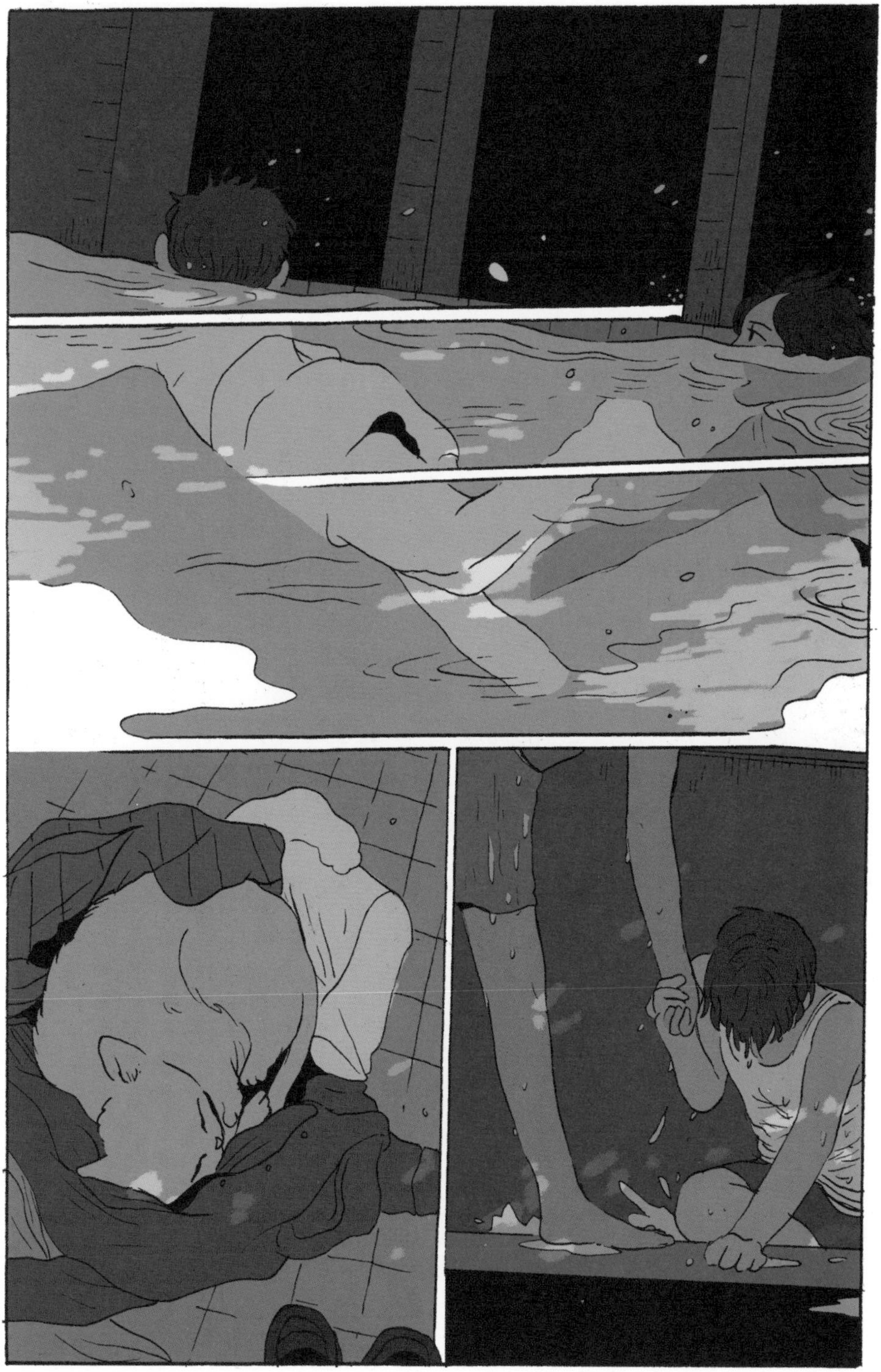

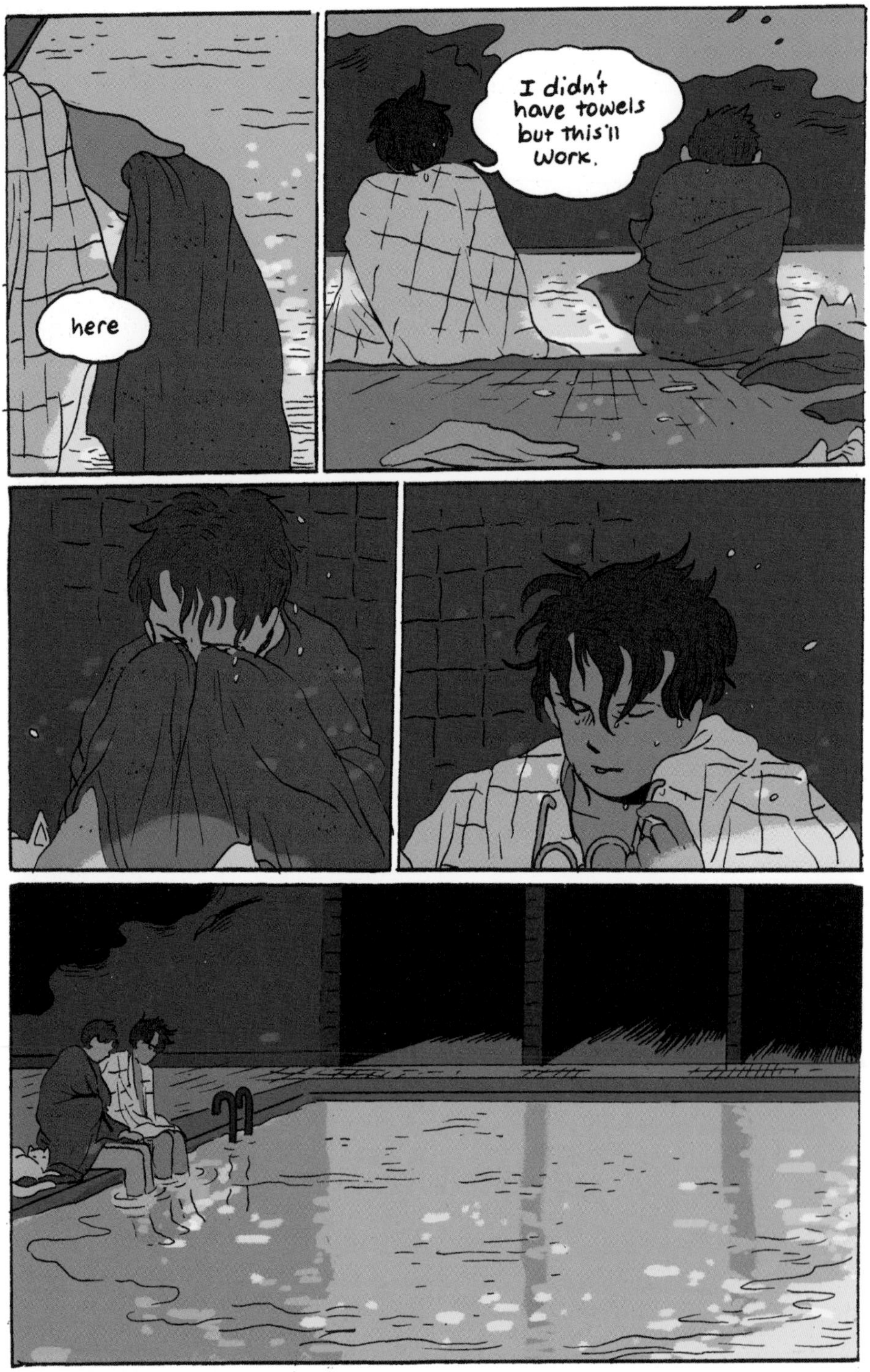
here
I didn't have towels but this'll work.

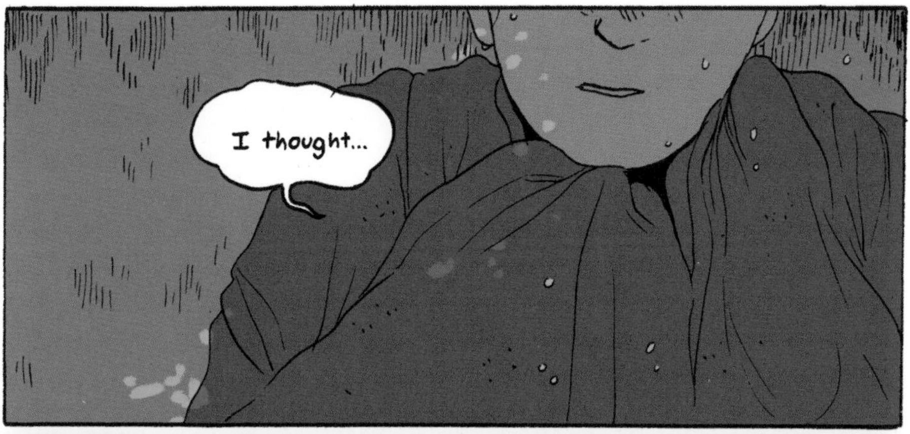
I thought...

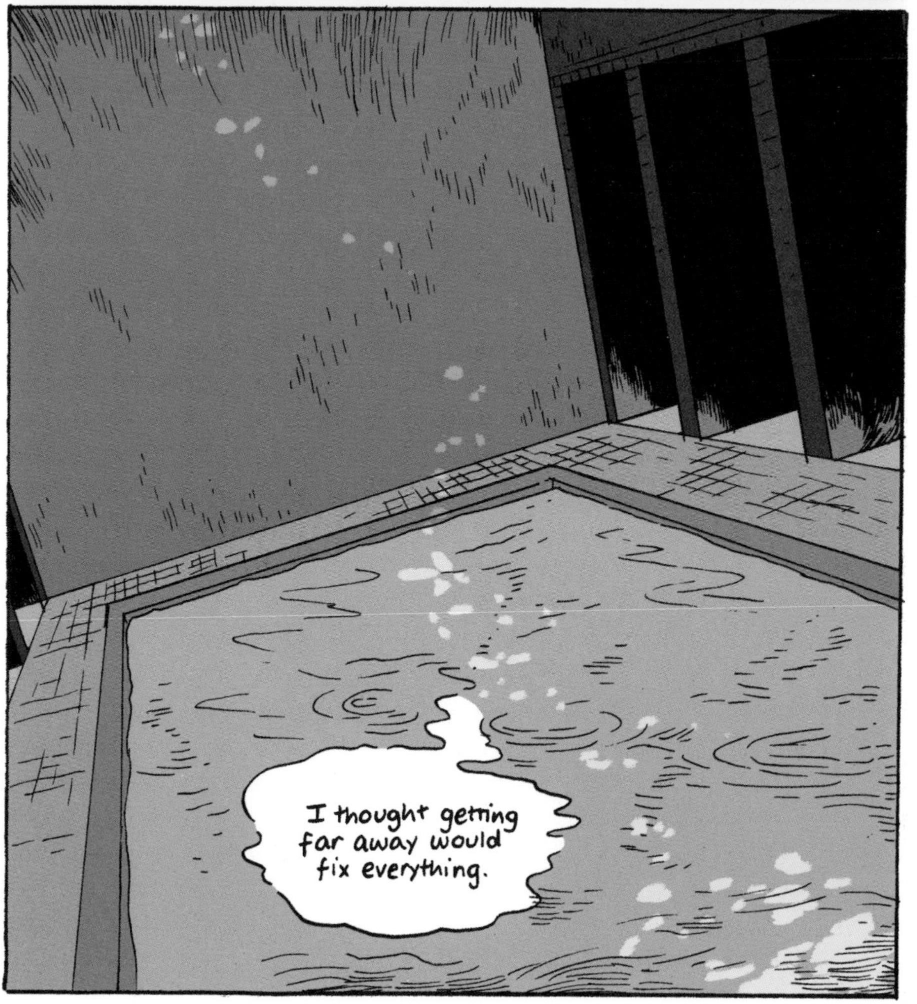
I thought getting far away would fix everything.

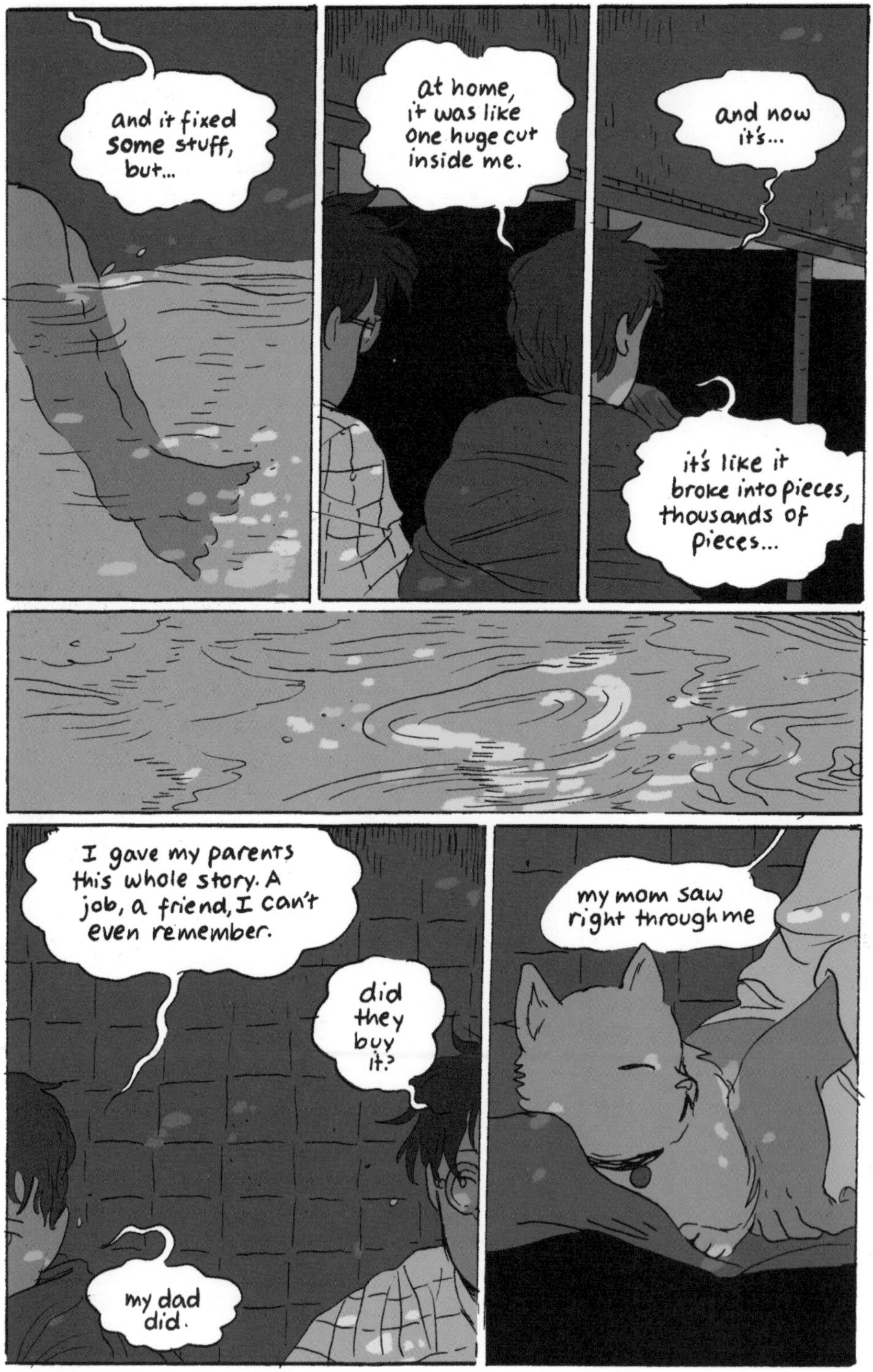
and it fixed some stuff, but...
at home, it was like one huge cut inside me.
and now it's...
it's like it broke into pieces, thousands of pieces...
I gave my parents this whole story. A job, a friend, I can't even remember.
did they buy it?
my dad did.
my mom saw right through me

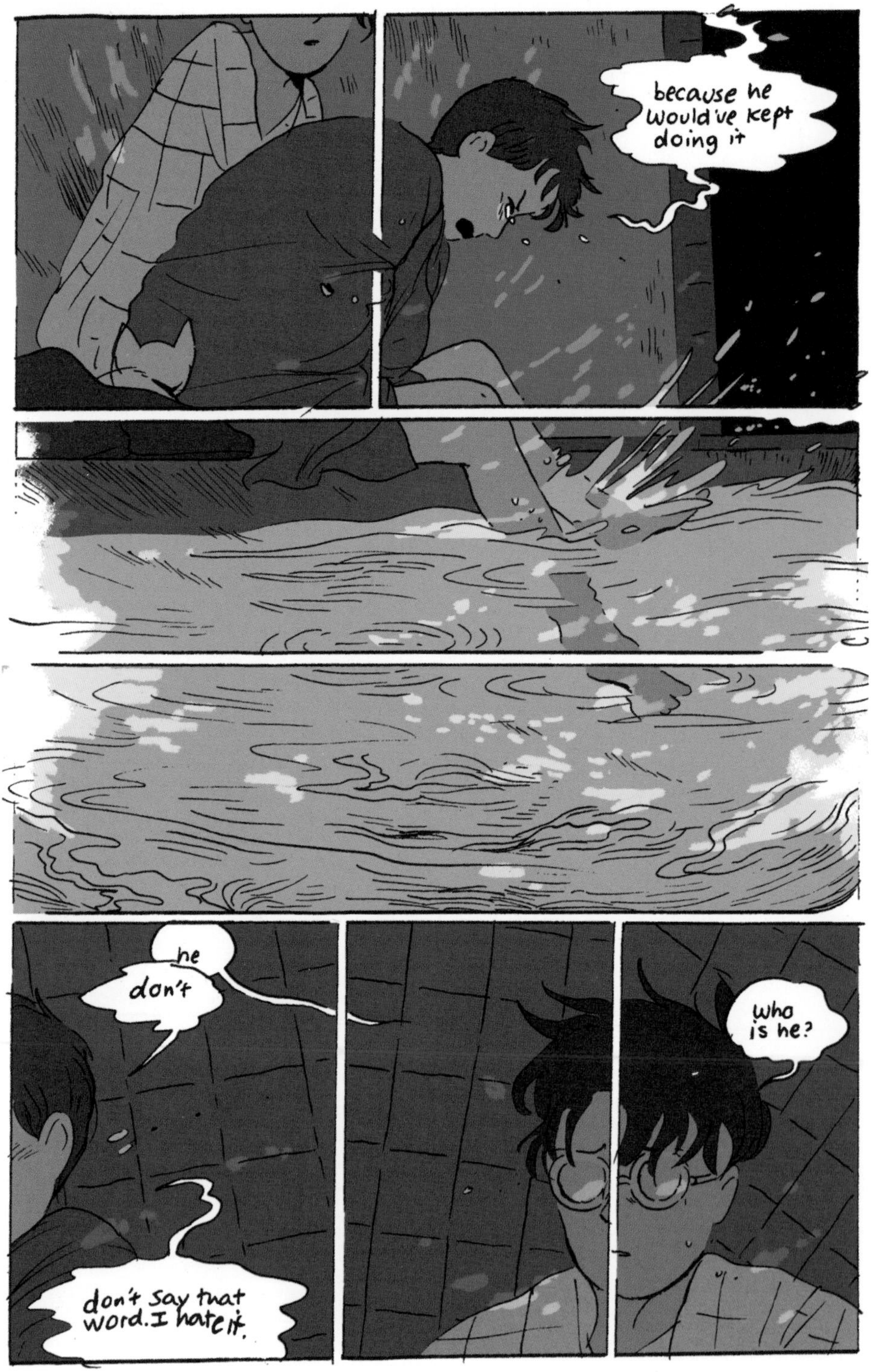
because he would've kept doing it
he
don't
don't say that word. I hate it.
who is he?

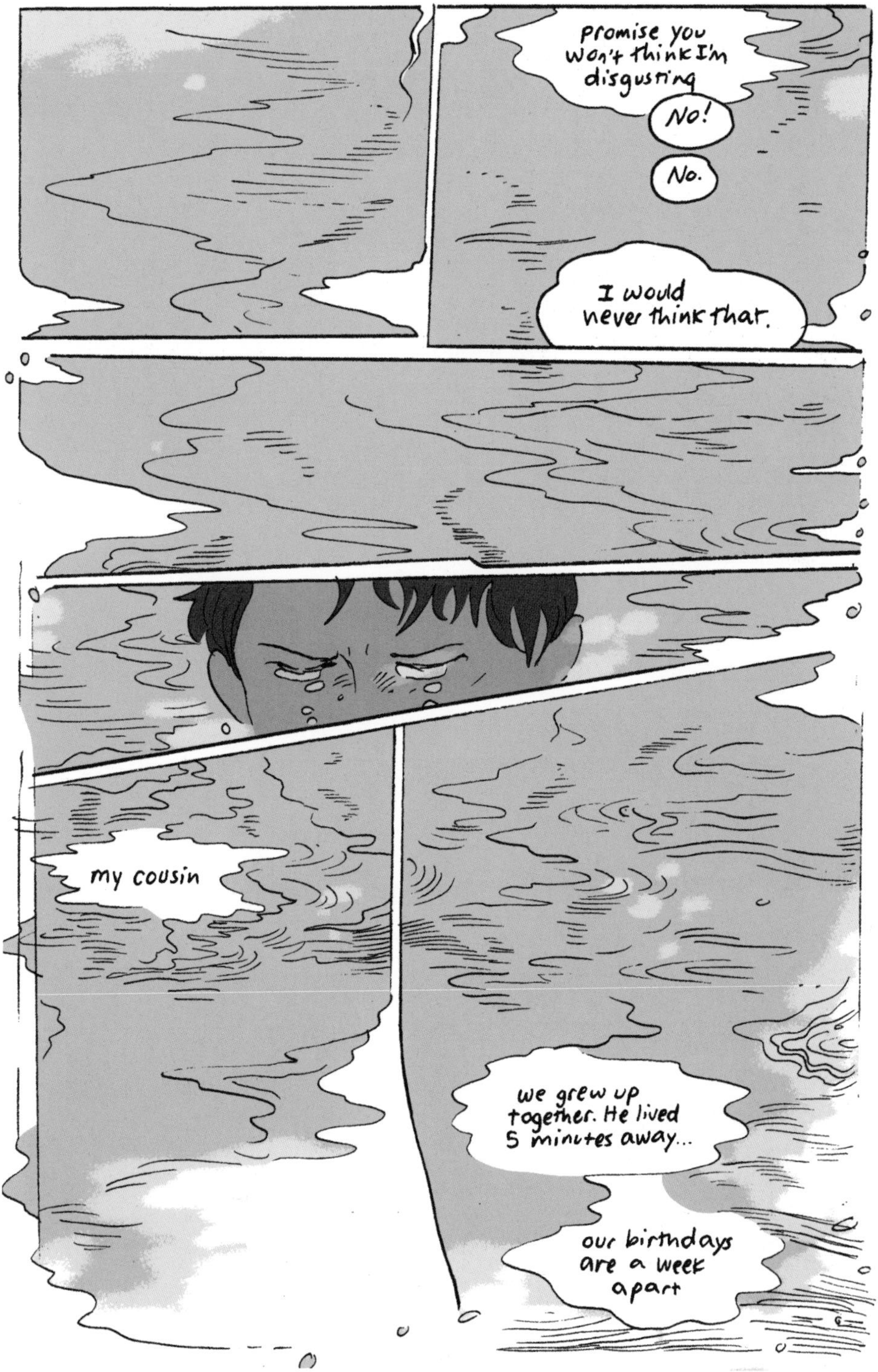
Promise you won't think I'm disgusting
No!
No.
I would never think that.
my cousin
we grew up together. He lived 5 minutes away...
our birthdays are a week apart

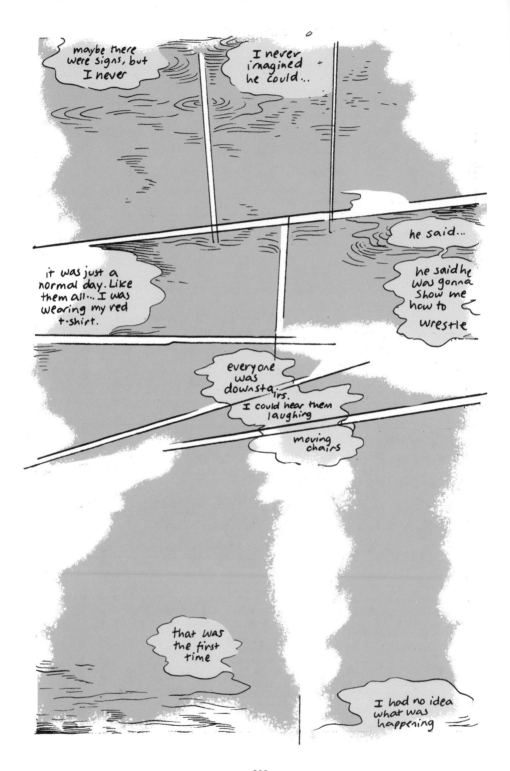

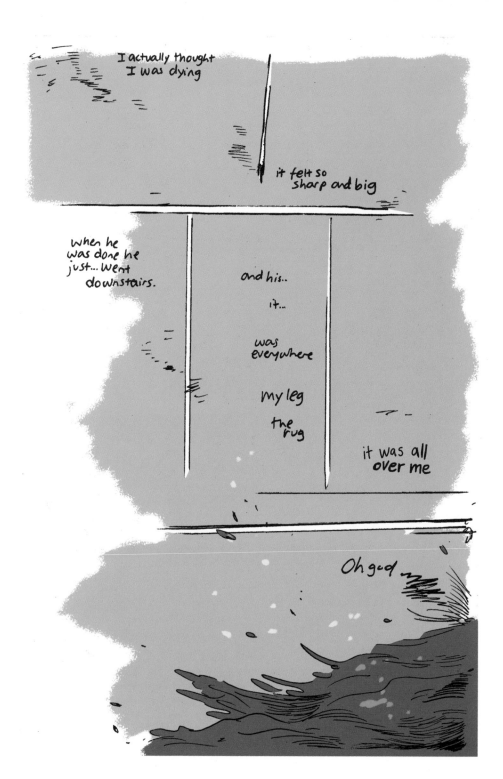

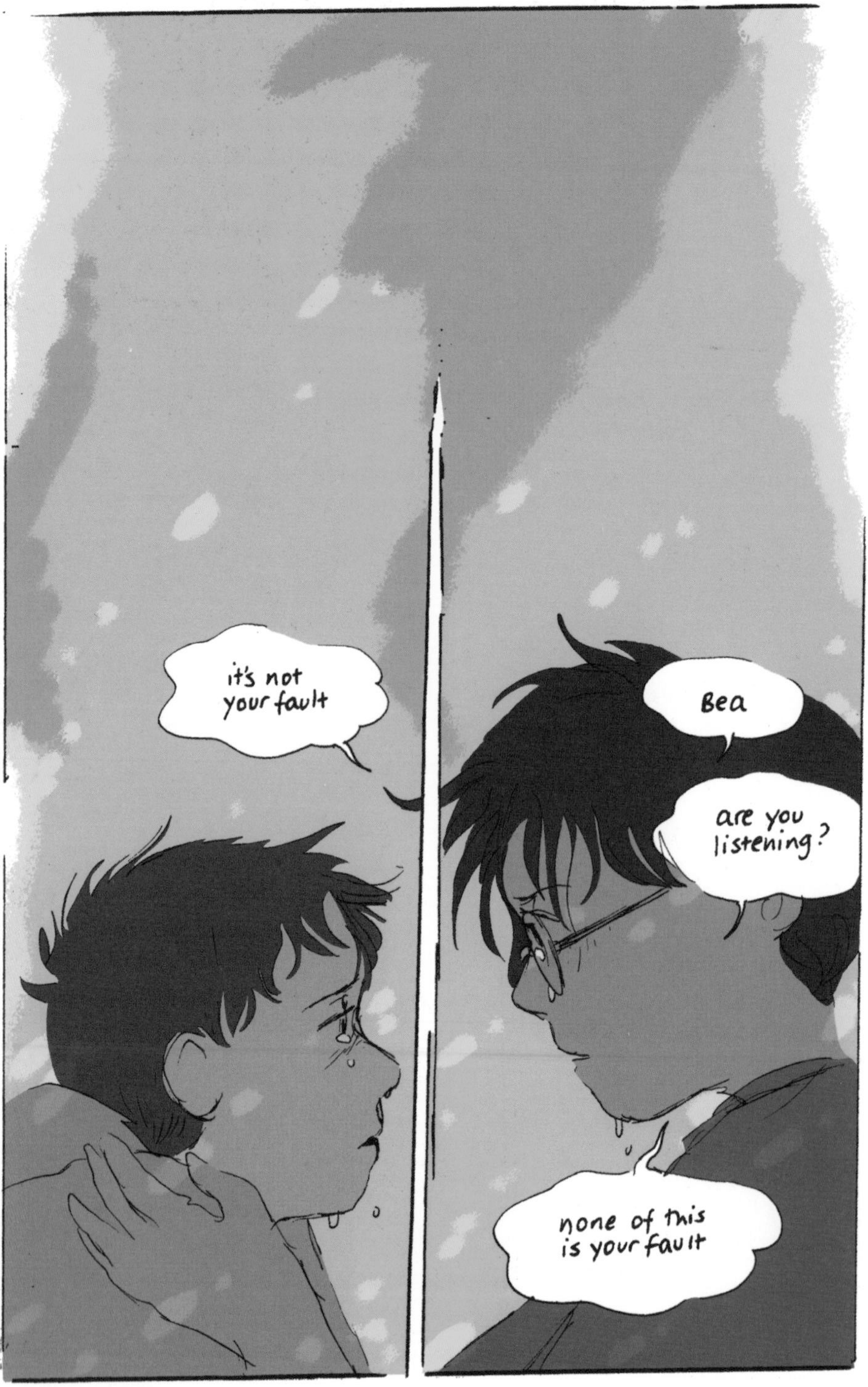
it's not your fault
Bea
are you listening?
none of this is your fault

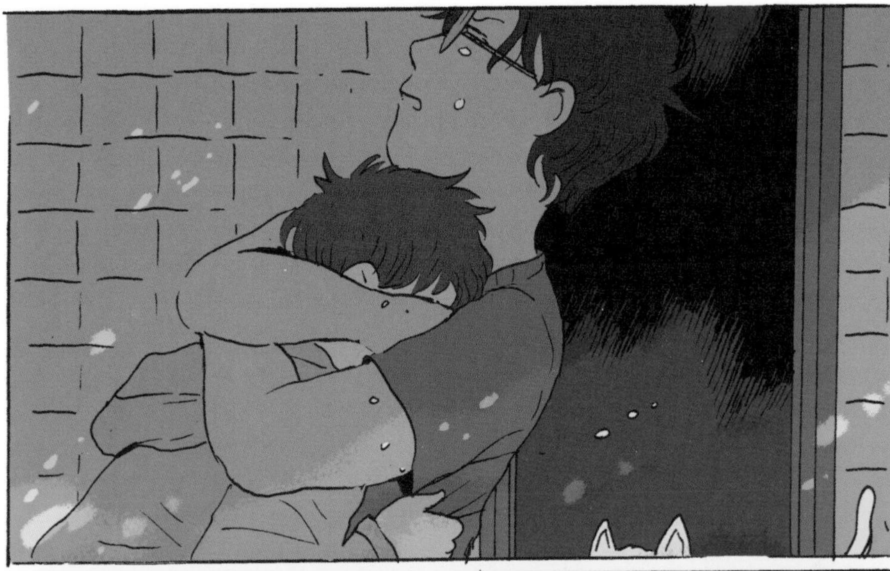

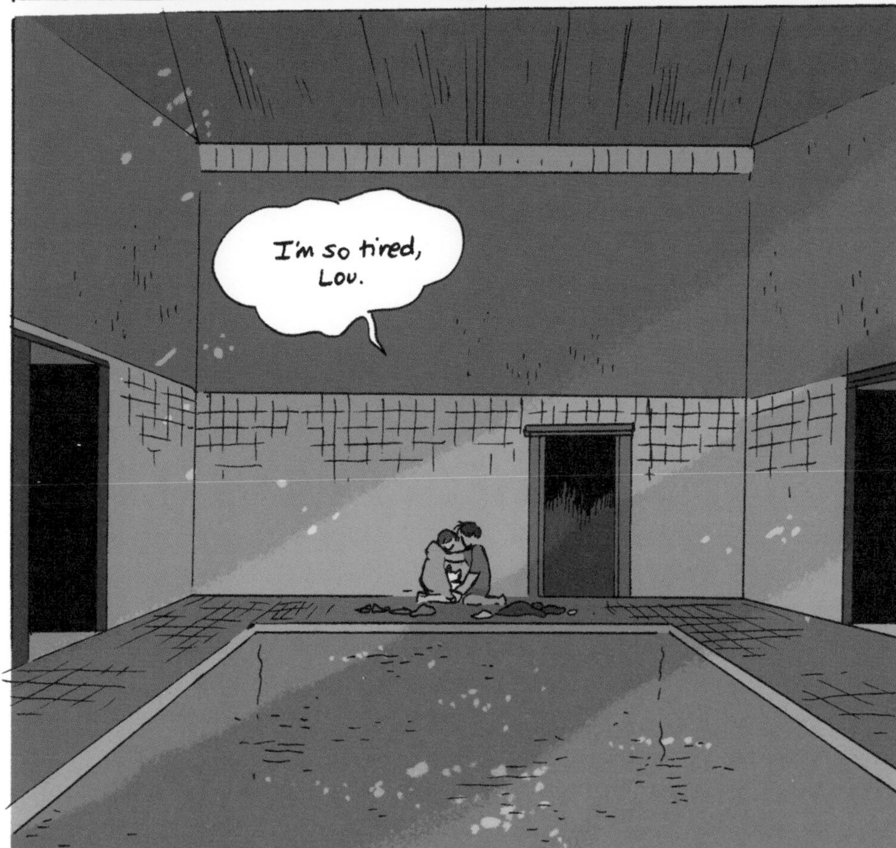
I'm so tired, Lou.

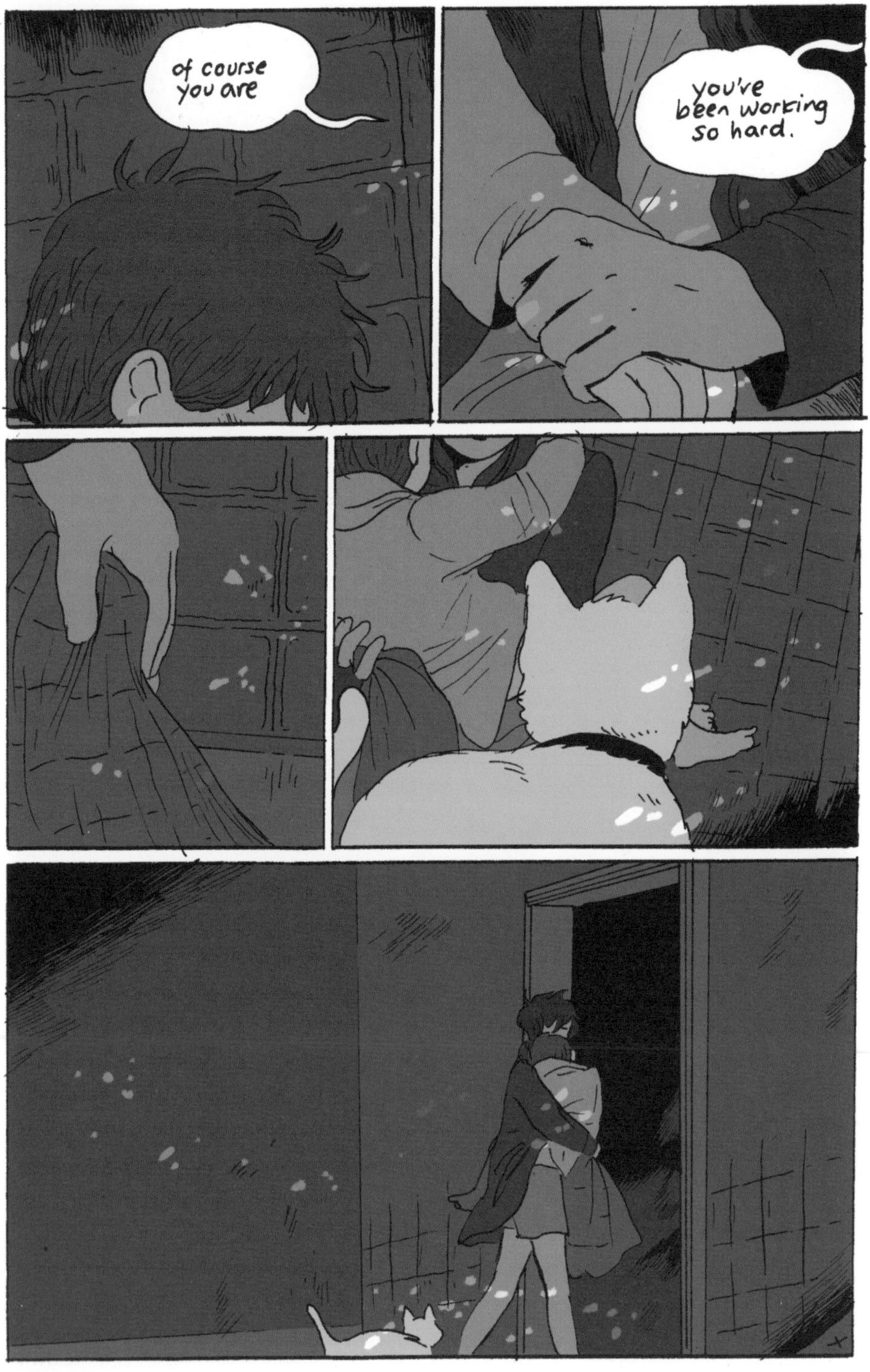
of course
you are
you've
been working
so hard.

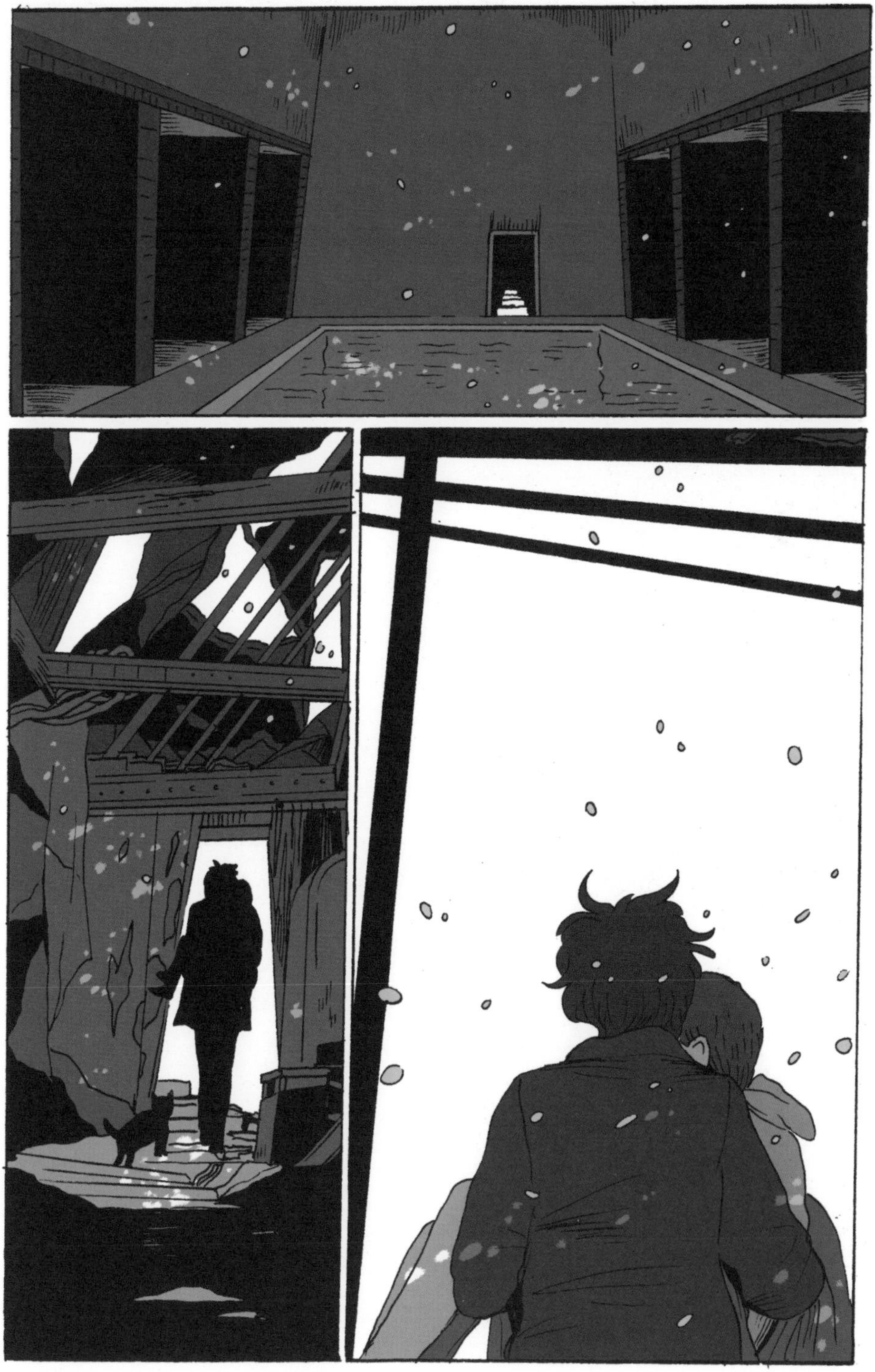

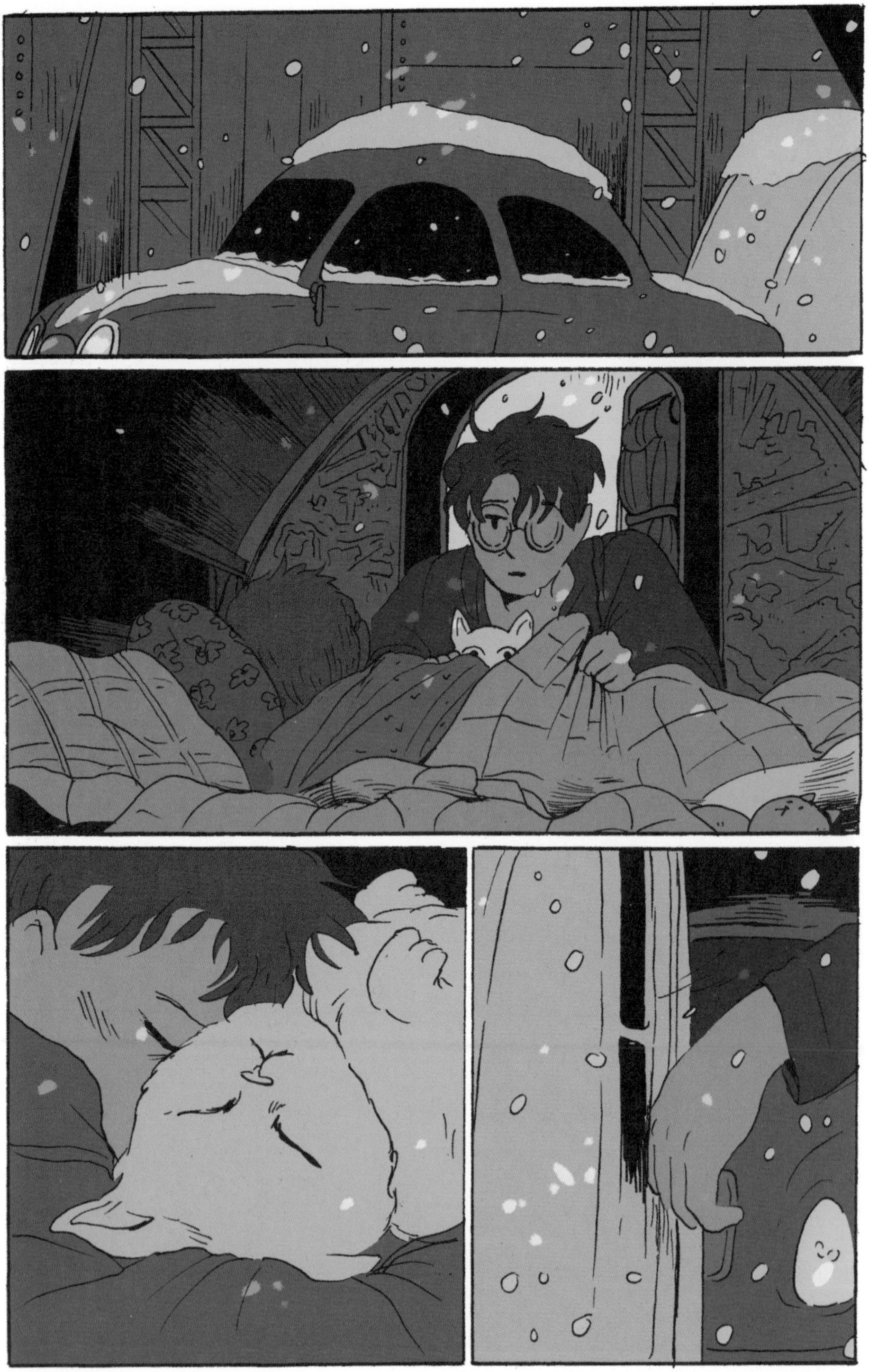

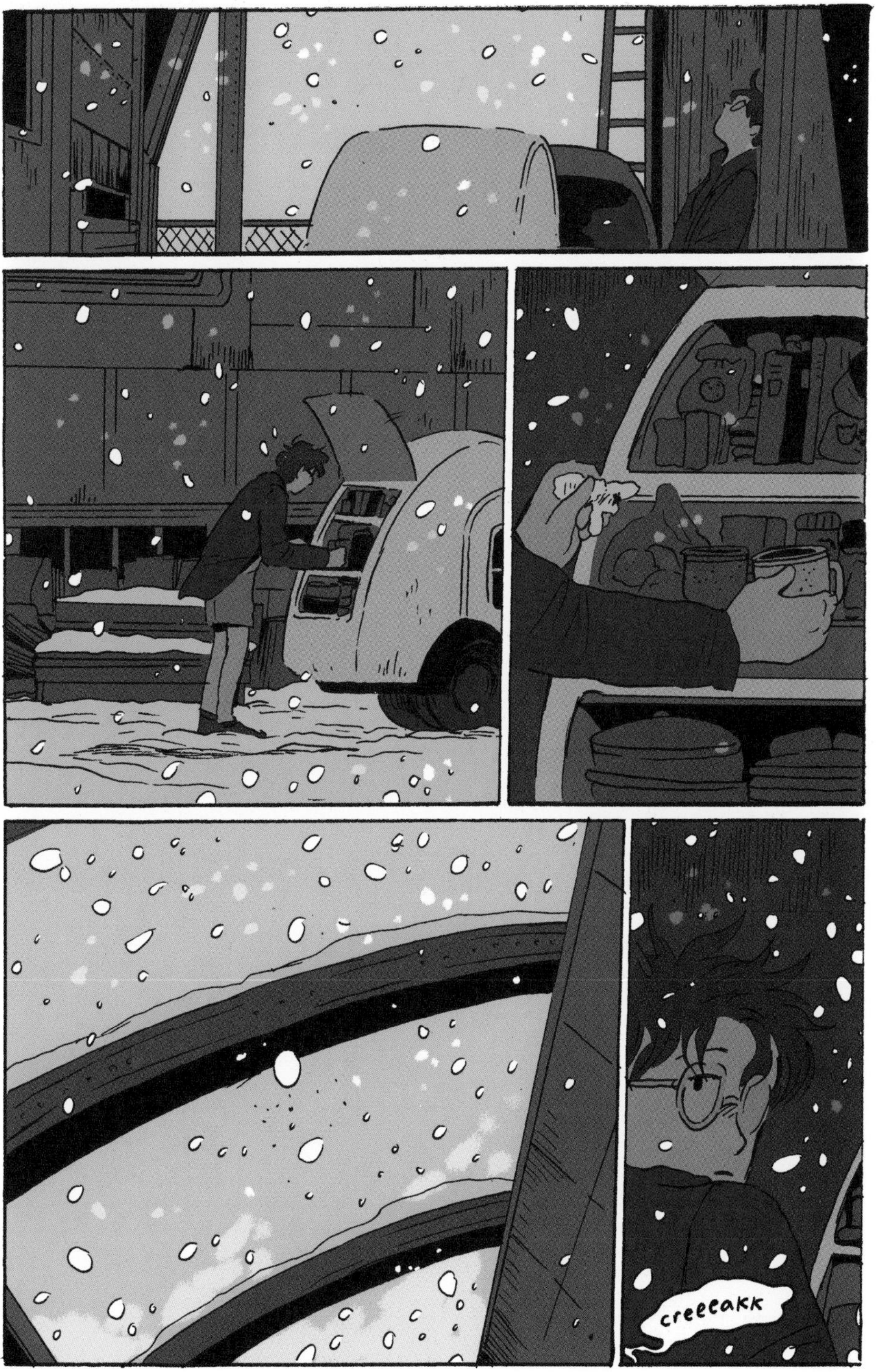
creeeakk

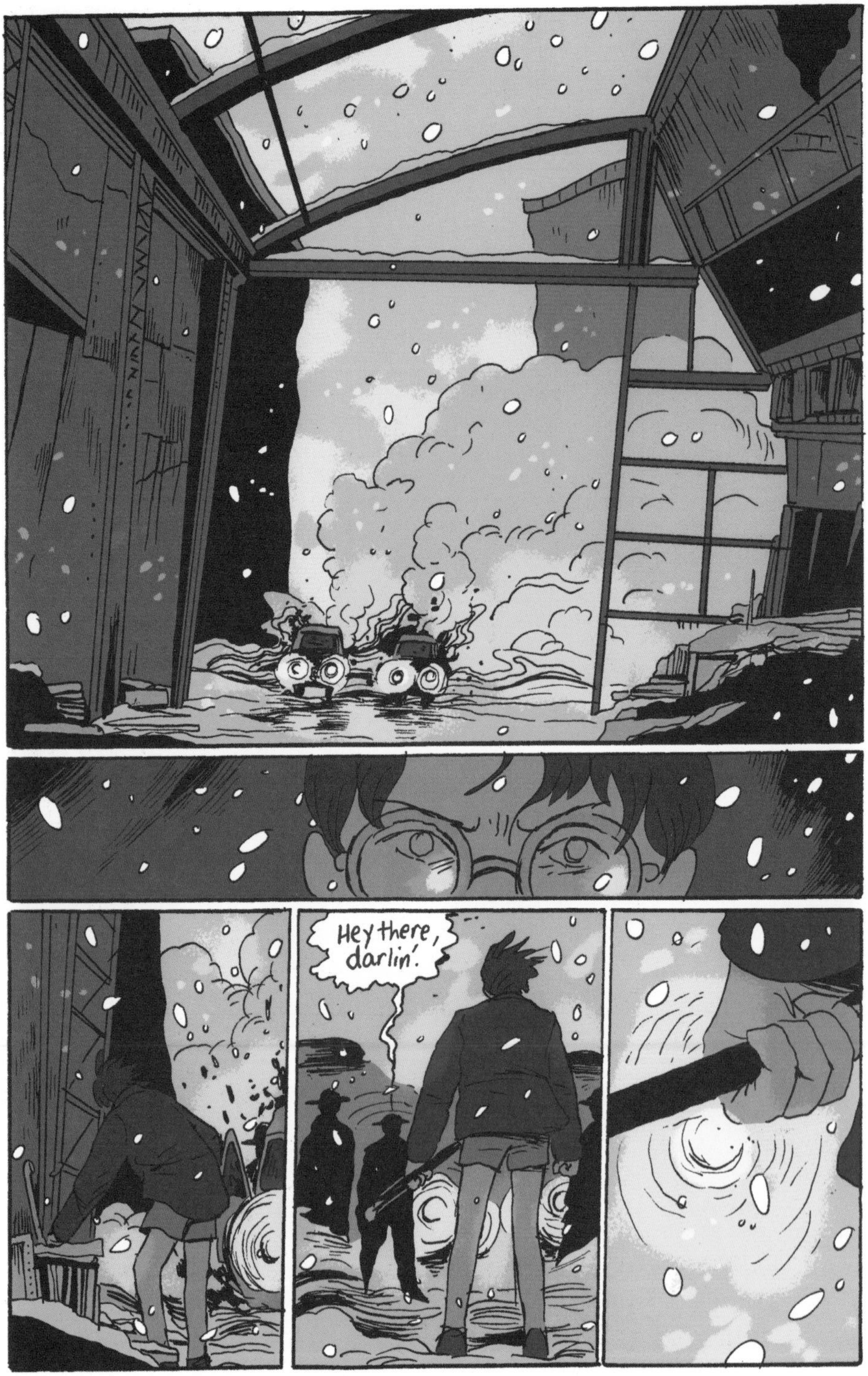
Hey there, darlin'.

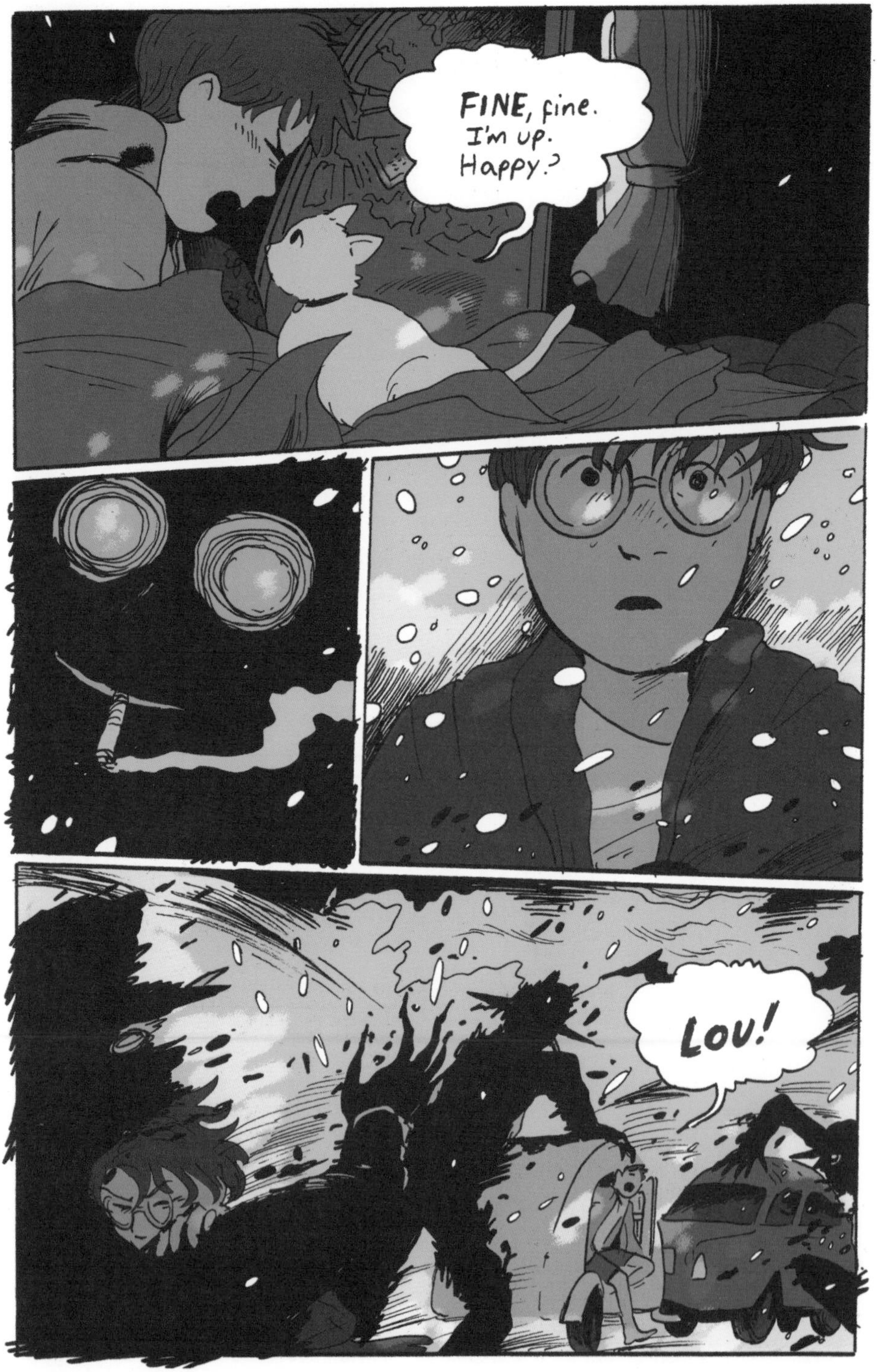
FINE, fine. I'm up. Happy?
LOU!

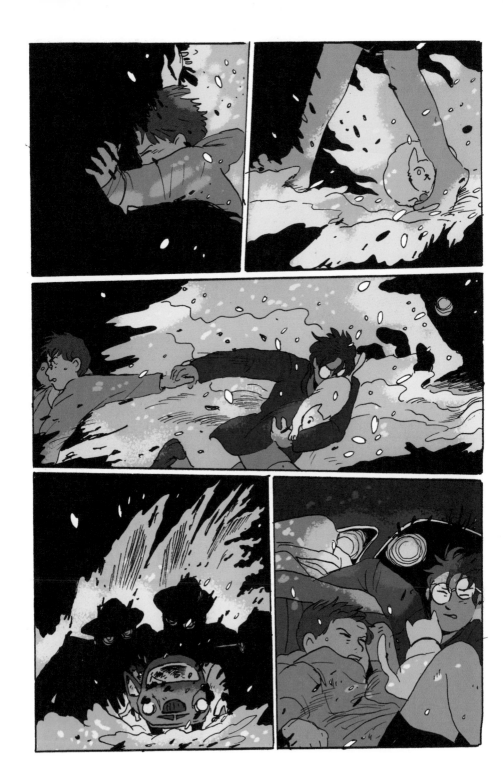

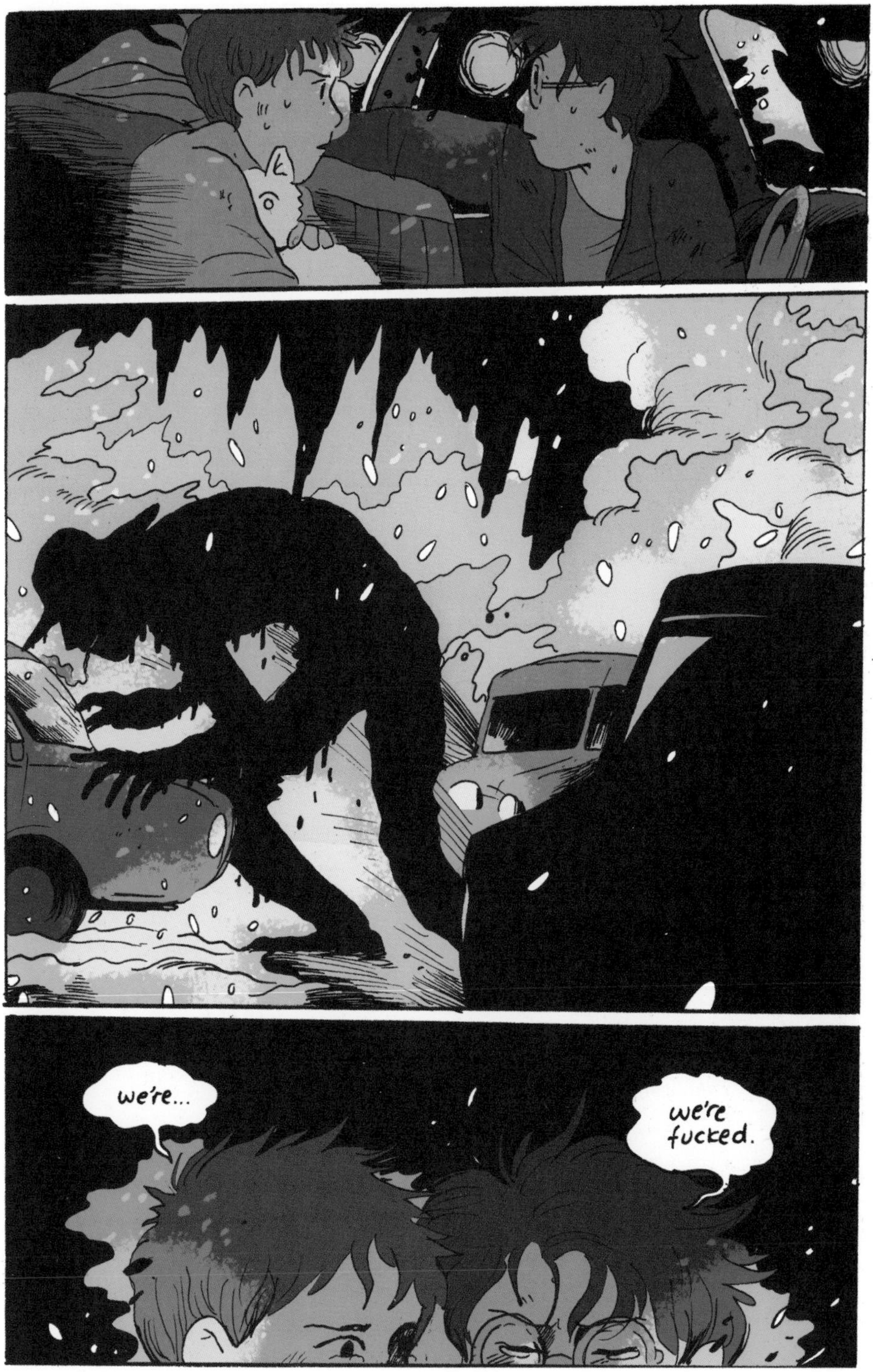
we're...
we're fucked.

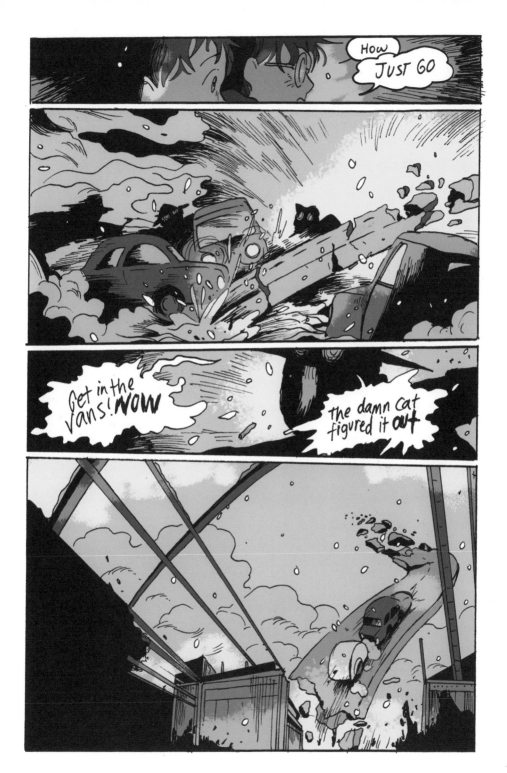

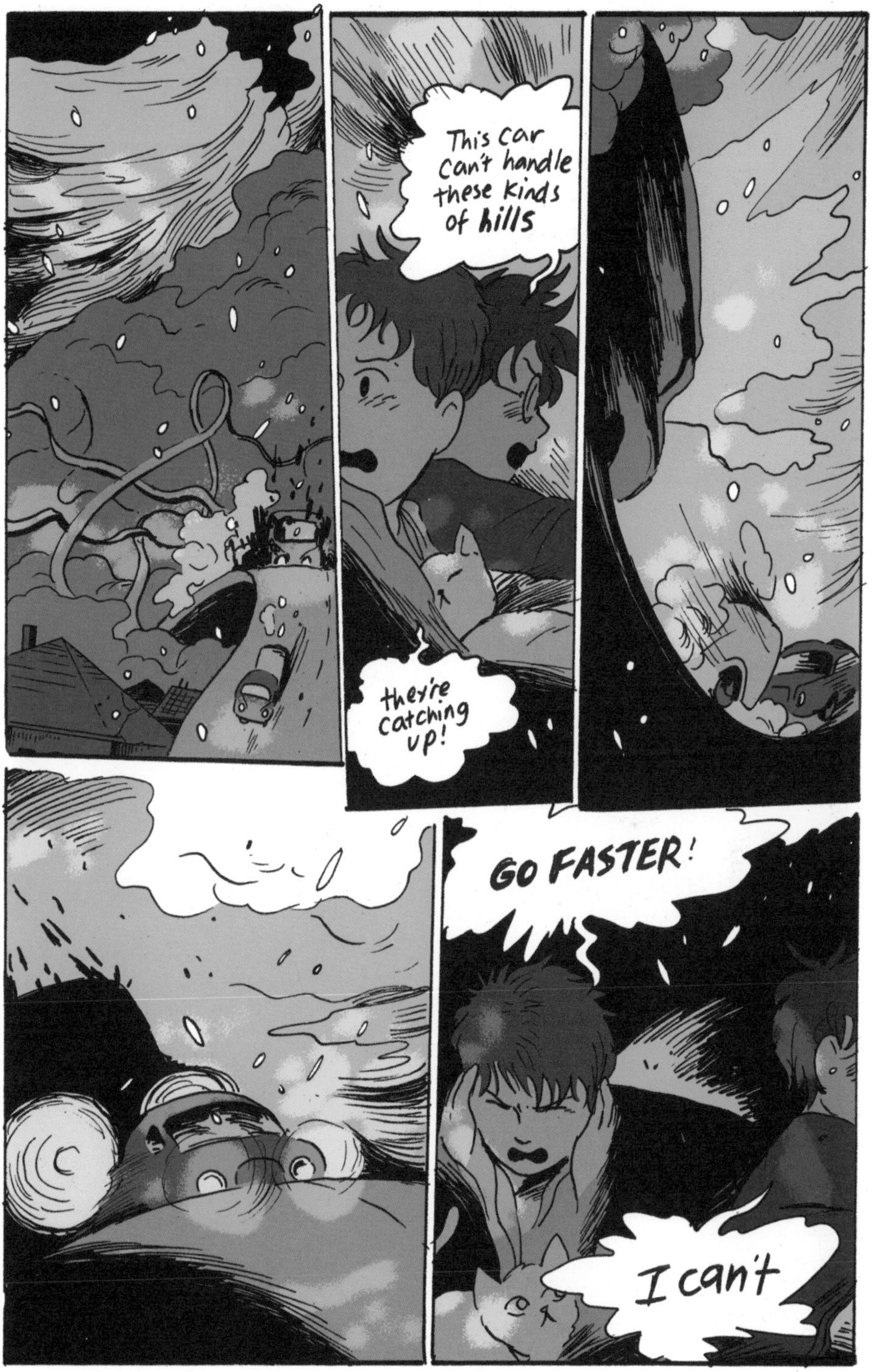
This car can't handle these kinds of hills
they're catching up!
GO FASTER!
I can't

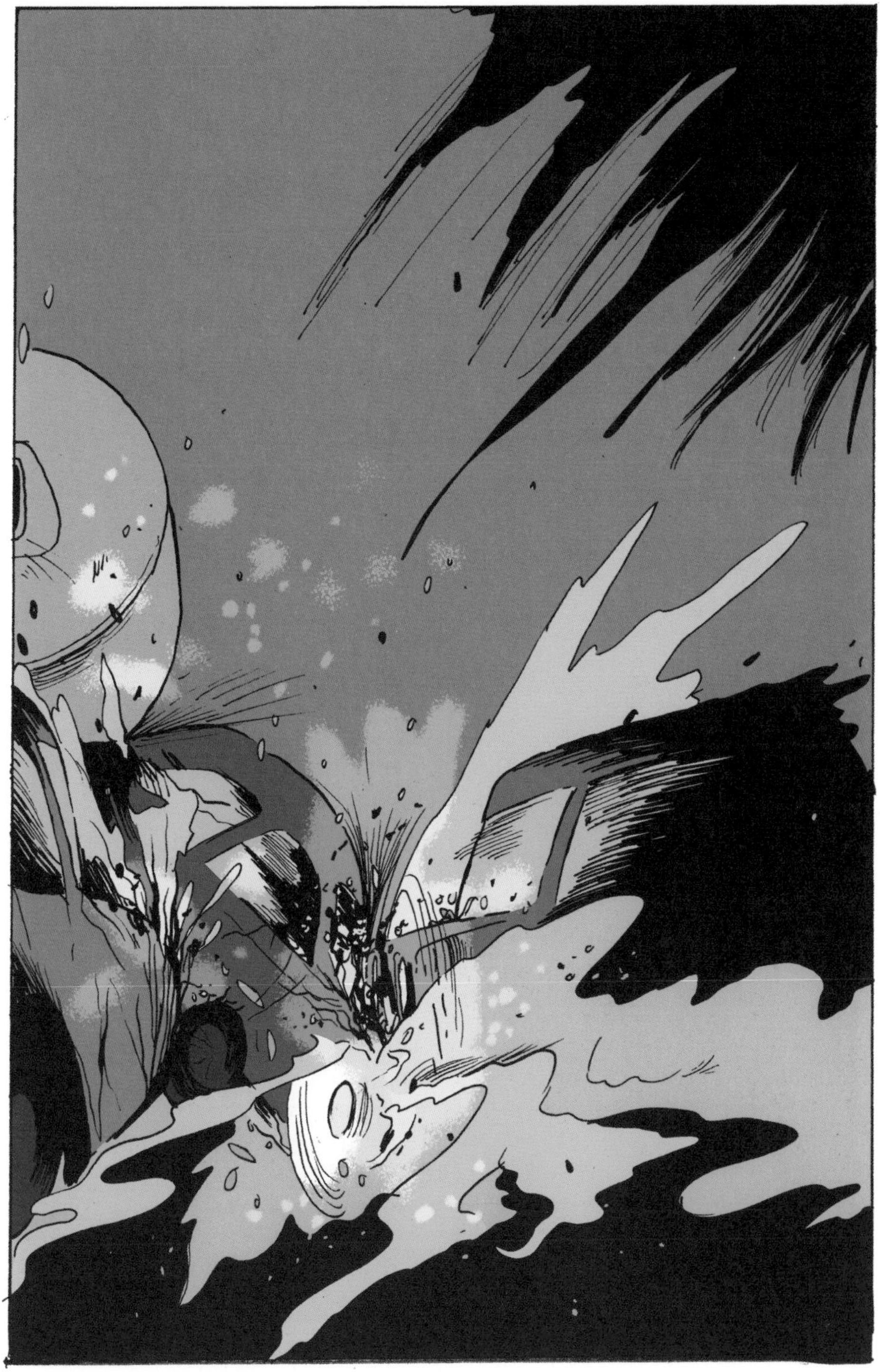

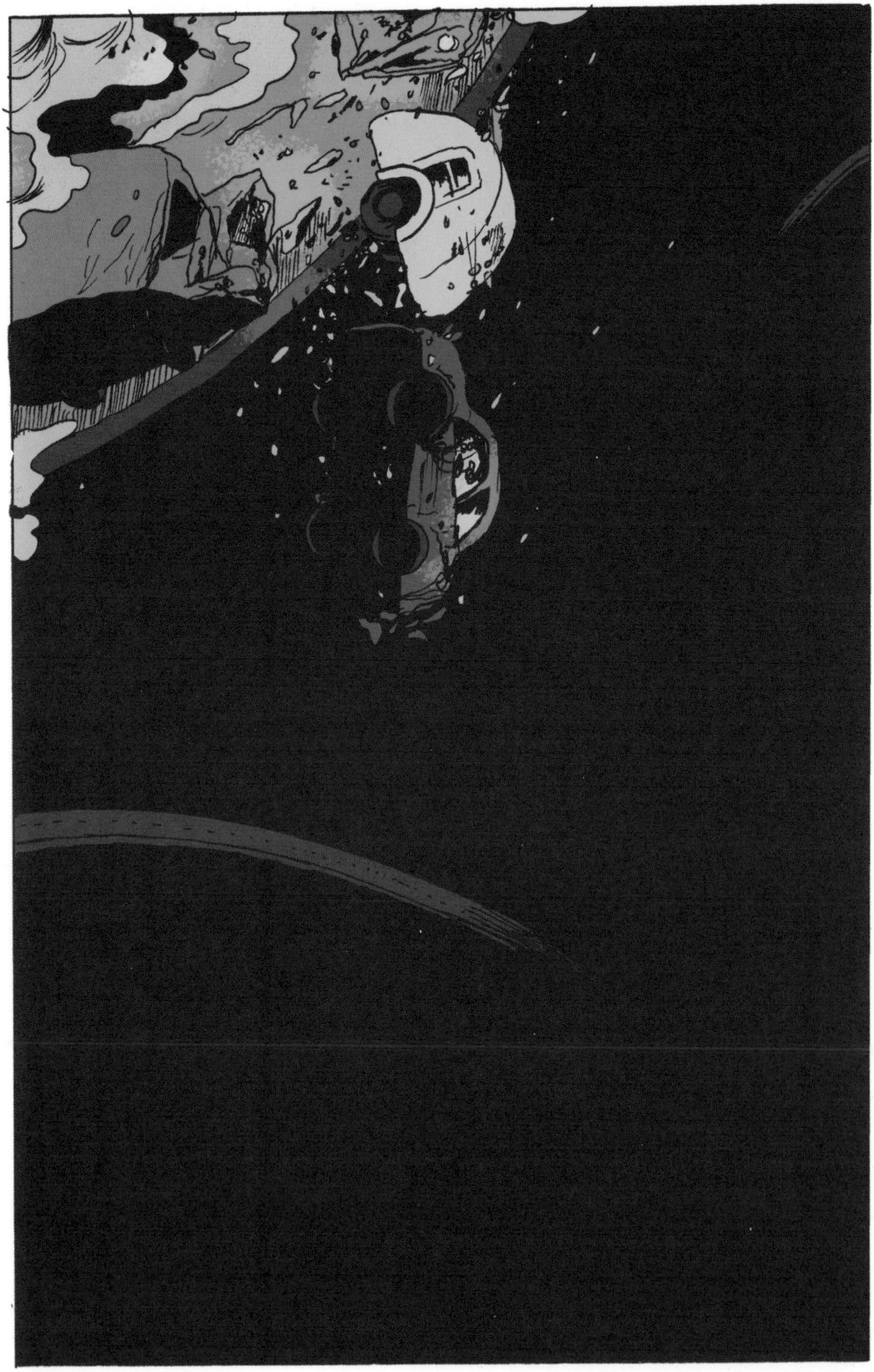

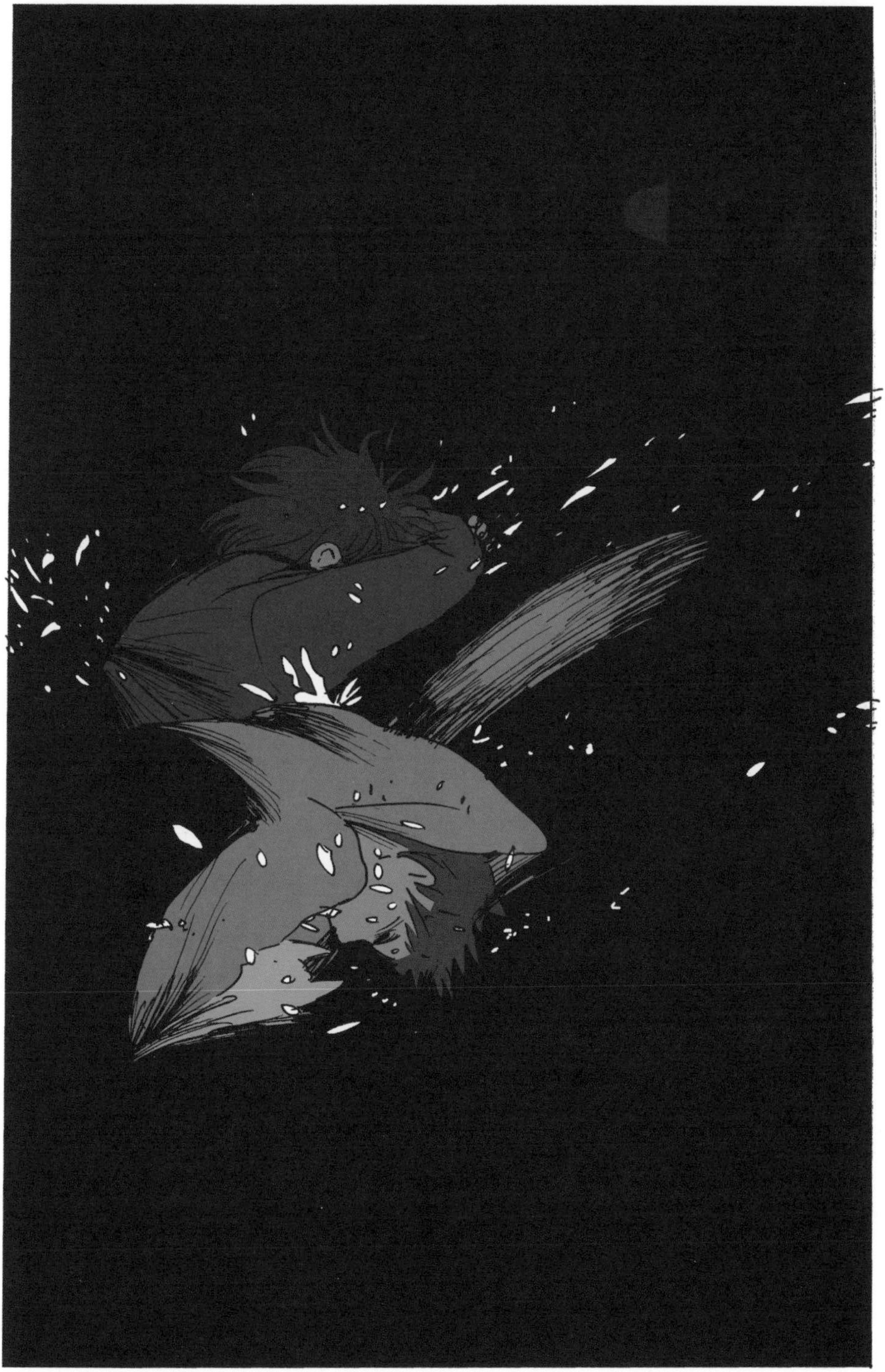

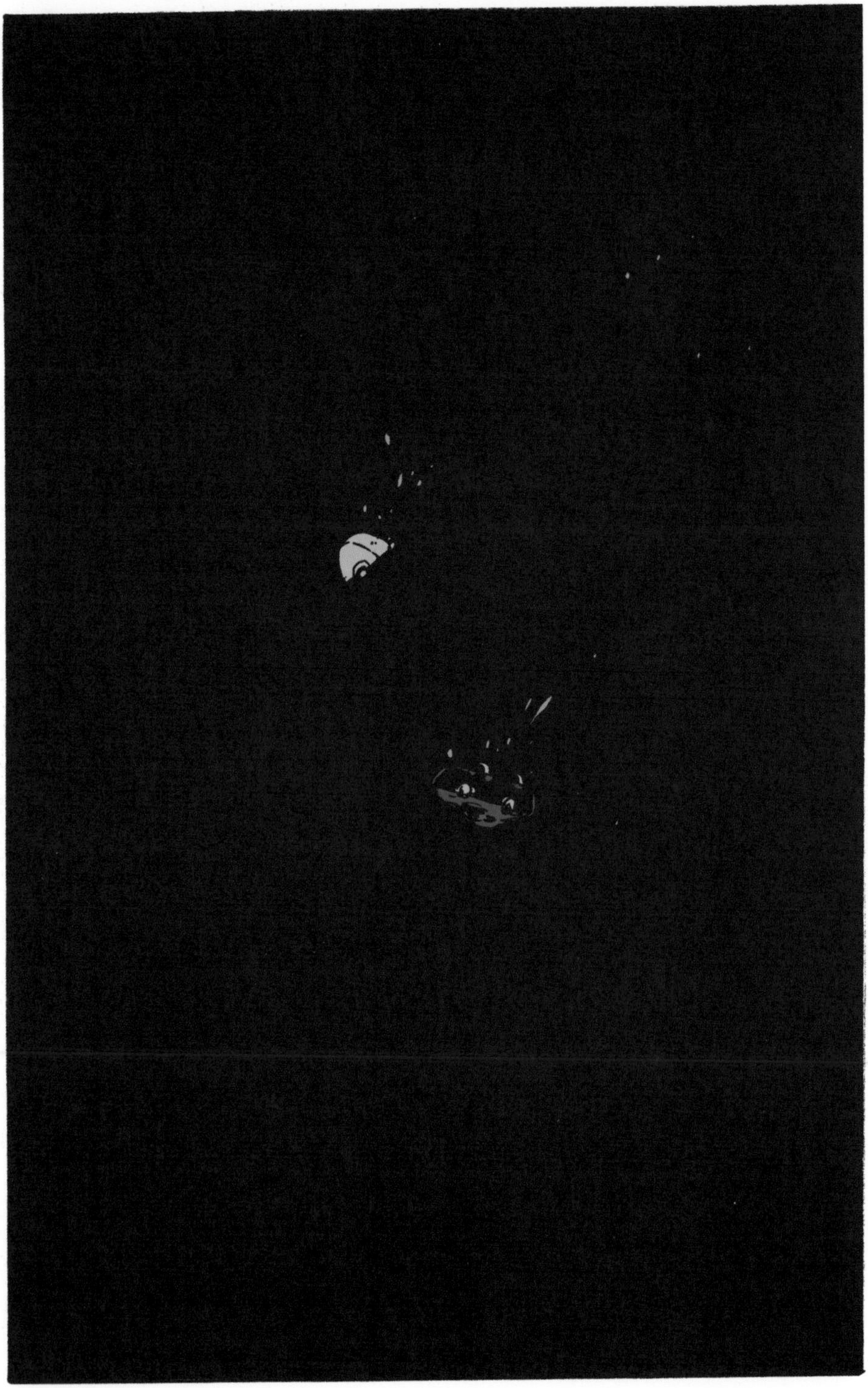

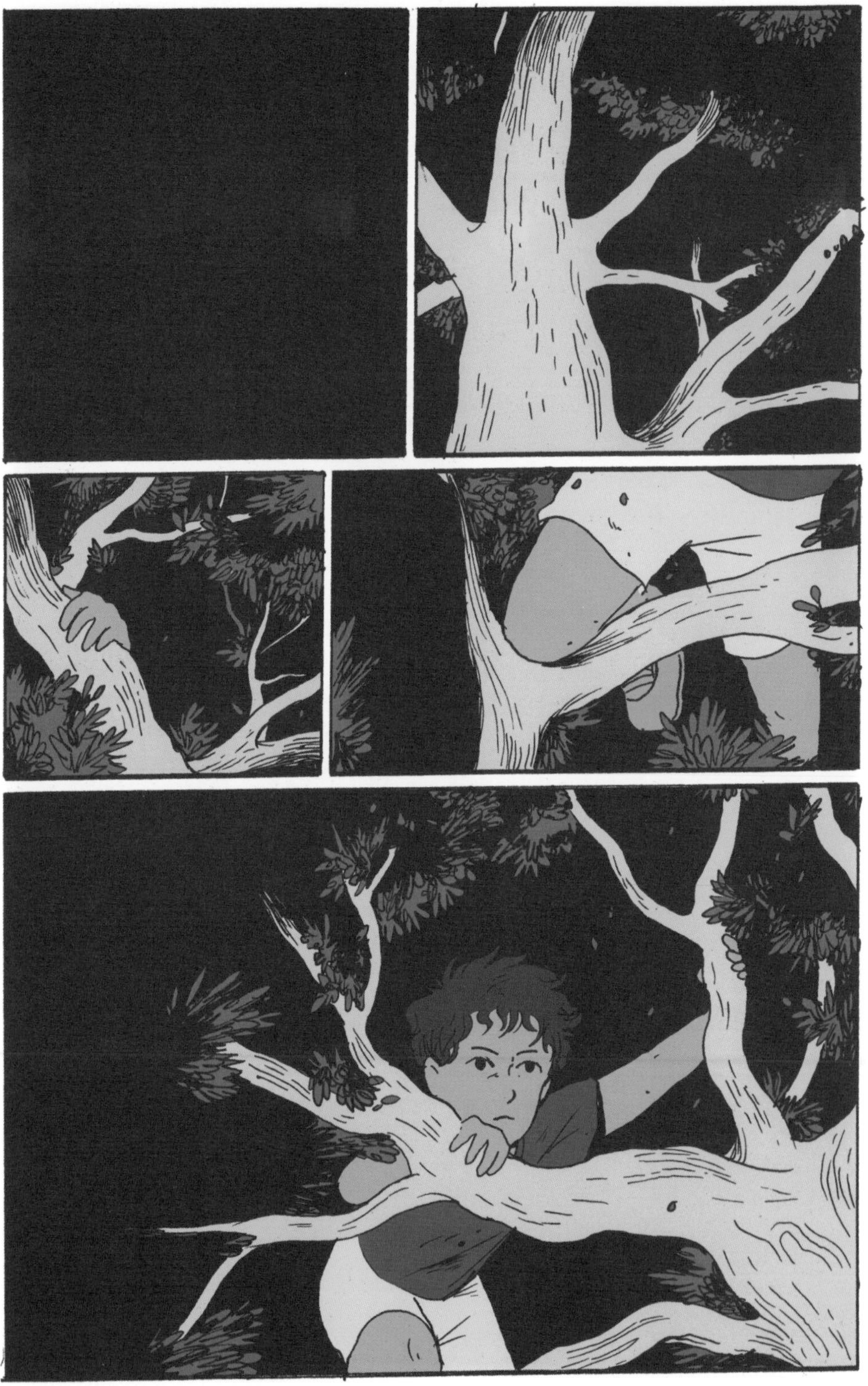

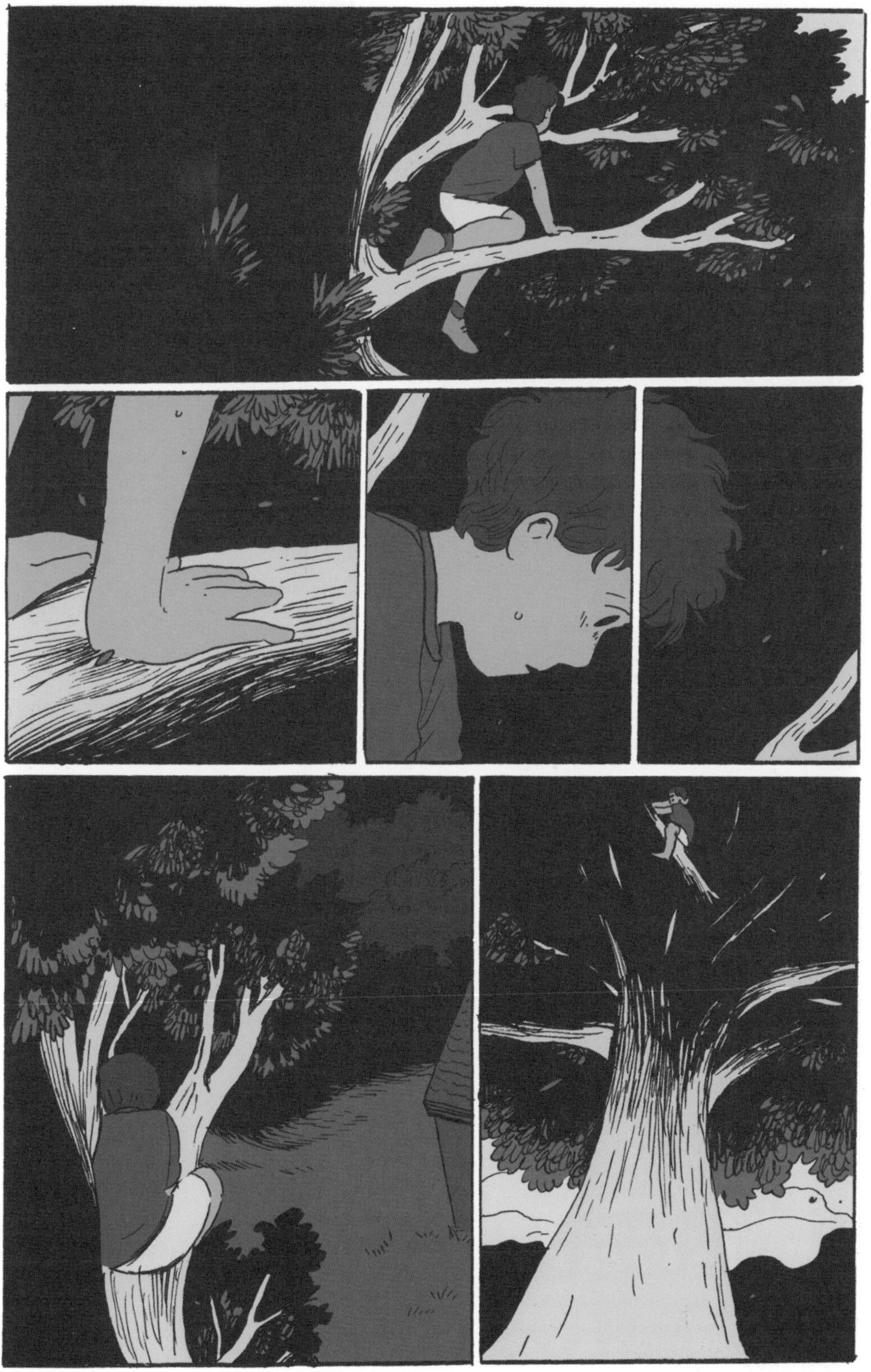

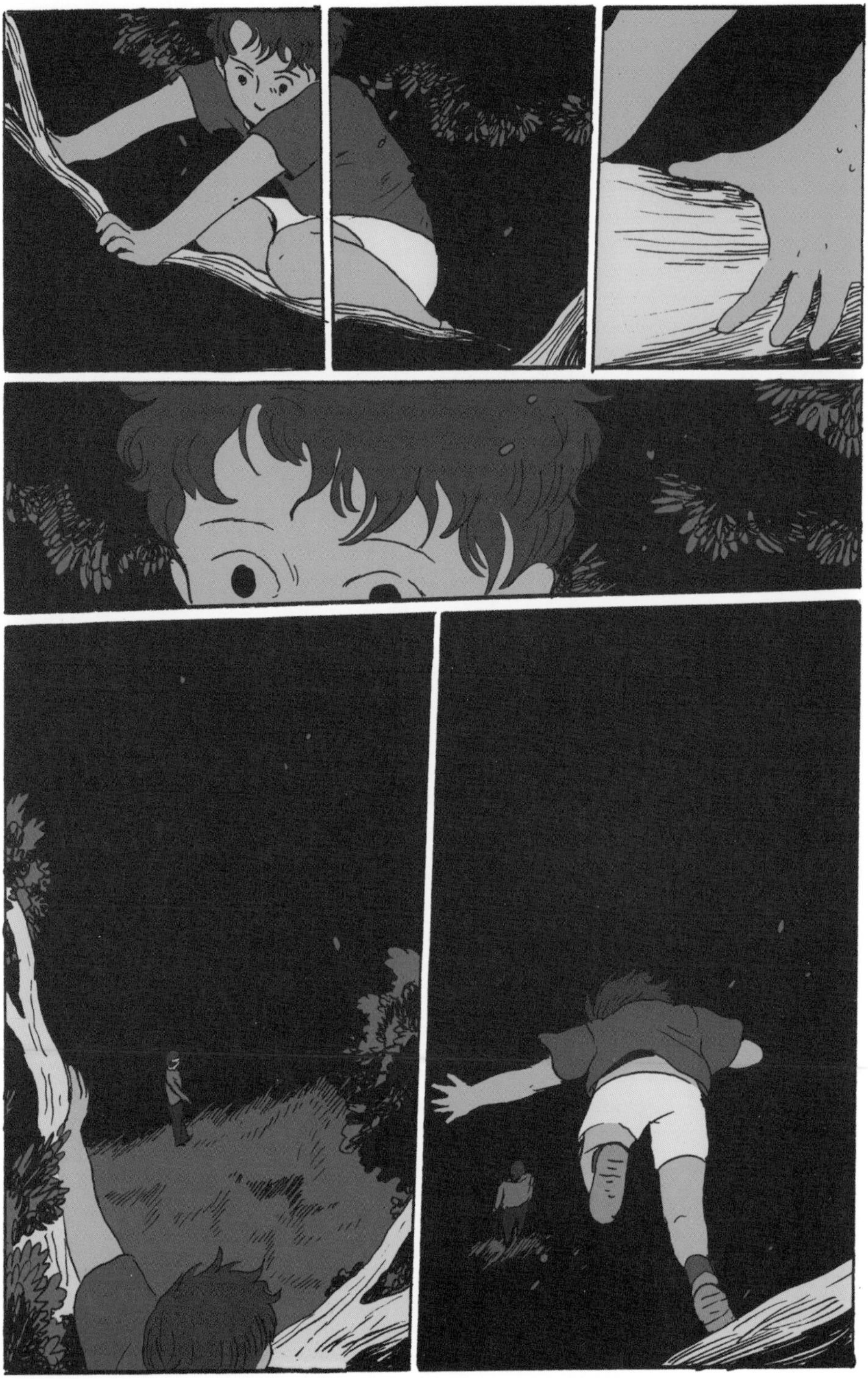

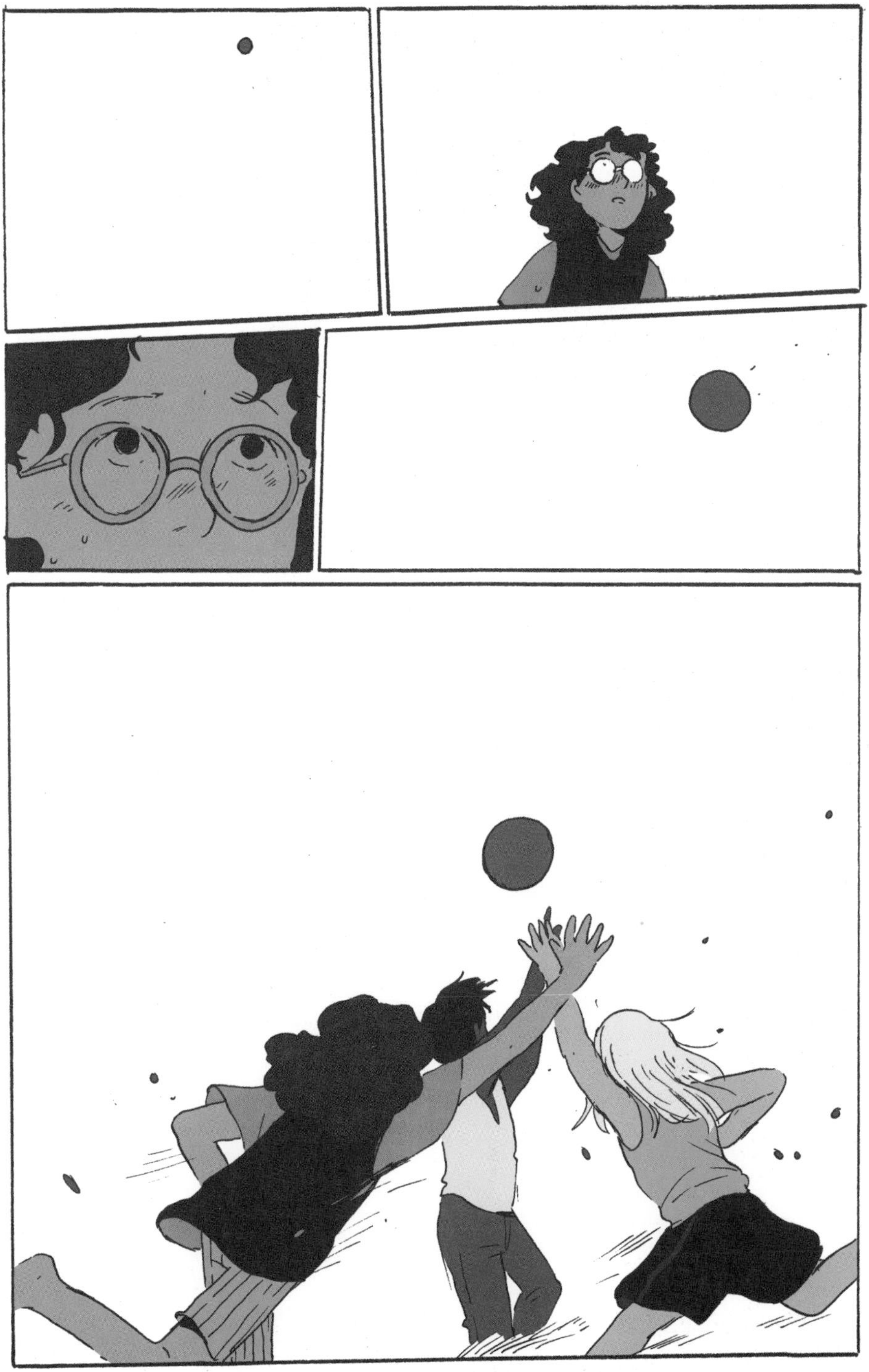

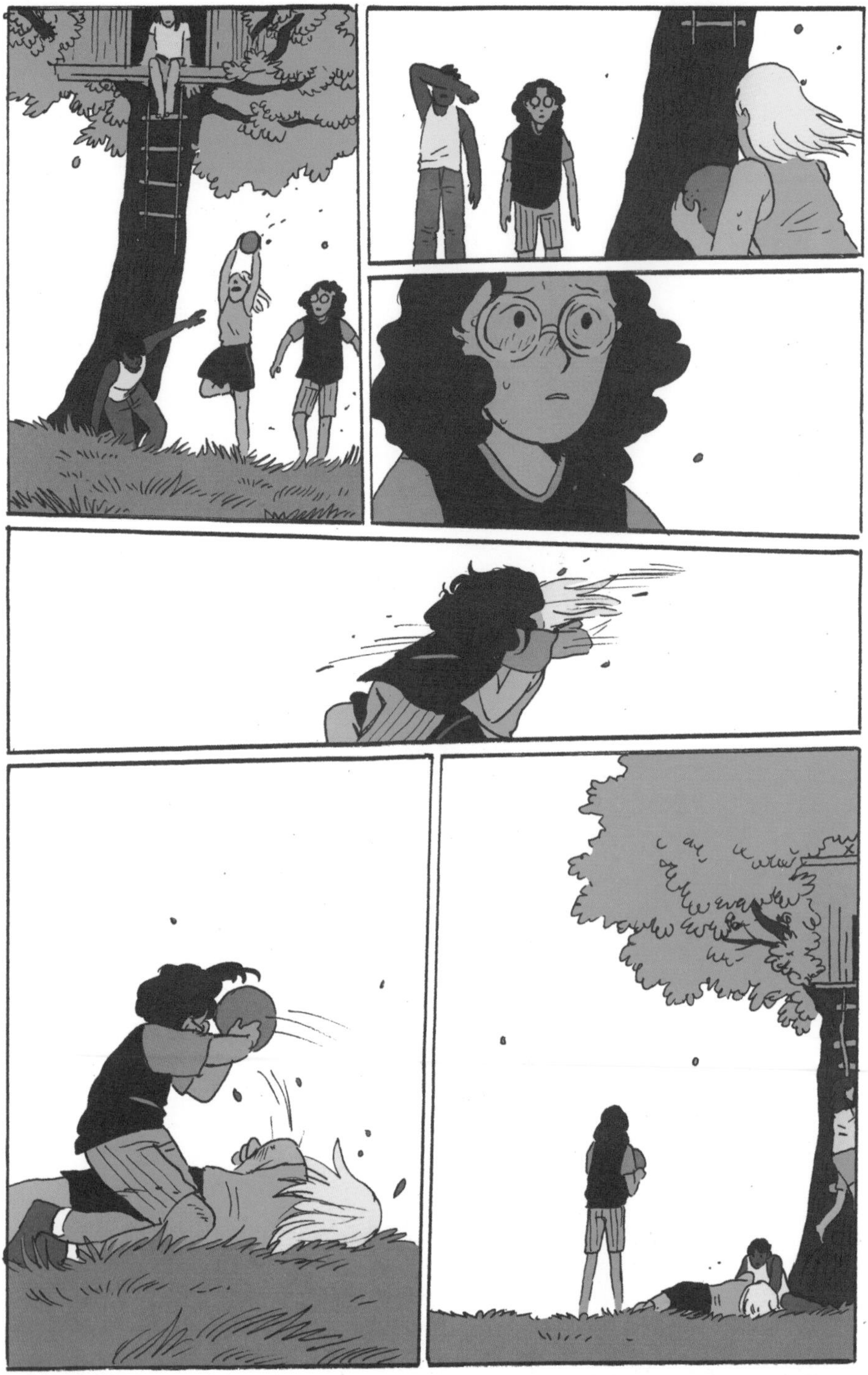

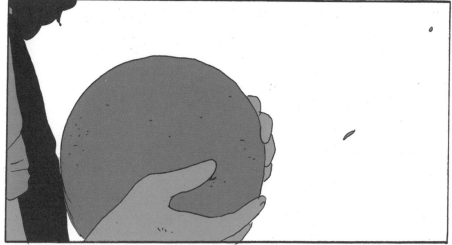

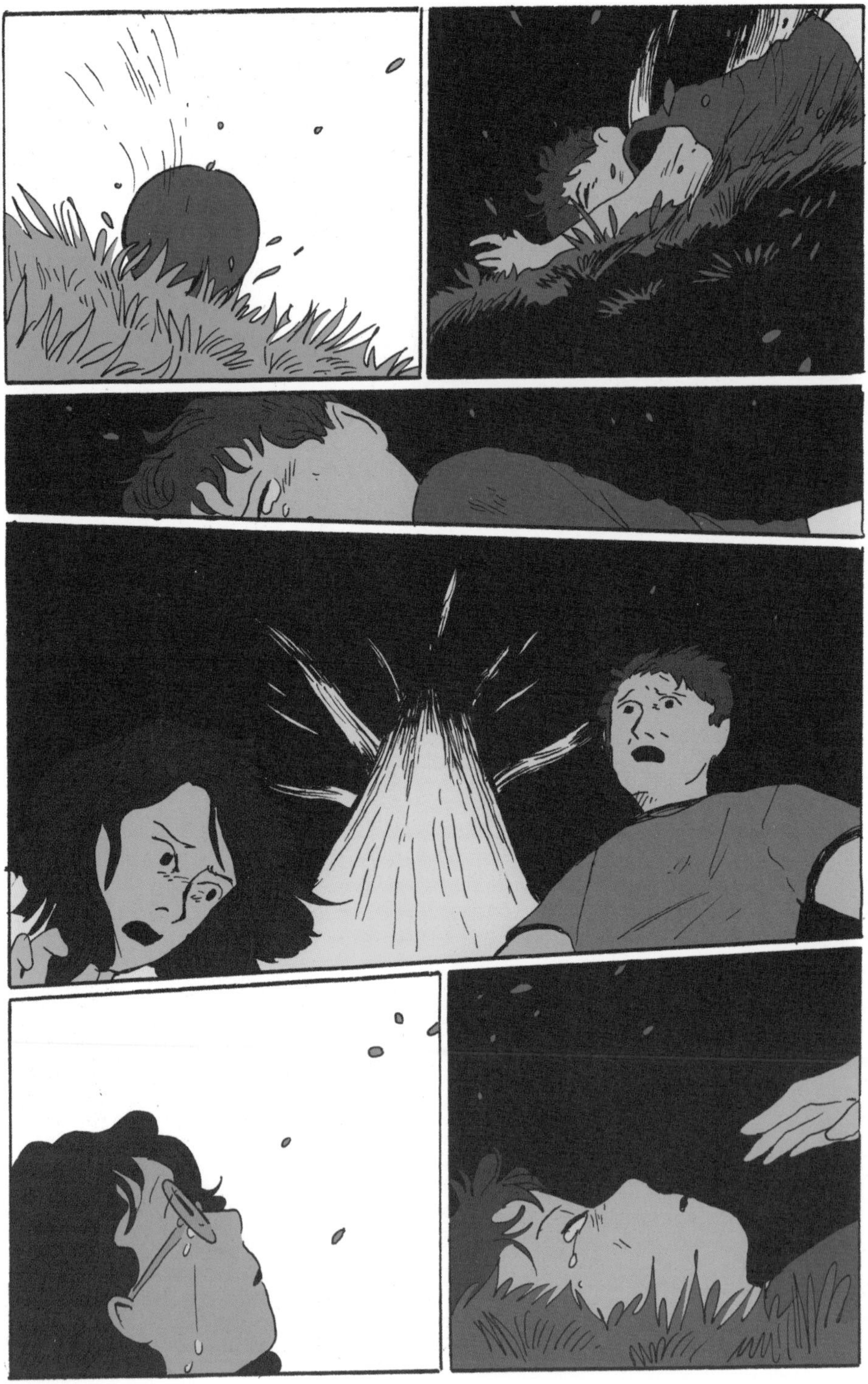

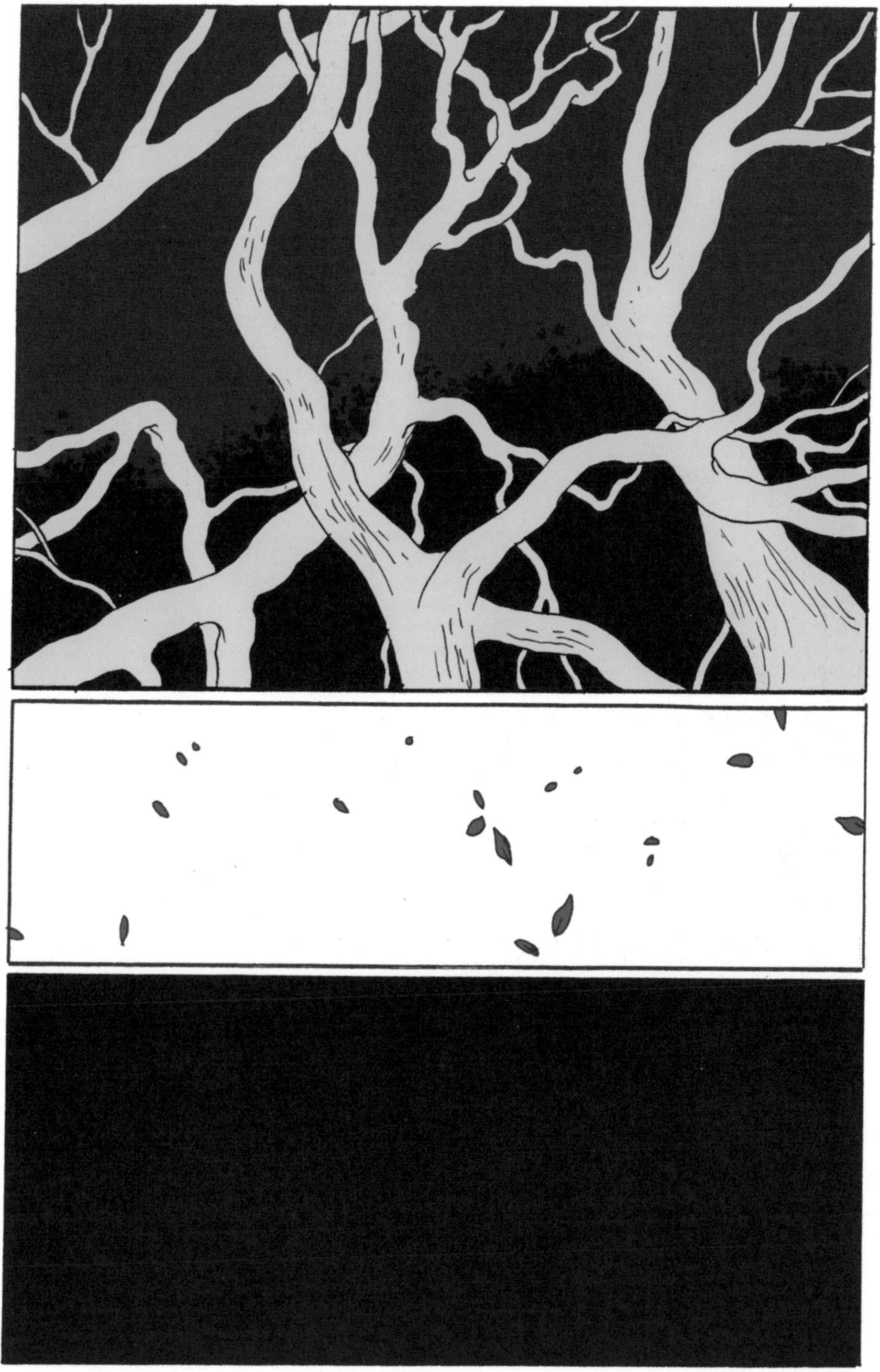

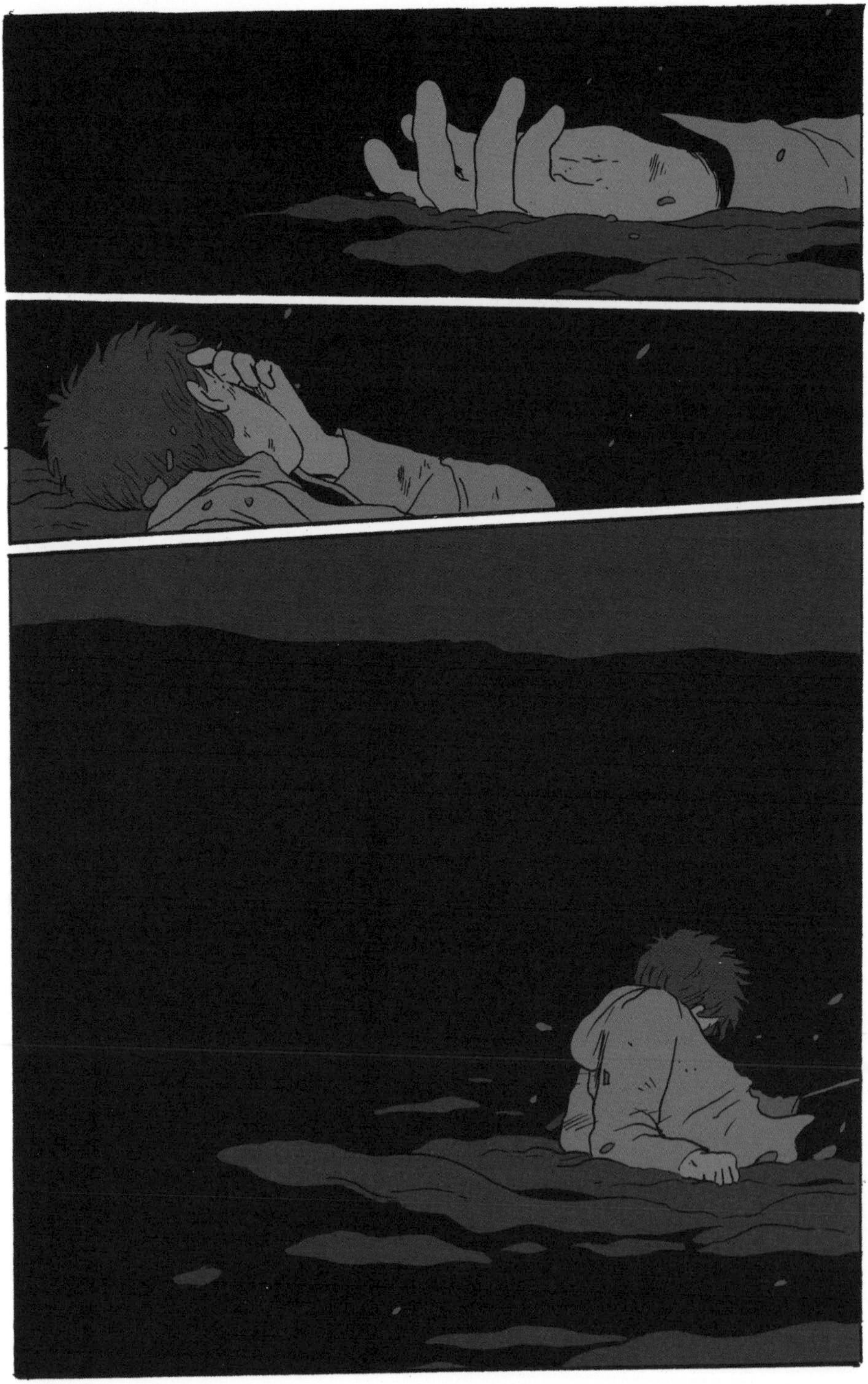

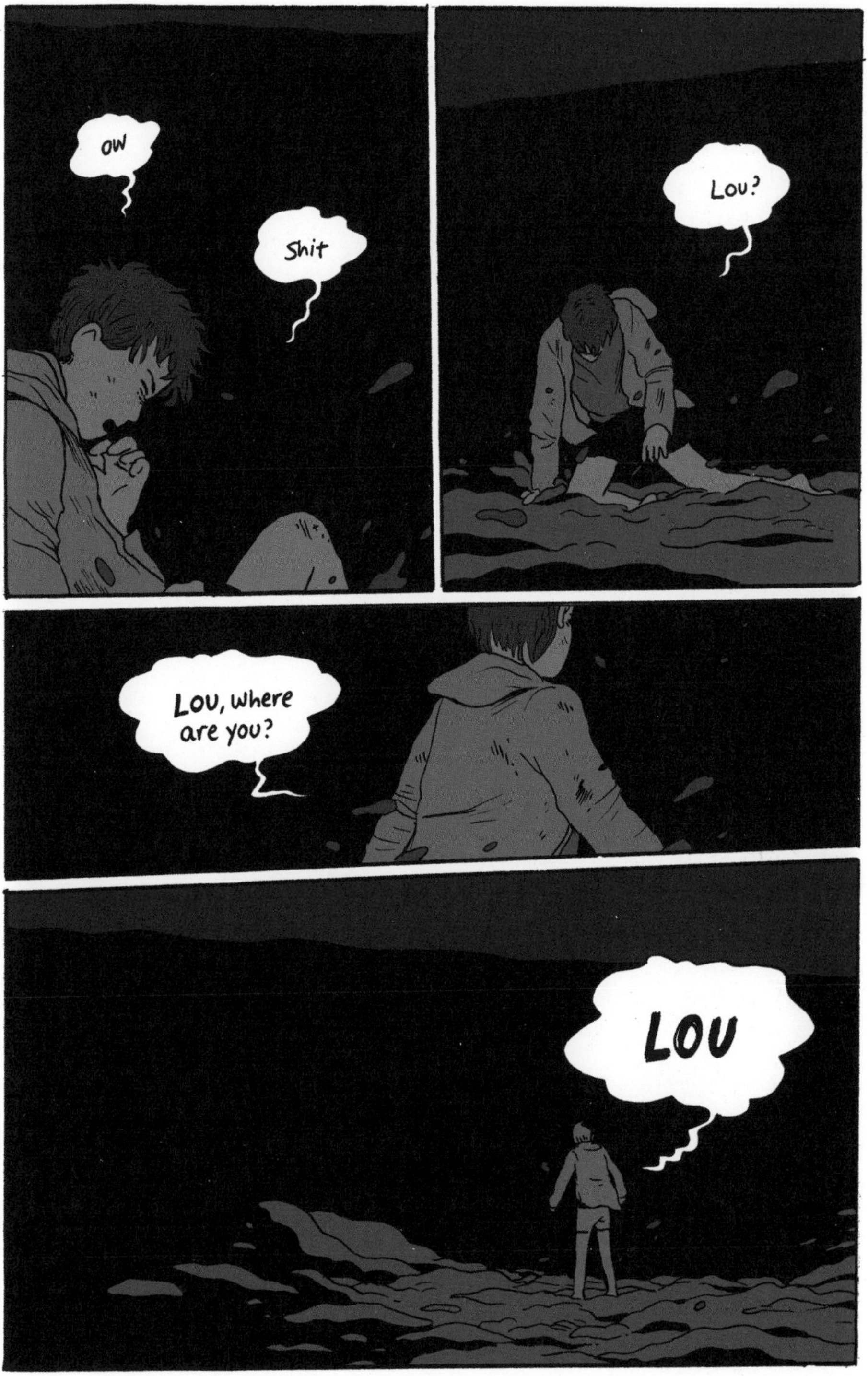
OW
Shit
Lou?
LOU, where are you?
LOU

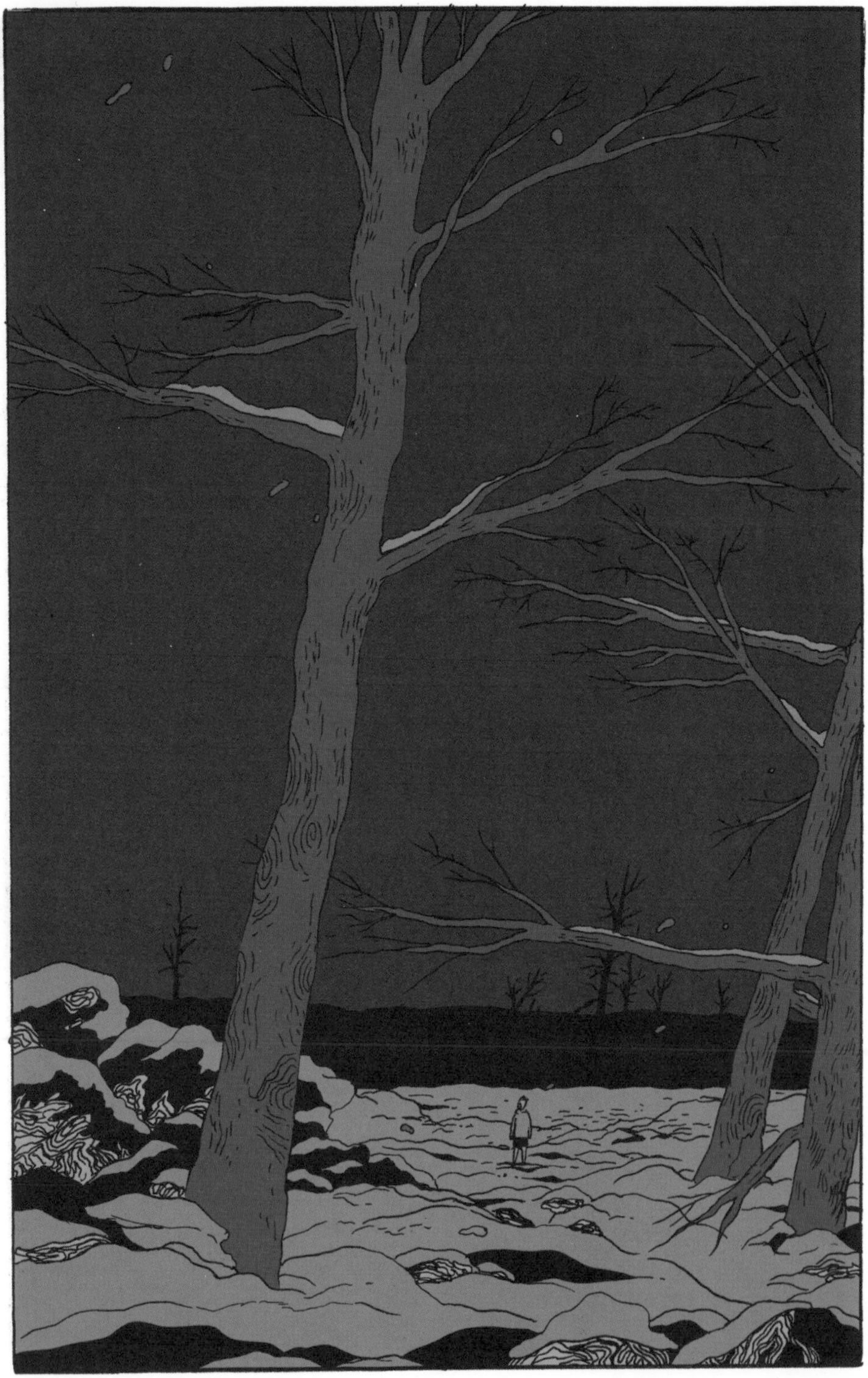

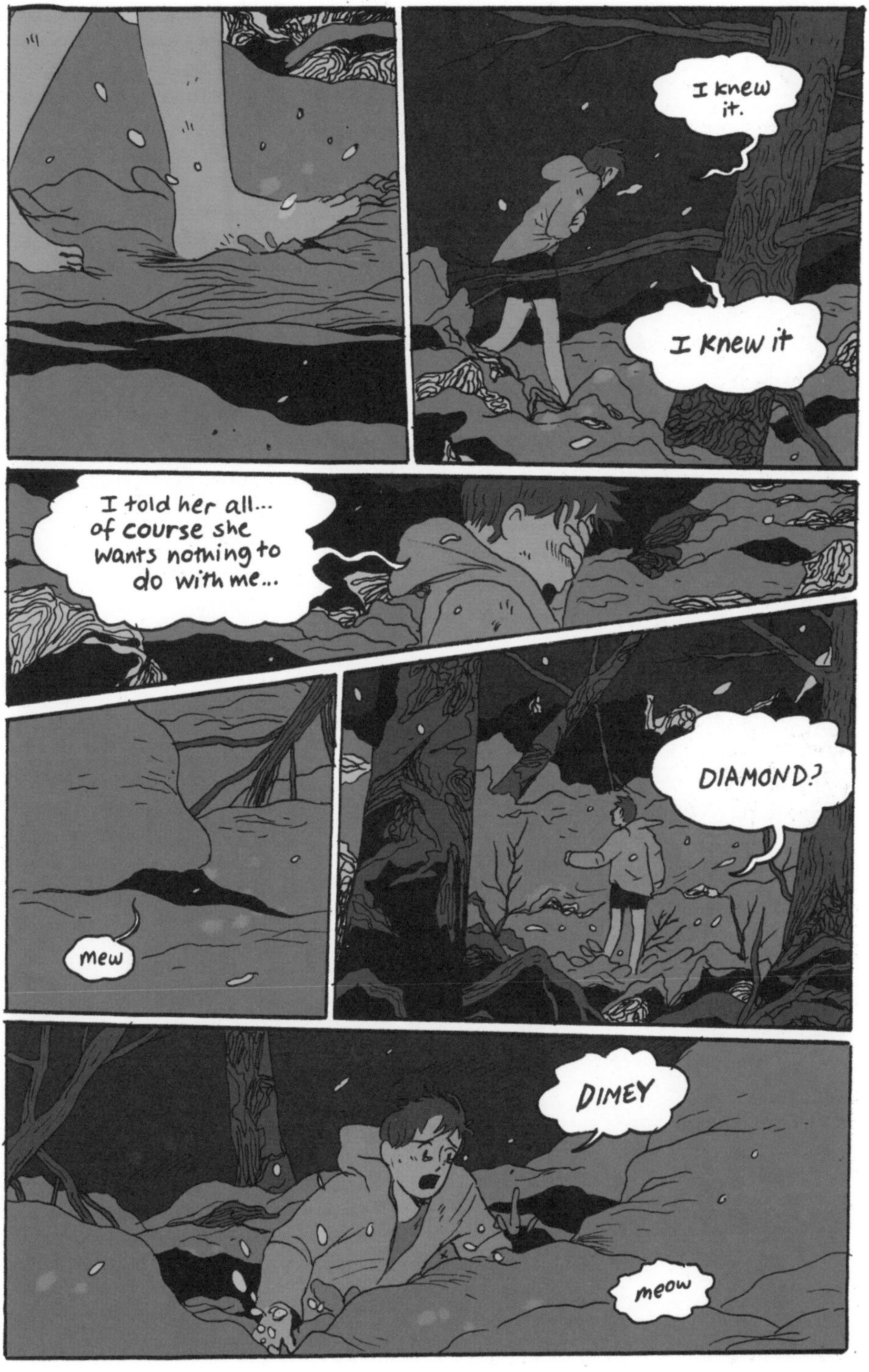
I knew it.
I knew it
I told her all... of course she wants nothing to do with me...
mew
DIAMOND?
DIMEY
meow

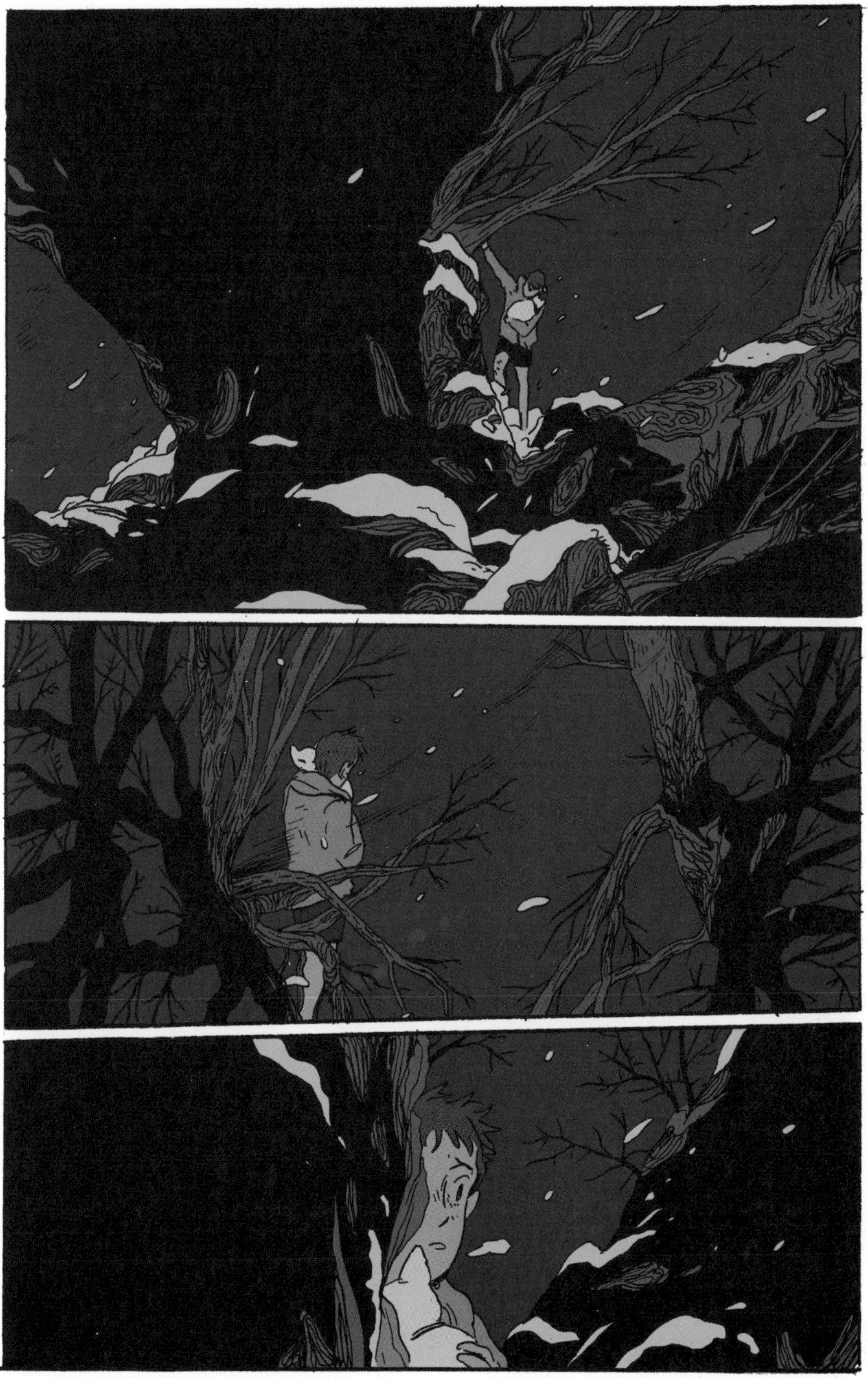

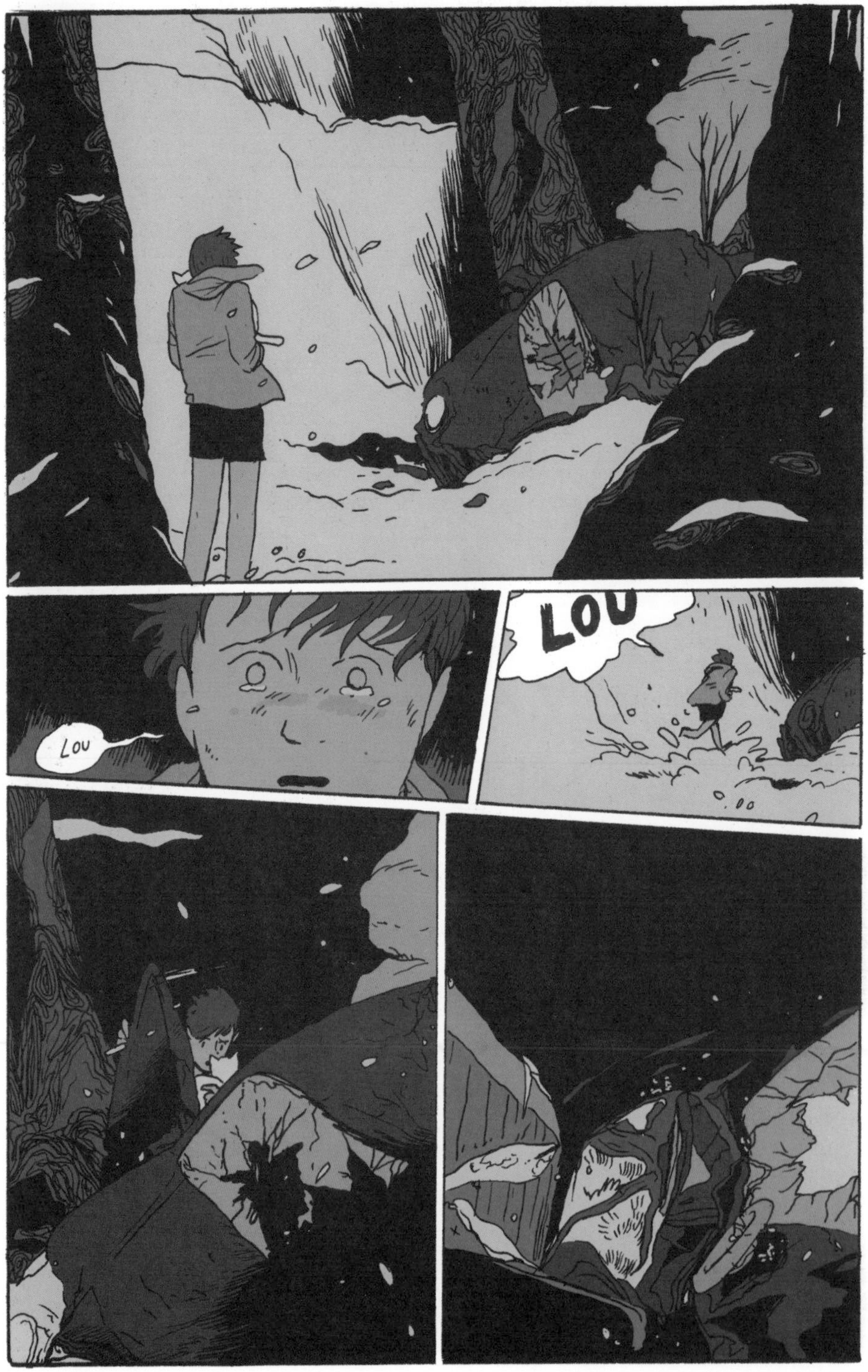
LOU
LOU

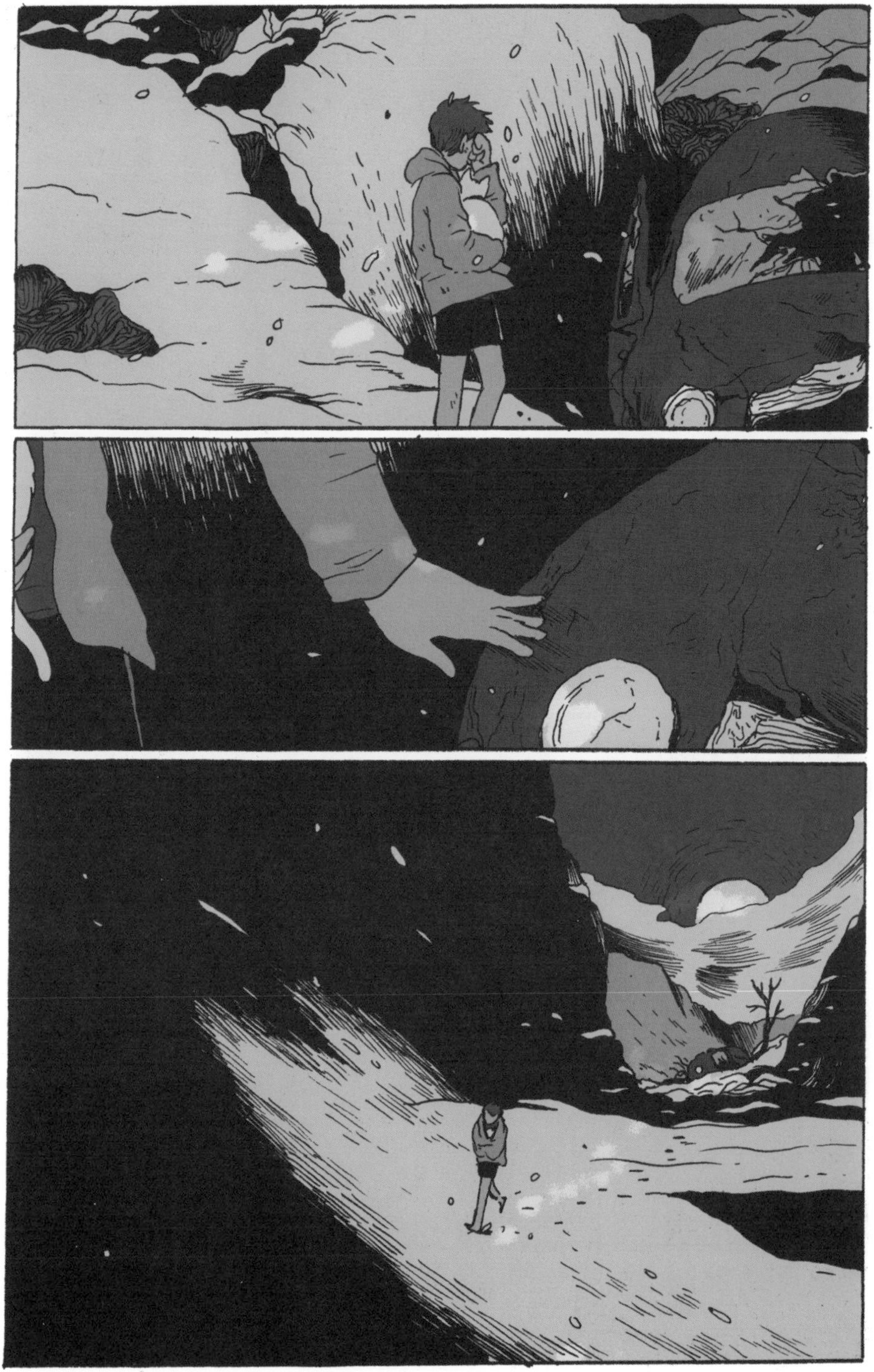

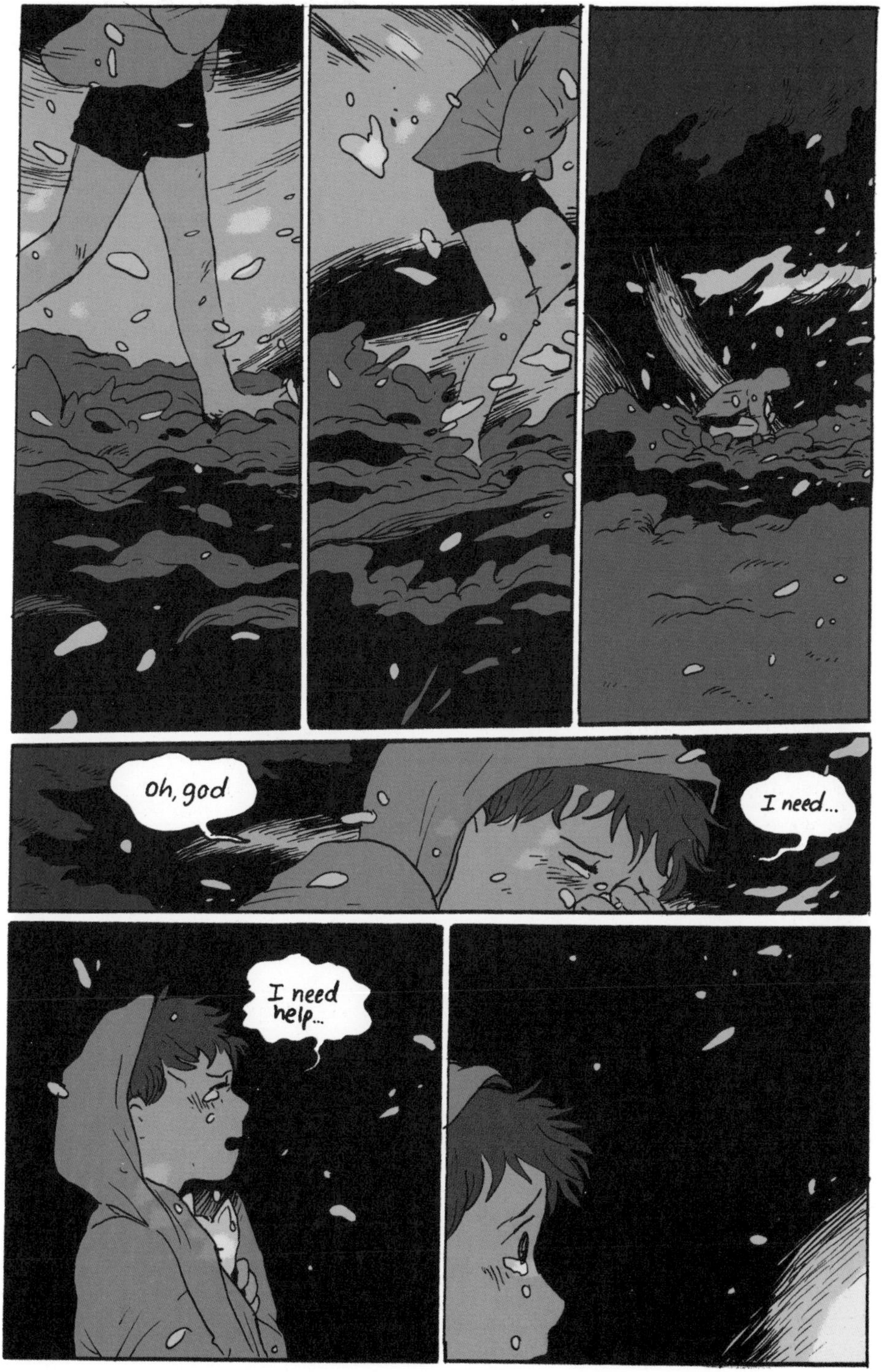
oh, god
I need...
I need help...

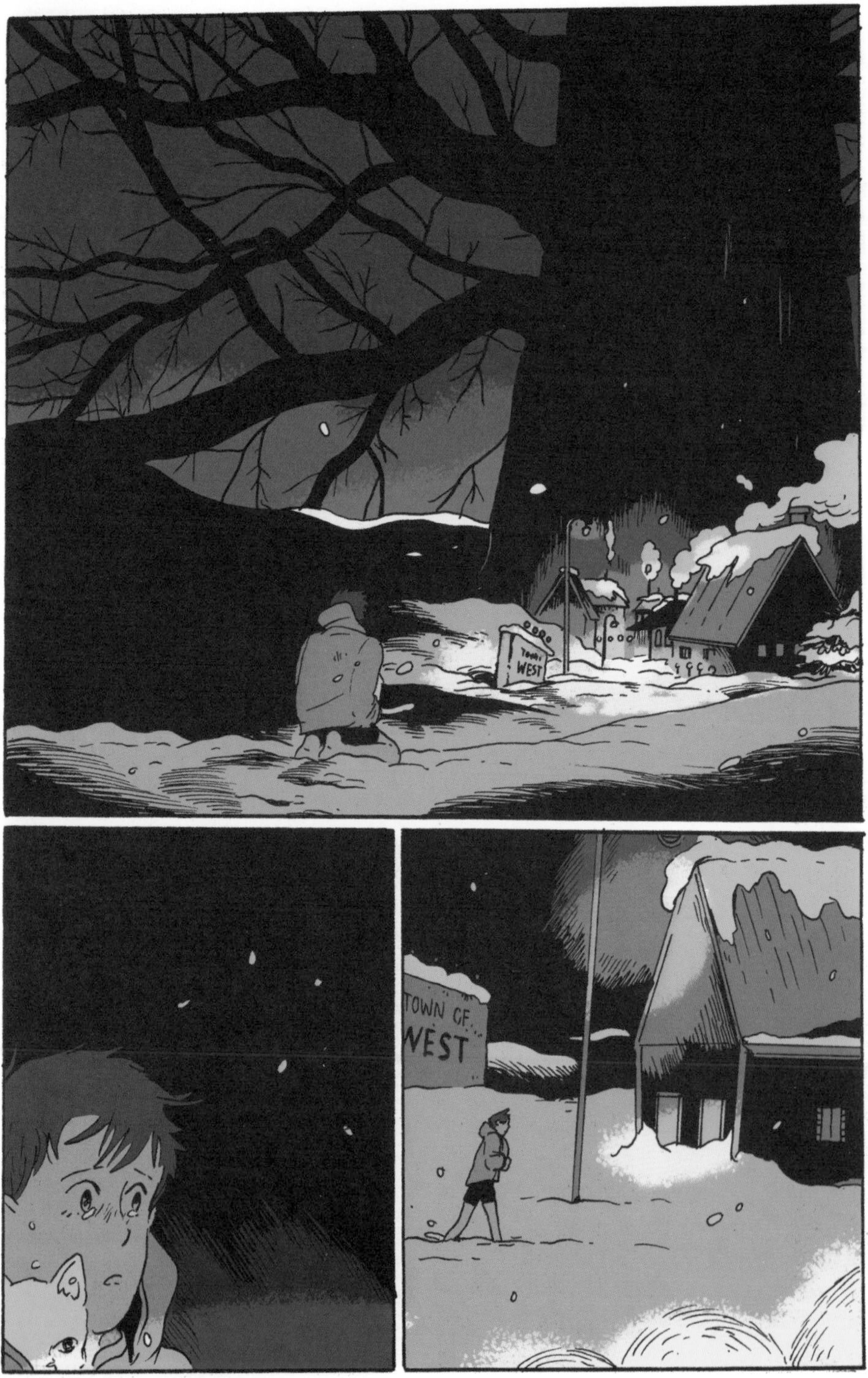
WEST
TOWN OF
WEST

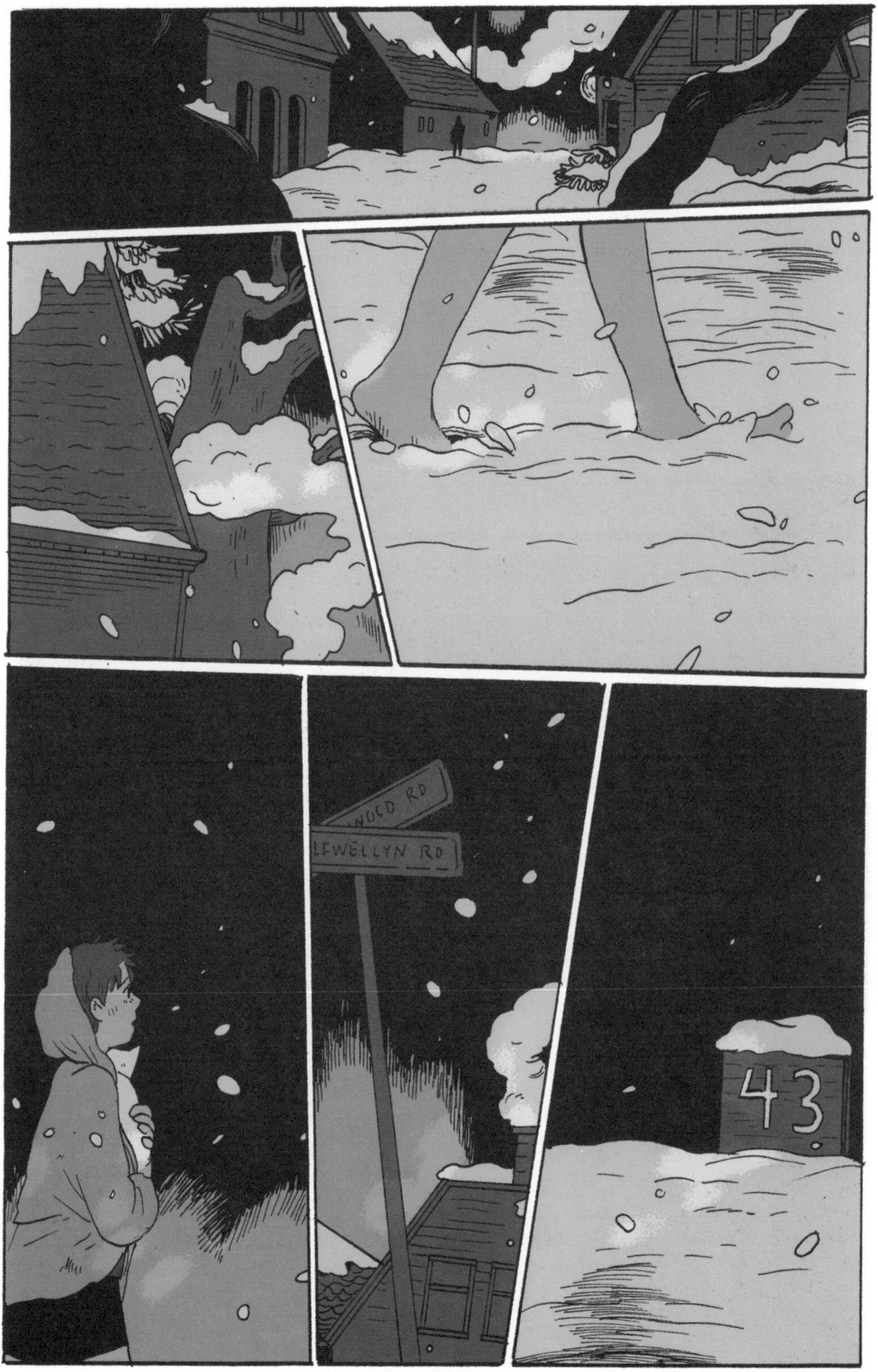
LEWELLYN RD
43

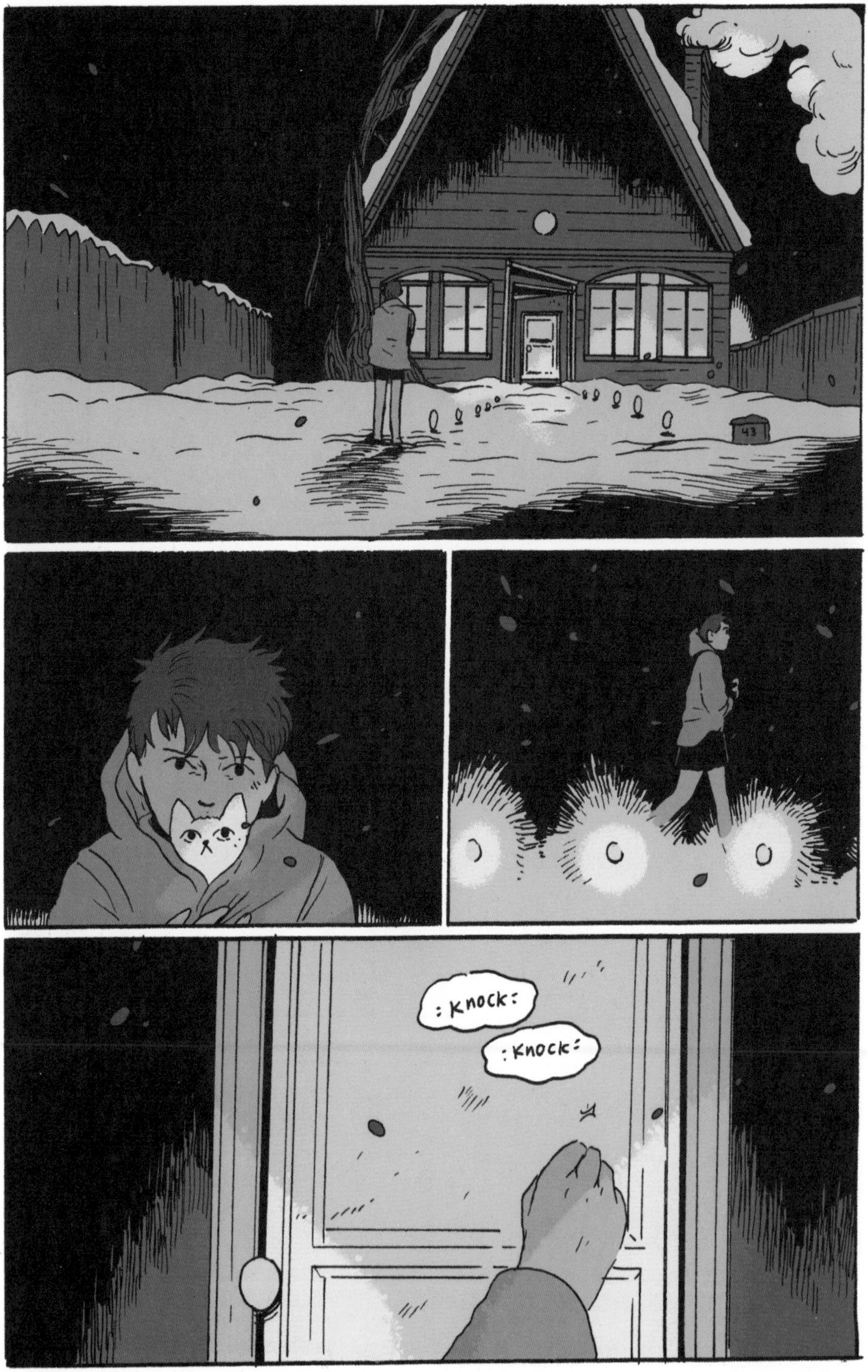
43
:Knock:
:Knock:

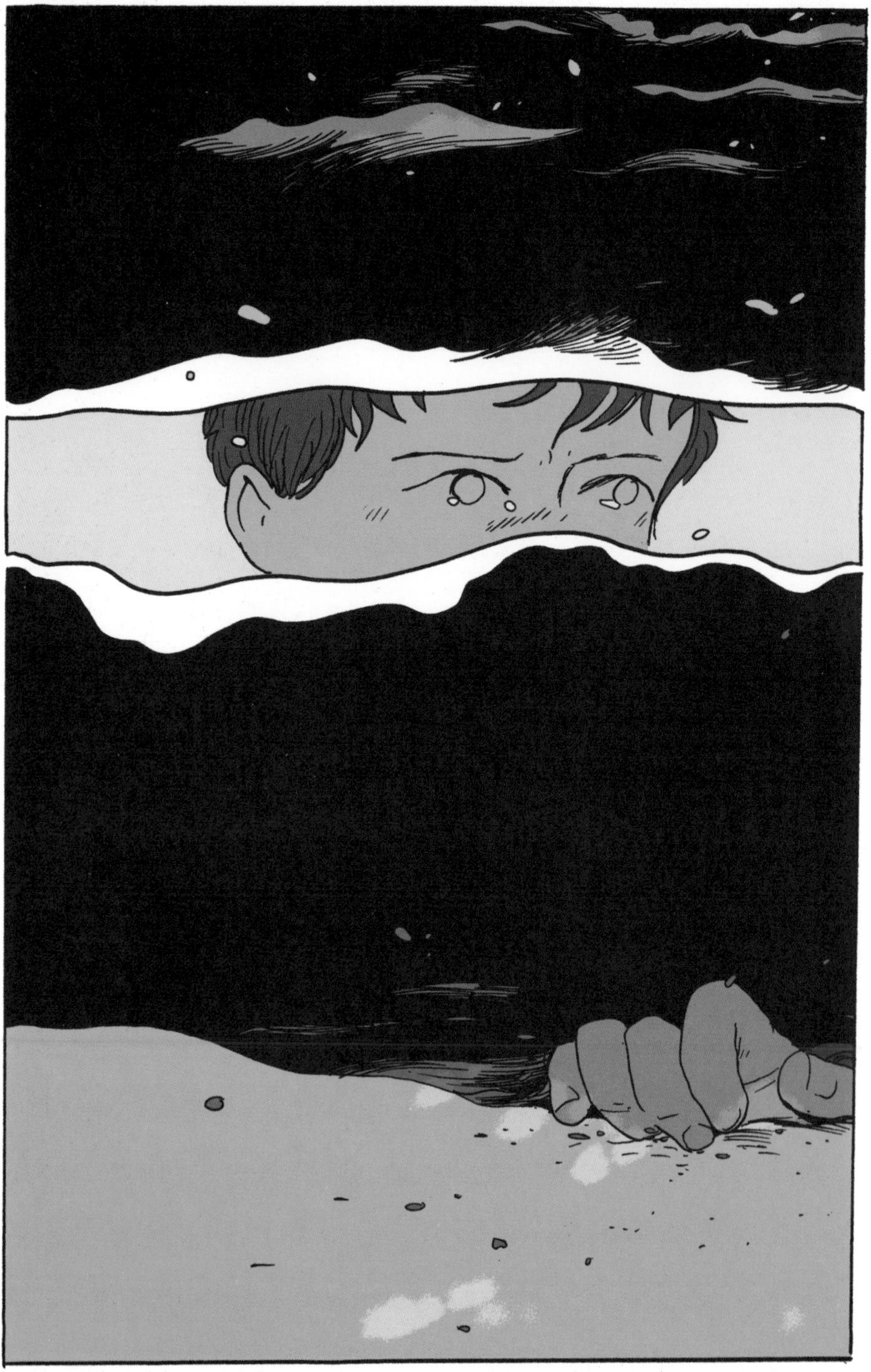

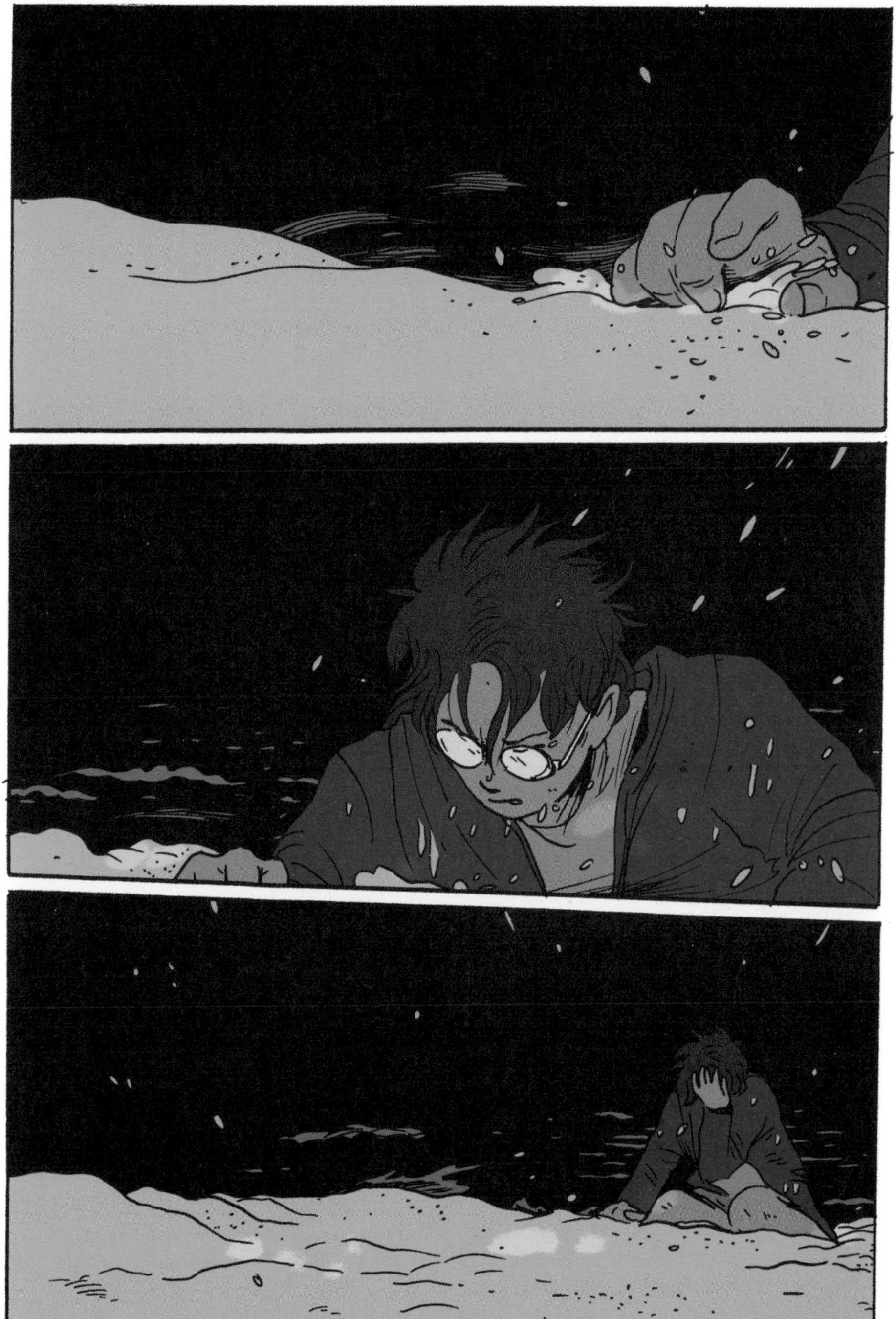

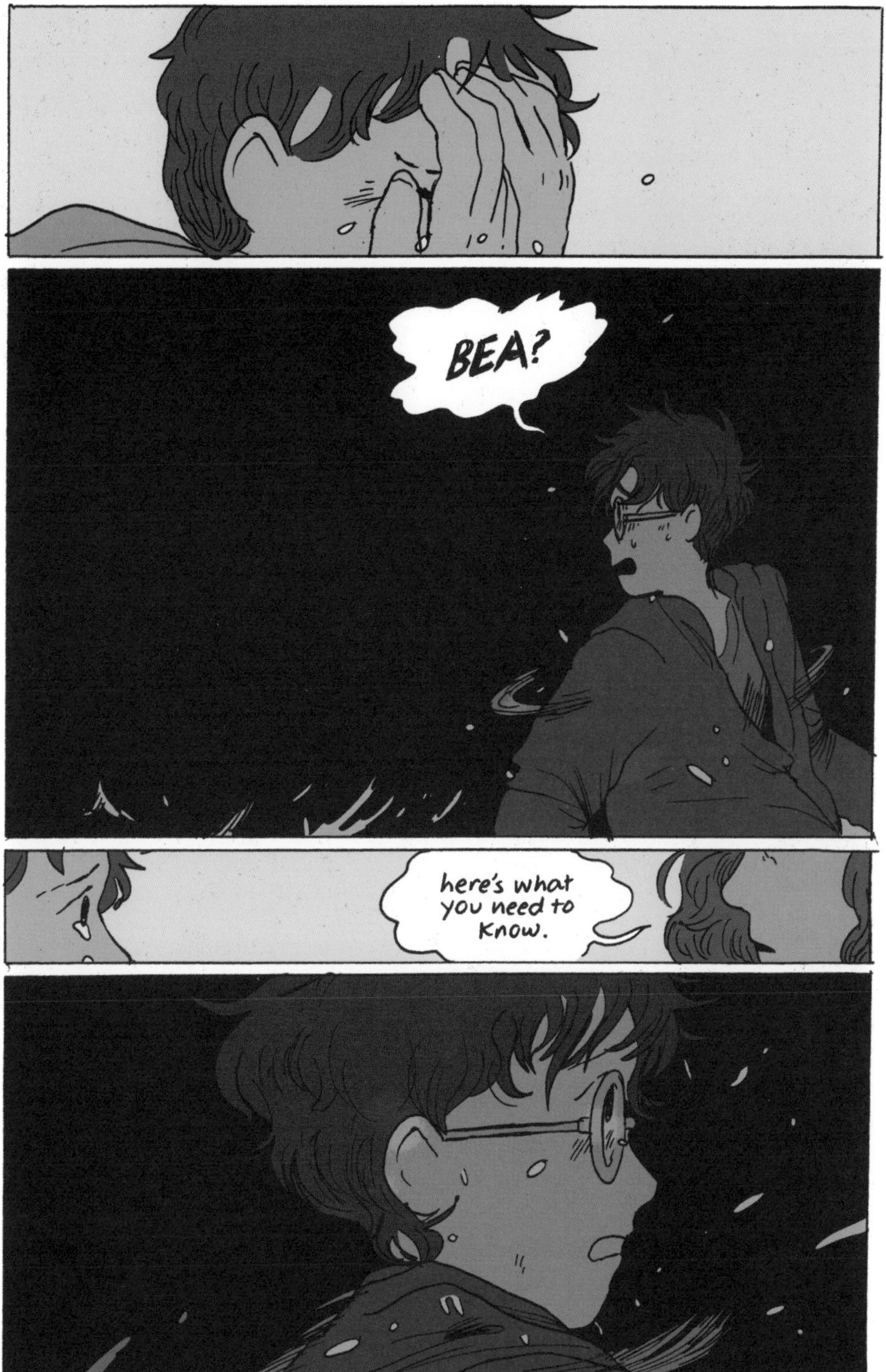
BEA?
here's what you need to know.

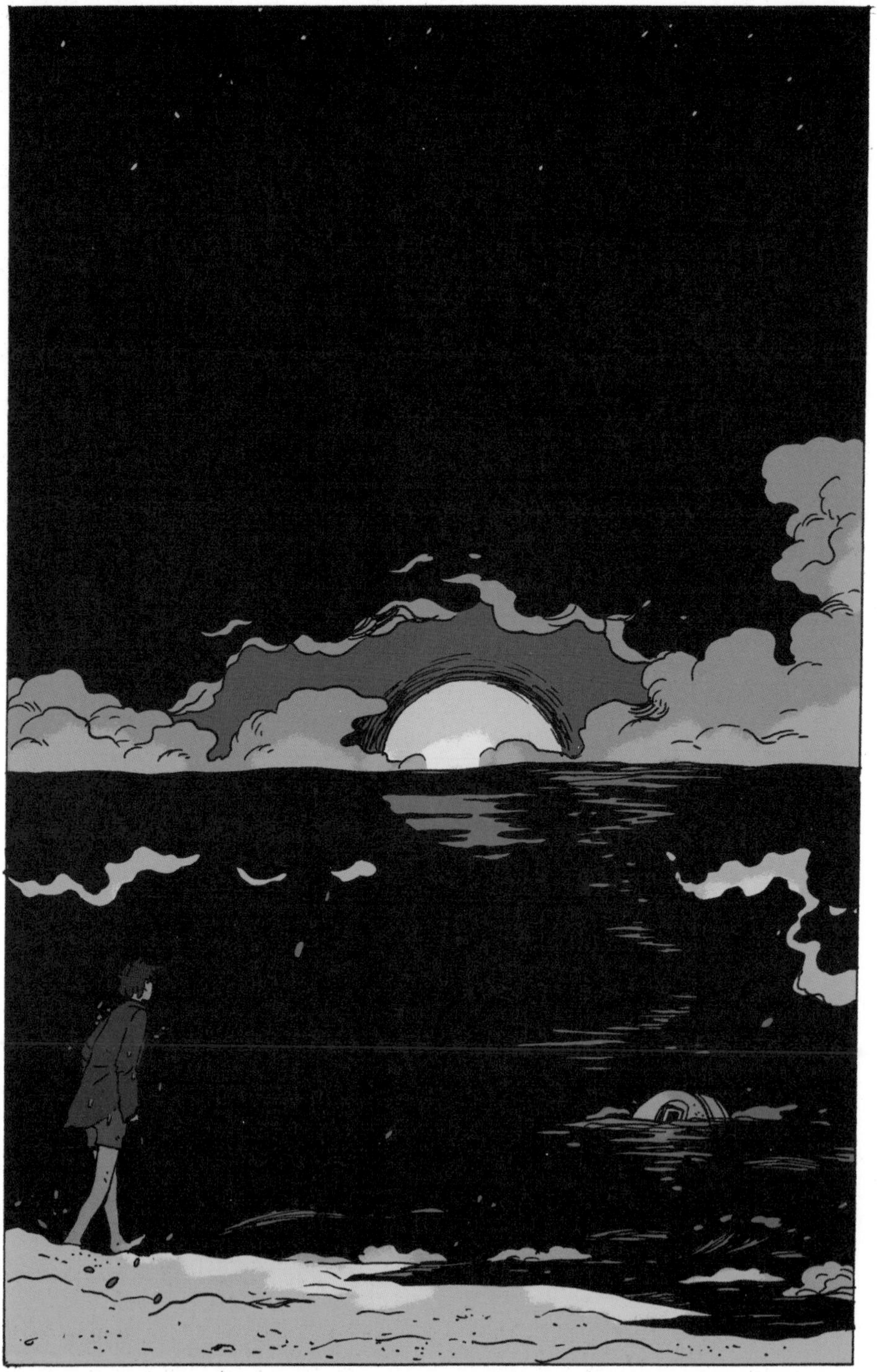

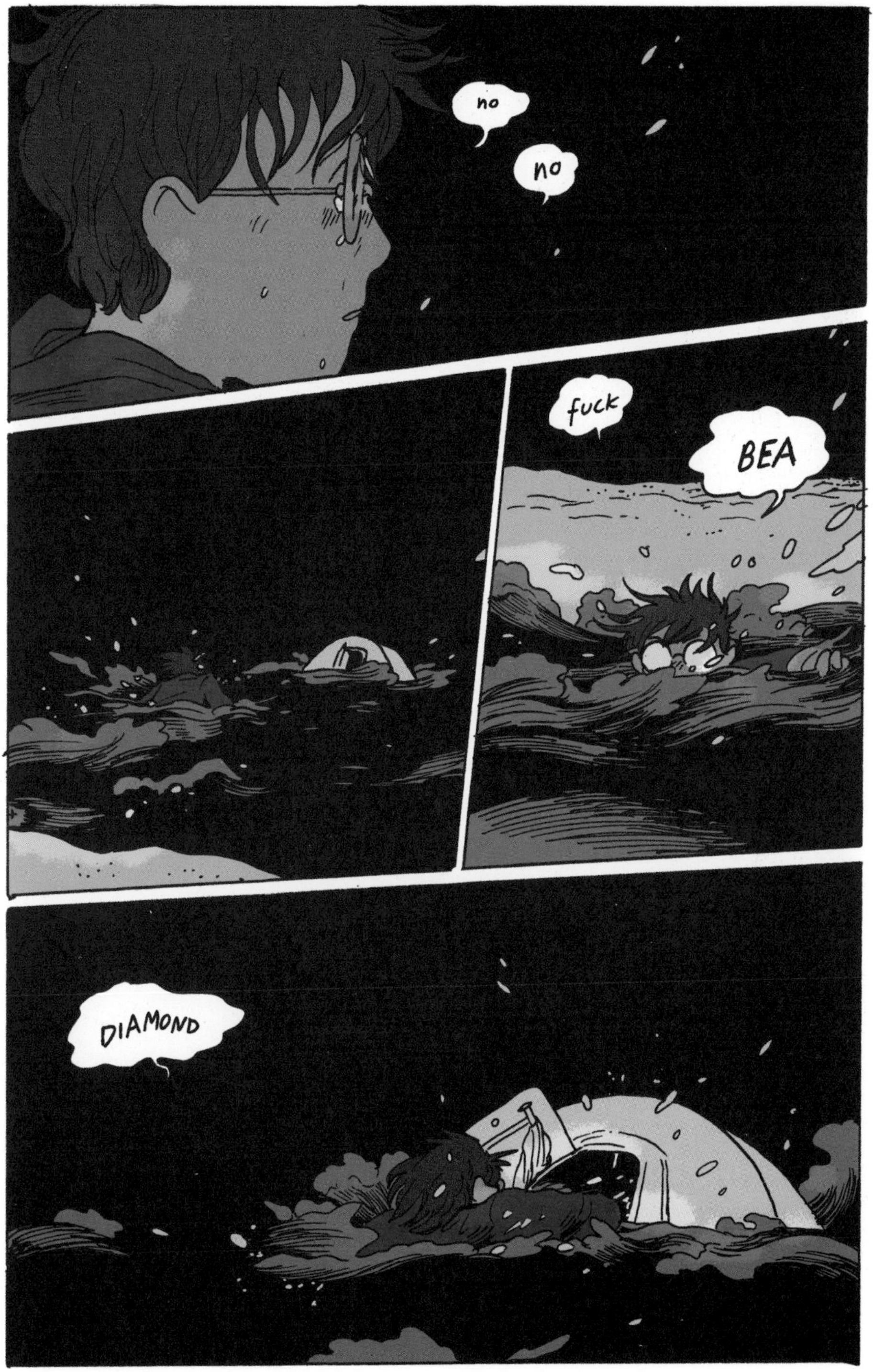
no
no
fuck
BEA
DIAMOND

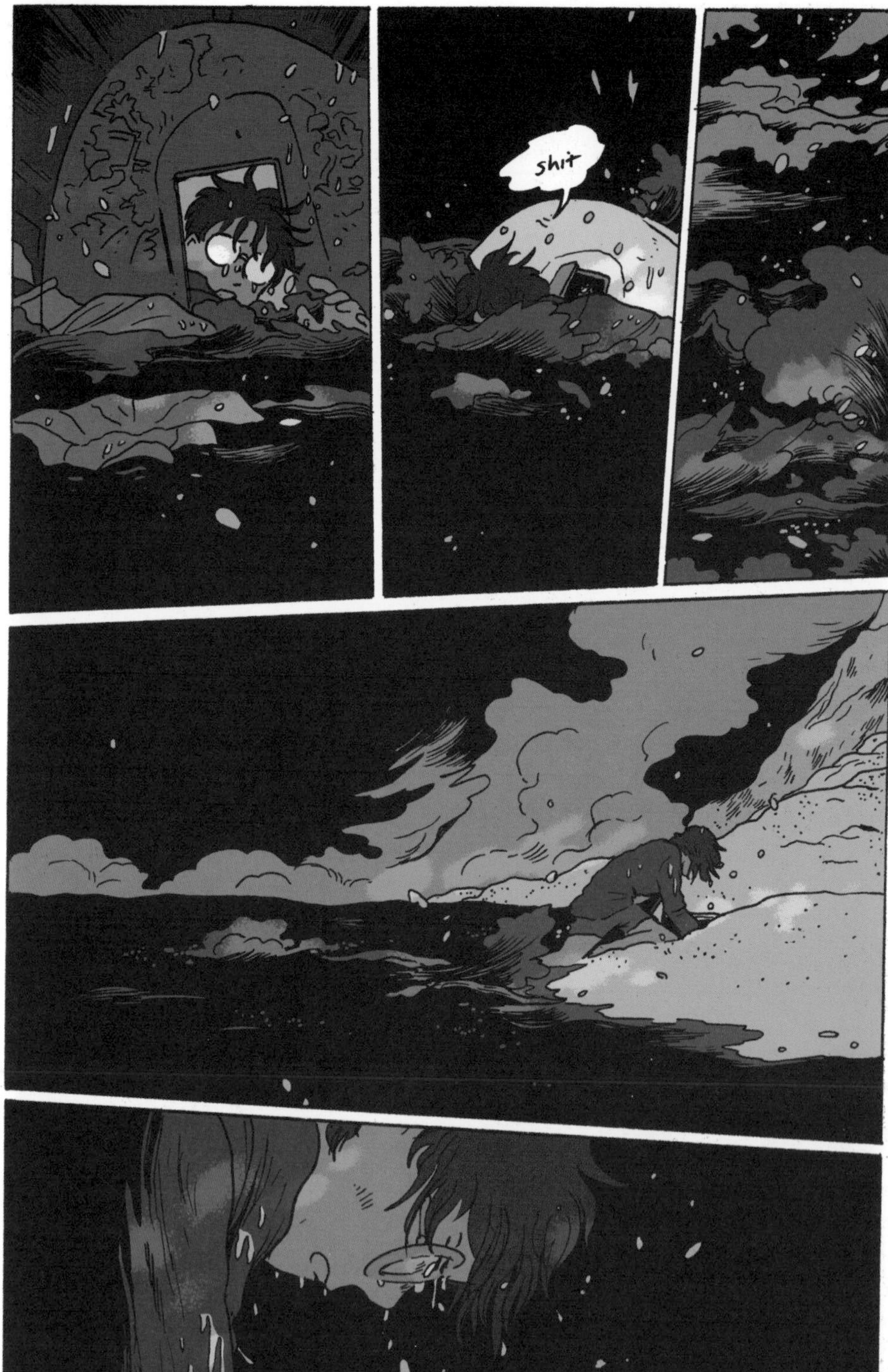
shit

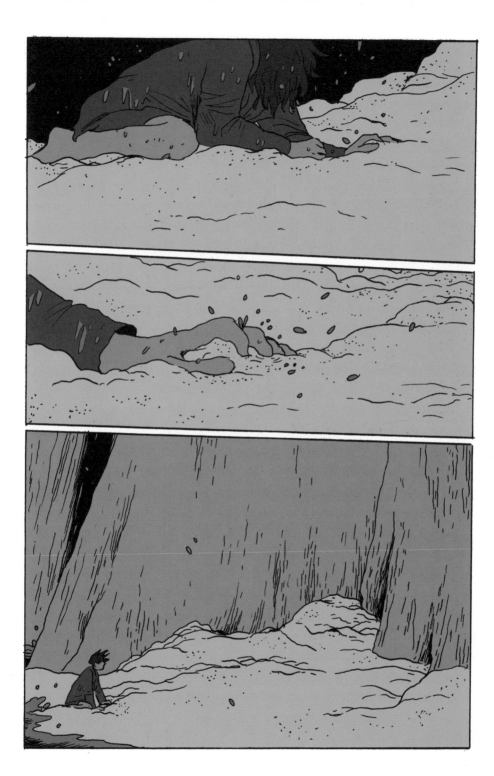

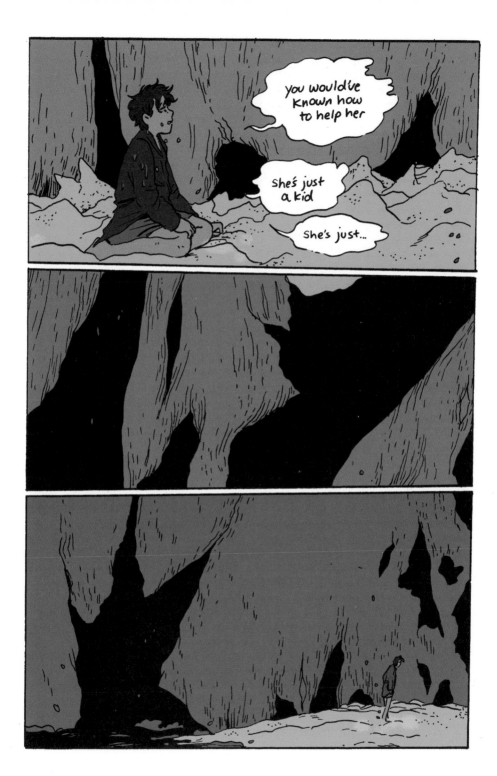

267

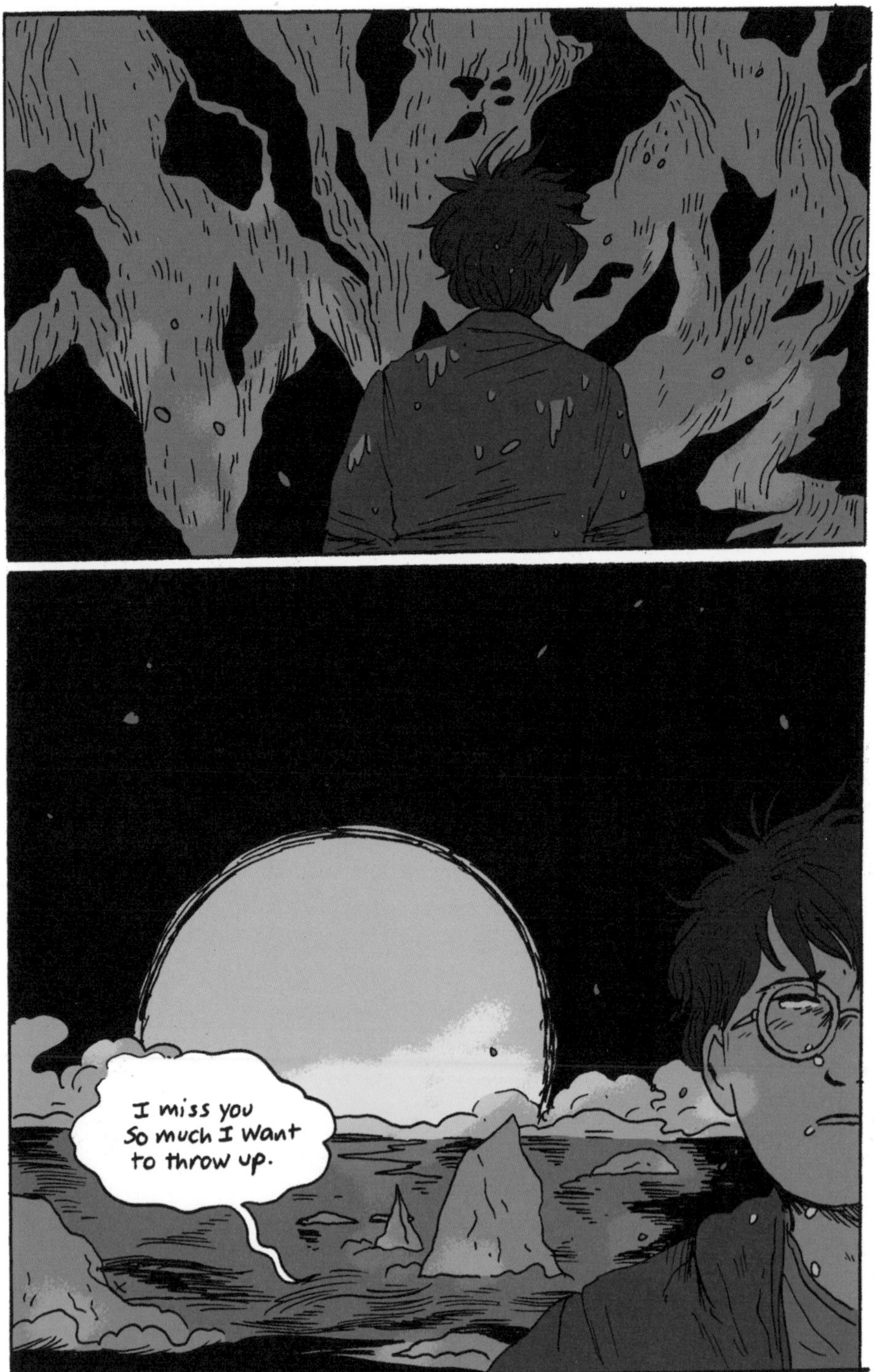
I miss you So much I want to throw up.

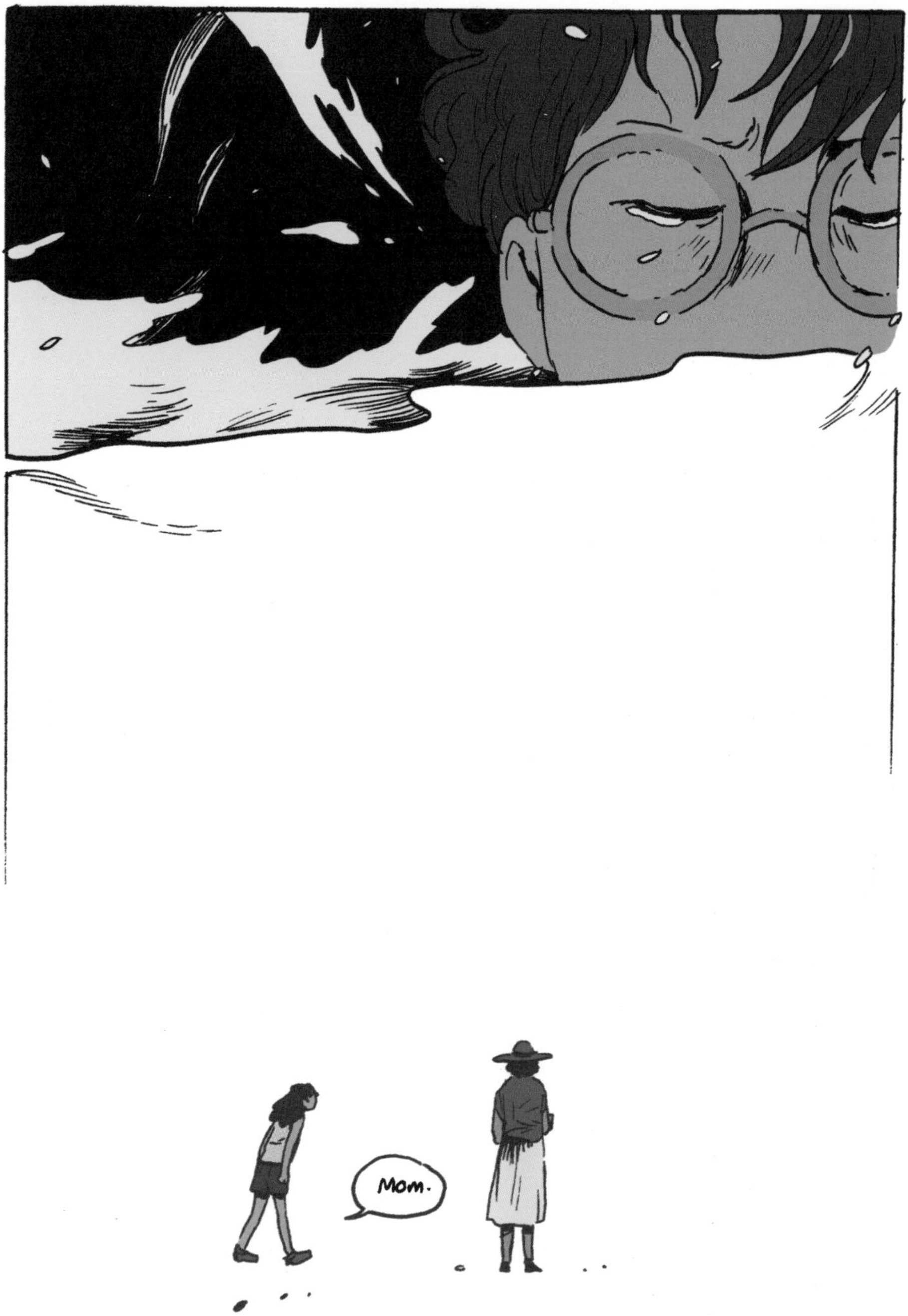

Mom.
MOM.

270

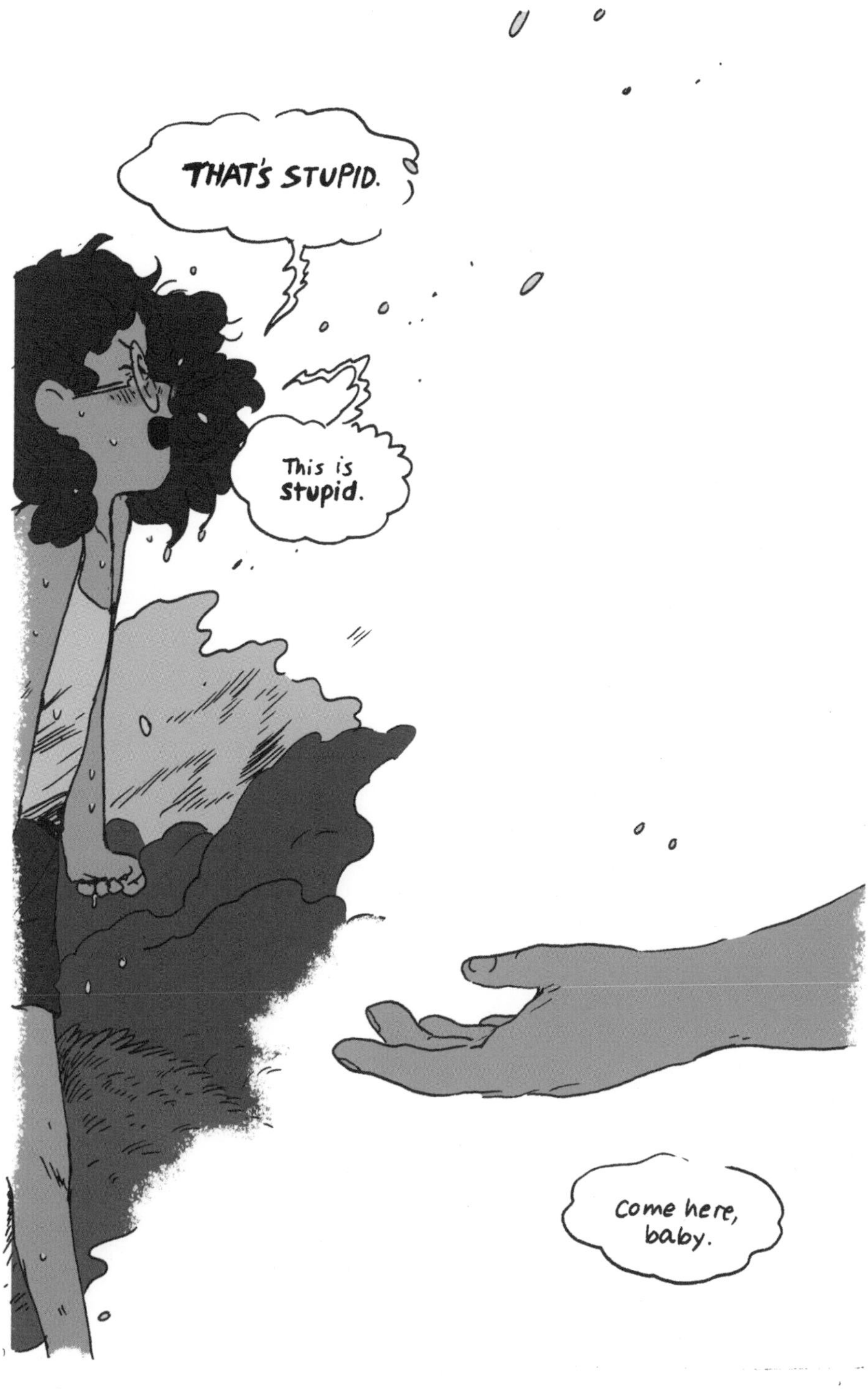
THAT'S STUPID.
This is stupid.
Come here, baby.

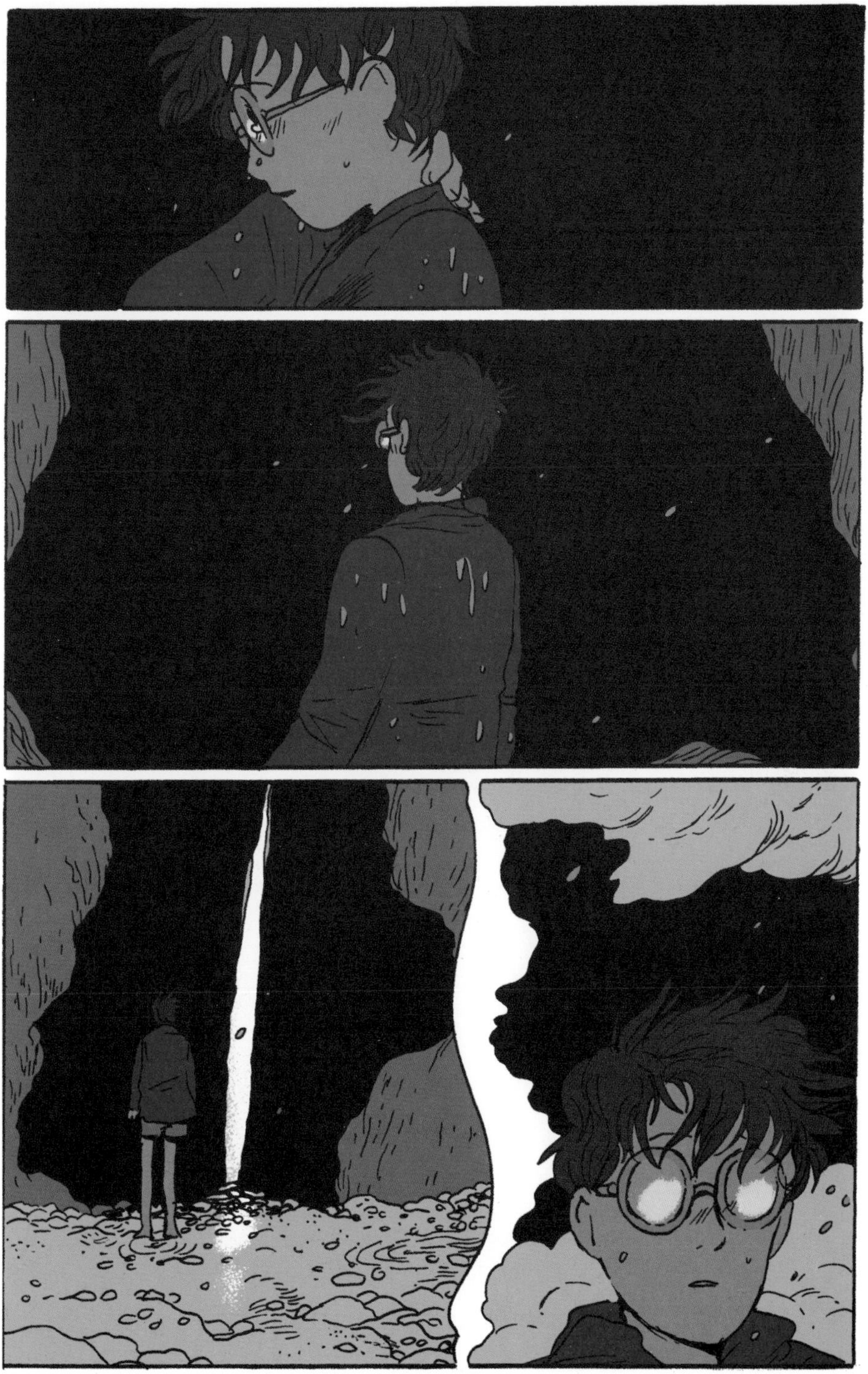

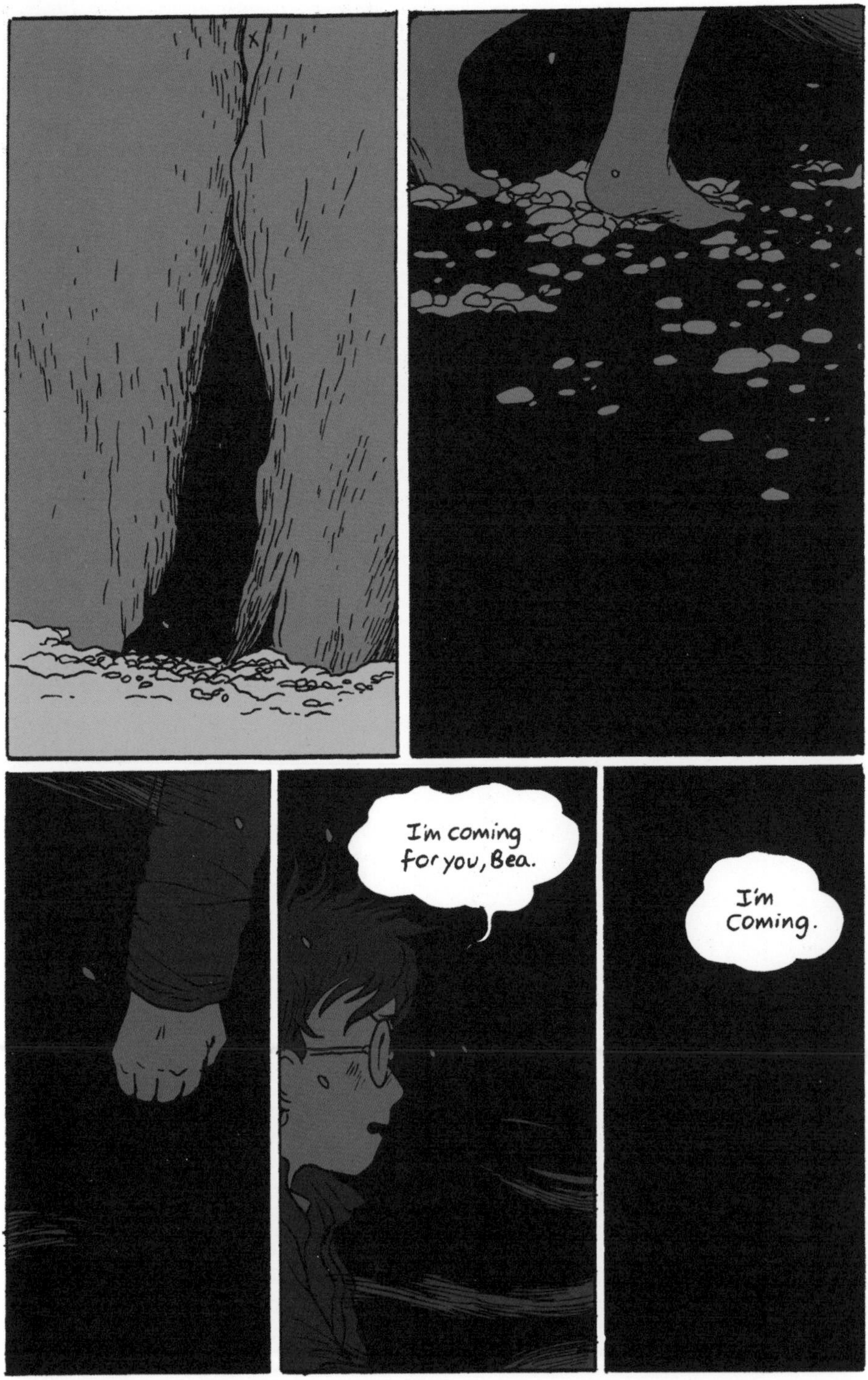
I'm coming for you, Bea.
I'm Coming.

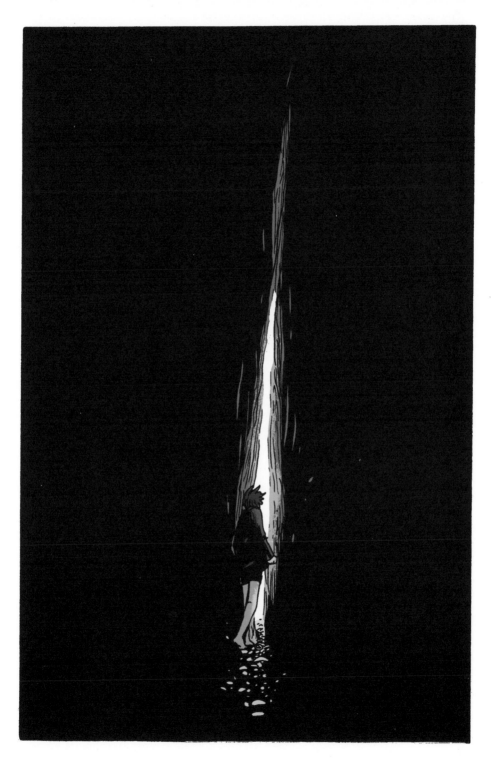

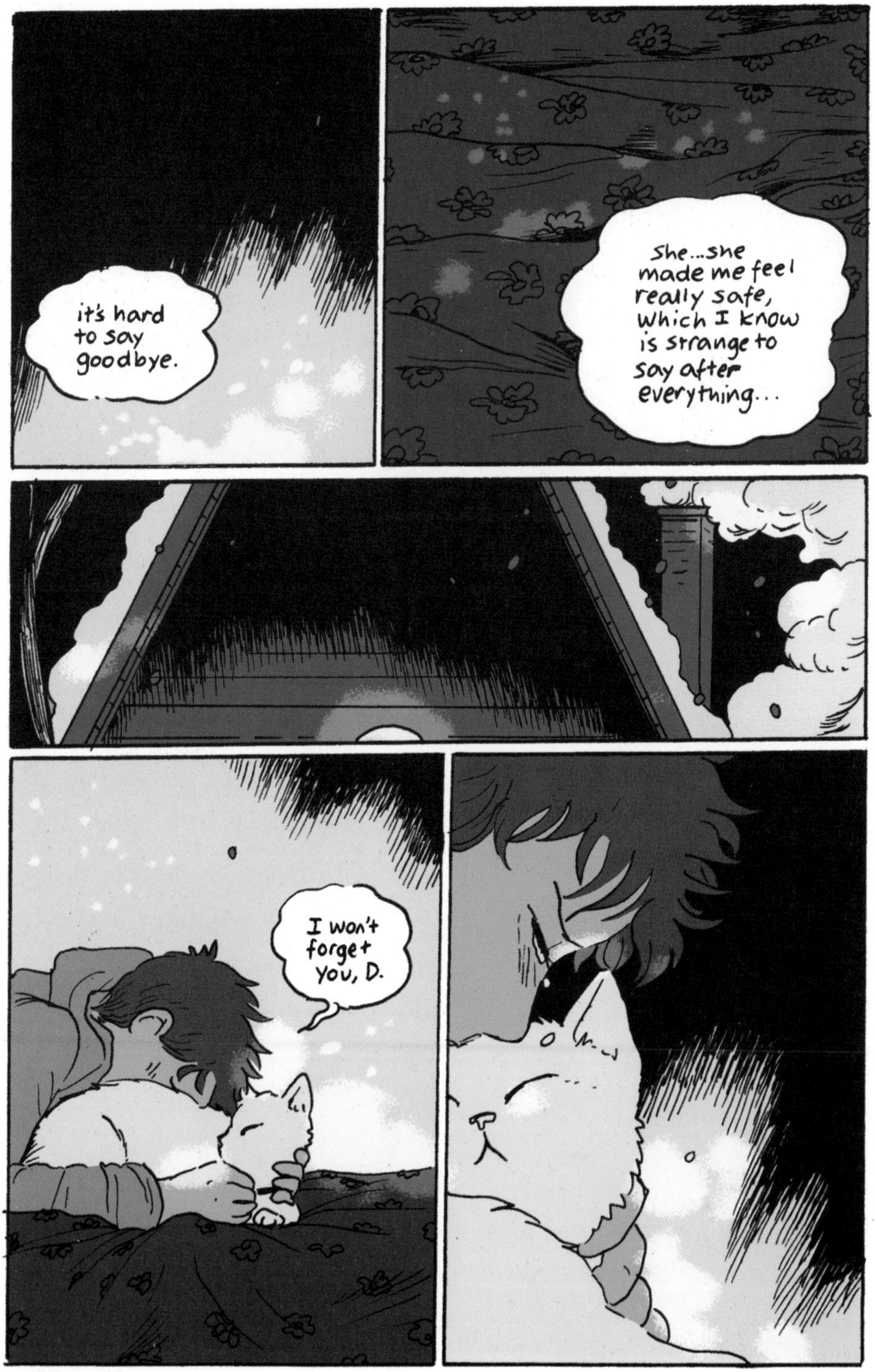
it's hard to say goodbye.
She...she made me feel really safe, which I know is strange to say after everything...
I won't forget you, D.

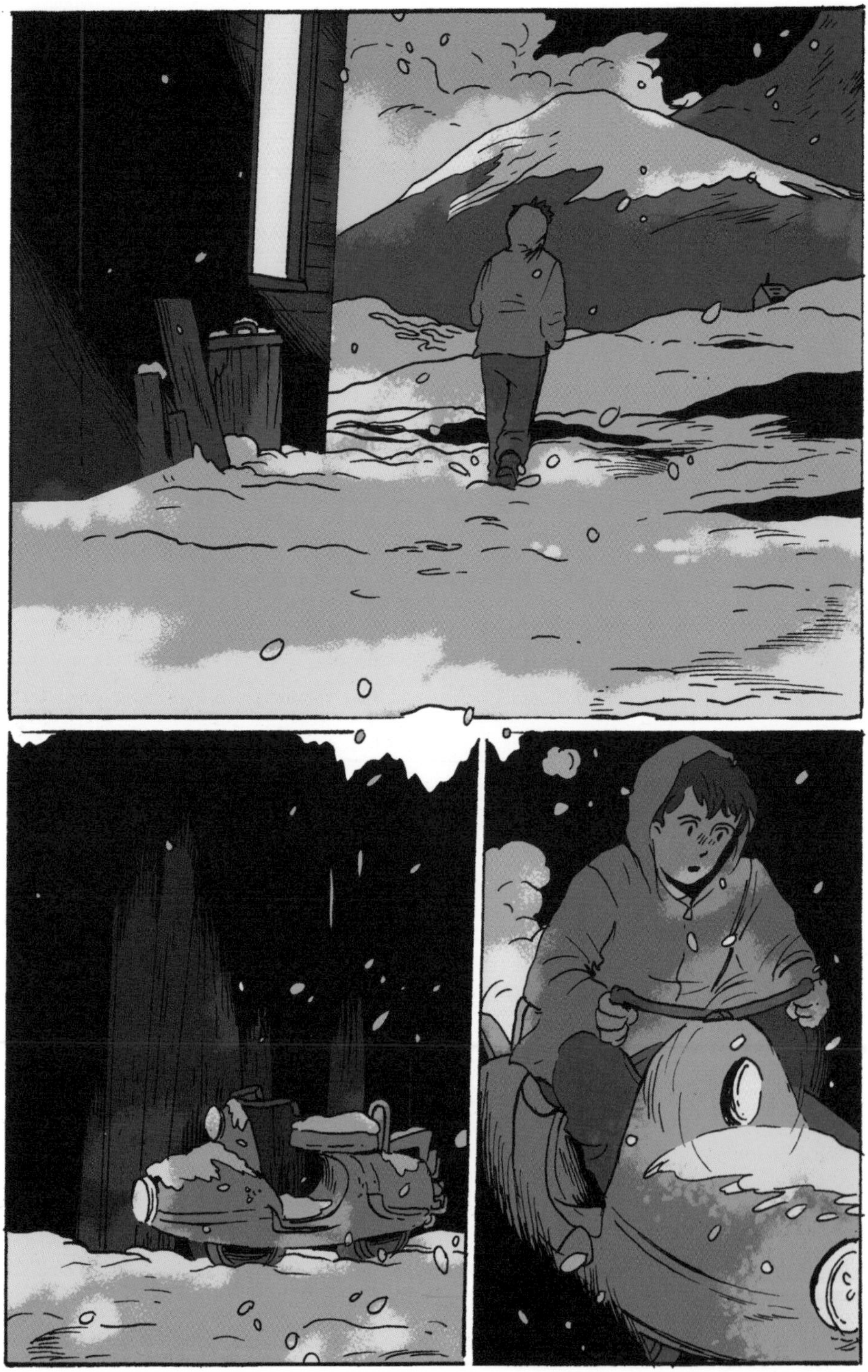

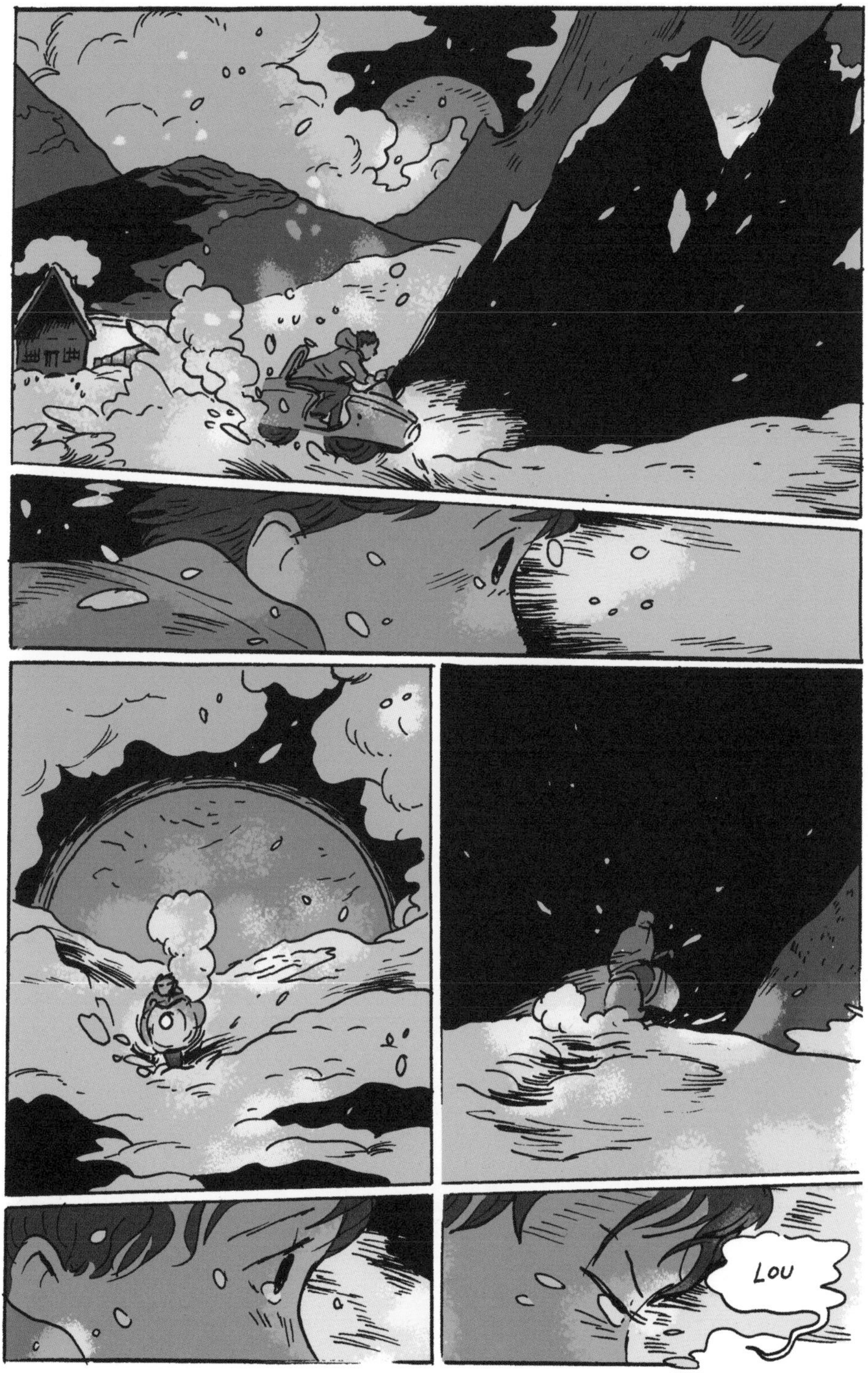
LOU

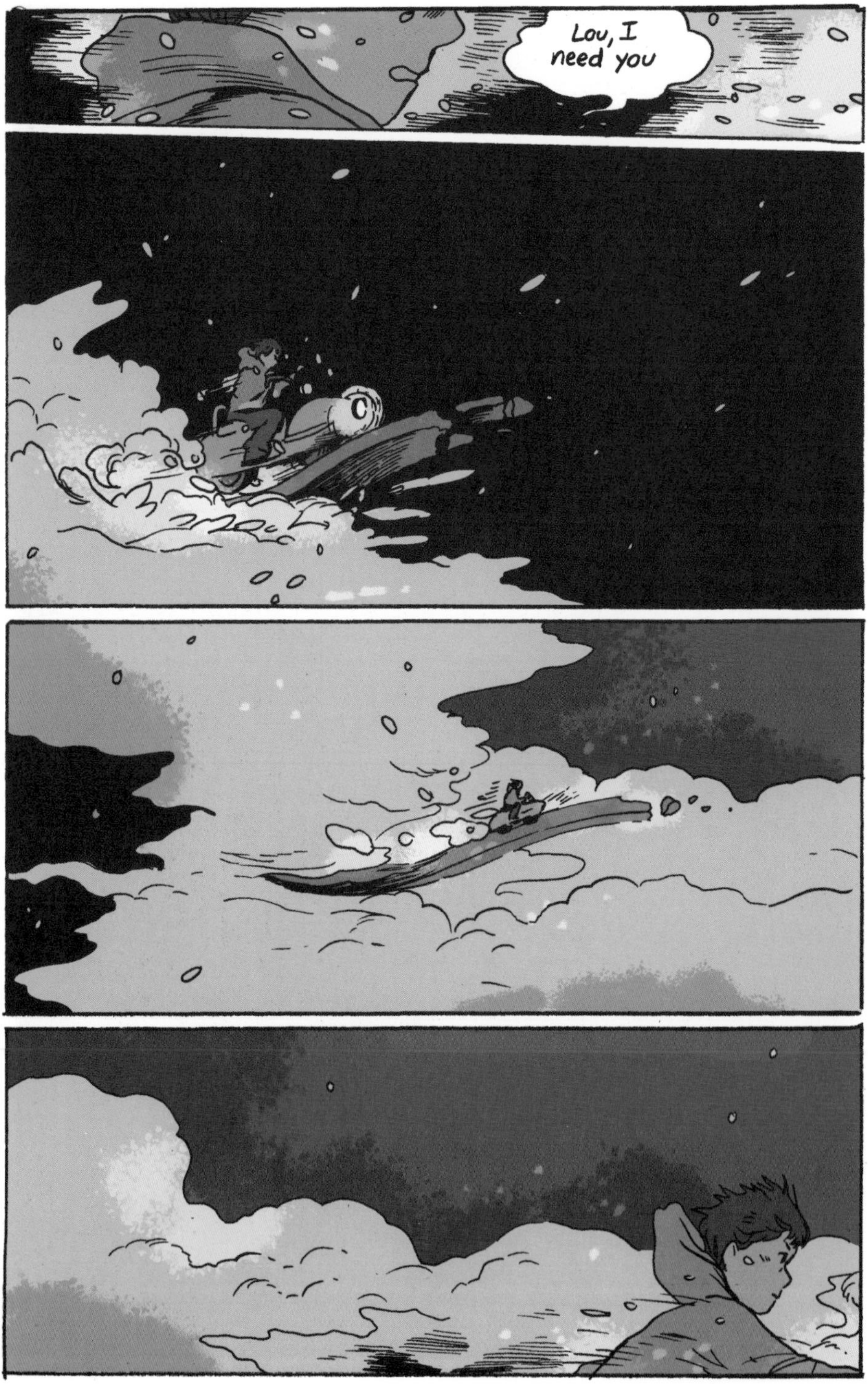
Lou, I need you

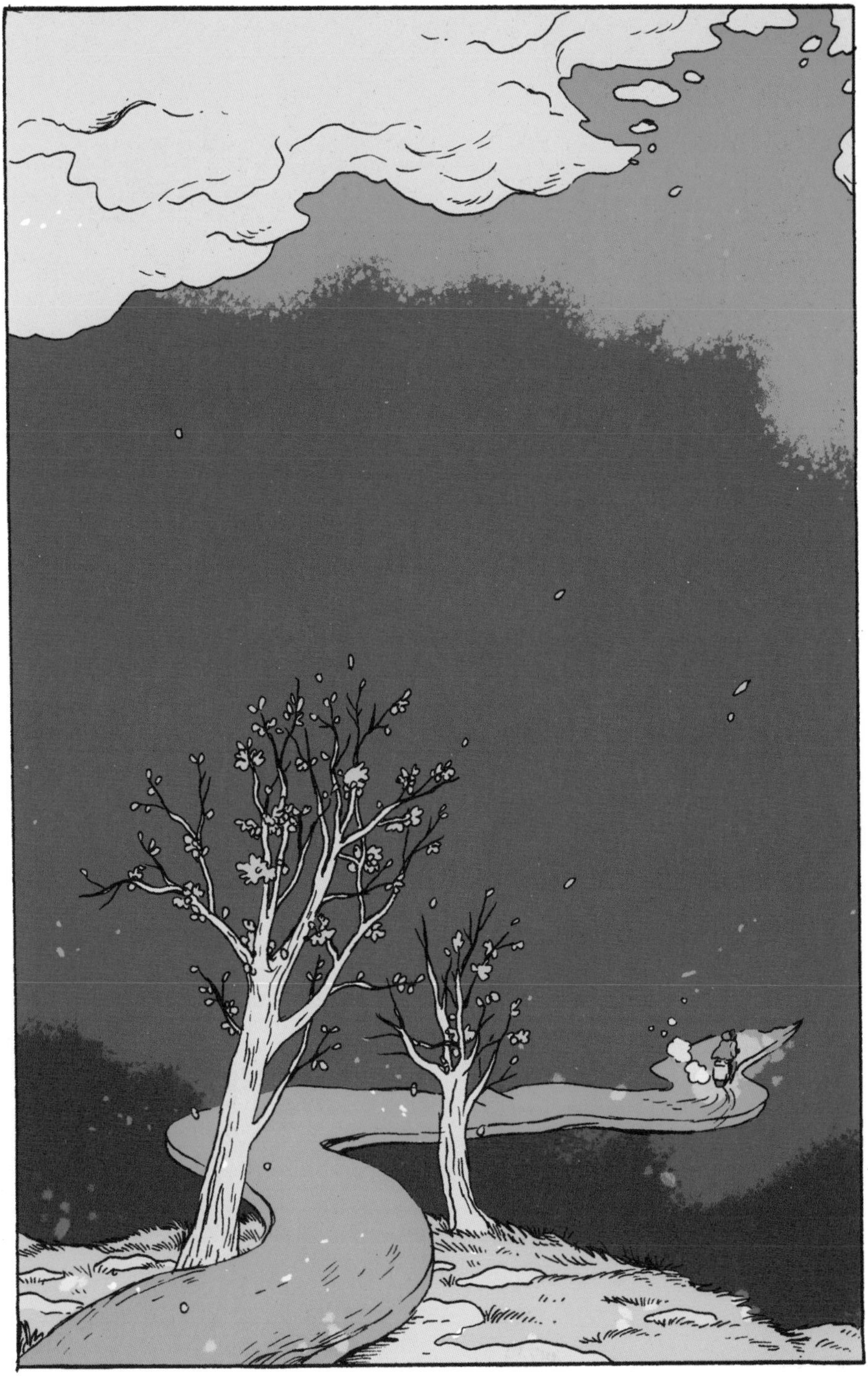

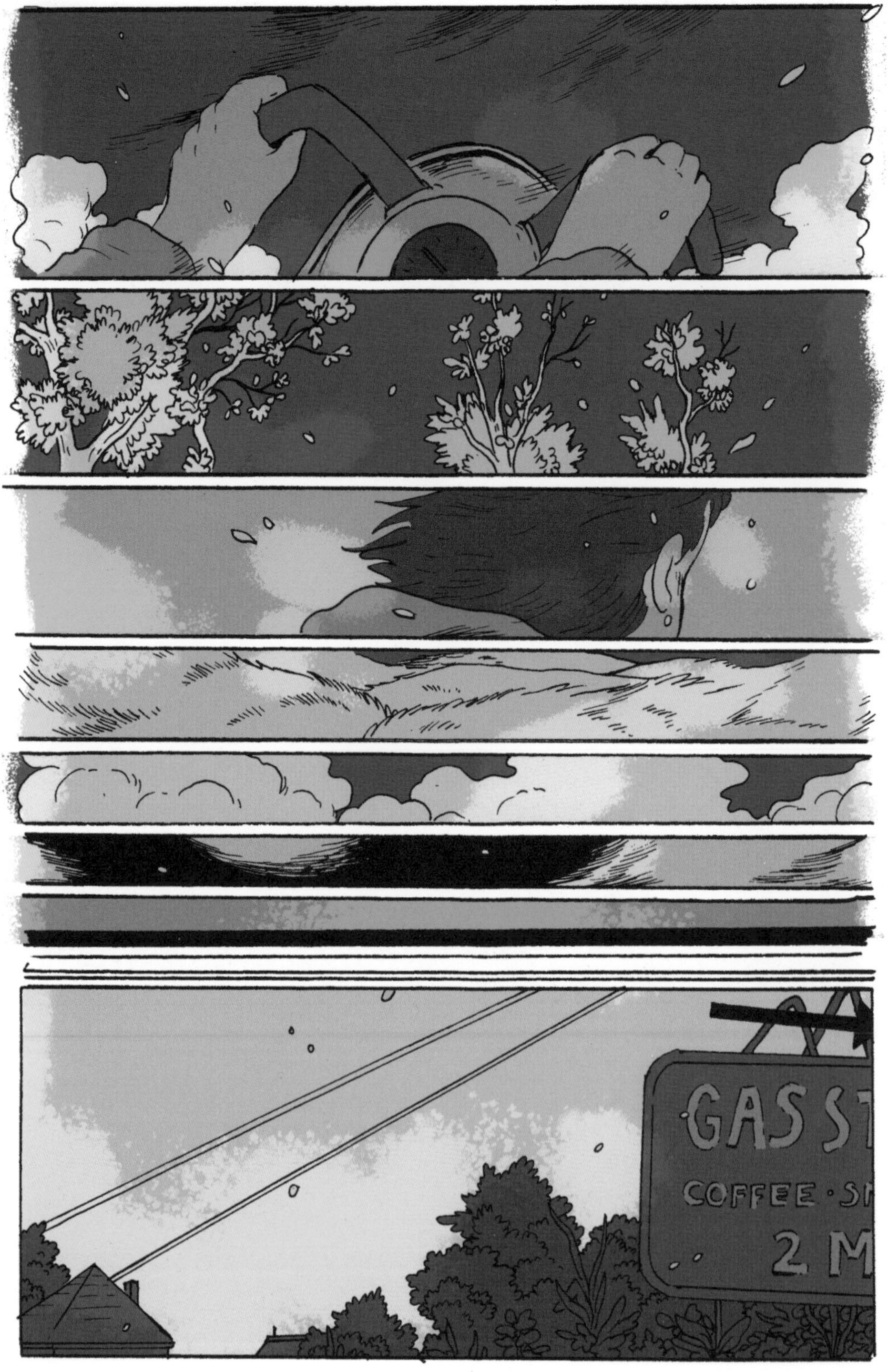
GAS ST
COFFEE · S
2 M

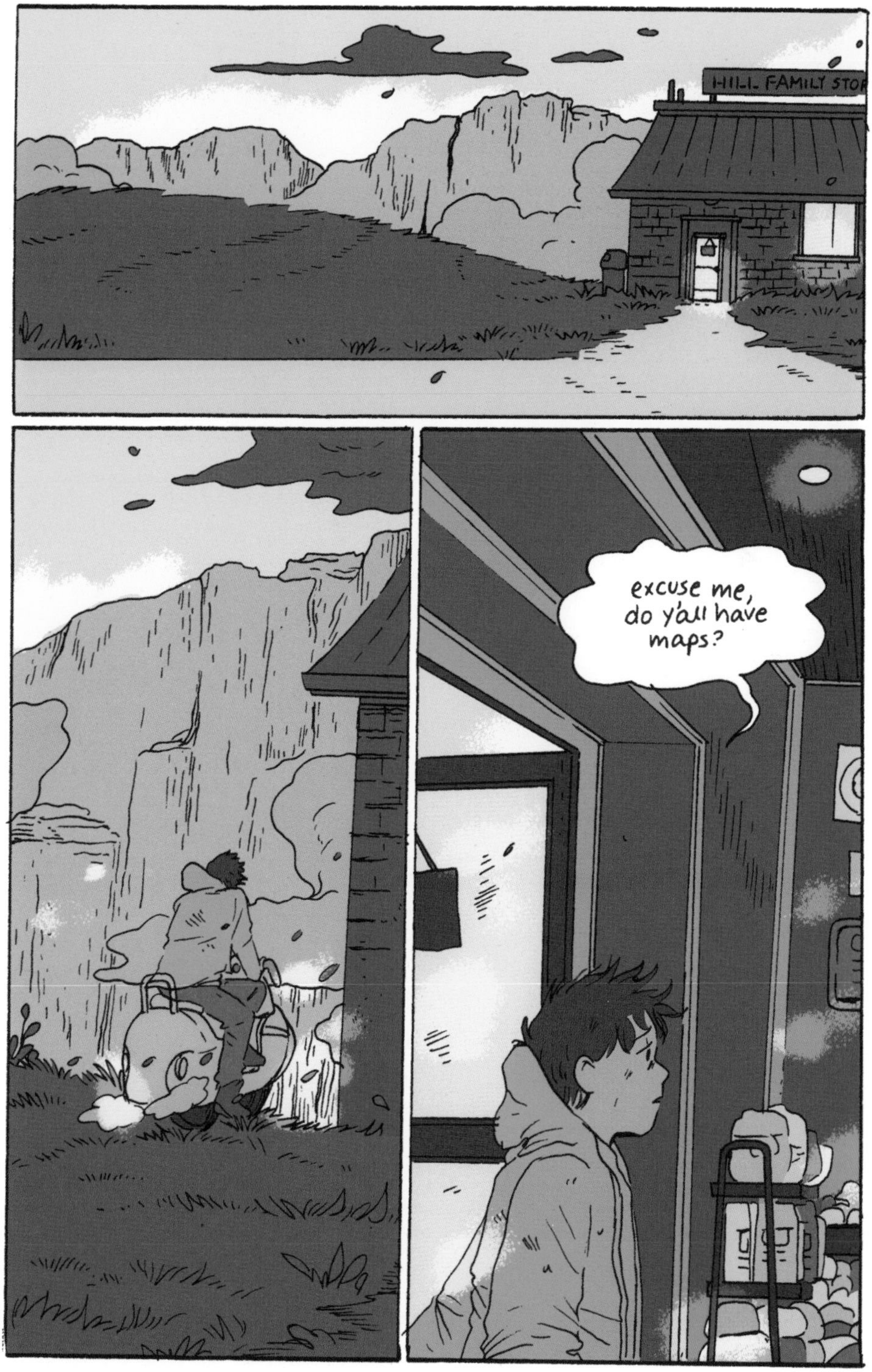
HILL FAMILY STO
excuse me, do y'all have maps?

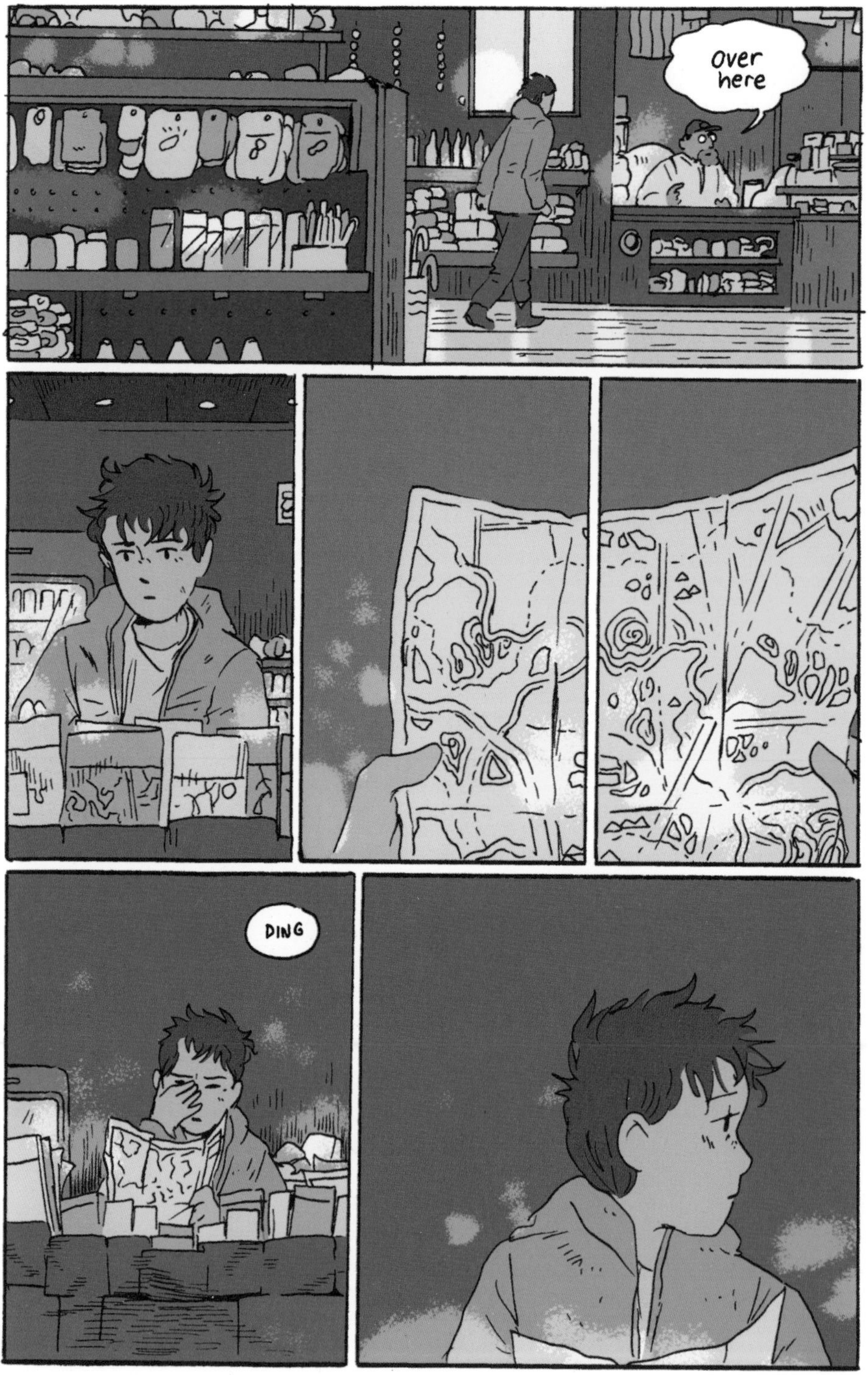
over here
DING

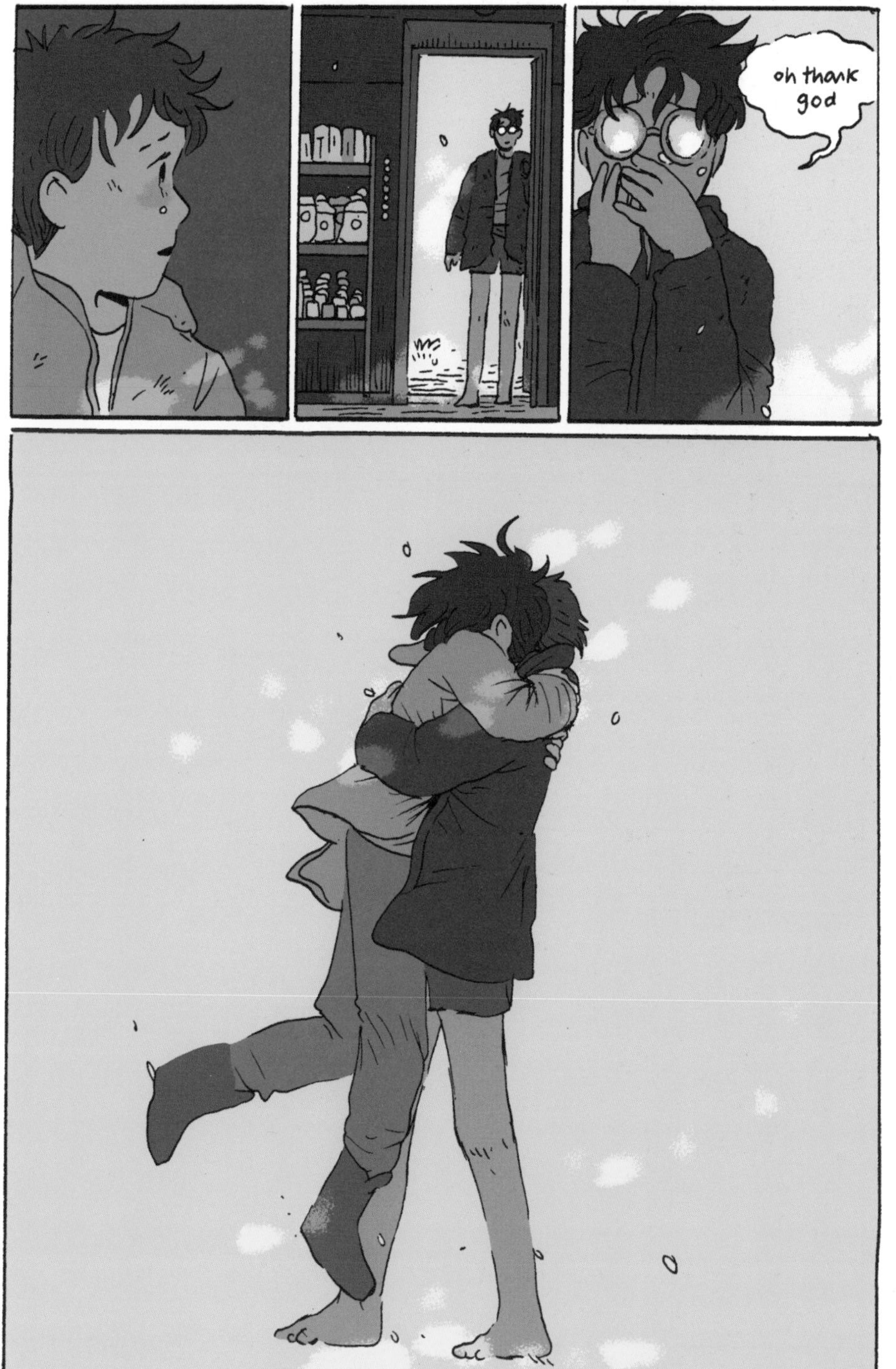
oh thank god

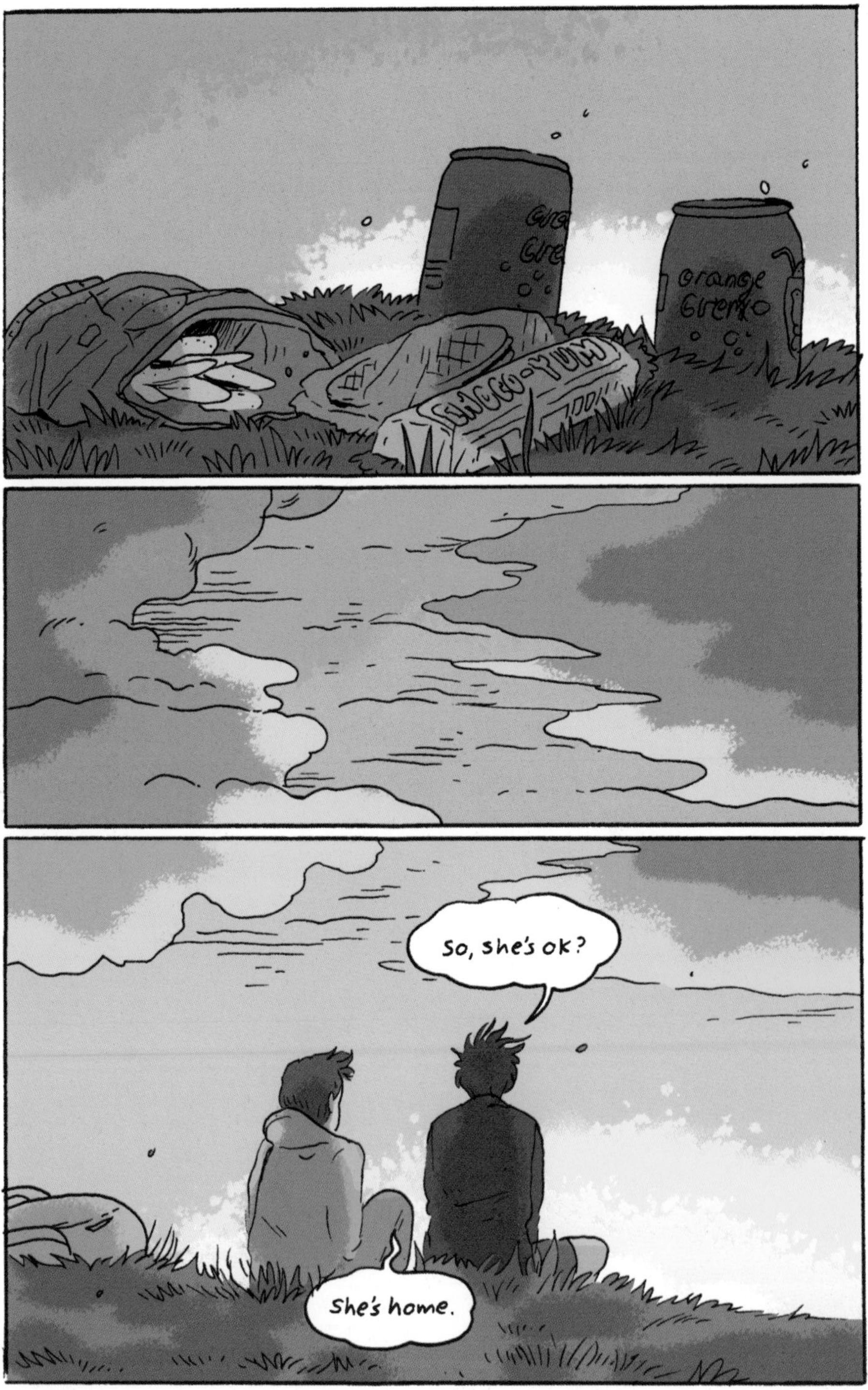

CHOCO-YUM
orange
Grenko
So, she's ok?
She's home.

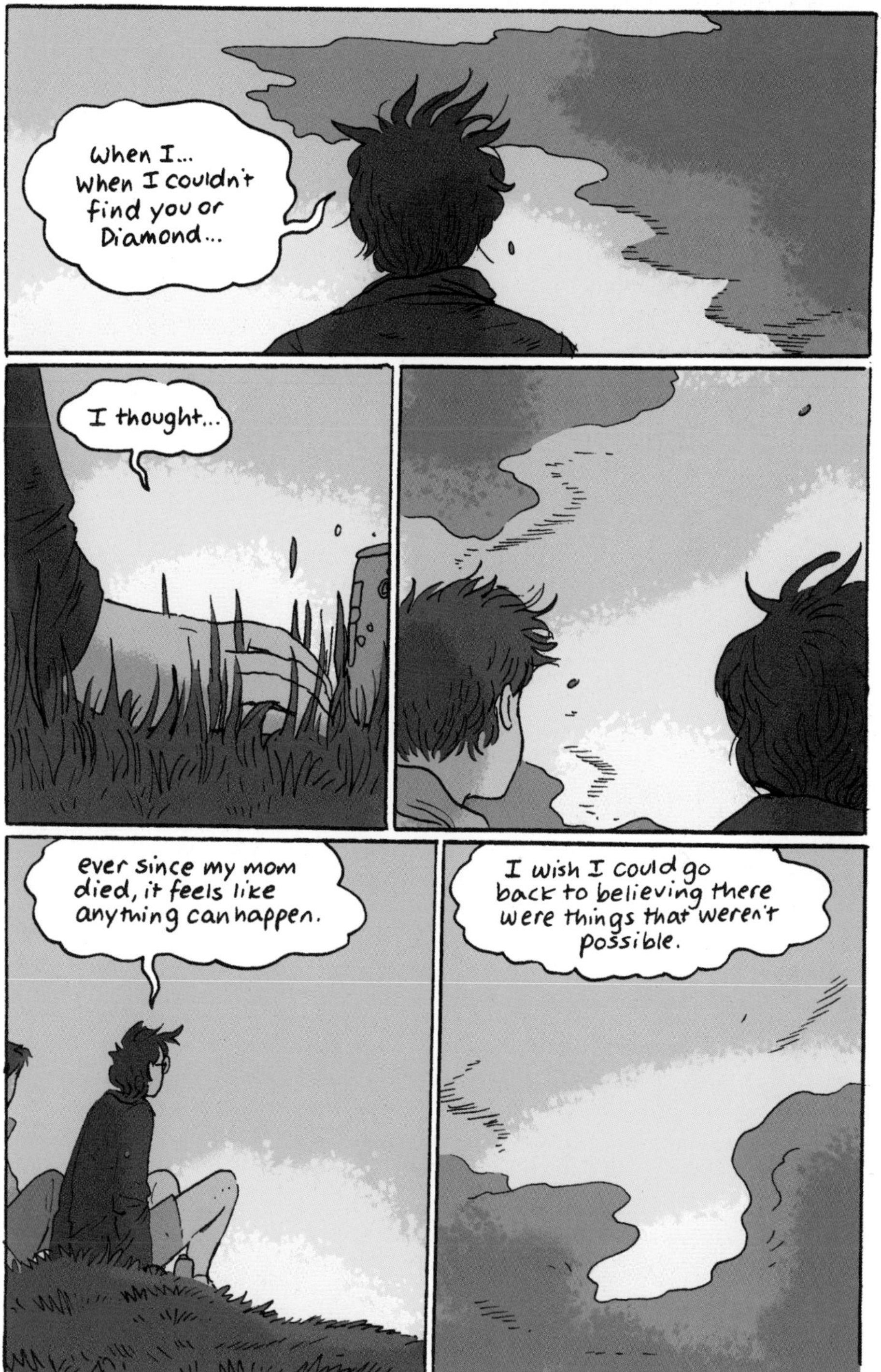
When I... When I couldn't find you or Diamond...
I thought...
ever since my mom died, it feels like anything can happen.
I wish I could go back to believing there were things that weren't possible.

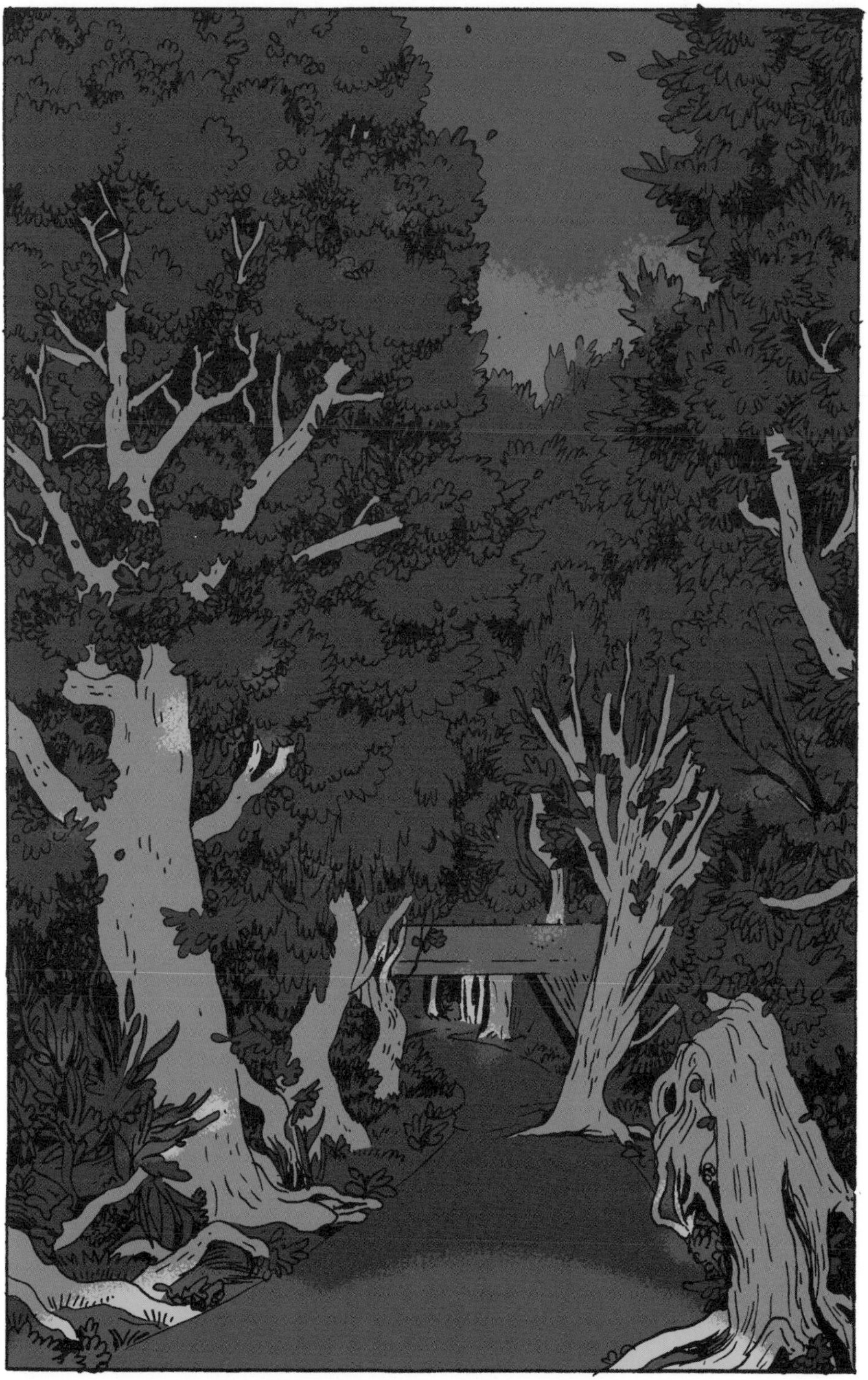

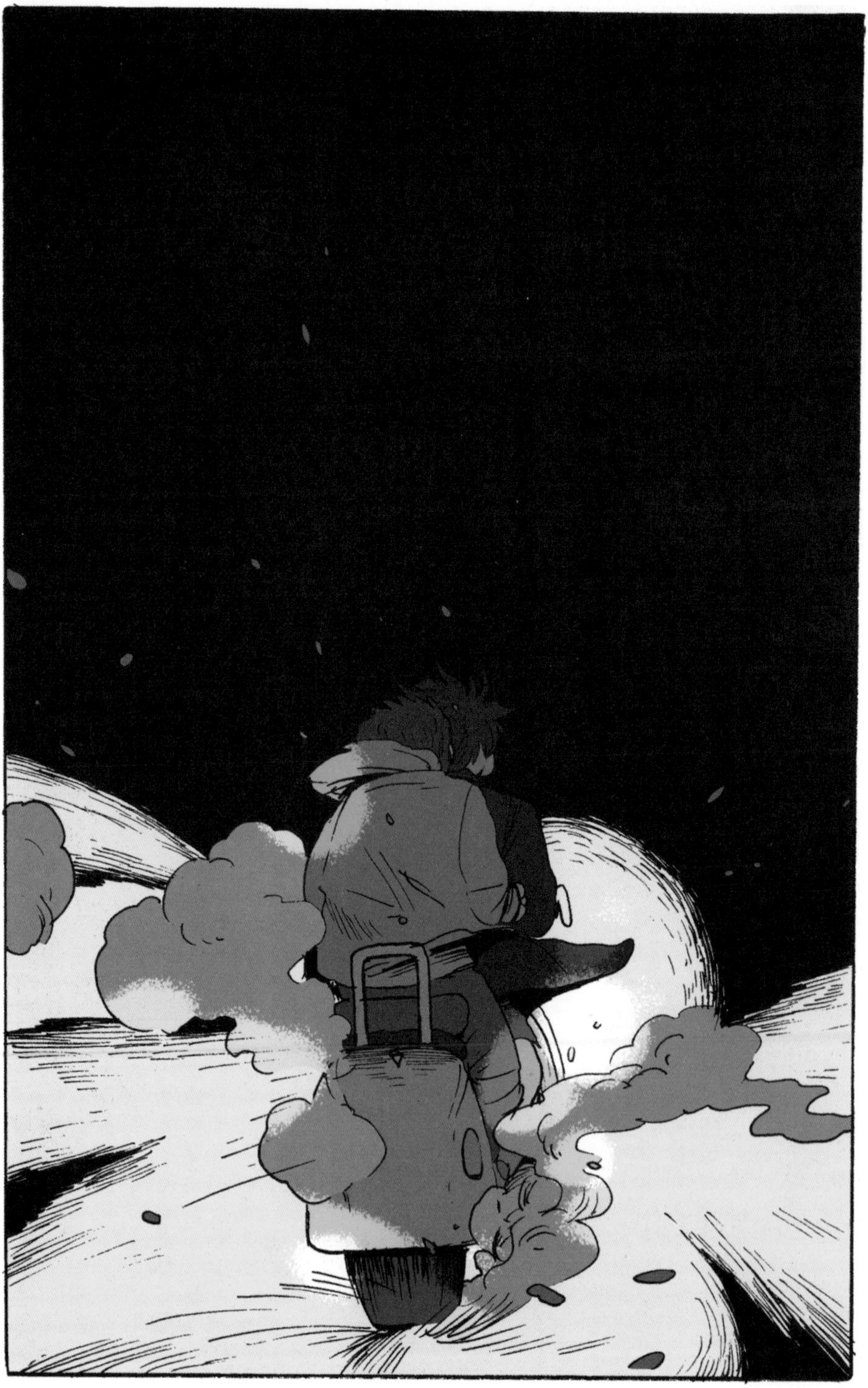

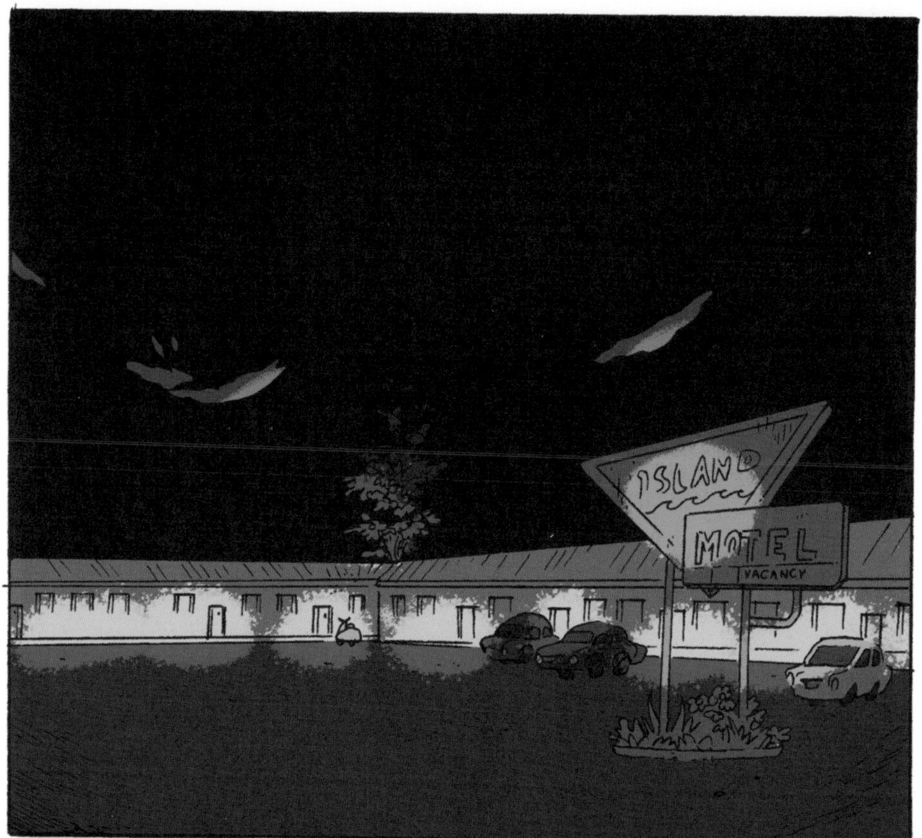
ISLAND
MOTEL
VACANCY

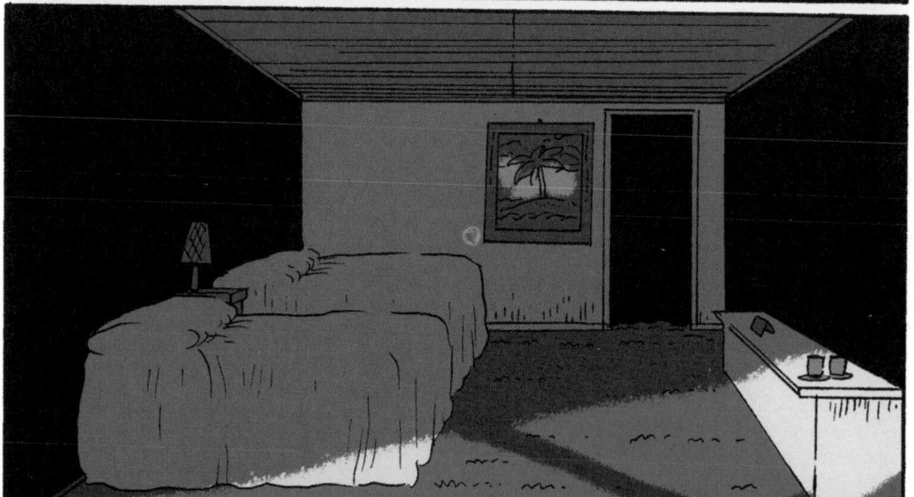

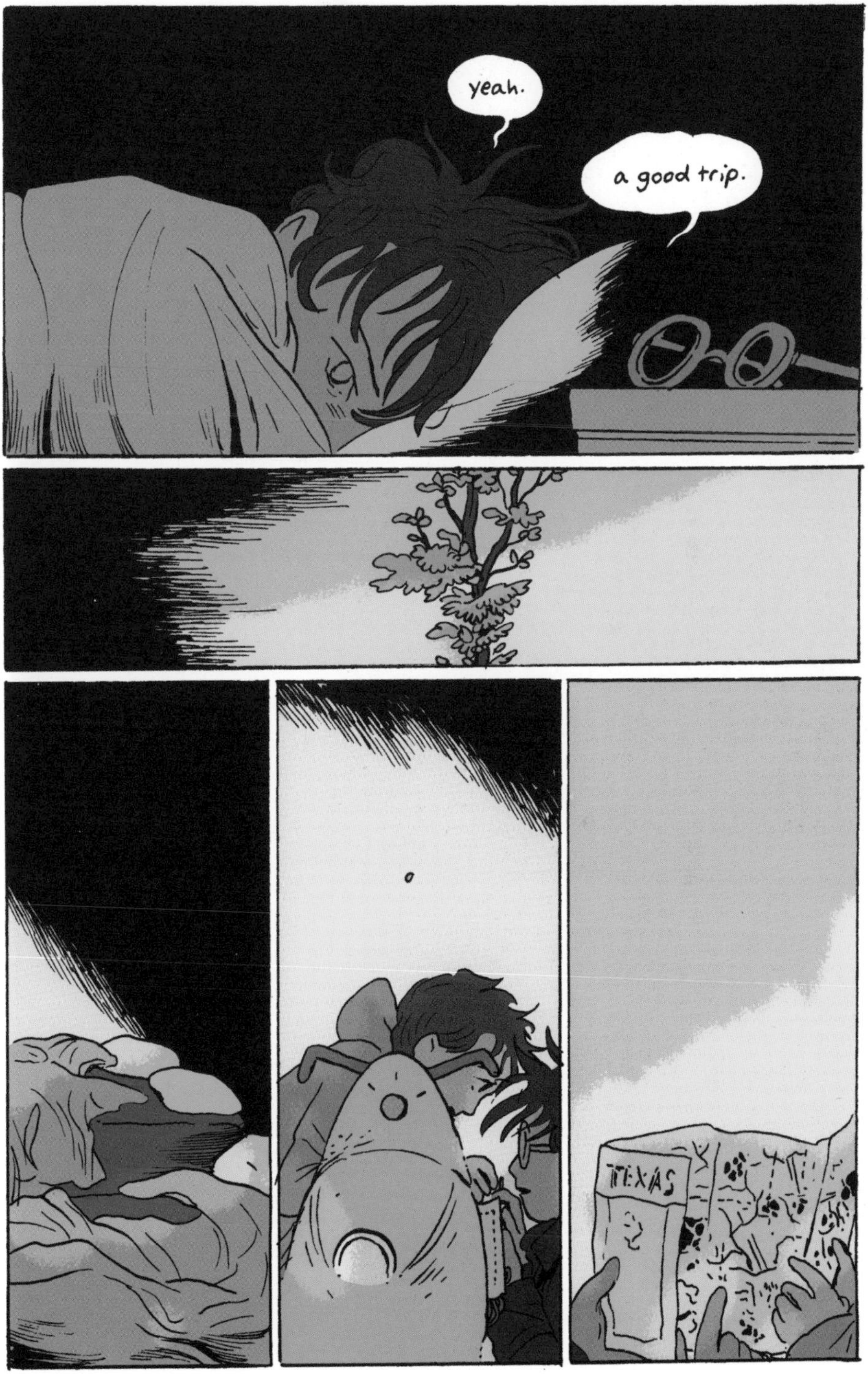
yeah.
a good trip.
TEXAS

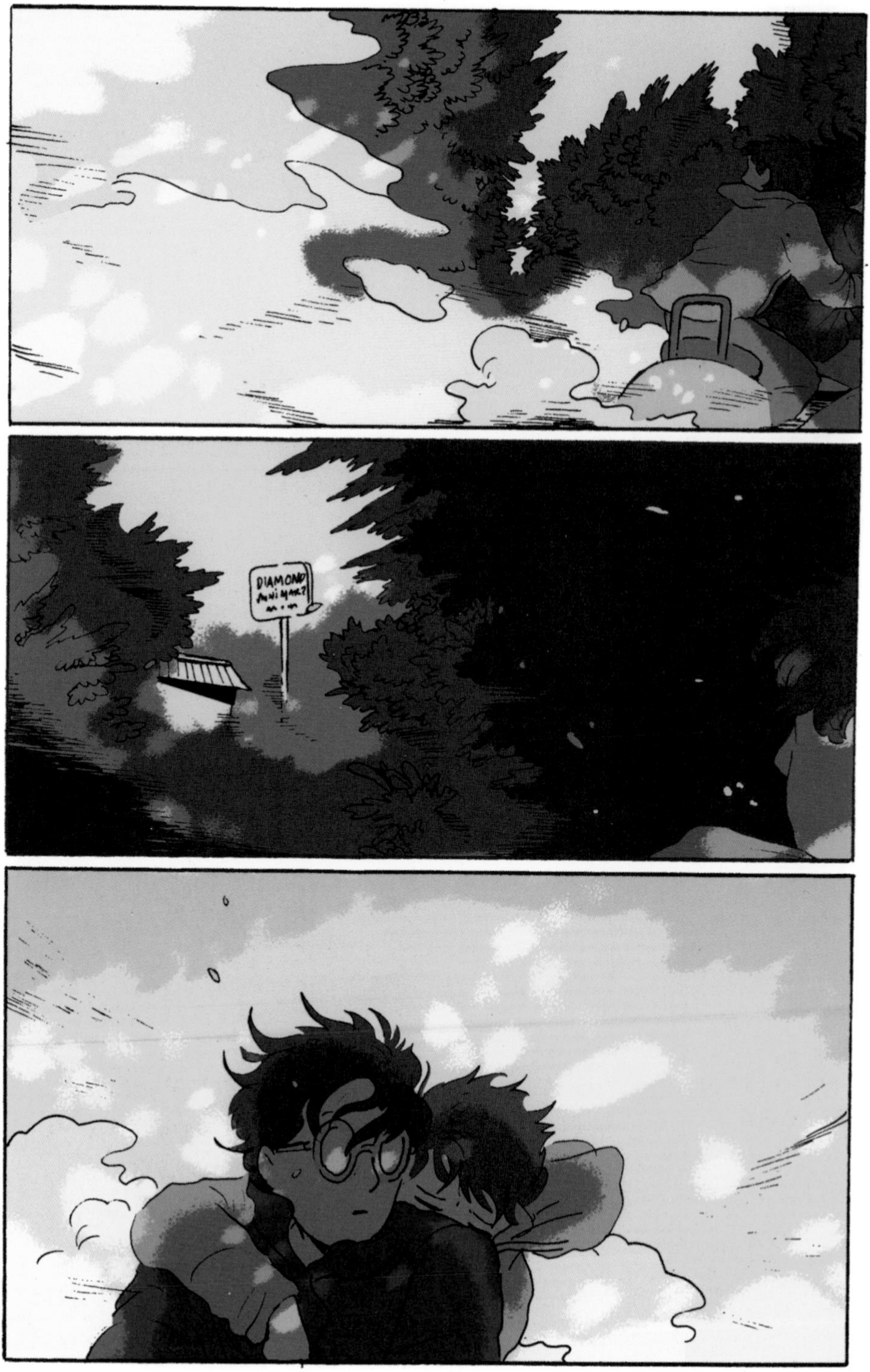
DIAMOND

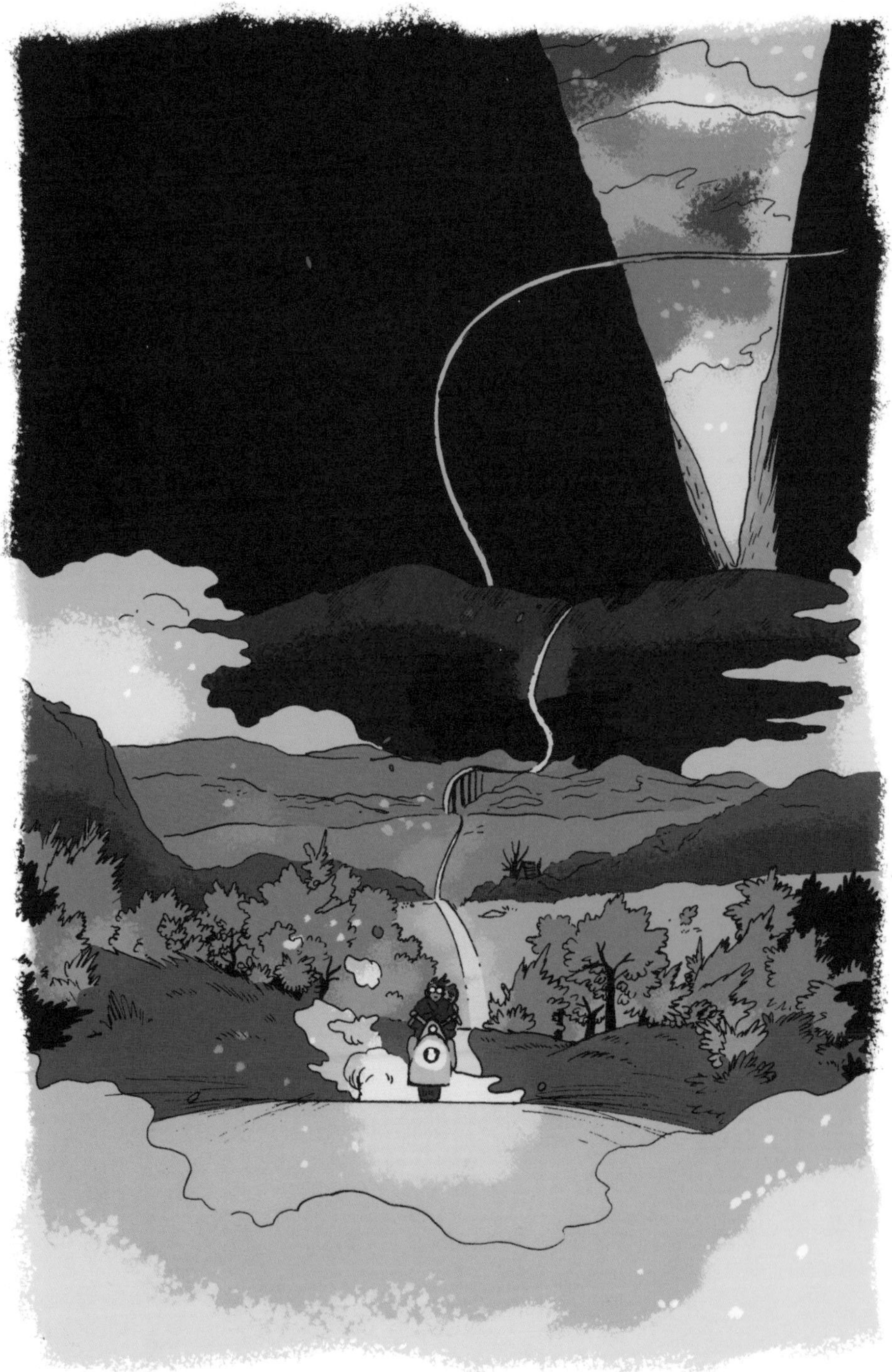

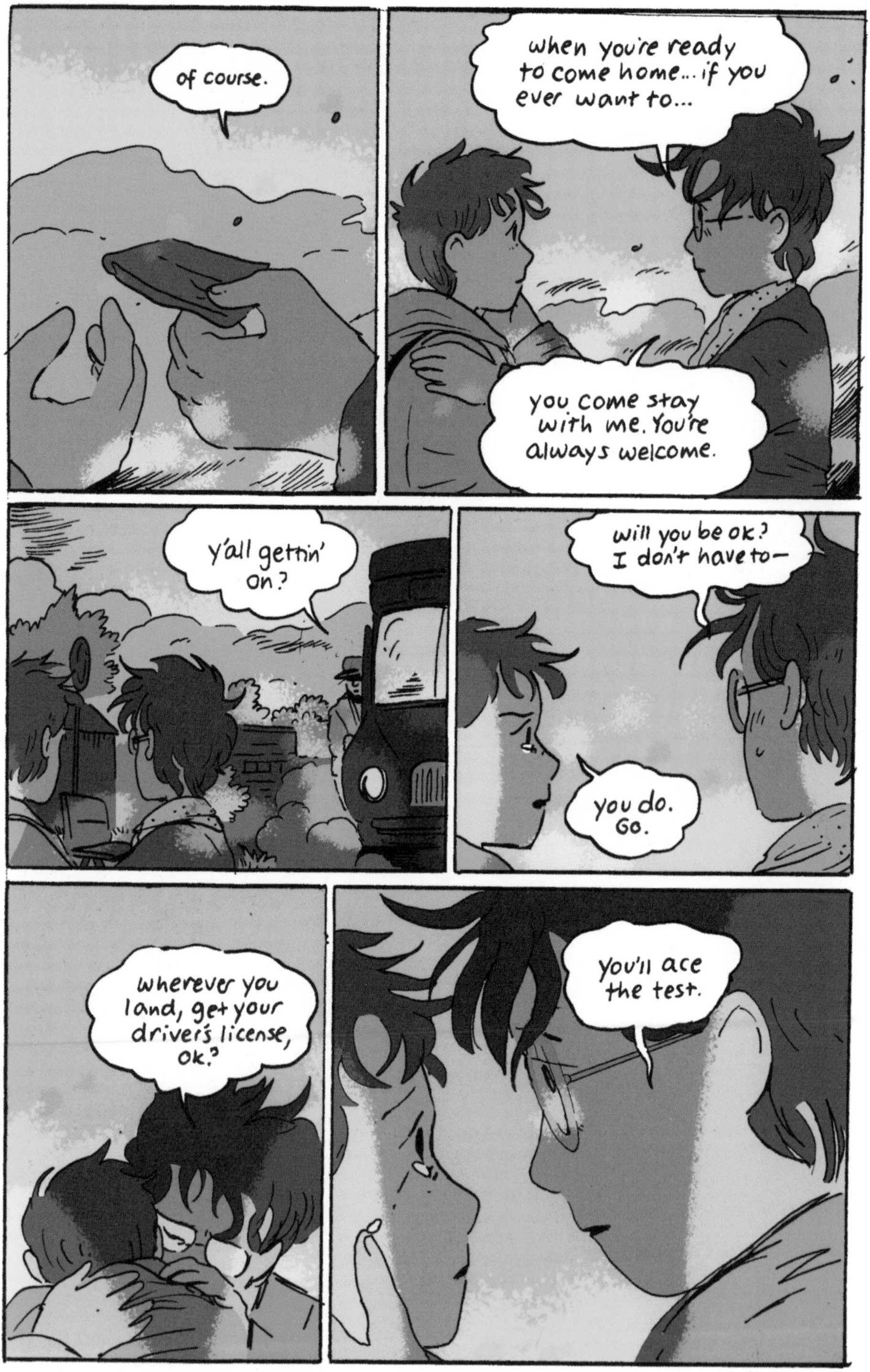
of course.
when you're ready to come home... if you ever want to...
you come stay with me. You're always welcome.
y'all gettin' on?
will you be ok? I don't have to—
you do. Go.
wherever you land, get your driver's license, ok?
you'll ace the test.

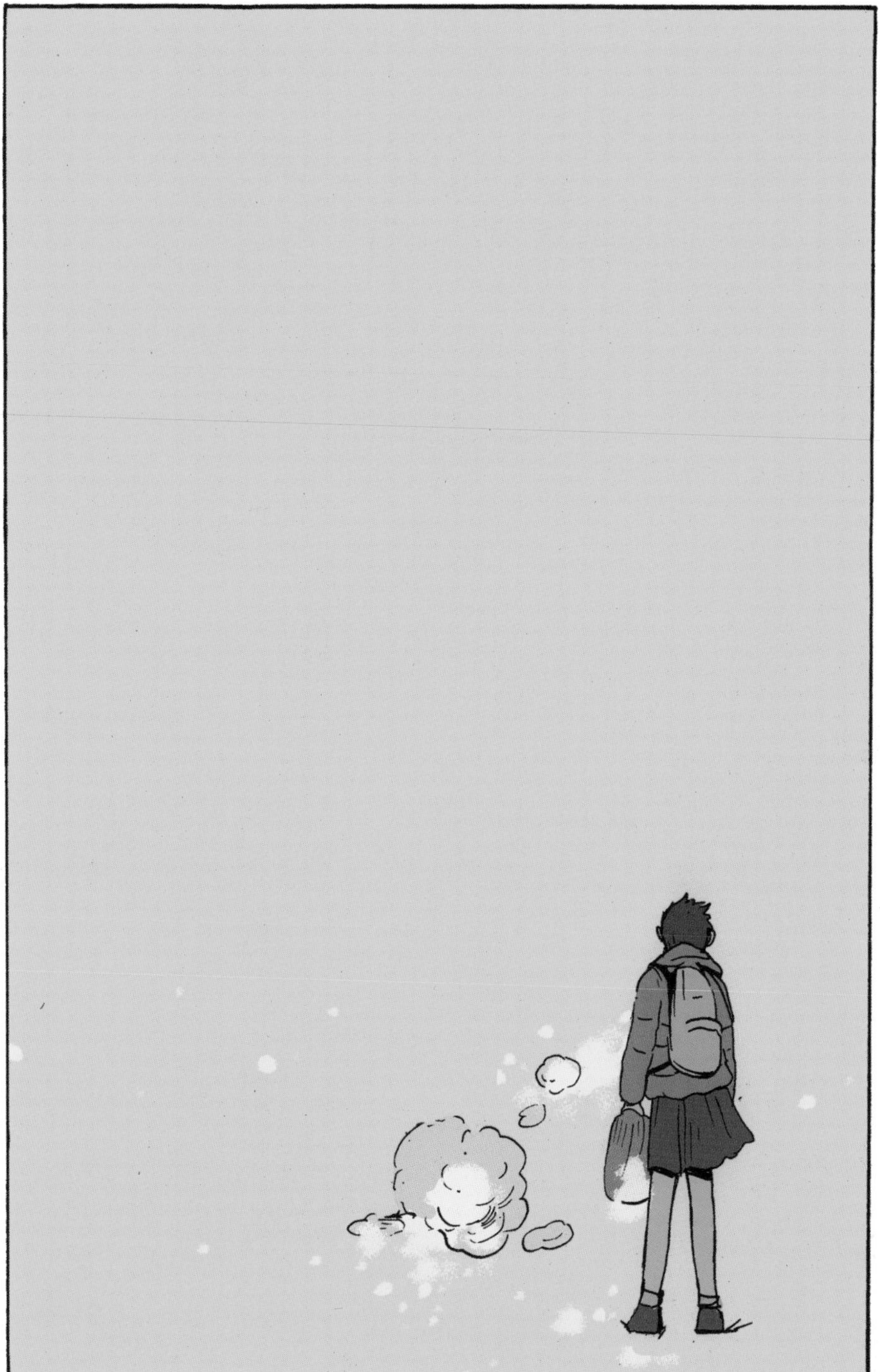

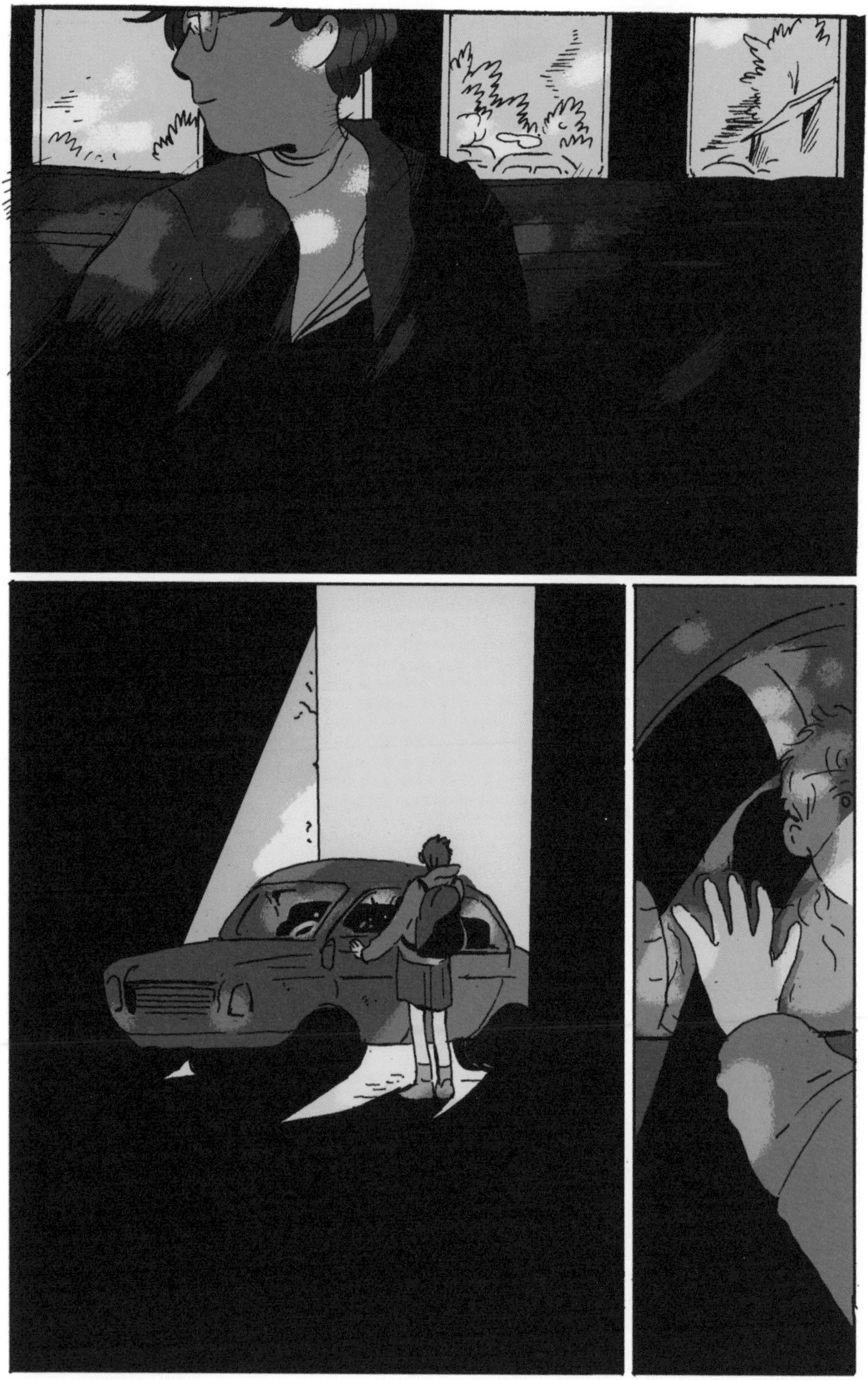

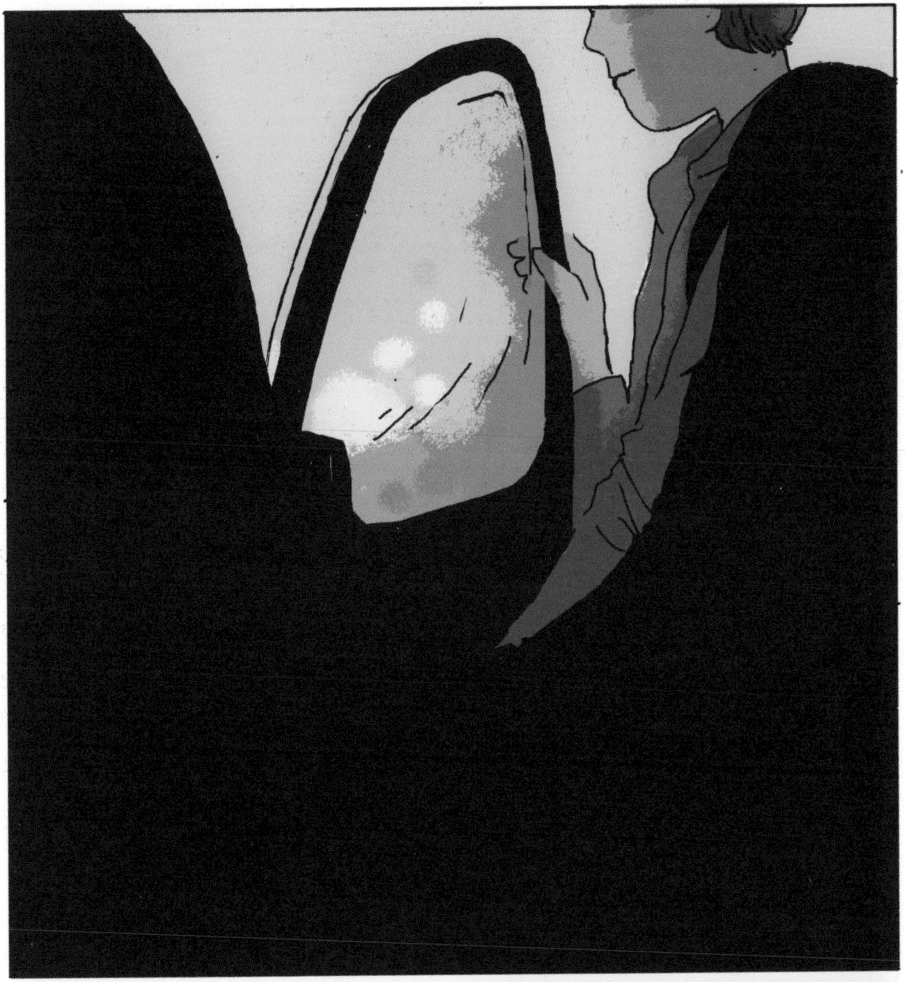

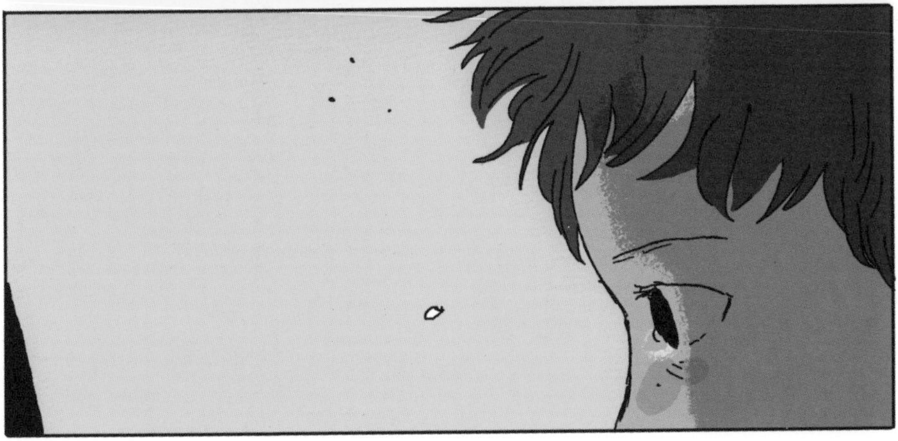

process...

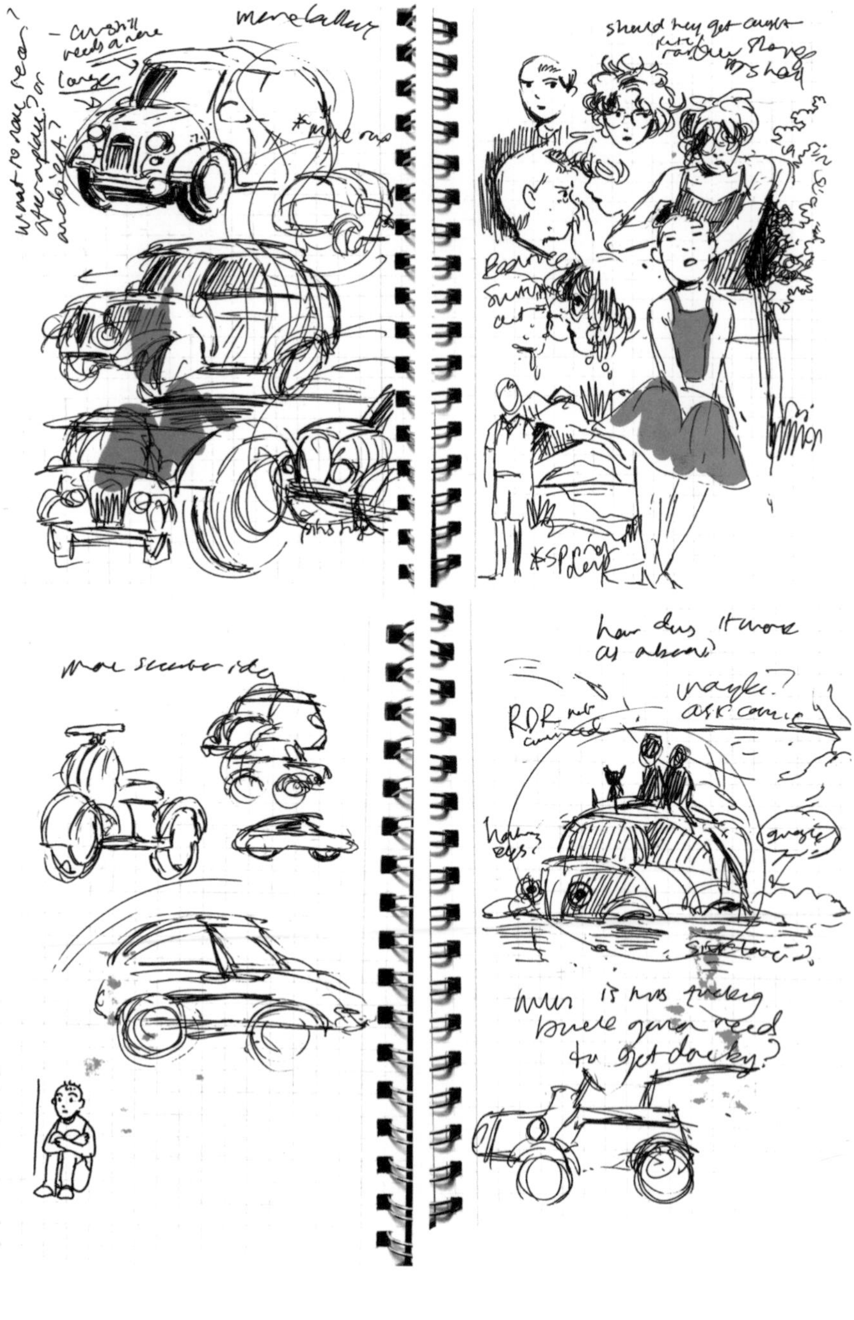

1st attempt at pencils

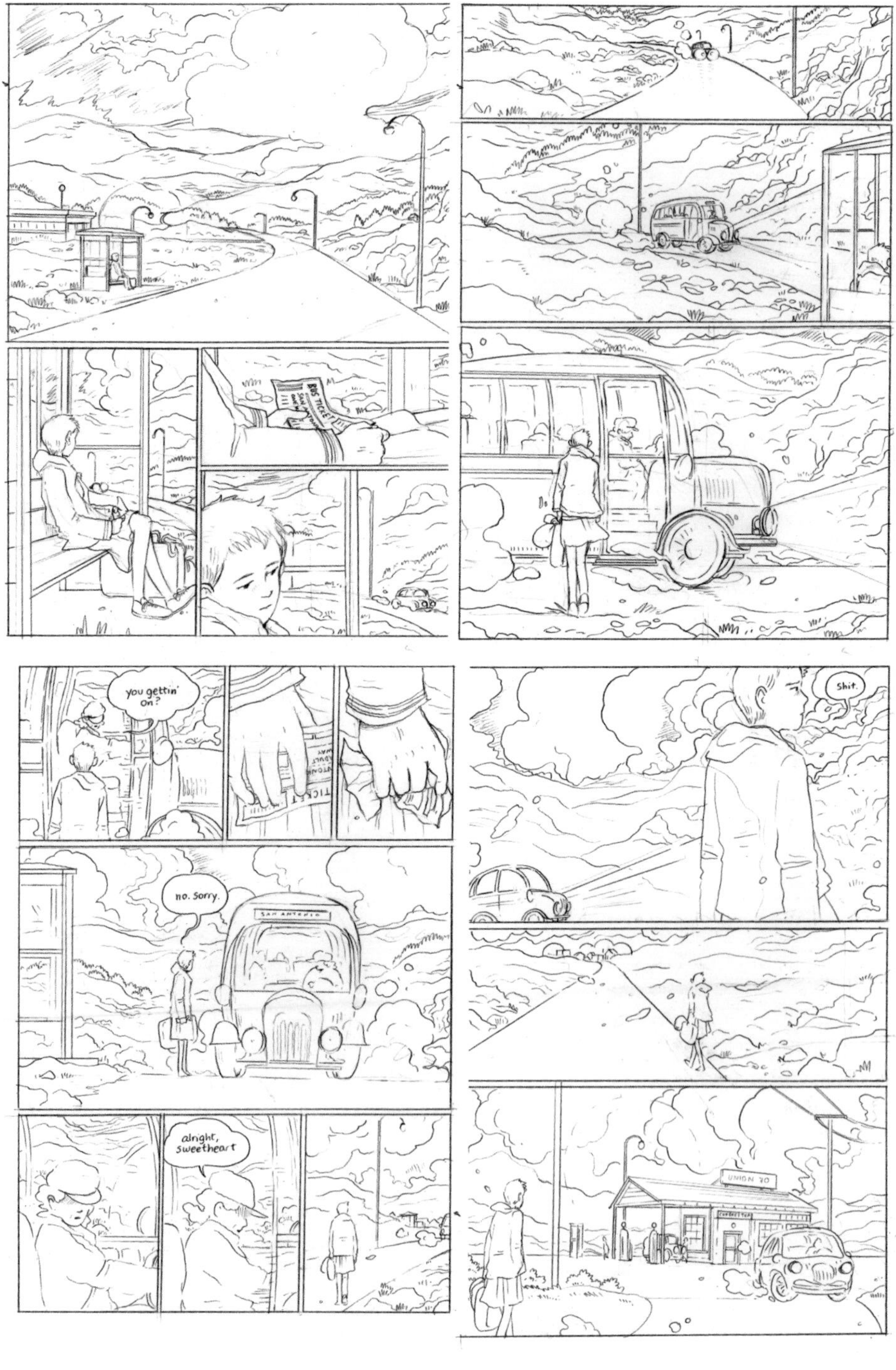
BUS TICKET
you gettin' on?
no. Sorry.
alright, sweetheart
Shit.
UNION 76

2nd go...

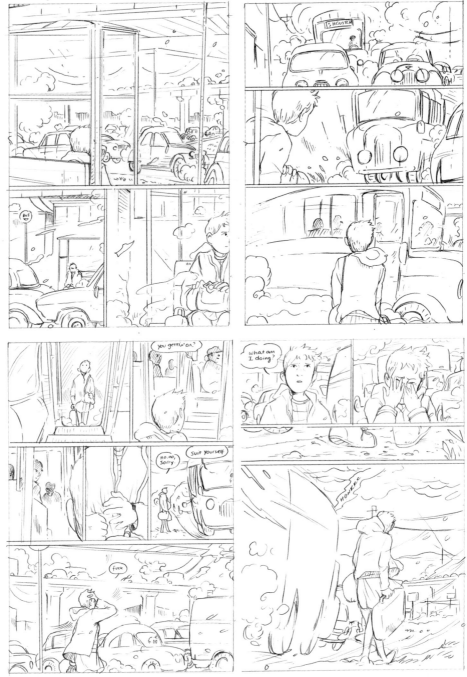

Inking...

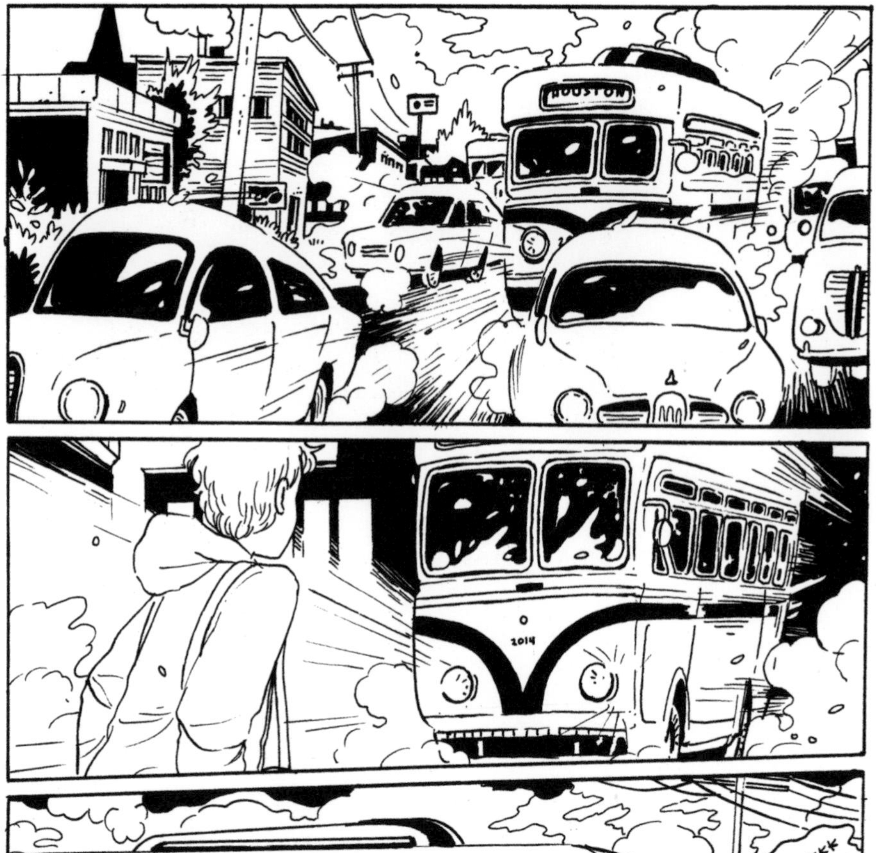
HOUSTON
2014
creeaaakkk

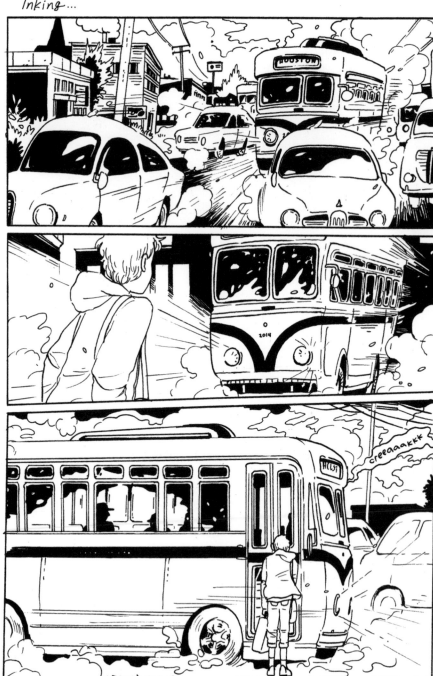

acknowledgments

there were many times working on this book
that I wanted to give up. It was the
support of people around me that got me
through it. I like to think that I have some sort
of never-ending well of energy and time and that
it is through sheer grit that I manage to make
long books in short times. But this is so far from
the truth. I am still here because of those of you
who continue to support me and love me.
Here are some of those people:

my First Second family. All of you
who have touched this book and helped it
get here.

Connie, my dear editor, who never gives up on me.

Seth, who values me more than I value myself.

My roommate and assistant, Annamarie, who
kept me fed and alive while making this book.

Jarad, who flatted this book in miraculous time
and helped me make it beautiful.

my family, whose support is more vast
than I can describe.

And of course, to you, for listening
    to what I had to say.

-t

Praise for Tillie Walden

spinning
tillie walden

A.V. Club Best Book of the Year
Paste Best Book of the Year
Wired Best Comic of the Year

"This beautiful story about sorrow, growth, and triumph will resonate in every reader's heart."
—**Laurie Halse Anderson**, author of *Speak*

ON A
SUNBEAM
TILLIE WALDEN

A.V. Club Best Book of the Year
A *Washington Post* "10 Best Graphic Novels of 2018"
A Chicago Public Library "Best of the Best 2018"

"Tillie Walden is the **future of comics**, and *On a Sunbeam* is her best work yet. It's a 'space' story unlike any you've ever read, with a rich, lived-in universe of complex characters."

—**Brian K. Vaughan**,
author of *Saga* and *Paper Girls*

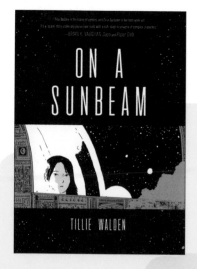

Tillie Walden is a cartoonist and illustrator from Austin, Texas. She is the creator of the graphic memoir *Spinning*, an Eisner Award winner, and *On a Sunbeam*, which was originally published as a webcomic. She is also the creator of the Ignatz Award winner *The End of Summer* and *I Love This Part*. Tillie is a graduate of the Center for Cartoon Studies, a comics MFA program in Vermont.

tilliewalden.com

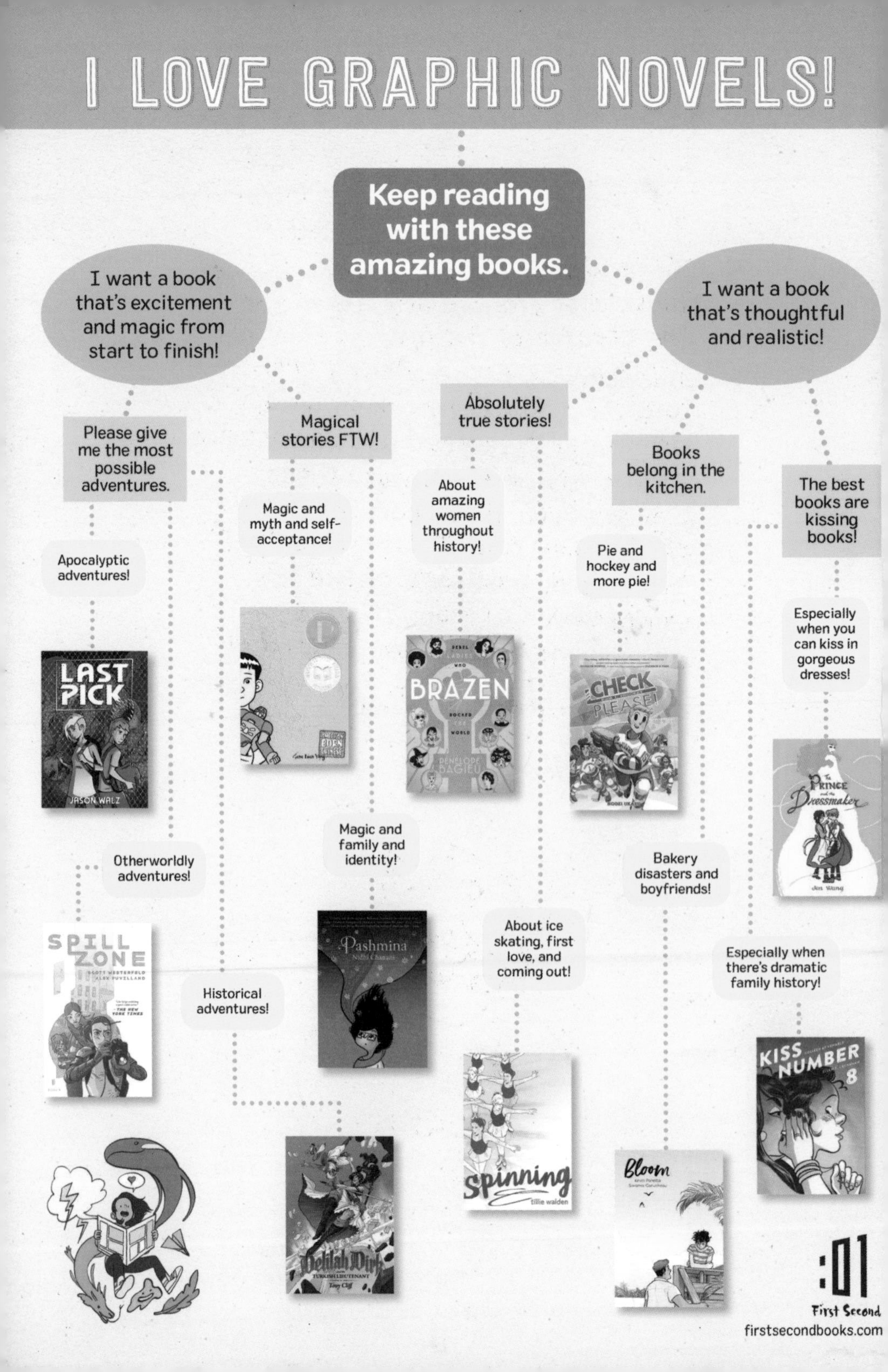

I LOVE GRAPHIC NOVELS!

Keep reading with these amazing books.

I want a book that's excitement and magic from start to finish!

I want a book that's thoughtful and realistic!

Please give me the most possible adventures.

Magical stories FTW!

Absolutely true stories!

Books belong in the kitchen.

The best books are kissing books!

Apocalyptic adventures!

Magic and myth and self-acceptance!

About amazing women throughout history!

Pie and hockey and more pie!

Especially when you can kiss in gorgeous dresses!

Otherworldly adventures!

Magic and family and identity!

Bakery disasters and boyfriends!

Historical adventures!

About ice skating, first love, and coming out!

Especially when there's dramatic family history!

:01
First Second
firstsecondbooks.com